Praise for Brandon Sanderson:

'Anyone looking for a different and refreshing fantasy novel will be delighted by this exceptional tale'

Michael Moorcock on *Warbreaker*

'Highly recommended to anyone hungry for a good read'

Robin Hobb on *The Final Empire*

'Brandon Sanderson is the real thing – an exciting storyteller with a unique and powerful vision'   David Farland

'Sanderson will be forever mentioned as one of the finest fantasy writers of this generation'   *Fantasy Faction*

'Sanderson is clearly a master of large-scale stories, splendidly depicting worlds as well as strong female characters'

Booklist

Also by Brandon Sanderson from Gollancz:

Mistborn
The Final Empire
The Well of Ascension
The Hero of Ages

The Alloy of Law

The Stormlight Archive
The Way of Kings Part One
The Way of Kings Part Two

Elantris
Warbreaker
Alcatraz
Legion and The Emperor's Soul

STEELHEART

BRANDON SANDERSON

GOLLANCZ

LONDON

First published in Great Britain in 2013 by Gollancz
An imprint of the Orion Publishing Group
Orion House, 5 Upper St Martin's Lane, London WC2H 9EA
An Hachette UK Company

A CIP catalogue record for this book is available
from the British Library

ISBN 978 0 575 10385 6 (Cased)
ISBN 978 0 575 10399 3 (Trade Paperback)

1 3 5 7 9 10 8 6 4 2

Printed in Great Britain by Clays Ltd, St Ives plc

The Orion Publishing Group's policy is to use papers that
are natural, renewable and recyclable products and made
from wood grown in sustainable forests. The logging and
manufacturing processes are expected to conform to the
environmental regulations of the country of origin.

www.brandonsanderson.com
www.orionbooks.co.uk
www.gollancz.co.uk

For Dallin Sanderson,

who fights evil each day with his smile

Prologue

I'VE seen Steelheart bleed.

It happened ten years ago; I was eight. My father and I were at the First Union Bank on Adams Street. We used the old street names back then, before the Annexation.

The bank was enormous. A single open chamber with white pillars surrounding a tile mosaic floor, broad doors that led deeper into the building. Two large revolving doors opened onto the street, with a set of conventional doors to the sides. Men and women streamed in and out, as if the room were the heart of some enormous beast, pulsing with a lifeblood of people and cash.

I knelt backward on a chair that was too big for me, watching the flow of people. I liked to watch people. The different shapes of faces, the hairstyles, the clothing, the expressions. Everyone showed so much *variety* back then. It was exciting.

1

"David, turn around, please," my father said. He had a soft voice. I'd never heard it raised, save for that one time at my mother's funeral. Thinking of his agony on that day still makes me shiver.

I turned around, sullen. We were to the side of the main bank chamber in one of the cubicles where the mortgage men worked. Our cubicle had glass sides, which made it less confining, but it still felt fake. There were little wood-framed pictures of family members on the walls, a cup of cheap candy with a glass lid on the desk, and a vase with faded plastic flowers on the filing cabinet.

It was an imitation of a comfortable home. Much like the man in front of us wore an imitation of a smile.

"If we had more collateral . . . ," the mortgage man said, showing teeth.

"Everything I own is on there," my father said, indicating the paper on the desk in front of us. His hands were thick with calluses, his skin tan from days spent working in the sun. My mother would have winced if she'd seen him go to a fancy appointment like this wearing his work jeans and an old T-shirt with a comic book character on it.

At least he'd combed his hair, though it was starting to thin. He didn't care about that as much as other men seemed to. "Just means fewer haircuts, Dave," he'd tell me, laughing as he ran his fingers through his wispy hair. I didn't point out that he was wrong. He would still have to get the same number of haircuts, at least until all of his hair fell out.

"I just don't think I can do anything about this," the mortgage man said. "You've been told before."

"The other man said it would be enough," my father replied, his large hands clasped before him. He looked concerned. Very concerned.

The mortgage man just continued to smile. He tapped the stack of papers on his desk. "The world is a much more dangerous place now, Mr. Charleston. The bank has decided against taking risks."

"Dangerous?" my father asked.

"Well, you know, the Epics . . ."

"But they *aren't* dangerous," my father said passionately. "The Epics are here to help."

Not this again, I thought.

The mortgage man's smile finally broke, as if he was taken aback by my father's tone.

"Don't you see?" my father said, leaning forward. "This isn't a dangerous time. It's a wonderful time!"

The mortgage man cocked his head. "Didn't your previous home get *destroyed* by an Epic?"

"Where there are villains, there will be heroes," my father said. "Just wait. They *will* come."

I believed him. A lot of people thought like he did, back then. It had only been two years since Calamity appeared in the sky. One year since ordinary men started changing. Turning into Epics — almost like superheroes from the stories.

We were still hopeful then. And ignorant.

"Well," the mortgage man said, clasping his hands on the table right beside a picture frame displaying a stock photo of smiling ethnic children. "Unfortunately, our underwriters don't agree with your assessment. You'll have to . . ."

They kept talking, but I stopped paying attention. I let my eyes wander back toward the crowds, then turned around again, kneeling on the chair. My father was too engrossed in the conversation to scold me.

So I was actually watching when the Epic strolled into the bank. I noticed him immediately, though nobody else seemed to pay him much heed. Most people say you can't tell an Epic from an ordinary man unless he starts using his powers, but they're wrong. Epics carry themselves differently. That sense of confidence, that subtle self-satisfaction. I've always been able to spot them.

Even as a kid I knew there was something different about that man. He wore a relaxed-fitting black business suit with a light tan shirt underneath, no tie. He was tall and lean, but *solid,* like a lot of Epics are. Muscled and toned in a way that you could see even through the loose clothing.

He strode to the center of the room. Sunglasses hung from his breast pocket, and he smiled as he put them on. Then he raised a finger and pointed with a casual tapping motion at a passing woman.

She vaporized to dust, clothing burning away, skeleton falling forward and clattering to the floor. Her earrings and wedding ring didn't dissolve, though. They hit the floor with distinct *ping*s I could hear even over the noise in the room.

The room fell still. People froze, horrified. Conversations stopped, though the mortgage man kept right on rambling, lecturing my father.

He finally choked off as the screaming began.

I don't remember how I felt. Isn't that odd? I can remember the lighting—those magnificent chandeliers up above, sprinkling the room with bits of refracted light. I can remember the lemon-ammonia scent of the recently cleaned floor. I can remember all too well the piercing shouts of terror, the mad cacophony as people scrambled for doors.

Most clearly, I remember the Epic smiling broadly—almost leering—as he pointed at people passing, reducing them to ash and bones with a mere gesture.

I was transfixed. Perhaps I was in shock. I clung to the back of my chair, watching the slaughter with wide eyes.

Some people near the doors escaped. Anyone who got too close to the Epic died. Several employees and customers huddled together on the ground or hid behind desks. Strangely, the room grew still. The Epic stood as if he were alone, bits of paper floating down through the air, bones and black ash scattered on the floor about him.

"I am called Deathpoint," he said. "It's not the cleverest of names,

I'll admit. But I find it memorable." His voice was eerily conversational, as if he were chatting with friends over drinks.

He began to stroll through the room. "A thought occurred to me this morning," he said. The room was large enough that his voice echoed. "I was showering, and it struck me. It asked . . . Deathpoint, why are you going to rob a bank today?"

He pointed lazily at a pair of security guards who had edged out of a side hallway just beside the mortgage cubicles. The guards turned to dust, their badges, belt buckles, guns, and bones hitting the floor. I could hear their bones knock against one another as they dropped. There are a lot of bones in a man's body, more than I'd realized, and they made a big mess when they scattered. An odd detail to notice about the horrible scene. But I remember it distinctly.

A hand clasped my shoulder. My father had crouched low before his chair and was trying to pull me down, to keep the Epic from seeing me. But I wouldn't move, and my father couldn't force me without making a scene.

"I've been planning this for weeks, you see," the Epic said. "But the thought only struck me this morning. Why? Why rob the bank? I can take anything I want anyway! It's ridiculous!" He leaped around the side of a counter, causing the teller cowering there to scream. I could just barely make her out, huddled on the floor.

"Money is worthless to me, you see," the Epic said. "*Completely* worthless." He pointed. The woman shriveled to ash and bone.

The Epic pivoted, pointing at several places around the room, killing people who were trying to flee. Last of all, he pointed directly at me.

Finally I felt an emotion. A spike of terror.

A skull hit the desk behind us, bouncing off and spraying ash as it clattered to the floor. The Epic had pointed not at me but at the mortgage man, who had been hiding by his desk behind me. Had the man tried to run?

The Epic turned back toward the tellers behind the counter. My father's hand still gripped my shoulder, tense. I could feel his worry for me almost as if it were a physical thing, running up his arm and into my own.

I felt terror then. Pure, immobilizing terror. I curled up on the chair, whimpering, shaking, trying to banish from my mind the images of the terrible deaths I'd just seen.

My father pulled his hand away. "Don't move," he mouthed.

I nodded, too scared to do anything else. My father glanced around his chair. Deathpoint was chatting with one of the tellers. Though I couldn't see them, I could hear when the bones fell. He was executing them one at a time.

My father's expression grew dark. Then he glanced toward a side hallway. Escape?

No. That was where the guards had fallen. I could see through the glass side of the cubicle to where a handgun lay on the ground, barrel buried in ash, part of the grip lying atop a rib bone. My father eyed it. He'd been in the National Guard when he was younger.

Don't do it! I thought, panicked. *Father, no!* I couldn't voice the words, though. My chin quivered as I tried to speak, like I was cold, and my teeth chattered. What if the Epic heard me?

I couldn't let my father do such a foolish thing! He was all I had. No home, no family, no mother. As he moved to go, I forced myself to reach out and grab his arm. I shook my head at him, trying to think of anything that would stop him. "Please," I managed to whisper. "The heroes. You said they'll come. Let them stop him!"

"Sometimes, son," my father said, prying my fingers free, "you have to help the heroes along."

He glanced at Deathpoint, then scrambled into the next cubicle. I held my breath and peeked very carefully around the side of the chair. I had to know. Even cowering and trembling, I had to see.

Deathpoint hopped over the counter and landed on the other side, our side. "And so, it doesn't matter," he said, still speaking in

6

a conversational tone, strolling across the floor. "Robbing a bank would give me money, but I don't need to *buy* things." He raised a murderous finger. "A conundrum. Fortunately, while showering, I realized something else: killing people every time you want something can be extremely inconvenient. What I needed to do was *frighten* everyone, show them my power. That way, in the future, nobody would deny me the things I wanted to take."

He leaped around a pillar on the other side of the bank, surprising a woman holding her child. "Yes," he continued, "robbing a bank for the money would be pointless—but showing what I can do . . . that is still important. So I continued with my plan." He pointed, killing the child, leaving the horrified woman holding a pile of bones and ash. "Aren't you glad?"

I gaped at the sight, the terrified woman trying to hold the blanket tight, the infant's bones shifting and slipping free. In that moment it all became so much more *real* to me. Horribly real. I felt a sudden nausea.

Deathpoint's back was toward us.

My father scrambled out of the cubicle and grabbed the fallen gun. Two people hiding behind a nearby pillar made for the closest doorway and pushed past my father in their haste, nearly knocking him down.

Deathpoint turned. My father was still kneeling there, trying to get the pistol raised, fingers slipping on the ash-covered metal.

The Epic raised his hand.

"What are you doing here?" a voice boomed.

The Epic spun. So did I. I think everyone must have turned toward that deep, powerful voice.

A figure stood in the doorway to the street. He was backlit, little more than a silhouette because of the bright sunlight shining in behind him. An amazing, herculean, awe-inspiring silhouette.

You've probably seen pictures of Steelheart, but let me tell you that pictures are completely inadequate. No photograph, video, or painting could *ever* capture that man. He wore black. A shirt, tight across an inhumanly large and strong chest. Pants, loose but not baggy. He didn't wear a mask, like some of the early Epics did, but a magnificent silver cape fluttered out behind him.

He didn't *need* a mask. This man had no reason to hide. He spread his arms out from his sides, and wind blew the doors open around him. Ash scattered across the floor and papers fluttered. Steelheart rose into the air a few inches, cape flaring out. He began to glide forward into the room. Arms like steel girders, legs like mountains, neck like a tree stump. He wasn't bulky or awkward, though. He was *majestic,* with that jet-black hair, that square jaw, an impossible physique, and a frame of nearly seven feet.

And those eyes. Intense, demanding, *uncompromising* eyes.

As Steelheart flew gracefully into the room, Deathpoint hastily raised a finger and pointed at him. Steelheart's shirt sizzled in one little section, like a cigarette had been put out on the cloth, but he showed no reaction. He floated down the steps and landed gently on the floor a short distance from Deathpoint, his enormous cape settling around him.

Deathpoint pointed again, looking frantic. Another meager sizzle. Steelheart stepped up to the smaller Epic, towering over him.

I knew in that moment that this was what my father had been waiting for. This was the hero everyone had been hoping would come, the one who would compensate for the other Epics and their evil ways. This man was here to save us.

Steelheart reached out, grabbing Deathpoint as he belatedly tried to dash away. Deathpoint jerked to a halt, his sunglasses clattering to the ground, and gasped in pain.

"I asked you a question," Steelheart said in a voice like rumbling thunder. He spun Deathpoint around to look him in the eyes. "What are you doing here?"

Deathpoint twitched. He looked panicked. "I . . . I . . ."

Steelheart raised his other hand, lifting a finger. "I have claimed this city, little Epic. It is *mine*." He paused. "And it is *my* right to dominate the people here, not yours."

Deathpoint cocked his head.

What? I thought.

"You seem to have strength, little Epic," Steelheart said, glancing at the bones scattered around the room. "I will accept your subservience. Give me your loyalty or die."

I couldn't believe Steelheart's words. They stunned me as soundly as Deathpoint's murders had.

That concept—*serve me or die*—would become the foundation of his rule. He looked around the room and spoke in a booming voice. "I am emperor of this city now. You will obey me. I own this land. I own these buildings. When you pay taxes, they come to me. If you disobey, you will die."

Impossible, I thought. *Not him too.* I couldn't accept that this incredible being was just like all the others.

I wasn't the only one.

"It's not supposed to be this way," my father said.

Steelheart turned, apparently surprised to hear anything from one of the room's cowering, whimpering peons.

My father stepped forward, gun down at his side. "No," he said. "You aren't like the others. I can see it. You're better than they are." He walked forward, stopping only a few feet from the two Epics. "You're here to save us."

The room was silent save for the sobbing of the woman who still clutched the remains of her dead child. She was madly, vainly trying to gather the bones, to not leave a single tiny vertebra on the ground. Her dress was covered in ash.

Before either Epic could respond, the side doors burst open. Men in black armor with assault rifles piled into the bank and opened fire.

Back then, the government hadn't given up yet. They still tried to fight the Epics, to subject them to mortal laws. It was clear from

9

the beginning that when it came to Epics, you didn't hesitate, you didn't negotiate. You came in with guns blazing and hoped that the Epic you were facing could be killed by ordinary bullets.

My father sprang away at a run, old battle instincts prompting him to put his back to a pillar nearer the front of the bank. Steelheart turned, a bemused look on his face, as a wave of bullets washed over him. They bounced off his skin, ripping his clothing but leaving him completely unscathed.

Epics like him are what forced the United States to pass the Capitulation Act that gave all Epics complete immunity from the law. Gunfire cannot harm Steelheart—rockets, tanks, the most advanced weapons of man don't even scratch him. Even if he could be captured, prisons couldn't hold him.

The government eventually declared men such as Steelheart to be natural forces, like hurricanes or earthquakes. Trying to tell Steelheart that he can't take what he wants would be as vain as trying to pass a bill that forbids the wind to blow.

In the bank that day, I saw with my own eyes why so many have decided not to fight back. Steelheart raised a hand, energy beginning to glow around it with a cool yellow light. Deathpoint hid behind him, sheltered from the bullets. Unlike Steelheart, he seemed to fear getting shot. Not all Epics are impervious to gunfire, just the most powerful ones.

Steelheart released a burst of yellow-white energy from his hand, vaporizing a group of the soldiers. Chaos followed. Soldiers ducked for cover wherever they could find it; smoke and chips of marble filled the air. One of the soldiers fired some kind of rocket from his gun, and it shot past Steelheart—who continued to blast his enemies with energy—to hit the back end of the bank, blowing open the vault.

Flaming bills exploded outward. Coins sprayed into the air and showered the ground.

Shouts. Screams. Insanity.

The soldiers died quickly. I continued to huddle on my chair, hands pressed against my ears. It was all so *loud*.

Deathpoint was still standing behind Steelheart. And as I watched, he smiled, then raised his hands, reaching for Steelheart's neck. I don't know what he was planning to do. Likely he had a second power. Most Epics as strong as he was possess more than one.

Maybe it would have been enough to kill Steelheart. I doubt it, but either way, we'll never know.

A single *pop* sounded in the air. The explosion had been so loud it left me deafened to the point that I barely recognized the sound as a gunshot. As the smoke from the explosion cleared, I could see my father. He stood a short distance in front of Steelheart with arms raised, his back to the pillar. He bore an expression of determination on his face and held the gun, pointing it at Steelheart.

No. Not at *Steelheart*. At Deathpoint, who stood just behind him.

Deathpoint collapsed, a bullet wound in his forehead. Dead. Steelheart turned sharply, looking at the lesser Epic. Then he looked back at my father and raised a hand to his face. There, on Steelheart's cheek just below his eye, was a line of blood.

At first I thought it must have come from Deathpoint. But when Steelheart wiped it away, it continued to bleed.

My father had shot at Deathpoint, but the bullet had passed by Steelheart first—and had grazed him on the way.

That bullet had *hurt* Steelheart, while the soldiers' bullets had bounced off.

"I'm sorry," my father said, sounding anxious. "He was reaching for you. I—"

Steelheart's eyes went wide, and he raised his hand before him, looking at his own blood. He seemed completely astounded. He glanced at the vault behind him, then looked at my father. In the settling smoke and dust, the two figures stood before each other—one a massive, regal Epic, the other a small homeless man with a silly T-shirt and worn jeans.

Steelheart jumped forward with blinding speed and slammed a hand against my father's chest, crushing him back against the white stone pillar. Bones shattered, and blood poured from my father's mouth.

"No!" I screamed. My own voice felt odd in my ears, like I was underwater. I wanted to run to him, but I was too frightened. I still think of my cowardice that day, and it sickens me.

Steelheart stepped to the side, picking up the gun my father had dropped. Fury burning in his eyes, Steelheart pointed the gun directly at my father's chest, then fired a single shot into the already-fallen man.

He does that. Steelheart likes to kill people with their own guns. It's become one of his hallmarks. He has incredible strength and can fire blasts of energy from his hands. But when it comes to killing someone he deems worth his special attention, he prefers to use their gun.

Steelheart left my father to slump down the pillar and tossed the handgun at his feet. Then he began to shoot blasts of energy in all directions, setting chairs, walls, counters, everything alight. I was thrown from my chair as one of the blasts struck nearby, and I rolled to the floor.

The explosions threw wood and glass into the air, shaking the room. In a few heartbeats, Steelheart caused enough destruction to make Deathpoint's murder spree seem tame. Steelheart laid waste to that room, knocking down pillars, killing anyone he saw. I'm not sure how I survived, crawling over the shards of glass and splinters of wood, plaster, and dust raining down around me.

Steelheart let out a scream of rage and indignation. I could barely hear it, but I could *feel* it shattering what windows remained, vibrating the walls. Then something spread out from him, a wave of energy. And the floor around him changed colors, transforming to metal.

The transformation spread, washing through the entire room at incredible speed. The floor beneath me, the wall beside me, the bits of glass on the ground—it all changed to steel. What we've learned now is that Steelheart's rage transforms inanimate objects around him into steel, though it leaves living things and anything close to them alone.

By the time his cry faded, most of the bank's interior had been changed completely to steel, though a large chunk of the ceiling was still wood and plaster, as was a section of one wall. Steelheart suddenly launched himself into the air, breaking through the ceiling and several stories to head into the sky.

I stumbled to my father, hoping he could do something, somehow stop the madness. When I got to him, he was spasming, blood covering his face, chest bleeding from the bullet wound. I clung to his arm, panicked.

Incredibly, he managed to speak, but I couldn't hear what he said. I was deafened completely by that point. My father reached out, a quivering hand touching my chin. He said something else, but I still couldn't hear him.

I wiped my eyes with my sleeve, then tried to pull his arm to get him to stand up and come with me. The entire building was shaking.

My father grabbed my shoulder, and I looked at him, tears in my eyes. He spoke a single word—one I could make out from the movement of his lips.

"Go."

I understood. Something huge had just happened, something that exposed Steelheart, something that terrified him. He was a new Epic back then, not very well known in town, but I'd heard of him. He was supposed to be invulnerable.

That gunshot had wounded him, and everyone there had seen him weak. There was no way he'd let us live—he had to preserve his secret.

Tears streaming down my cheeks, feeling like an utter coward for leaving my father, I turned and ran. The building continued to tremble with explosions; walls cracked, sections of the ceiling crumbled. Steelheart was trying to bring it down.

Some people ran out the front doors, but Steelheart killed them from above. Others ran out side doors, but those doorways only led deeper into the bank. Those people were crushed as most of the building collapsed.

I hid in the vault.

I wish I could claim that I was smart for making that choice, but I'd simply gotten turned around. I vaguely remember crawling into a dark corner and curling up into a ball, crying as the rest of the building fell apart. Since most of the main room had been turned to metal by Steelheart's rage, and the vault was steel in the first place, those areas didn't crumble as the rest of the building did.

Hours later, I was pulled out of the wreckage by a rescue worker. I was dazed, barely conscious, and the light blinded me as I was dug free. The room I had been in had sunk partially, lurched on its side, but it was still strangely intact, the walls and most of the ceiling now made of steel. The rest of the large building was rubble.

The rescue worker whispered something in my ear. "Pretend to be dead." Then she carried me to a line of corpses and put a blanket over me. She'd guessed what Steelheart might do to survivors.

Once she went back to look for other survivors, I panicked and crawled from beneath the blanket. It was dark outside, though it should have only been late afternoon. Nightwielder was upon us; Steelheart's reign had begun.

I stumbled away and limped into an alley. That saved my life a second time. Moments after I escaped, Steelheart returned, floating down past the rescue lights to land beside the wreckage. He carried someone with him, a thin woman with her hair in a bun. I would later learn she was an Epic named Faultline, who had the power to move earth. Though she would one day challenge Steelheart, at that point she served him.

She waved her hand and the ground began to shake.

I fled, confused, frightened, pained. Behind me, the ground opened up, swallowing the remnants of the bank—along with the corpses of the fallen, the survivors who were receiving medical attention, and the rescue workers themselves. Steelheart wanted to leave no evidence. He had Faultline bury all of them under hundreds of feet of earth, killing anyone who could possibly speak of what had happened in that bank.

Except me.

Later that night, he performed the Great Transfersion, an awesome display of power by which he transformed most of Chicago—buildings, vehicles, streets—into steel. That included a large portion of Lake Michigan, which became a glassy expanse of black metal. It was there that he built his palace.

I know, better than anyone else, that there are no heroes coming to save us. There are no good Epics. None of them protect us. Power corrupts, and absolute power corrupts absolutely.

We live with them. We try to exist *despite* them. Once the Capitulation Act was passed, most people stopped fighting. In some areas of what we now call the Fractured States, the old government is still marginally in control. They let the Epics do as they please, and try to continue as a broken society. Most places are chaos, though, with no law at all.

In a few places, like Newcago, a single godlike Epic rules as a tyrant. Steelheart has no rivals here. Everyone knows he's invulnerable. Nothing harms him: not bullets, not explosions, not electricity. In the early years, other Epics tried to take him down and claim his throne, as Faultline attempted.

They're all dead. Now it's very rare that any of them tries.

However, if there's one fact we can hold on to, it's this: *every* Epic has a weakness. Something that invalidates their powers, something that turns them back into an ordinary person, if only for a moment. Steelheart is no exception; the events on that day in the bank prove it.

My mind holds a clue to how Steelheart might be killed. Something about the bank, the situation, the gun, or my father himself was able to counteract Steelheart's invulnerability. Many of you probably know about that scar on Steelheart's cheek. Well, as far as I can determine, I'm the only living person who knows how he got it.

I've seen Steelheart bleed.

And I *will* see him bleed again.

PART ONE

1

I skidded down a stairwell and crunched against steel gravel at the bottom. Sucking in air, I dashed through one of the dark understreets of Newcago. Ten years had passed since my father's death. That fateful day had become known by most people as the Annexation.

I wore a loose leather jacket and jeans, and had my rifle slung over my shoulder. The street was dark, even though it was one of the shallow understreets with grates and holes looking up into the sky.

It's always dark in Newcago. Nightwielder was one of the first Epics to swear allegiance to Steelheart, and is a member of his inner circle. Because of Nightwielder there are no sunrises, and no moon to speak of, just pure darkness in the sky. All the time, every day. The only thing you can see up there is Calamity, which looks kind of like a bright red star or comet. Calamity began to shine one year before men started turning into Epics. Nobody knows why or how it still shines through the darkness. Of course, nobody knows why the Epics started appearing, or what their connection is to Calamity either.

I kept running, cursing myself for not leaving earlier. The lights along the ceiling of the understreet flickered, their coverings tinted blue. The understreet was littered with its typical losers: addicts at corners, dealers—or worse—in alleyways. There were some furtive groups of workers going to or from their jobs, thick coats and collars flipped up to hide their faces. They walked hunched over, eyes on the ground.

I'd spent most of the last decade among people like them, working at a place we simply called the Factory. Part orphanage, part school, it was mostly a way to exploit children for free labor. At least the Factory had given me a room and food for the better part of ten years. That had been way better than living on the street, and I hadn't minded for one moment working for my food. Child labor laws were relics of a time when people could care about such things.

I pushed my way past a pack of workers. One cursed at me in a language that sounded vaguely Spanish. I looked up to see where I was. Most intersections were marked by spray-painted street names on the gleaming metallic walls.

When the Great Transfersion caused the better part of the Old City to be turned into solid steel, that included the soil and rock, dozens—maybe hundreds—of feet down into the ground. During the early years of his reign, Steelheart pretended to be a benevolent—if ruthless—dictator. His Diggers had cut out several levels of understreets, complete with buildings, and people had flowed to Newcago for work.

Life had been difficult here, but it had been chaos everywhere else—Epics warring with one another over territory, various paragovernmental or state military groups trying to claim land. Newcago was different. Here you could be casually murdered by an Epic who didn't like the way you looked at him, but at least there was electricity, water, and food. People adapt. That's what we do.

Except for the ones who refuse to.

Come on, I thought, checking the time on my mobile, which I wore in the forearm mount of my coat. *Blasted rail line outage.* I took another shortcut, barreling through an alleyway. It was dim, but after ten years of living in perpetual gloom, you got used to it.

I passed huddled forms of sleeping beggars, then leaped over one sprawled in the street at the end of the alleyway and burst out onto Siegel Street, a wider thoroughfare that was better lit than most. Here, one level underground, the Diggers had hollowed out rooms that people used as shops. They were closed up for the moment, though more than a few had someone watching out front with a shotgun. Steelheart's police theoretically patrolled the understreets, but they rarely came to help except in the worst cases.

Originally, Steelheart had spoken of a grand underground city that would stretch down dozens of levels. That was before the Diggers had gone mad, before Steelheart had given up the pretense of caring about the people in the understreets. Still, these upper levels weren't terrible. At least there was a sense of organization, and plenty of burrowed-out holes to use as homes.

The lights in the ceiling here were faintly green and yellow, alternating. If you knew the color patterns of the various streets, you could navigate pretty well through the understreets. The top levels, at least. Even veterans of the city tended to avoid the lower levels, called the steel catacombs, where it was too easy to get lost.

Two blocks to Schuster Street, I thought, glancing through a gap in the ceiling toward the better-lit, gleaming skyscrapers above. I jogged the two blocks, then swerved into a stairwell going up, feet falling on steel steps that reflected the dim, half-functional lights.

I scrambled out onto a metal street, then immediately ducked into an alleyway. A lot of people said that the overstreets weren't nearly as dangerous as the understreets, but I never felt comfortable on them. I never felt safe anywhere, to be honest, not even at the Factory with the other kids. But up here . . . up here there were Epics.

Carrying a rifle around the understreets was common practice, but up here it could draw attention from Steelheart's soldiers or a passing Epic. It was best to remain hidden. I crouched beside some boxes in the alleyway, catching my breath. I glanced at my mobile, tapping over to a basic map of the area, then looked up.

Directly across from me was a building with red neon lettering. The Reeve Playhouse. As I watched, people began pouring out the front, and I breathed a sigh of relief. I'd made it just as the play ended.

The people were all overstreeters, in dark suits and colorful dresses. Some would be Epics, but most would not. Instead they were those who had somehow gotten ahead in life. Perhaps Steelheart favored them for tasks they performed, or perhaps they had simply been born to rich parents. Steelheart could take anything he wanted, but to have an empire he needed people to help rule. Bureaucrats, officers in his army, accountants, trading gurus, diplomats. Like the upper crust of an old-school dictatorship, these people lived off the crumbs that Steelheart left behind.

That meant they were almost as culpable as the Epics in keeping the rest of us oppressed, but I didn't bear them much ill will. The way the world was these days, you did what you had to in order to survive.

They had an old-fashioned style—it was the current trend. The men wore hats, and the women's dresses looked like those from pictures I'd seen of old Prohibition days. It was a direct contrast to the modern steel buildings and the distant thumping of an advanced Enforcement copter.

The opulent people suddenly began moving out of the way,

making room for a man in a bright red pinstriped suit, a red fedora, and a deep red and black cape.

I ducked down a little lower. It was Fortuity. He was an Epic with precognition powers. He could guess the numbers that would come up on a dice roll, for instance, or foretell the weather. He could also sense danger, and that elevated him to High Epic status. You couldn't kill a man like him with a simple rifle shot. He would know the shot was coming and would dodge it before you pulled the trigger. His powers were so well attuned that he could avoid a machine-gun barrage, and he would also know if his food had been poisoned or if a building was rigged with explosives.

High Epics. They're blasted hard to kill.

Fortuity was a moderately high-ranking member of Steelheart's government. Not part of his innermost circle, like Nightwielder, Firefight, or Conflux, but powerful enough to be feared by most of the minor Epics in town. He had a long face and a hawkish nose. He strolled to the curb in front of the playhouse, lighting a cigarette as the other patrons spilled out behind him. Two women in sleek gowns hung on his elbows.

I itched to unsling my rifle and take a shot at him. He was a sadistic monster. He claimed his powers worked best when practicing an art called extispicy: the reading of the entrails of dead creatures to divine the future. Fortuity preferred to use human entrails, and he liked them fresh.

I held myself back. The moment I decided to try to shoot him, his powers would activate. Fortuity had nothing to fear from a lone sniper. He probably thought he didn't have anything to fear at all. If my information was right, the next hour would prove him very wrong on that count.

Come on, I thought. *This is the best time to move against him. I'm right. I've got to be.*

Fortuity took a drag on his cigarette, nodding to a few people who passed by. He had no bodyguards. Why would he need

23

bodyguards? His fingers glittered with rings, though wealth was meaningless to him. Even without Steelheart's rules granting him the right to take what he wanted, Fortuity could win a fortune in any gambling house on any day he chose.

Nothing happened. Had I been wrong? I'd been so *sure*. Bilko's information was usually up to date. Word in the understreets was that the Reckoners were back in Newcago. Fortuity *was* the Epic they'd target. I knew this. I'd made a habit—maybe even a quest—of studying the Reckoners. I—

A woman walked past Fortuity. Tall, lithe, and golden-haired, and perhaps twenty years old, she wore a thin red dress with a plunging neckline. Even with two beauties on his arms, Fortuity turned and stared at her. She hesitated, glancing back at him. Then she smiled and walked up, hips undulating back and forth.

I couldn't hear what they said, but in the end, this newcomer displaced the other women. She led Fortuity down the road, whispering in his ear and laughing. The other two women waited behind, arms crossed, not daring to complain. Fortuity did *not* like his women to speak back to him.

This had to be it. I wanted to get ahead of them, but couldn't do so on the street itself. Instead I moved back through a few alleyways. I knew the area perfectly; studying maps of the theater district was what had almost made me late.

I hustled around the back of a building, sticking to the shadows, and arrived at another alleyway. From here I could peek out and see the same road, but from another angle. Fortuity ambled along the steel sidewalk outside.

The area was lit by lamps hanging from streetlights. The streetlights themselves had been turned to steel during the transfersion—electronics and bulbs included. They no longer worked, but they did provide a convenient place to hang lanterns.

Those lanterns left pools of light that the pair moved through, in and out. I held my breath, watching closely. Fortuity was packing a

24

weapon for certain. The suit was tailored to hide the bulge under his arm, but I could still make out where his holster was.

Fortuity didn't have any directly offensive powers, but that didn't really matter. His precognition powers meant he never missed with a handgun, no matter how wild the shot seemed. If he decided to kill you, you had a couple of seconds to respond, or you'd be dead.

The woman didn't appear to be carrying a weapon, though I couldn't be certain. That dress showed plenty of curves. A gun strapped to her thigh, perhaps? I looked closer as she moved into another pool of light, though I found myself staring at her, rather than looking for weapons. She was gorgeous. Eyes that glittered, bright red lips, golden hair. And that low neckline . . .

I shook myself. *Idiot,* I thought. *You have a purpose. Women interfere with things like a purpose.*

But even a ninety-year-old blind priest would stop and stare at this woman. If he weren't blind, that is. *Dumb metaphor,* I thought. *I'll have to work on that one.* I have trouble with metaphors.

Focus. I raised my rifle, leaving on the safety and using the scope for its zoom. Where were they going to hit him? The street here ran through several blocks of gloomy darkness—broken only by the lanterns—before intersecting Burnley Street. That was a major hub of the local dance scene. Likely the woman had enticed Fortuity to join her at a club. The quickest route was through this dark, less-populated street.

The empty street was a very good sign. The Reckoners rarely struck at an Epic who was in too public an area. They didn't like innocent casualties. I tilted the rifle up and scanned the skyrise windows with my scope. Some of the glass-turned-steel windows had been cut out and replaced with glass again. Was anyone up there watching?

I'd been hunting the Reckoners for years. They were the only ones who still fought back, a shadowy group that stalked, entrapped, and assassinated powerful Epics. The Reckoners, *they* were the heroes. Not what my father had imagined—no Epic powers, no flashy costumes. They didn't stand for truth, the American ideal, or any such nonsense.

They just killed. One by one. Their goal was to eliminate each and every Epic who thought himself or herself above the law. And since that was pretty much *every* Epic, they had a lot of work to do.

I continued scanning windows. How would they try to kill Fortuity? There would only be a few ways to go about it. They might try to catch him in a situation impossible to escape. A precog's powers would lead him down the safest path of self-preservation, but if you set up a situation where *every* path led to death, you could kill him.

We call that a checkmate, but they're really hard to set up. More likely, the Reckoners knew Fortuity's weakness. Every Epic has at least one—an object, a state of mind, an action of some sort—that allows you to void their powers.

There, I thought, heart leaping as—through the scope—I spotted a dark figure huddled in a window on the third floor of a building across the street. I couldn't make out details, but he was probably tracking Fortuity with a rifle and scope of his own.

This was it. I smiled. I'd actually found them. After all of my practicing and searching, I'd *found* them.

I kept looking, even more eager. The sniper would just be one piece of the plot to kill the Epic. My hands began to sweat. Other people get excited by sporting events or action films, but I don't have time for prefabricated thrills. This, however . . . getting the chance to watch the Reckoners in action, seeing one of their traps firsthand . . . Well, it was literally the fulfillment of one of my grandest dreams, even if it was only the first step in my plans. I hadn't come just to watch an Epic be assassinated. Before the night's end, I intended to find a way to make the Reckoners let me join them.

"Fortuity!" yelled a nearby voice.

I quickly lowered my rifle, pulling back against the side of the alleyway. A figure ran past the opening a moment later. He was a stout man in a smoking jacket and slacks.

"Fortuity!" he yelled again. "Wait up!" I raised my weapon again, using the scope to inspect the newcomer. Was this part of the Reckoners' trap?

No. That was Donny "Curveball" Harrison, a minor Epic with only a single power, the ability to fire a handgun without ever running out of bullets. He was a bodyguard and hit man in Steelheart's organization. There was no way he was part of the Reckoners' plan—they didn't work with Epics. Ever. The Reckoners hated the Epics. They only killed the worst of them, but they would *never* let one join their team.

Cursing softly to myself, I watched Curveball confront Fortuity and the woman. She looked concerned, full lips pursed, gorgeous eyes narrowed. Yes, she was worried. She was one of the Reckoners for certain.

Curveball started talking, explaining something, and Fortuity frowned. What was going on?

I turned my attention back to the woman. *There's something about her . . .* , I thought, my eyes lingering. She was younger than I'd originally thought, probably eighteen or nineteen, but something in those eyes made her *seem* much older.

Her look of concern was gone in a moment, replaced by what I realized was intentional vapidity as she turned to Fortuity and gestured onward. Whatever the trap was, she needed him to be farther down the street. That made sense. Trapping a precog is *tough*. If his danger senses got even a faint whiff of a trap, he'd bolt. She *had* to know his weakness, but probably didn't want to try to exploit it until they were more isolated.

Even then, it might not work. Fortuity would still be an armed man, and many Epic weaknesses were notoriously tricky to exploit.

I kept watching. Whatever Curveball's problem was, it didn't seem to have anything to do with the woman. He kept gesturing back toward the playhouse. If he convinced Fortuity to return . . .

The trap would never be sprung. The Reckoners would pull out, vanish, pick a new target. I could spend years searching for another chance like this one.

I couldn't let that happen. Taking a deep breath, I lowered my rifle and slung it over my shoulder. Then I stepped out onto the street and took off toward Fortuity.

It was time to hand the Reckoners my résumé.

2

I hustled down the dark street on a steel sidewalk, passing in and out of pockets of light.

I might have just decided to do something very, very stupid. Like eating-meat-sold-by-shady-understreet-vendors stupid. Maybe even stupider. The Reckoners planned their assassinations with extreme care. It hadn't been my intention to interfere—only to watch, then try to get them to take me on. By stepping out of that alleyway, I changed things. Interfered with the plan, whatever it was. There was a chance that everything was going just as it was supposed to— that Curveball was accounted for.

But maybe not. No plan was perfect, and even the Reckoners failed. Sometimes they pulled out, their target left alive. It was better to retreat than risk capture.

I didn't know which situation this was, but I had to at least try to help. If I missed this opportunity, I'd curse myself for years.

All three people—Fortuity, Curveball, and the beauty with the dangerous air—turned toward me as I ran up. "Donny!" I said. "We need you back at the Reeve!"

Curveball frowned at me, eyeing my rifle. He reached under his jacket for his gun, but didn't pull it out. Fortuity, in his red suit and deep red cape, raised an eyebrow at me. If I'd been a danger, his powers would have warned him. I wasn't planning to do anything to him in the next few minutes, though, so he got no warning.

"Who are *you*?" Curveball demanded.

I stopped. "Who am I? Sparks, Donny! I've worked for Spritzer for three years now. Would it *kill* you to try remembering people's names once in a while?"

My heart was thumping, but I tried not to show it. Spritzer was the guy who ran the Reeve Playhouse. Spritz wasn't an Epic, but he was in Steelheart's pay—pretty much anyone with any influence in the city was.

Curveball studied me suspiciously, but I knew he didn't give much mind to the lowlife thugs around him. In fact, he probably would have been shocked by how much I knew about him, along with most of the Epics in Newcago.

"Well?" I demanded. "You coming?"

"You don't give lip to me, boy. What are you, a door guard?"

"I went on the Idolin raid last summer," I said, crossing my arms. "I'm moving up, Donny."

"You call me sir, idiot," Curveball snapped, lowering his hand from his jacket. "If you were 'moving up,' you wouldn't be running messages. What's this nonsense about going back? He said he needed Fortuity to run some odds for him."

I shrugged. "He didn't tell me *why*; he just sent me to get you. Said to say that he'd been wrong, and you weren't to bother Fortuity." I looked to Fortuity. "I don't think the Spritz knew about . . . er . . . that you had plans, sir." I nodded to the woman.

There was a long, uncomfortable pause. I was so nervous, you could have scratched off a lottery ticket by holding it against my knuckles. Finally, Fortuity sniffed. "Tell Spritz that he's forgiven, this time. He should know better—I'm not his personal calculator." He turned, sticking out his elbow to the woman and walking away, obviously assuming that she'd jump at his whim.

As she turned to follow, she glanced at me, long lashes fluttering above deep blue eyes. I found myself smiling.

Then I realized that if I'd fooled Fortuity, I'd probably fooled her too. That meant she—and the Reckoners—now thought I was one of Steelheart's lackeys. They were always careful not to endanger civilians, but they had nothing at all against taking out a few hit men or thugs.

Aw, sparks, I thought. *I should have winked at her! Why didn't I wink at her?*

Would that have looked stupid? I'd never really practiced winking. Could you do it the wrong way, though? It was a simple thing.

"Something wrong with your eye?" Curveball asked.

"Er, got a lash in it," I said. "Sir. Sorry. Um, we should get back." The thought of the Reckoners setting off their trap in time to take out Curveball—and me—as a nice side effect suddenly made me very, very nervous.

I hurried down the sidewalk, splashing through some puddles. Rain didn't evaporate quickly in the darkness, and with the steel ground, there wasn't anywhere for it to go. The Diggers had created some drainage, along with pipes to circulate air in the understreets, but their eventual madness had disrupted those plans and they'd never finished.

Curveball followed me at a moderate speed. I slowed down, matching his pace, worried he might come up with a reason to go back for Fortuity.

"What's your hurry, kid?" he growled.

In the distance, the woman and Fortuity had stopped beneath a streetlight, where they had taken to searching one another's mouths with their tongues.

"Stop staring," Curveball said, walking past. "He could gun us down without even looking and nobody would care."

It was true. Fortuity was a powerful enough Epic that—so long as he didn't interfere with one of Steelheart's plans—he could do whatever he pleased. Curveball himself didn't have that kind of immunity. You still had to be careful when you were at his level. Steelheart wouldn't care if a minor Epic like Curveball got himself stabbed in the back.

I tore my eyes away and joined Curveball. He lit up a cigarette as he walked, a flash of light in the dark, followed by the coal-red sizzle of the tip hanging in the air before him. "Sparks, Spritz," he said. "Could have sent one of you lackeys out after Fortuity in the first place. I hate looking like a slontze."

"You know how Spritz is," I said absently. "He figured that sending you would be less offensive to Fortuity, since you're an Epic."

"Suppose that's right." Curveball took a pull on his cigarette. "Whose team are you in?"

"Eddie Macano's," I said, naming one of the underlings in Spritz's organization. I glanced over my shoulder. They were *still* going at it. "He was the one who made me run after you. Didn't want to do it himself. Too busy trying to pick up one of those girls Fortuity left behind. Whatta slontze, eh?"

"Eddie Macano?" Curveball said, turning toward me. The red tip of his cigarette lit his perplexed face a scarlet orange. "He died in that skirmish with the underbloods two days back. I was there. . . ."

I froze. *Whoops.*

Curveball reached for his gun.

Ǝ

HANDGUNS have one distinct advantage over rifles — they're fast. I didn't even try to beat him to the draw. I ducked to the side, running as fast as I could toward an alleyway.

In the near distance, somebody screamed. *Fortuity*, I thought. *Did he see me run? But I'm not standing in the light, and he wasn't watching. This is something else. The trap must have—*

Curveball opened fire on me.

The thing about handguns is that they're blasted difficult to aim. Even trained, practiced professionals miss more often than they hit. And if you level the gun out in front of you sideways—like you think you're in some stupid action movie—you'll hit even *less* often.

That was exactly what Curveball did, flashes from the front of his gun lighting the darkness. A bullet hit the ground near me, spraying sparks as it ricocheted off the steel pavement. I skidded into an alleyway and pressed myself back against the wall, out of Curveball's direct line of sight.

Bullets continued to spray against the wall. I didn't dare look out, but I could hear Curveball cursing and yelling. I was too panicked to count shots. A magazine like his couldn't hold more than a dozen or so bullets—

Oh, right, I thought. *His Epic power.* The man could keep blasting away and never run out of bullets. Eventually he'd round the corner and get a direct shot.

Only one thing to do. I took a deep breath, letting my rifle slide off my shoulder and catching it with my hand. I dropped to one knee in the mouth of the alleyway, putting myself at risk, and raised the rifle. The burning cigarette gave me a sight on Curveball's face.

A bullet hit the wall above me. I prepared to squeeze the trigger.

"Stop it, you slontze!" a voice called, interrupting Curveball. A figure moved between us in the dim light just as I fired. The shot missed. That was *Fortuity*.

I lowered my gun as another shot rang out from high above. The sniper. A bullet struck the ground nearby, almost hitting Fortuity— but he jerked sideways at just the right moment. His danger sense.

Fortuity ran awkwardly, and as he got closer to a lantern, I saw why. He was handcuffed. Still, he was escaping; whatever the Reckoners' plan was, it looked like it had fallen apart.

Curveball and I glanced at each other, then he took off following Fortuity, firing a few stray shots in my direction. Having infinite bullets didn't make him any better a shot, however, and they all went wide.

I climbed to my feet and looked the other direction, toward where the woman had been. Was she all right?

A loud *crack* sounded in the air, and Curveball screamed, dropping to the ground. I smiled, right until a second shot fired and a spray of sparks exploded from the wall beside me. I cursed, ducking back into my alleyway. A second later the woman in the sleek red dress spun into the alleyway, holding a tiny derringer pistol and pointing it directly at my face.

People firing handguns missed, on average, from over ten paces—but I wasn't sure of the statistics when the pistol was fifteen inches from your face. Probably not so good for the target.

"Wait!" I said, holding up my hands, letting my rifle fall in its strap on my shoulder. "I'm trying to help! Didn't you see Curveball firing at me?"

"Who do you work for?" the woman demanded.

"Havendark Factory," I said. "I used to drive a cab, though I—"

"Slontze," she said. Gun still trained on me, she raised her hand to her head, touching one finger to her ear. I could see an earring there that was probably tethered to her mobile. "Megan here. Tia. Blow it."

An explosion sounded nearby and I jumped. "What was that!"

"The Reeve Playhouse."

"You *blew up* the Reeve?" I said. "I thought the Reckoners didn't hurt innocents!"

That froze her, gun still pointed at me. "How do you know who we are?"

"You're hunting Epics. Who else would you be?"

"But—" She cut off, cursing softly, raising her finger again. "No time. Abraham. Where is the mark?"

I couldn't hear the reply, but it obviously satisfied her. A few more explosions sounded in the distance.

She eyed me, but my hands were still raised, and she *must* have seen Curveball firing on me. She apparently decided I wasn't a threat. She lowered her gun and hurriedly reached down, breaking the stiletto heels off her shoes. Then she grabbed the side of her dress and ripped it off.

I gaped.

I normally consider myself somewhat levelheaded, but it's not every day that you find yourself in a darkened alleyway with a gorgeous woman who rips off most of her clothing. Underneath she wore a low-cut tank top and a pair of spandex biker shorts. I was pleased to note that the gun holster was, indeed, strapped to her right thigh. Her mobile was hooked to the outside of the sheath.

She tossed the dress aside—it had been designed to come off easily. Her arms were lean and firm, and the wide-eyed naivety she'd shown earlier was completely gone, replaced with a hard edge and a determined expression.

I took a step, and in a heartbeat her pistol was trained on my forehead again. I froze.

"Out of the alleyway," she said, gesturing.

I nervously did as asked, walking back onto the street.

"On your knees, hands on head."

"I don't really—"

"Down!"

I got down on my knees, feeling stupid, raising my hands to my head.

"Hardman," she said, finger to her ear. "If Knees here so much as *sneezes*, put a slug through his neck."

"But—" I began.

She took off at a run down the street, moving much more quickly now that she'd removed the heels and the dress. That left me alone. I felt like an idiot kneeling there, hairs on my neck prickling as I thought of the sniper who had his weapon trained on me.

How many agents did the Reckoners have here? I couldn't imagine them trying anything like this without at least two dozen. Another explosion shook the ground. Why the blasts? They'd alert Enforcement, Steelheart's soldiers. Lackeys and thugs were bad enough; Enforcement wielded advanced guns and the occasional armor unit—twelve-foot-tall robotic suits of power armor.

The next explosion was closer, just down the block. Something must have gone wrong in their original plan, otherwise Fortuity wouldn't have gotten away from the woman in red. Megan? Was that what she'd said her name was?

This was one of their contingency plans. But what were they trying to do?

A figure burst out of an alleyway nearby, almost making me jump. I held still, cursing that sniper, but I did turn my head slightly to look. The figure wore red, and still had handcuffs on. Fortuity.

The explosions, I realized. *They were to scare him back this way!*

He crossed the street, then turned to run in my direction. Megan—if that was really her name—burst from the same road he'd appeared out of. She turned this way, trying to chase him down, but behind her—in the distance—another group of figures rushed out from a different street.

They were four of Spritz's thugs, in suits and carrying submachine guns. They pointed at Megan.

I watched from the other side of the street as Megan and Fortuity passed me. The thugs were approaching from my right, and Megan and Fortuity were running to my left, all of us on the same darkened street.

Come on! I thought at the sniper up above. *She doesn't see them! They'll gun her down. Take them out!*

Nothing. The thugs leveled their guns. I felt sweat trickle down the back of my neck. Then, teeth clenched, I rolled to the side, whipping my rifle out and drawing a bead on one of them.

I took a deep breath, concentrated, and squeezed the trigger, fully expecting to be shot in the head from above.

4

A handgun is like a firecracker—unpredictable. Light a firecracker, toss it, and you never really know where it's going to land or the damage it's going to do. The same's true when you shoot a handgun.

An Uzi is even worse—it's like a string of firecrackers. Much more likely to hurt something, but still awkward and unruly.

A rifle is elegant. It's an extension of your will. Take aim, squeeze the trigger, make things happen. In the hands of an expert with stillness inside of him, there's nothing more deadly than a good rifle.

The first thug fell to my shot. I inched the gun to the side, then squeezed again. The second went down. The other two lowered their weapons, dodging.

Look. Squeeze. Three down. The last one was full-out running by the time I focused on him, and he managed to get behind cover. I hesitated, spine itching—waiting to feel the bullet from the sniper hit my back. It didn't come. Hardman, it appeared, had realized that I was a good guy.

I stood up hesitantly. It wasn't the first time I'd killed, unfortunately. It didn't happen often, but once or twice, I'd had to protect myself in the understreets. This was different, but I didn't have time to think about it.

I shoved those emotions aside, and not knowing what else to do, I turned to the left and took off at a dead run down the street after Fortuity and the Reckoner woman. The Epic cursed and weaved toward a side street. The streets were all empty. Our explosions and gunfire had caused anyone nearby to clear out—this sort of thing wasn't uncommon in Newcago.

Megan dashed after Fortuity, and I was able to cut to the side and meet up with her. She glared at me as we barreled down the cross street, shoulder to shoulder, after the Epic.

"I told you to stay put, Knees!" she yelled.

"Good thing I ignored you! I just saved your life."

"That's why I haven't shot you. Get out of here."

I ignored her, aiming my rifle as I ran and taking a shot at the Epic. It went wide   it was too hard to run and fire at the same time. *He's fast!* I thought, annoyed.

"That's useless," the girl said. "You can't hit him."

"I can slow him down," I said, lowering the rifle, running past a pub with lights off and doors closed. A group of nervous patrons watched from one of the windows. "Dodging will throw him off balance."

"Not for long."

"We need to both fire at once," I said. "We can pin him between two bullets, so either way he dodges, he'll hit one of them. Checkmate."

"Are you insane?" she said, still running. "That would be near impossible."

She was right. "Well, let's use his weakness, then. I know you know what it is—otherwise you'd never have gotten those handcuffs on him."

"It won't help," she said, dodging around a lamppost.

"It worked for you. Tell me what it is. I'll use it."

"Slontze," she cursed at me. "His danger sense is weakened if he's attracted to you. So unless he finds you a *whole* lot prettier than I do, it's *not* going to help."

Oh, I thought. Well, that was a problem.

"We need to—" Megan began, but then cut off, raising her finger to her ear as we ran. "No! I can do this! I don't *care* how close they are!"

They're trying to get her to pull out, I realized. It wouldn't be long before Enforcement arrived.

Ahead of us an unfortunate driver, probably on the way to the club district, pulled around the corner. The car screeched to a halt, and Fortuity cut in front of it, heading to the right down another alleyway that would lead him toward more populated streets.

I got an idea.

"Take this," I said, tossing my rifle to Megan. I whipped out my extra magazine and tossed it to her as well. "Fire at him. Slow him down."

"What?" Megan demanded. "Who are you to give me—"

"Do it!" I said, skidding to a stop beside the car. I pulled open the passenger door. "Out," I said to the woman behind the wheel.

The bystander got out and scurried away, leaving the keys in the ignition. In a world full of Epics with the legal right to take any vehicle they want, few people ask questions. Steelheart is brutal with thieves who aren't Epics, so most would never try what I'd just done.

Outside the car, Megan cursed, then raised my rifle expertly and took a shot. She had good aim, and Fortuity—just a little ways down the alleyway—stumbled to the right, his danger sense prompting him to dodge out of the way. As I'd hoped, it slowed him considerably.

I gunned the engine. It was a nice sporty coupe, and it looked practically new. Pity, that.

I tore off down the street. I'd told Megan that I'd been a cab-driver. Which was true; I'd tried it a few months back, right after graduating from the Factory. I hadn't mentioned, however, that the job had lasted only one day; I'd proven terrible at it.

You never know how much you'll like something until you try it out. It had been one of my father's famous sayings. The cab company hadn't expected me to "try out" driving for the first time in one of their cars. But how else was a guy like me supposed to get behind a wheel? I was an orphan who had been owned by the Factory for most of my life. My type didn't exactly make big money, and the understreets don't have room for cars anyway.

Regardless, driving had proven a tad more difficult than I'd expected it to be. I screeched around the corner of the dark street, the gas pedal pressed to the floor, barely in control. I knocked down a stop sign and a street sign on my way, but I made it down the block in a matter of heartbeats and screeched around another corner. I hit a few trash cans as I went up over the curb, but managed to retain control as I turned and pulled the car to a stop facing south.

I was pointing it directly down the alleyway. Fortuity was still stumbling through it toward me, tripping on refuse and boxes as Megan slowed him.

There was a pop, Fortuity dodged, and my windshield suddenly cracked—a bullet blasting through it about an inch from my head. My heart leaped. Megan was still shooting.

You know, David, I thought to myself. *You really need to start thinking your plans through a little more carefully.*

I slammed the pedal down, roaring into the alleyway. It was just barely wide enough for the car, and sparks flew up on the left side as I veered a hair too far in that direction, shearing off the side mirror.

The headlights shone on a figure in a red leisure suit, hands cuffed together, cape flapping behind him. He'd lost his hat while running. His eyes were wide. There was nowhere for him to go in either direction.

Checkmate.

Or so I thought. As I got close, Fortuity leaped into the air and slammed his feet into the front of my windshield with superhuman dexterity.

That utterly shocked me. Fortuity wasn't supposed to have any enhanced physical abilities. Of course, for a man like him—who avoided danger so easily—there may not have been many opportunities to display such things. Either way, his feet hit my windshield in an expert maneuver only someone with super reflexes could have managed. He pushed off and jumped backward, the windshield shattering into pebbled glass, using the momentum of the car to throw himself into a backflip.

I slammed on the brakes and blinked as the glass sprayed my face. The car screeched to a halt in a shower of sparks. Fortuity landed his flip with poise.

I shook my head, dazed. *Yeah, super reflexes,* a piece of my mind thought. *I should have realized. Perfect complement to a precog portfolio.* Fortuity was wise to keep the secret. Many a powerful Epic had realized that hiding one or two abilities gave them an edge when another Epic tried to kill them.

Fortuity ran forward. I could see him glaring at me, lips curling up in a sneer. He was a monster—I'd documented over a hundred murders tied to him. And from the look in his eyes, he intended to add my name to that list.

He leaped into the air, toward the hood of the car.

Crack! Crack!

Fortuity's chest exploded.

5

FORTUITY'S corpse slammed down onto the hood of the car. Megan stood behind him, my rifle in one hand—held at the hip— her pistol in the other hand. The car's headlights bathed her in light. "Sparks!" she cursed. "I can't believe that actually worked."

She fired both at once, I realized. *She checkmated him in the air with two shots.* It had probably only worked because he'd been jumping—in midair it would have been harder for him to jerk out of the way. But still, shooting like that was incredible. A gun in each hand, one of them a rifle?

Sparks, I thought, echoing her. We'd actually won.

Megan pulled Fortuity's body off the hood and checked for a pulse. "Dead," she said. Then she shot the body twice in the head. "And double dead, to be certain."

At that moment about a dozen of Spritz's thugs appeared at the end of the alleyway, sporting Uzis.

I swore, scrambling into the back seat of the car. Megan jumped onto the hood and slid through the shattered windshield, ducking down in the passenger seat as a hailstorm of bullets slammed into the vehicle.

I tried to open the back door—but, of course, the walls of the alleyway were too close. The back window shattered and puffs of stuffing flew from the seats as they were shredded by Uzi fire.

"Calamity!" I said. "Glad it's not *my* car."

Megan rolled her eyes at me, then pulled something out of her top. A small cylinder, like a lipstick case. She twisted the bottom, waited for a lull in the bullets, then lobbed it out the front window.

"What was that?" I yelled over the shots.

I was answered by an explosion that shook the car, blowing scraps of trash from the alleyway across us. The bullets stopped for a moment, and I could hear men crying out in pain. Megan—still toting my rifle—hopped over the torn-up seat and lithely slipped through the broken back window, then ran for it.

"Hey!" I said, crawling out after her, bits of safety glass falling from my clothing. I jumped to the ground and dashed to the end of the alleyway, cutting to the side just as the survivors from the explosion started firing again.

She can shoot like a dream and she carries tiny grenades in her top, a bit of my addled mind thought. *I think I might be in love.*

I heard a low rumbling over the gunfire, and an armored truck pulled around the corner ahead, roaring toward Megan. It was huge and green, imposing, with enormous headlights. And it looked an awful lot like . . .

"A garbage truck?" I asked, running up to join Megan.

A tough-looking black man rode in the passenger seat. He pushed open the door for Megan. "Who's that?" the man asked, nodding to me. He spoke with a faint French accent.

"A slontze," she said, tossing my rifle back to me. "But a useful one. He knows about us, but I don't think he's a threat."

Not exactly a glowing recommendation, but good enough. I smiled as she climbed into the cab, pushing the man to the middle seat.

"Do we leave him?" asked the man with the French accent.

"No," said the driver. I couldn't make him out; he was just a shadow, but his voice was solid and resonant. "He comes with us."

I smiled, eagerly stepping up into the truck. Could the driver be Hardman, the sniper? He'd seen how helpful I'd been. The people inside reluctantly made room for me. Megan slipped into the back seat of the crew cab beside a wiry man wearing a leather camouflage jacket and holding a very nice-looking sniper rifle. *He* was probably Hardman. To his other side was a middle-aged woman with shoulder-length red hair. She wore spectacles and business attire.

The garbage truck pulled away, moving faster than I'd have thought possible. Behind us a group of the thugs came out of the alley, firing on the truck. It didn't do much good, though we weren't out of danger quite yet. Overhead I heard the distinctive sound of Enforcement copters. There would probably be a few high-level Epics on the way too.

"Fortuity?" the driver asked. He was an older man, perhaps in his fifties, and wore a long, thin black coat. Oddly, he had a pair of goggles tucked into the breast pocket of the coat.

"Dead," Megan said from behind.

"What went wrong?" the driver asked.

"Hidden power," she said. "Super reflexes. I got him cuffed, but he slipped away."

"There was also that one," the guy in the camo jacket—I was pretty sure that was Hardman—said. "He came up in the middle of it all, caused a wee bit of trouble." He had a distinctive Southern accent.

"We'll talk about him later," the driver said, taking a corner at high speed.

My heart started to beat more quickly, and I glanced out the window, searching the sky for copters. It wouldn't be long before Enforcement was told what to look for, and the truck was rather conspicuous.

"We should have just shot Fortuity in the first place," said the man with the French accent. "Derringer to the chest."

"Wouldn't have worked, Abraham," the driver said. "His abilities were too strong—even attraction could only do so much. We needed to do something nonlethal first—trap him, then shoot him. Precogs are tough."

He had that part right, probably. Fortuity had possessed a *very* strong danger sense. Likely the plan had been for Megan to cuff him and maybe lock him to the lamppost. Then, when he was partially immobilized, she could have rammed her derringer into his chest and fired. If she'd tried that first, his power might have warned him. It would have depended on how attracted he was to her.

"I wasn't expecting him to be so strong," Megan said, sounding disappointed with herself as she pulled on a brown leather jacket and a pair of cargo pants. "I'm sorry, Prof. I shouldn't have let him get away from me."

Prof. Something about that name struck me.

"It's done," the driver—Prof—said, pulling the garbage truck to a jarring halt. "We ditch the machine. It's been compromised."

Prof opened the door and we piled out.

"I—" I began to say, planning to introduce myself. The older man they called Prof, however, shot me a menacing glare over the hood of the garbage truck. I cut myself short, choking on my words. Standing in the shadows, with his long jacket and that grizzled face, hair peppered with grey, that man looked *dangerous*.

The Reckoners pulled a few packs of equipment out of the back of the garbage truck, including a massive machine gun that Abraham now toted. They led me down a set of steps into the understreets. From there the team hustled through a set of twists and turns. I did a pretty good job keeping track of where we were going until they led me down a long flight of stairs, several levels deep, into the steel catacombs.

Smart people stayed away from the catacombs. The Diggers had gone mad before the tunnels were finished. The ceiling lights rarely worked, and the square-shaped tunnels through the steel changed size as you progressed.

The team was silent as they continued down the passages, turning up the lights on their mobiles, which most wore strapped to the fronts of their jackets. I'd wondered if the Reckoners would carry mobiles, and the fact that they wore them made me feel better about mine. I mean, *everyone* knew that the Knighthawk Foundry was neutral, and that mobile connections were completely secure. The Reckoners' using the network was just another indication that Knighthawk was reliable.

We walked for a time, the Reckoners moving quietly, carefully. Several times Hardman went ahead to scout; Abraham watched our rear with that wicked-looking machine gun of his. It was hard to keep my bearings—down in the steel catacombs it felt like a subway system that halfway through development had turned into a rat's maze.

There were choke points, tunnels that went nowhere, and unnatural angles. In some places electrical cords jutted from the walls like those creepy arteries you find in the middle of a chunk of chicken. In other places the steel walls weren't solid, but instead had patches of paneling that had been ripped into by people searching for something worth selling. Scrap metal, however, was worthless in Newcago. There was more than enough of *that* lying around.

We passed groups of teenagers with dark expressions standing beside burning trash cans. They seemed displeased to have their solace invaded, but nobody interfered with us. Perhaps it was due to Abraham's enormous gun. The thing had gravatonics glowing blue on the bottom to help him lift it.

We worked our way through those tunnels for over an hour. Occasionally we passed vents blowing air. The Diggers had gotten some things working down here, but most of it made no sense. Still, there was fresh air. Sometimes.

Prof led the way in that long black coat. *It's a lab coat,* I realized as we turned another corner. *One that's been dyed black.* He wore a black buttoned shirt beneath it.

The Reckoners were obviously worried about being followed, but I felt they overdid it. I was hopelessly lost after fifteen minutes, and Enforcement *never* came down to this level. There was an unspoken agreement. Steelheart ignored those living in the steel catacombs, and they didn't do anything to bring his judgment down upon them.

Of course . . . the Reckoners changed that truce. An important Epic had been assassinated. How would Steelheart react to that?

Eventually the Reckoners led me around a corner that looked like every other one—only this time it led to a small room cut into the steel. There were a lot of these places in the catacombs. Places where the Diggers had planned to put a restroom, a small shop, or a dwelling.

Hardman the sniper took up position at the door. He'd taken out a camo ball cap and put it on his head, and there was an unfamiliar emblem on the front. It looked like some kind of royal crest or something. The other four Reckoners arranged themselves facing me. Abraham got out a large flashlight and clicked a button that lit up the sides, turning it into a lantern. He set it on the floor.

Prof crossed his arms, his face emotionless, inspecting me. The woman with the red hair stood beside him. She seemed more thoughtful. Abraham still carried his large gun, and Megan took off her leather jacket and strapped on an underarm gun holster. I tried not to stare, but that was like trying not to blink. Only . . . well, kind of the opposite.

I took a hesitant step backward, realizing I was cornered. I'd begun to think that I was on my way toward being accepted into their team. But looking into Prof's eyes, I realized that was *not* the case. He saw me as a threat. I hadn't been brought along because I'd been helpful; I'd been brought along because he hadn't wanted me wandering free.

I was a captive. And this deep in the steel catacombs, nobody would notice a scream or a gunshot.

6

"TEST him, Tia," Prof said.

I shied back, holding my rifle nervously. Behind Prof, Megan leaned against a wall, jacket back on, handgun strapped under her arm. She spun something in her hand. The extra magazine for my rifle. She'd never returned it.

Megan smiled. She'd tossed my rifle back to me up above, but I had a sinking suspicion that she'd emptied the chamber, leaving the gun unloaded. I started to panic.

The redhead—Tia—approached me, holding some kind of device. It was flat and round, the size of a plate, but had a screen on one side. She pointed it at me. "No reading."

"Blood test," Prof said, face hard.

Tia nodded. "Don't force us to hold you down," she said to me, removing a strap from the side of the device; it was connected to the disc by cords. "This will prick you, but it won't do you any harm."

"What is it?" I demanded.

"A dowser."

A dowser . . . a device that tested if one was an Epic or not. "I . . . thought those were just myths."

Abraham smiled, enormous gun held beside him. He was lean and muscled and seemed very calm, as opposed to the tension displayed by Tia and even Prof. "Then you won't mind, eh, my friend?" he asked with his French accent. "What does it matter if a *mythological* device pricks you?"

That didn't comfort me, but the Reckoners were a group of practiced assassins who killed High Epics for a living. There wasn't much I could do.

The woman wrapped my arm with a wide strap, a bit like what you use to measure blood pressure. Wires led from it to the device in her hand. There was a small box on the inside of the strap, and it pricked me.

Tia studied the screen. "He's clean for certain," she said, looking at Prof. "Nothing on the blood test either."

Prof nodded, seeming unsurprised. "All right, son. It's time for you to answer a few questions. Think very carefully before you reply."

"Okay," I said as Tia removed the strap. I rubbed my arm where I'd been pricked.

"How," Prof said, "did you find out where we were going to strike? Who told you that Fortuity was our target?"

"Nobody told me."

His expression grew dark. Beside him, Abraham raised an eyebrow and hefted his gun.

"No, really!" I said, sweating. "Okay, so I heard from some people on the street that you might be in town."

51

"We didn't tell anyone our mark," Abraham said. "Even if you knew we were here, how did you know the Epic we'd try to kill?"

"Well," I said, "who *else* would you hit?"

"There are thousands of Epics in the city, son," Prof said.

"Sure," I replied. "But most are beneath your notice. You target High Epics, and there are only a few hundred of those in Newcago. Among them, only a couple dozen have a prime invincibility—and you *always* pick someone with a prime invincibility.

"However, you also wouldn't go after anyone *too* powerful or *too* influential. You figure they'd be well protected. That rules out Nightwielder, Conflux, and Firefight—pretty much Steelheart's whole inner circle. It also rules out most of the burrow barons.

"That leaves about a dozen targets, and Fortuity was the worst of the lot. All Epics are murderers, but he'd killed the most innocents by a long shot. Plus, that twisted way he played with people's entrails is *exactly* the sort of atrocity the Reckoners would want to stop." I looked at them, nervous, then shrugged. "Like I said. Nobody had to tell me. It's obvious who you'd end up picking."

The small room grew silent.

"Ha!" said the sniper, who still stood by the doorway. "Lads and ladies, I think this means we might be getting a *tad* predictable."

"What's a prime invincibility?" Tia asked.

"Sorry," I said, realizing they wouldn't know my terms. "It's what I call an Epic power that renders conventional methods of assassination useless. You know, regeneration, impervious skin, precognition, self-reincarnation, that kind of thing." A High Epic was someone who had one of those. I'd never heard of one who had two, fortunately.

"Let us pretend," Prof said, "that you really did figure it out on your own. That still doesn't explain how you knew where we'd spring our trap."

"Fortuity always sees the plays at Spritz's place on the first Saturday of the month," I said. "And he always goes to look for amusement afterward. It's the only reliable time when you'd find him alone and in a mind-set where he could be baited into a trap."

Prof glanced at Abraham, then at Tia. She shrugged. "I don't know."

"I think he's telling the truth, Prof," Megan said, her arms crossed, jacket open at the front. *Don't . . . stare . . . ,* I had to remind myself.

Prof looked at her. "Why?"

"It makes sense," she said. "If Steelheart had known who we were going to hit, he'd have had something more elaborate planned for us than one boy with a rifle. Besides, Knees here *did* try to help. Kind of."

"I helped! You'd be dead if it weren't for me. Tell her, Hardman."

The Reckoners looked confused.

"Who?" Abraham asked.

"Hardman," I said, pointing at the sniper by the door.

"My name's Cody, kid," he said, amused.

"Then where's Hardman?" I asked. "Megan told me he was up above, watching with his rifle to . . ." I trailed off.

There never was a sniper up above, I realized. *At least, not one specifically told to watch me.* Megan had just said that to make me stay put.

Abraham laughed deeply. "Got caught by the old invisible sniper gag, eh? Had you kneeling there thinking you'd be shot any moment. Is that why she calls you Knees?"

I blushed.

"All right, son," Prof said. "I'm going to be nice to you and pretend none of this ever happened. Once we're out that door, I want you to count to a thousand really slowly. Then you can leave. If you try to follow us, I'll shoot you." He waved to the others.

"No, wait!" I said, reaching for him.

The other four each had a gun out in a flash, all pointed at my head.

I gulped, then lowered my hand. "Wait, please," I said a little more timidly. "I want to join you."

"You want to what?" Tia asked.

"Join you," I said. "That's why I came today. I didn't intend to get involved. I just wanted to apply."

"We don't exactly accept applications," Abraham said.

Prof studied me.

"He *was* somewhat helpful," Megan said. "And I . . . will admit that he is a decent shot. Maybe we should take him on, Prof."

Well, whatever else happened, I'd managed to impress her. That seemed almost as great a victory as taking down Fortuity.

Eventually Prof shook his head. "We aren't recruiting, son. Sorry. We're going to leave, and I don't want to *ever* see you anywhere near one of our operations again—I don't want to even get a hint of you being in the same town as us. Stay in Newcago. After today's mess, we won't be coming back here for a long while."

That seemed to settle it for all of them. Megan gave me a shrug, an almost apologetic one that seemed to indicate she'd said what she had as thanks for saving her from the thugs with the Uzis. The others gathered around Prof, joining him as he walked to the door.

I stood behind, feeling impotent and frustrated.

"You're failing," I said to them, my voice growing soft.

For some reason this made Prof hesitate. He glanced back at me, most of the others already out the door.

"You never go for the real targets," I said bitterly. "You always pick the safe ones, like Fortuity. Epics you can isolate and kill. Monsters, yes, but relatively unimportant ones. Never the *real* monsters, the Epics who broke us and turned our nation to rubble."

"We do what we can," Prof said. "Getting ourselves killed trying to take out an invincible Epic wouldn't serve anyone."

"Killing men like Fortuity won't do much either," I said. "There are too many of them, and if you keep picking targets like him, nobody's going to worry about you. You're only an annoyance. You can't change the world that way."

"We're not trying to," Prof said. "We're just killing Epics."

"What would you have us do, lad?" Hardman—I mean, Cody—said, amused. "Take on Steelheart himself?"

"Yes," I said fervently, stepping forward. "You want to change things, you want to make them afraid? He's the one to attack! Show them that nobody's above our vengeance!"

Prof shook his head. He continued on his way, black lab coat rustling. "I made this decision years ago, son. We have to fight the battles we have a chance of winning."

He walked out into the hallway. I was left alone in the small room, the flashlight they'd left behind giving a cold glow to the steel chamber.

I had failed.

7

I stood in the still, quiet box of a room lit by the abandoned flashlight. It appeared to be running low on charge, but the steel walls reflected the dim light well.

No, I thought.

I strode from the room, heedless of the warnings. *Let them shoot me.*

Their retreating figures were backlit by their mobiles, a group of dark forms in the cramped hallway.

"Nobody else fights," I called after them. "Nobody else even tries! You're the only ones left. If even *you're* scared of men like Steelheart, then how can anyone ever think any differently?"

The Reckoners continued walking.

"Your work means something!" I yelled. "But it's not enough! So long as the most powerful of the Epics consider themselves immune, nothing will change. So long as you leave them alone, you're essentially *proving* what they've always said! That if an Epic is strong enough, he can take what he wants, do what he wants. You're saying they deserve to rule."

The group kept walking, though Prof—toward the rear—seemed to hesitate. It was only for a moment.

I took a deep breath. There was only one thing left to try. "I've seen Steelheart bleed."

Prof stiffened.

That made the others pause. Prof looked over his shoulder at me. "*What?*"

"I've seen Steelheart bleed."

"Impossible," Abraham said. "The man is perfectly impervious."

"I've seen it," I said, heart thumping, face sweating. I'd never told anyone. The secret was too dangerous. If Steelheart knew that someone had survived the bank attack that day, he'd hunt me down. There would be no hiding, no running. Not if he thought I knew his weakness.

I didn't, not completely. But I had a clue, perhaps the only one anyone had.

"Making up lies won't get you on our team, son," Prof said slowly.

"I'm not lying," I said, meeting his eyes. "Not about this. Give me a few minutes to tell my story. At least listen."

"This is foolishness," Tia said, taking hold of Prof's arm. "Prof, let's go."

Prof didn't respond. He studied me, eyes searching my own, as if looking for something. I felt strangely exposed before him, naked. As if he could see my every wish and sin.

He walked slowly back to me. "All right, son," he said. "You've got fifteen minutes." He gestured back toward the room. "I'll listen to what you have to say."

We walked back into the small room amid a few grumbles from some of the others. I was beginning to place the members of the team. Abraham, with his large machine gun and beefy arms—he had to be the heavy-weapons man. He'd be around to lay down cover at Enforcement officers if something went wrong. He'd intimidate information out of people when needed, and would probably work the heavy machinery if the plan called for it.

Red-haired Tia, narrow-faced and articulate, was probably the team's scholar. Judging from her clothes, she wouldn't be involved in confrontations, and the Reckoners needed people like her—someone who knew exactly how Epic powers worked, and who could help decipher their targets' weaknesses.

Megan had to be point woman. She would be the one who went into danger, who moved the Epic into position. Cody, with his camo and sniper rifle, was most likely fire support. I was guessing that after Megan neutralized the Epic's powers in some way, Cody would pick them off or checkmate them with precision fire.

Which left Prof. Team leader, I supposed. Maybe a second point man, if they needed one? I hadn't quite placed him yet, though something itched at me regarding his name.

As we entered the room again, Abraham looked interested in what I was going to say. On the other hand, Tia looked annoyed, and Cody actually looked amused. The sniper leaned back against the wall and relaxed, crossing his arms to watch the hallway. The rest of them surrounded me, waiting.

I smiled at Megan, but her face had become impassive. Cold, even. What had changed?

I took a deep breath. "I've seen Steelheart bleed," I repeated. "It happened ten years ago, when I was eight. My father and I were at the First Union Bank on Adams Street. . . ."

I fell silent, story finished, my last words hanging in the air. *And I intend to see him bleed again.* It sounded like bravado to me now, standing before a group of people who had dedicated their lives to killing Epics.

My nervousness had evaporated while telling the story. It felt oddly relaxing to finally share it, giving voice to those terrible events. At last, someone else knew. If I were to die, there would be others who had the information I alone had carried. Even if the Reckoners decided not to go after Steelheart, the knowledge would exist, perhaps to be used someday. Assuming they believed me.

"Let's sit," Prof finally said, settling down. The others joined him, Tia and Megan reluctantly, but Abraham was still relaxed. Cody remained standing by the door, keeping guard.

I sat down, setting my rifle across my lap. I had the safety on, even though I was pretty sure it wasn't loaded.

"Well?" Prof asked of his team.

"I've heard of it," Tia admitted grudgingly. "Steelheart destroyed the bank on the Day of Annexation. The bank rented out some of the offices on the upper floor—nothing too important, some assessors and bookkeepers who did government work. Most lorists I've talked to assume that Steelheart hit the building because of those offices."

"Yes," Abraham agreed. "He attacked many city buildings that day."

Prof nodded thoughtfully.

"Sir—" I began.

He cut me off. "You've had your say, son. It's a show of respect that we're talking about this where you can hear. Don't make me regret it."

"Er, yes sir."

"I *have* always wondered why he attacked the bank first," Abraham continued.

"Yeah," Cody said from the doorway. "It was an odd choice. Why take out a bunch of accountants, *then* move on to the mayor?"

"But this is not a good enough reason to change our plans,"

Abraham added, shaking his head. He nodded to me, enormous gun over his shoulder. "I'm sure you're a wonderful person, my friend, but I do not think we should base decisions on information given by someone we only just met."

"Megan?" Prof asked. "What do you think?"

I glanced at her. Megan sat a little apart from the others. Prof and Tia seemed the most senior of this particular cell of the Reckoners. Abraham and Cody often chimed in their thoughts, as close friends would. But what of Megan?

"I think this is stupid," she said, her voice cold.

I frowned. *But . . . just a few minutes ago, she was the friendliest toward me!*

"You stood up for him before," Abraham said, as if voicing my own thoughts.

That made her scowl. "That was before I heard this wild story. He's lying, trying to get onto our team."

I opened my mouth to protest, but a glance from Prof made me bite off the comment.

"You sound like you're considering it," Cody said to Prof.

"Prof?" Tia said. "I know that look. Remember what happened with Duskwatch."

"I remember," he said. He studied me further.

"What?" Tia asked.

"He knows about the rescue workers," Prof said.

"The rescue workers?" Cody asked.

"Steelheart covered up that he killed the rescue workers," Prof said softly. "Few know of what he did to them and the survivors—of what happened at the First Union building. He didn't kill anyone who went to help at other city buildings he'd destroyed. He only killed the rescue workers at First Union.

"Something *is* different about his destruction of the bank," Prof continued. "We know he entered that one, and spoke to the people inside. He didn't do that elsewhere. They say he came out of First

Union enraged. Something happened inside. I've known that for a while. The other cell leaders know it as well. We assumed that whatever made him angry had to do with Deathpoint." Prof sat with one hand on his knee, and he tapped his finger in thought, studying me. "Steelheart got his scar that day. Nobody knows how."

"I do," I said.

"Perhaps," Prof said.

"Perhaps," Megan said. "Perhaps not. Prof, he could have heard of the murders and known of Steelheart's scar, then fabricated the rest! There'd be no way to prove it, because if he's right, then he and Steelheart are the only witnesses."

Prof nodded slowly.

"Hitting Steelheart would be near impossible," Abraham said. "Even if we *could* figure out his weakness, he's got guards. Strong ones."

"Firefight, Conflux, and Nightwielder," I said, nodding. "I've got a plan for dealing with each of them. I think I've figured out their weaknesses."

Tia frowned. "You have?"

"Ten years," I said softly. "For ten years, all I've done is plan how to get to him."

Prof still seemed thoughtful. "Son," he said to me. "What did you say your name was?"

"David."

"Well, David. You guessed we were going to hit Fortuity. What would you guess we'd do next?"

"You'll leave Newcago by nightfall," I said immediately. "That's always what a team does after springing a trap. Of course, there *is* no nightfall here. But you'll be gone in a few hours, then go rejoin the rest of the Reckoners."

"And what would be the next Epic we'd be planning to hit?" Prof asked.

"Well," I said, thinking quickly, remembering my lists and

projections. "None of your teams have been active in the Middle Grasslands or Caliph lately. I'd guess your next target would be either the Armsman in Omaha, or Lightning, one of the Epics in Snowfall's band out in Sacramento."

Cody whistled softly. Apparently I'd guessed pretty well—which was fortunate. I hadn't been too sure. I tended to be right about a quarter of the time lately, guessing where Reckoner cells would strike.

Prof suddenly moved to stand. "Abraham, prep Hole Fourteen. Cody, see if you can get a false trail set up that will lead to Caliph."

"Hole Fourteen?" Tia said. "We're staying in the city?"

"Yes," Prof said.

"Jon," Tia said, addressing Prof. His real name, probably. "I can't—"

"I'm not saying that we're going to hit Steelheart," he said, holding up a hand. He pointed at me. "But if the kid has figured out what we're going to do next, someone else might have too. That means we need to change. Immediately. We'll go to ground here for a few days." He looked at me. "As for Steelheart . . . we'll see. First I want to hear your story again. I want to hear it a dozen times. Then I'll decide what to do next."

He held out a hand to me. I took it hesitantly, letting him pull me to my feet. There was something in this man's eyes, something I didn't expect to see. A hatred of Steelheart nearly as deep as my own. It was manifest in the way he said the Epic's name, the way his lips turned down, the way his eyes narrowed and seemed to *burn* as he spoke the word.

It seemed like the two of us understood each other in that moment.

Prof, I thought. *Professor, PhD. The man who founded the Reckoners is named Jonathan Phaedrus. P-h . . . d.*

This wasn't just a team commander, a chief of one of the Reckoner cells. This was Jon Phaedrus himself. Their leader and founder.

8

"SO . . . ," I said as we left the room. "Where's this place we're going? Hole Fourteen?"

"You don't need to know that," Prof said.

"Can I have my rifle magazine back?"

"No."

"Do I need to know any . . . I don't know. Secret handshakes? Special identifiers? Codes so other Reckoners know I'm one of them?"

"Son," Prof said, "you're *not* one of us."

"I know, I know," I said quickly. "But I don't want anyone to surprise us and think I'm an enemy or something, and—"

"Megan," Prof said, jerking his thumb at me. "Entertain the kid. I need to think." He walked on ahead, joining Tia, and the two of them began speaking quietly.

Megan gave me a scowl. I probably deserved it, for yammering questions at Prof like that. I was just so nervous. Phaedrus himself, the founder of the Reckoners. Now that I knew what to look for, I recognized him from the descriptions—sparse though they were—that I'd read.

The man was a legend. A god among freedom fighters and assassins alike. I was starstruck, and the questions had just dribbled out. In truth I was proud of myself for not asking for an autograph on my gun.

My behavior hadn't earned me points with Megan, however, and she obviously didn't like being put on babysitting detail either. Cody and Abraham were talking ahead, which left Megan and me walking beside each other as we moved at a brisk pace down one of the darkened steel tunnels. She was silent.

She really was pretty. And she was probably around my age, maybe just a year or two older. I still wasn't certain why she'd turned cold toward me. Maybe some witty conversation would help with that. "So, uh," I said. "How long have you . . . you know, been with the Reckoners? And all?"

Smooth.

"Long enough," she said.

"Were you involved in any of the recent kills? Gyro? Shadowblight? Earless?"

"Maybe. I doubt Prof would want me sharing specifics."

We walked in silence for a time longer.

"You know," I said, "you're not really very entertaining."

"What?"

"Prof told you to entertain me," I said.

"That was just to deflect your questions onto someone else. I doubt you'll find anything I do to be particularly entertaining."

"I wouldn't say that," I said. "I liked the striptease."

She glared at me. *"What?"*

"Out in the alley," I said. "When you . . ."

Her expression was so frigid you could have used it to liquid-cool a high-fire-rate stationary gun barrel. Or maybe some drinks. Chill drinks—that was a better metaphor.

I didn't think she'd appreciate me using it right then, though. "Never mind," I said.

"Good," she said, turning away from me and continuing on.

I breathed out, then chuckled. "For a moment there I thought you'd shoot me."

"I only shoot people when the job calls for it," she said. "You're trying to make small talk; you're simply not very good at it. That's not a shooting offense."

"Er, thanks."

She nodded, businesslike, which wasn't exactly the reaction I'd have hoped for from a pretty girl whose life I'd saved. Granted, she was the first girl—pretty or not—whose life I'd saved, so I didn't have much of a baseline.

Still, she'd been kind of warm to me before, hadn't she? Maybe I just needed to work a little harder. "So what *can* you tell me?" I asked. "About the team, or the other members."

"I'd prefer to discuss another topic," she said. "One that doesn't involve secrets about the Reckoners *or* my clothing, please."

I fell silent. Truth was, I didn't *know* about much other than the Reckoners and the Epics in town. Yes, I'd had some schooling at the Factory, but only basic kinds of stuff. And before that I'd lived a year scavenging on the streets, malnourished, barely avoiding death.

"I guess we could talk about the city," I said. "I know a lot about the understreets."

"How old are you?" Megan said.

"Eighteen," I said, defensive.

"And is anyone going to come looking for you? Are people going to wonder where you went?"

I shook my head. "I hit my majority two months ago. Got kicked out of the Factory where I worked."

That was the rule. You only worked there until you were eighteen; after that you found another job.

"You worked at a factory?" she asked. "For how long?"

"Nine years or so," I said. "Weapons factory, actually. Made guns for Enforcement." Some understreeters, particularly the older ones, grumbled about how the Factory exploited children for labor. That was a stupid complaint, made by old people who remembered a different world. A safer world.

In my world, people who gave you the chance to work in exchange for food were saints. Martha saw to it that her workers were fed, clothed, and protected, even from one another.

"Was it nice?"

"Kind of. It's not slave labor, like people think. We got paid." Kind of. Martha saved wages to give us when we were no longer owned by the Factory. Enough to establish ourselves, find a trade.

"It was a good place to grow up, all things considered," I said wistfully as we walked. "Without the Factory, I doubt I'd have ever learned to fire a gun. The kids aren't supposed to use the weapons, but if you're good, Martha—she ran the place—turns a blind eye." More than one of her kids had gone on to work for Enforcement.

"That's interesting," Megan said. "Tell me more."

"Well, it's . . ." I trailed off, looking at her. Only now did I realize she'd been walking along, eyes forward, barely paying attention. She was just asking things to keep me talking, maybe even to keep me from bothering her in more invasive ways.

"You're not even listening," I accused.

"You seemed like you wanted to talk," she said curtly. "I gave you the chance."

Sparks, I thought, feeling like a slontze. We fell silent as we walked, which seemed to suit Megan just fine.

"You don't know how aggravating this is," I finally said.

She gave me a glance, her emotions hidden. "Aggravating?"

"Yes, aggravating. I've spent the last ten years of my life studying the Reckoners and the Epics. Now that I'm with you, I'm told I'm not allowed to ask questions about important things. It's aggravating."

"Think about something else."

"There *is* nothing else. Not to me."

"Girls."

"None."

"Hobbies."

"None. Just you guys, Steelheart, and my notes."

"Wait," she said. "Notes?"

"Sure," I said. "I worked in the Factory during the days, always listening for rumors. I spent my free days spending what little money I had buying newspapers or stories off those who traveled abroad. I got to know a few information brokers. Each night I'd work on the notes, putting it all together. I knew I'd need to be an expert on Epics, so I became one."

She frowned deeply.

"I know," I said, grimacing. "It sounds like I don't have a life. You're not the first to tell me that. The others at the Factory—"

"Hush," she said. "You wrote about Epics, but what about us? What about the Reckoners?"

"Of course I wrote it down," I said. "What was I supposed to do? Keep it in my head? I filled a couple notebooks, and though most of it was guesswork, I'm pretty good at guessing. . . ." I trailed off, realizing why she looked so worried.

"Where is it all?" she asked softly.

"In my flat," I said. "Should be safe. I mean, none of those goons got close enough to see me clearly."

"And the woman you pulled out of her car?"

I hesitated. "Yeah, she saw my face. She *might* be able to describe me. But, I mean, that wouldn't be enough for them to track me, right?"

Megan was silent.

Yes, I thought. *Yes, it might be enough.* Enforcement was very good at its job. And unfortunately, I had a few incidents in my past, such as the taxi wreck. I was on file, and Steelheart would give Enforcement a great deal of motivation to follow every lead regarding Fortuity's death.

"We need to talk to Prof," Megan said, towing me by the arm toward where the others were walking ahead.

9

PROF listened to my explanation with thoughtful eyes. "Yes," he said as I finished. "I should have seen this. It makes sense."

I relaxed. I'd been afraid he'd be furious.

"What's the address, son?" Prof asked.

"Fifteen thirty-two Ditko Place," I said. It was carved into the steel around a park in one of the nicer areas of the understreets. "It's small, but I live alone. I keep it locked tight."

"Enforcement won't need a key," Prof said. "Cody, Abraham, go to this place. Set a firebomb, make sure nobody is inside, and blow the entire room."

I felt a sudden jolt of alarm, as if someone had hooked up my toes to a car battery. *"What?"*

"We can't have Steelheart getting that information, son," Prof said. "Not just the information about us, but the information on the other Epics you collected. If it's as detailed as you say, he could use it against the other powerful Epics in the region. Steelheart already has too much influence. We need to destroy that intel."

"You can't!" I exclaimed, my voice echoing in the narrow, steel-walled tunnel. Those notes were my life's work! Sure, I hadn't been around *that* long, but still . . . ten years of effort? Losing it would be like losing a hand. Given the option, I'd rather lose the hand.

"Son," Prof said, "don't push me. Your place here is fragile."

"You *need* that information," I said. "It's important, sir. Why would you burn hundreds of pages of information about the powers of Epics and their possible weaknesses?"

"You said you gathered it through hearsay," Tia said, her arms crossed. "I doubt there's anything in it that we don't know already."

"Do you know Nightwielder's weakness?" I asked, desperate.

Nightwielder. He was one of Steelheart's High Epic bodyguards, and his powers created the perpetual darkness over Newcago. He was a shadowy figure himself, completely incorporeal, immune to gunfire or weapons of any kind.

"No," Tia admitted. "And I doubt you do either."

"Sunlight," I said. "He becomes solid in sunlight. I've got pictures."

"You have *pictures* of Nightwielder in corporeal form?" Tia asked.

"I think so. The person I bought them from wasn't certain, but I'm reasonably sure."

"Hey, lad," Cody called. "You want to buy Loch Ness from me? I'll give you a good price."

I glared at him, and he just shrugged. Loch Ness was in Scotland, I knew that much, and it seemed that the crest on Cody's cap might be some kind of Scottish or English deal. But his accent didn't match.

"Prof," I said, turning back to him. "Phaedrus, sir, please. You have to see my plan."

"Your plan?" He didn't seem surprised that I'd worked out his name.

"For killing Steelheart."

"You have a plan?" Prof asked. "For killing the most powerful Epic in the country?"

"That's what I told you before."

"I thought you wanted to join us to get us to do it."

"I need help," I said. "But I didn't come empty-handed. I've got a detailed plan. I think it will work."

Prof just shook his head, looking bemused.

Suddenly, Abraham laughed. "I like him. He has . . . something. *Un homme téméraire*. You sure we aren't recruiting, Prof?"

"Yes," Prof said flatly.

"At least look at my plan before you burn it," I said. "Please."

"Jon," Tia said. "I'd like to see these pictures. They're likely fake, but even so . . ."

"Fine," Prof said, tossing something to me. The magazine for my rifle. "Change of plans. Cody, you take Megan and the boy and go to his place. If Enforcement is there and looks like they're going to take this information, destroy it. But if the site looks safe, bring it back." He eyed me. "Whatever you can't carry easily, destroy. Understood?"

"Sure," Cody said.

"Thank you," I said.

"It's not a favor, son," Prof said. "And I hope it's not a mistake either. Go on. We may not have much time before they track you."

It was getting quiet in the understreets by the time we neared Ditko Place. You'd think that, with the perpetual darkness, there wouldn't really be a "day" or a "night" in Newcago, but there is. People tend to want to sleep when everyone else sleeps, so we settle into routines.

Of course, there are a minority who don't like to do as told, even when it comes to something simple. I was one of those. Being up all night means being awake when everyone else is sleeping. It's quieter, more private.

The ceiling lights were set to a clock somewhere, and they colored to deeper shades when it was night. The change was subtle, but we learned to notice it. So, even though Ditko Place was near the surface, there wasn't much motion on the streets. People were sleeping.

We arrived at the park, a large underground chamber carved from the steel. It had numerous holes in the ceiling for fresh air, and blue-violet lights shone from spotlights around the rim. The center of the tall chamber was cluttered with rocks brought in from outside—real rocks, not ones that had been turned to steel. There was also wooden playground equipment, moderately well maintained, that had been scavenged from somewhere. In the daytime the place would fill with children—the ones too young to work, or the ones with families who could afford not to have them work. Old women and men would gather to knit socks or do other simple work.

Megan raised her hand to still us. "Mobiles?" she whispered.

Cody sniffed. "Do I look like some amateur?" he asked. "It's on silent."

I hesitated, then took mine off the place on my shoulder and double-checked. Fortunately it was on silent. I took out the battery anyway, just in case. Megan moved quietly out of the tunnel and across the park toward the shadow of a large rock. Cody went next, then I followed, keeping low and moving as quietly as I could, passing large stones growing lichen.

Up above a few cars rumbled by on the roadway that ran past the openings in the ceiling. Late-night commuters heading home. Sometimes they'd throw trash down on us. A surprising number of the rich still had ordinary jobs. Accountants, teachers, salesmen, computer technicians—though Steelheart's datanet was open only to his most trusted. I'd never seen a real computer, just my mobile.

It was a different world above, and jobs that had once been common were now held by only the privileged. The rest of us worked factories or sewed clothing in the park while watching children play.

I reached the rock and crouched beside Cody and Megan, who were stealthily inspecting the two far walls of the chamber, where the dwellings were cut. Dozens of holes in the steel provided homes of various sizes. Metal fire escapes had been harvested from unused buildings above and set up here to give access to the holes.

"So, which one is it?" Cody asked.

I pointed. "See that door on the second level, far right? That's it."

"Nice," Cody said. "How'd y'all afford a place like this?" He asked it casually, but I could tell that he was suspicious. They all were. Well, I suppose that was to be expected.

"I needed a room by myself for my research," I said. "The factory where I worked saves all of your wages when you're a kid, then gives them to you in four yearly chunks when you hit eighteen. It was enough to get me a year in my own room."

"Cool," Cody said. I wondered if my explanation passed his test or not. "It doesn't look like Enforcement has made it here yet. Maybe they couldn't match you from the description."

I nodded slowly, though beside me Megan was looking around, her eyes narrowed.

"What?" I asked.

"It looks too easy. I don't trust things that look too easy."

I scanned the far walls. There were a few empty trash bins and some motorbikes chained up beside a stairwell. Some chunks of metal had been etched by enterprising street artists. They weren't supposed to do that, but the people encouraged them, quietly. It was one of the only forms of rebellion the common people ever engaged in.

"Well, we can wait here staring until they *do* come," Cody said, rubbing his face with a leathery finger, "or we can just go. Let's be on with it." He stood up.

One of the large trash bins shimmered.

"Wait!" I said, grabbing Cody and pulling him down, my heart leaping.

"What?" he said, anxious, unslinging his rifle. It was of a very fine make, old but well maintained, with a large scope and a state-of-the-art suppressor on the front. I'd never been able to get my hands on one of those. The cheaper ones worked poorly, and I found it too hard to aim with them.

"There," I said, pointing at the trash bin. "Watch it."

He frowned but did what I asked. My mind raced, sorting through fragments of remembered research. I needed my notes. Shimmering . . . illusionist Epic . . . who was that?

Refractionary, I thought, seizing on a name. *A class C illusionist with personal invisibility capabilities.*

"What am I watching for?" Cody asked. "Did you get spooked by a cat or something—" He cut off as the bin shimmered again. Cody frowned, then crouched down farther. "What is that?"

"An Epic," Megan said, her eyes narrowing. "Some of the lesser Epics with illusion powers have trouble maintaining an exact illusion."

"Her name is Refractionary," I said softly. "She's pretty skilled, capable of creating complex visual manifestations. But she's not terribly powerful, and her illusions always have tells to them. Usually they shimmer as if light is reflecting off them."

Cody aimed his rifle, sighting on the trash bin. "So you're saying that bin isn't really there. It's hiding something else. Enforcement officers, probably?"

"I'd guess so," I said.

"Can she be harmed by bullets, lad?" Cody asked.

"Yes, she's not a High Epic. But Cody, she might not be in there."

"You just said—"

"She's a class C illusionist," I explained. "But her secondary power is class B personal invisibility. Illusions and invisibility often go hand in hand. Anyway, she can make herself invisible, but not anything else—others, she has to create an illusion around. I'd be certain she's hiding an Enforcement squad in that fake trash bin illusion, but if she's smart—and she is—she'll be somewhere else."

I felt an itch in the small of my back. I *hated* illusionist Epics. You never knew where they'd be. Even the weakest of them—class D or E, by my own notation system—could make an illusion big enough for themselves to hide in. If they had personal invisibility, it was even worse.

"There," Megan whispered, pointing toward a large piece of playground equipment—a kind of wooden fort for climbing. "See those boxes on the top of that playground tower? They just shimmered. Someone's hiding in them."

"That's only big enough for one person," I whispered. "From that position, whoever is there could see right into my apartment through the door. Sniper?"

"Most likely," Megan said.

"Refractionary is close, then," I said. "She'll need to be able to see both that playground equipment and the fake garbage bins to keep the illusions going. The range on her powers isn't great."

"How do we draw her out?" Megan asked.

"She likes to be involved, from what I remember," I said. "If we can get the Enforcement soldiers to move, she'll stay close to them, in case she needs to give orders or make illusions to support them."

"Sparks!" Cody whispered. "How do you know all of this, lad?"

"Weren't you listening?" Megan asked softly. "This is what he does. It's what he has built his life around. He studies them."

Cody stroked his chin. He looked as if he'd assumed everything I said before was bravado. "You know her weakness?"

"It's in my notes," I said. "I'm trying to remember. Uh . . . well, illusionists usually can't see if they turn themselves completely invisible. They need light to strike their irises. So you can watch for the eyes. But a really skilled illusionist can make their eyes match the color of their surroundings. But that's not really her weakness, more a limitation of illusions themselves."

What was it? "Smoke!" I exclaimed, then blushed at the sound of it. Megan shot me a glare. "It's her weakness," I whispered. "She always avoids people who are smoking, and stays away from any kind of fire. It's pretty well known, and reasonably substantiated, as far as Epic weaknesses go."

"Guess we're back to starting the place on fire after all," Cody said. He seemed excited by the prospect.

"What? No."

"Prof said—"

"We can still get the information," I said. "They're waiting for me, but they only sent a minor Epic. That means they want me, but they haven't sorted through that the Reckoners were behind the assassination tonight—or maybe they don't know how I was involved. They probably haven't cleaned out my room yet, even if they did break in and scan through what's there."

"Excellent reason to burn the place," Megan said. "I'm sorry, but if they're that close . . ."

"But see, it's essential that we go in now," I said, growing more anxious. "We have to see what has been disturbed, if anything. That'll tell us what they've discovered. We burn the place down now, and we blind ourselves."

The other two hesitated.

"We can stop them," I said. "And we might be able to kill us an Epic in the process. Refractionary has plenty of blood on her hands. Just last month someone cut her off in traffic. She created an illusion of the road turning up ahead and drove the offender off the freeway and into a home. Six dead. Children were in the car."

Epics had a distinct, even incredible, lack of morals or conscience. That bothered some people, on a philosophical level. Theorists, scholars. They wondered at the sheer inhumanity many Epics manifested. Did the Epics kill because Calamity chose—for whatever reason—only terrible people to gain powers? Or did they kill because such amazing power twisted a person, made them irresponsible?

There were no conclusive answers. I didn't care; I wasn't a scholar. Yes, I did research, but so did a sports fan when he followed his team. It didn't matter to me why the Epics did what they did any more than a baseball fan wondered at the physics of a bat hitting a ball.

Only one thing mattered—Epics gave no thought for ordinary human life. A brutal murder was a fitting retribution, in their minds, for the most minor of infractions.

"Prof didn't approve hitting an Epic," Megan said. "This isn't in the procedures."

Cody chuckled. "Killing an Epic is always in the procedures, lass. You just haven't been with us long enough to understand."

"I have a smoke grenade in my room," I said.

"What?" Megan asked. "How?"

"I grew up working at a munitions plant," I said. "We mostly made rifles and handguns, but we worked with other factories. I got to pick up the occasional goody from the QC reject pile."

"A smoke grenade is a goody?" Cody asked.

I frowned. What did he mean? Of course it was. Who wouldn't want a smoke grenade when offered one? Megan actually showed the faintest of smiles. She understood.

I don't get you, girl, I thought. She carried explosives in her shirt and was an excellent shot, but she was worried about procedures when she got a chance to kill an Epic? And as soon as she caught me looking at her, her expression grew cold and aloof once again.

Had I done something to offend her?

"If we can get that grenade, I can use it to negate Refractionary's powers," I said. "She likes to stay near her teams. So if we can draw the soldiers into an enclosed space, she'll probably follow. I can blow the grenade, then shoot her when it makes her appear."

"Good enough," Cody said. "But how are we going to manage all of that *and* get your notes?"

"Easy," I said, reluctantly handing my rifle to Megan. I'd have a better chance of fooling them if I wasn't armed. "We give them the thing they're waiting for. Me."

10

I crossed the street toward my flat, hands in the pockets of my jacket, fingering the roll of industrial tape I usually kept there. The other two hadn't liked my plan, but they hadn't come up with anything better. Hopefully they'd be able to fulfill their parts in it.

I felt completely naked without my rifle. I had a couple of handguns stashed in my room, but a man wasn't really dangerous unless he had a rifle. At least, he wasn't consistently dangerous. Hitting something with a handgun always felt like an accident.

Megan did it, I thought. *She not only hit, but hit a High Epic in the middle of a dodge, firing two guns at once, one from the hip.*

She'd shown emotion during our fight with Fortuity. Passion, anger, annoyance. The second two toward me, but it had been something. And then, for a few moments after he fell . . . there had been a connection. Satisfaction, and appreciation of me that had come out when she'd spoken on my behalf to Prof.

Now that was gone. What did it mean?

I stopped at the edge of the playground. Was I really thinking about a girl *now*? I was only about five paces from where a group of Enforcement officers were hiding, probably with automatic or energy weapons trained on me.

Idiot, I thought, heading up the metal stairway toward my apartment. They'd wait to see if I got out anything incriminating before grabbing me. Hopefully.

Climbing steps like that, with my back to the enemy, was excruciating. I did what I always did when I grew afraid. I thought of my father falling, bleeding beside that pillar in the broken bank lobby while I hid. I hadn't helped.

I would never be that coward again.

I reached the door to my apartment, then fiddled with the keys. I heard a distant scrape but pretended not to notice. That would be the sniper on top of the playground equipment nearby, repositioning to aim at me. Yes, from this angle I saw for certain. That playground piece was just tall enough that the sniper would be able to shoot through the door into my apartment.

I stepped inside my single room. No hallways or anything else, just a hole cut into the steel, like most dwellings in the understreets. It might not have had a bathroom or running water, but I was still living quite well, by understreets standards. A whole room for a single person?

I kept it messy. Some old, disposable noodle bowls sat in a pile beside the door, smelling of spice. Clothing was strewn across the floor. I had a bucket of two-day-old water sitting on the table, and dirty, beat-up silverware sat in a pile beside it.

I didn't use those to eat. They were for show. So was the clothing; I didn't wear any of it. My actual clothing—four sturdy outfits, always clean and washed—was folded in the trunk beside my mattress on the floor. I *kept* my room messy, intentionally. It actually itched at me, as I liked things neat.

I'd found that sloppiness put people off guard. If my landlady came snooping up here, she'd find what she expected. A teenager just into his majority blowing his earnings on an easy life for a year before responsibility hit him. She wouldn't poke or prod for secret compartments.

I hurried to the trunk. I unlocked it and pulled out my backpack—already packed with a change of clothing, spare shoes, some dry rations, and two liters of water. There was a handgun in a pouch on one side, and the smoke grenade was in a pouch on the other side.

I walked to my mattress and unzipped the case. Inside was my life. Dozens of folders, filled with clippings from newspapers or scraps of information. Eight notebooks filled with my thoughts and findings. A larger notebook with my indexes.

Maybe I should have brought all of this with me when going to watch the Fortuity hit. After all, I'd hoped to leave with the Reckoners. I'd debated it but had eventually decided that it wouldn't be reasonable. There was so much of it, for one thing. I could lug it all if I needed to, but it slowed me down.

And it was just too precious. This research was the most valuable thing in my life. Collecting some of it had nearly gotten me killed—spying on Epics, asking questions better left unasked, making payments to shady informants. I was proud of it, not to mention frightened about what might happen to it. I'd thought it safer here.

Boots shook the metal landing of the stairway outside. I looked over my shoulder and saw one of the most feared sights in the understreets: fully geared Enforcement officers. They stood on the landing, automatic rifles in their hands, sleek black helmets on their heads, military-grade armor on their chests, knees, arms. There were three of them.

Their helmets had black visors that came down over their eyes, leaving their mouths and chins exposed. The eye shields gave them night vision and glowed faintly green, with a strange smoky pattern that swirled and undulated across the front. It was transfixing, which was said to be the point.

I didn't need to act to make my eyes go wide, my muscles taut.

"Hands on your head," the lead officer said, rifle up at his shoulder and the barrel trained on me. "Down on your knees, subject."

That was what they called people, *subject*. Steelheart didn't bother with any kind of silly pretense that his empire was a republic or a representative government. He didn't call people *citizens* or *comrades*. They were subjects of his empire. That was that.

I quickly raised my hands. "I didn't do anything!" I whined. "I was just there to watch!"

"HANDS UP, KNEES DOWN!" the officer yelled.

I complied.

They entered the room, leaving the doorway conspicuously open so that their sniper had a view through the door. From what I'd read, these three would be part of a five-person squad known as a Core. Three regular troops, one specialist—in this case a sniper—and one minor Epic. Steelheart had about fifty Cores like this.

Almost all of Enforcement was made of special-operations teams. If there was any large-scale fighting to be done, something *very* dangerous, Steelheart, Nightwielder, Firefight, or maybe Conflux—who was head of Enforcement—would deal with it personally. Enforcement was used for the smaller problems in the city, the ones Steelheart didn't want to bother with himself. In a way he didn't need Enforcement. They were like a homicidal dictator's version of valet parking attendants.

One of the three soldiers kept an eye on me while the other two rifled through the contents of my mattress. *Is she in here?* I wondered. *Invisible somewhere?* My instincts, and my memory of researching her, told me she'd be near.

I just had to hope she was in the room. I couldn't move until

Cody and Megan fulfilled their part of my plan, though, so I waited, tense, for them to do so.

The two soldiers pulled notebooks and folders out from between the two pieces of foam that made up my mattress. One flipped through the notes. "This is information on Epics, sir," he said.

"I thought I'd be able to see Fortuity fight another Epic," I said, staring at the floor. "When I found out something terrible was happening, I tried to get away. I was only there to see what would happen, you know?"

The officer began looking through the notebooks. The soldier watching me seemed uncomfortable about something. He kept glancing at me, then at the others.

I felt my heart thumping, waiting. Megan and Cody would attack soon. I had to be ready.

"You are in serious trouble, subject," the officer said, tossing one of my notebooks to the floor. "An Epic, and an important one, is dead."

"I didn't have anything to do with it!" I said. "I swear. I—"

"Bah." The lead officer pointed toward one of the other soldiers. "Gather this up."

"Sir," said the soldier watching me. "He's probably telling the truth."

I hesitated. That voice . . .

"Roy?" I said, shocked. He'd hit majority the year before me . . . and had joined Enforcement after that.

The officer glanced back at me. "You know this subject?"

"Yes," Roy said, sounding reluctant. He was a tall redhead. I'd always liked him. He'd been an adjunct at the Factory, which was a position Martha gave to senior boys—they were meant to stop the young or weaker workers from being picked on. He'd done his job well.

"You didn't say anything?" the lead officer said, his voice hard.

"I . . . sir, I'm sorry. I should have. He's always had a fascination with Epics. I've seen him cross half the city on foot and wait in the rain just because he heard a new Epic might be passing through town. If he heard something about two of them fighting, he'd have gone to watch, whether it was a good idea or not."

"Sounds exactly like the kind of person who should be off the streets," the officer said. "Gather this. Son, you're going to come tell us *exactly* what you saw. If you do a good job, perhaps you might even live through the night. It—"

A gunshot sounded outside. The officer's face blossomed red, the front of his helmet exploding as a bullet hit him.

I rolled toward my backpack. Cody and Megan had done their job, quietly taking down the sniper and getting into position to support me.

I ripped open the Velcro on the side of my pack and pulled out my handgun, then fired rapidly at Roy's thighs. The bullets hit an open spot in his advanced plastic armor, dropping him, though I almost missed. Sparking pistols.

The other soldier fell to a well-placed shot from Cody, who would be on that playground equipment outside. I didn't stop to make sure the third soldier was dead—Refractionary might be in the room, armed and ready to shoot. I pulled out the smoke grenade and removed the pin.

I dropped the grenade. A burst of grey smoke jetted from the canister, filling the room. I held my breath, handgun up. Refractionary's powers would be negated when the smoke touched her. I waited for her to appear.

Nothing happened. She wasn't in the room.

Smothering a curse, still holding my breath, I glanced at Roy. He was trying to move, holding his leg and trying to point his rifle toward me. I leaped through the smoke and kicked the rifle aside. Then I pulled his sidearm out of its holster and tossed it. Both guns would be useless to me; they'd be keyed to his gloves.

Roy's hand was in his pocket. I put my gun to his temple and yanked his hand out. He'd been trying to dial his mobile. I cocked the gun, and he dropped the mobile.

"It's too late anyway, David," Roy spat, then started coughing at the smoke. "Conflux will know the moment we go offline. Other Cores are on their way here. They'll send spying eyes down to watch. Those are probably already here."

Breath still held, I checked the pockets on his cargo pants. There were no other weapons.

"You're being a fool, David," Roy said, coughing. I ignored him and scanned the room. I had to start breathing, and the smoke was getting overpowering.

Where was Refractionary? On the landing, maybe. I kicked the smoke grenade out, hoping she was there.

Nothing. Either I had her weakness wrong, or she'd decided not to join her team in coming to get me.

What if she was sneaking up on Megan and Cody? They'd never see her coming.

I glanced down. Roy's mobile.

Worth a try.

I snatched the phone and opened the address book. Refractionary was listed under her Epic name. Most Epics preferred to use them.

I dialed.

Almost immediately, a gunshot sounded from the playground outside.

I couldn't hold my breath any longer. I ducked outside, staying low, and kicked the smoke grenade off the landing. I started down the stairwell and took a deep breath.

Then, eyes watering, I scanned the playground. Cody knelt on top of the playground equipment, rifle out. At the base of the tower, Megan stood with her gun out, a body in black and yellow at her feet. Refractionary.

Megan fired again into the body, just to be certain, but the woman was obviously dead.

Another Epic eliminated.

11

MY first move was to go back in and toss Roy's rifle, which he had been crawling toward, out the door. Then I checked on the two other soldiers. One was dead; the other had a weak pulse—but he wasn't going to be waking anytime soon.

Time to move quickly. I pulled the notebooks from my mattress and stuffed them in my backpack. Six thick notebooks and one index caused the backpack to bulge. I thought for a moment, then took my extra pair of shoes out of the pack. I could buy new shoes, but I couldn't replace these notebooks.

The last two fit, and beside them I slid the folders about Steelheart, Nightwielder, and Firefight. After a moment I added the one about Conflux. It was the thinnest. Very little was known about the clandestine High Epic who ran Enforcement.

Roy was still coughing, though the smoke had cleared out. He pulled off his helmet. It was surreal to see that familiar face—one I'd known for years—wearing the uniform of the enemy. We hadn't been friends; I didn't really have those, but I'd looked up to him.

"You're working with the Reckoners," Roy said.

I needed to try to lay down a false trail, get him to think I was working for someone else. "What?" I said, doing my best to look baffled.

"Don't try to hide it, David. It's obvious. Everyone knows the Reckoners hit Fortuity."

I knelt down beside him, pack slung over my shoulder. "Look, Roy, don't let them heal you, okay? I know Enforcement has Epics who can do that. Don't let them, if you can manage it."

"What, why—"

"You want to be laid out sick for this next part, Roy," I said softly, intensely. "Power is going to change hands in Newcago. Limelight is coming for Steelheart."

"Limelight?" Roy said. "Who the hell is that?"

I walked over to the rest of my folders, then reluctantly took a can of lighter fluid from my trunk and poured it on the bed.

"You're working for an Epic?" Roy whispered. "You really think anyone can challenge Steelheart? Sparks, David! How many rivals has he killed?"

"This is different," I said, then got out some matches. "Limelight is different." I lit the match.

I couldn't take the remaining folders. They were source material, facts and articles for the information I'd collected in my notebooks. I wanted to take them, but there was no more room in my bag.

I dropped the match. The bed started aflame.

"One of your friends might still be alive," I said to Roy, nodding to the two Enforcement officers who were down. The leader had been shot in the head, but the other one only in the side. "Get him out. Then stay out of things, Roy. Dangerous days are coming."

I slung the pack over my shoulder and hastened out the door and onto the stairwell. I met Megan on the way down the steps.

"Your plan failed," she said quietly.

"Worked well enough," I said. "An Epic is dead."

"Only because she left her mobile on vibrate," Megan said, hurrying down the steps beside me. "If she hadn't been sloppy . . ."

"We were lucky," I agreed. "But we still won."

Mobiles were just a part of daily life. The people might live in hovels, but they all had a mobile for entertainment.

We met Cody at the base of the playground tower near Refractionary's corpse. He handed back my rifle. "Lad," he said, "that was *awesome*."

I blinked. I'd been expecting another berating, like Megan had given me.

"Prof is going to be jealous he didn't come himself," Cody said, slinging his rifle over his shoulder. "Were you the one who called her?"

"Yeah," I said.

"Awesome," Cody said again, slapping me on the back.

Megan didn't look nearly as pleased. She gave Cody a sharp look, then reached for my pack.

I resisted.

"You need two hands for the rifle," she said, pulling it free and slinging it over her shoulder. "Let's move. Enforcement will . . ." She trailed off as she noticed Roy barely managing to tow the other Enforcement officer out of the burning room and onto the landing.

I felt bad, but only a little. Copters were thumping above; he'd have help soon. We scurried across the park, heading toward the tunnels that led deeper into the understreets.

"You left them alive?" Megan asked as we ran.

"This was more useful," I said. "I laid us a false trail. I told him a lie that I was working for an Epic who wants to challenge Steelheart. Hopefully it will keep them from searching for the Reckoners." I hesitated. "Besides. They're not our enemies."

"Of course they are," she snapped.

"No," Cody said, jogging beside her. "He's right, lass. They aren't. They may work for the enemy, but they're just regular folks. They do what they can to get by."

"We can't think like that," she said as we reached a branching tunnel. She glared at me, eyes cold. "We can't show them mercy. They won't show it to us."

"We can't become them, lass," Cody said, shaking his head. "Listen to Prof talk about it sometime. If we have to do what the Epics do to beat them, then it's not worth it."

"I've heard him talk," she said, still looking at me. "I'm not worried about him. I'm worried about Knees here."

"I'll shoot an Enforcement officer if I have to," I said, meeting her eyes. "But I won't get distracted hunting them down. I have a goal. I'll see Steelheart dead. That is all that matters."

"Bah," she said, turning away from me. "That's not an answer."

"Let's keep moving," Cody said, nodding toward a stairwell down to deeper tunnels.

"He's a scientist, lad," Cody explained as we walked through the narrow corridors of the steel catacombs. "Studied Epics in the early days, created some pretty remarkable devices, based on what we learned from them. That's why he's called Prof, other than that last-name thing."

I nodded thoughtfully. Now that we were deep, Cody had relaxed. Megan was still stiff. She walked ahead, holding her mobile and using it to send Prof a report on the mission. Cody had his set to flashlight, hooked to the upper left of his camo jacket. I'd removed the network card from mine, which he said was a good idea until Abraham or Tia had a chance to tweak it.

It turned out that they didn't trust even the Knighthawk Foundry. The Reckoners usually left their mobiles linked only to one another, and had the transmissions encrypted on both ends, not using the regular network. Until I got the encryption too, I could at least use my mobile as a camera or a glorified flashlight.

Cody walked with a relaxed posture, rifle up on his shoulder, arm looped over it and hand hanging down. I seemed to have earned his approval with Refractionary's death.

"So where did he work?" I asked, hungry for information about Prof. There were so many rumors about the Reckoners, but few real facts.

"Don't know," Cody admitted. "Nobody's sure what Prof's past is, though Tia probably knows something. She doesn't talk about it. Abe and I have bets going 'bout what Prof's specific workplace was. I'm pretty sure he was at some kind of secret government organization."

"Really?" I asked.

"Sure," Cody said. "I wouldn't be surprised if it was the same one that caused Calamity."

That was one of the theories, that the United States government—or sometimes the European Union—had somehow set off Calamity while trying to start a superhuman project. I thought it was pretty far-fetched. I'd always figured it was some kind of comet that got caught in Earth's gravity, but I didn't know if the science of that made any sense. Maybe it was a satellite. That could fit Cody's theory.

He wouldn't be the only one who thought it reeked of conspiracy. There *were* a lot of things about the Epics that didn't add up.

"Oh, you got that look," Cody said, pointing at me.

"That look?"

"Y'all think I'm crazy."

"No. No, of course not."

"You do. Well, it's okay. I know what I know, even if Prof rolls his eyes whenever I say anything about it." Cody smiled. "But that's another story. As for Prof's line of work, I think it *must* have been some kind of weapons facility. He created the tensors, after all."

"The tensors?"

"Prof wouldn't want you talking about that," Megan said, looking over her shoulder. "Nobody gave authorization for *him* to know about it," she added, glancing at me.

"I'm giving it," Cody said, relaxed. "He's going to see anyway, lass. And *don't* quote Prof's rules at me."

She closed her mouth; she looked like she'd been about to do just that.

"The tensors?" I asked again.

"Something Prof invented," Cody said. "Either right before or right after he left the lab. He's got a couple of things like that, inventions that give us our main edge against the Epics. Our jackets are one of those—they can take a lot of punishment—and the tensors are another."

"But what *are* they?"

"Gloves," Cody said. "Well, devices in the form of gloves. They create vibrations that disrupt solid objects. Works best on dense stuff, like stone and metal, some kinds of wood. Turns that kind of material to dust, but won't do anything to a living animal or person."

"You're kidding." In all my years of research I'd never heard of any technology like that.

"Nope," Cody said. "They're difficult to use, though. Abraham and Tia are the most skilled. But you'll see—the tensors, they let us go where we're not supposed to be. Where we're not expected to be."

"That's amazing," I said, my mind racing. The Reckoners *did* have a reputation for being able to get where nobody thought they could. There were stories . . . Epics killed in their own chambers, well guarded and presumed safe. Near-magical escapes by the Reckoners.

A device that could turn stone and metal to powder . . . You could get through locked doors, regardless of the security devices. You could sabotage vehicles. Maybe even knock down buildings. Suddenly, some of the most baffling mysteries surrounding the Reckoners made sense to me. How they'd gotten in to trap Daystorm, how they'd escaped the time when Calling War had nearly cornered them.

They'd have to be clever about how they entered, so as to not leave obvious holes that gave them away. But I could see how it would work. "But why . . . ," I asked, dazed, "why are you telling me this?"

"As I said, lad," Cody explained. "You're going to see them at work soon anyway. Might as well prepare you for it. Besides, you already know so much about us that one more thing won't matter."

"Okay." I said it lightly, then caught the somber tone of his voice. He'd left something unsaid: I already knew so much that I couldn't be allowed to go free.

Prof had given me my chance to leave. I'd insisted they bring me. At this point I either convinced them utterly that I wasn't a threat and joined them, or they left me behind. Dead.

I swallowed uncomfortably, my mouth suddenly dry. *I asked for this,* I told myself sternly. I'd known that once I joined them—if I joined them—I wouldn't ever be leaving. I was in, and that was that.

"So . . ." I tried to force myself not to dwell on the fact that this man—or any of them—might someday decide I needed to be shot in the name of the common good. "So how did he figure these gloves out? The tensors? I've never heard of anything *like* them."

"Epics," Cody said, his voice growing amiable again. "Prof let it drop once. The technology came from studying an Epic who could do something similar. Tia says it happened in the early days—before society collapsed, some Epics were captured and held. Not all of them are so powerful they can escape captivity with ease. Different labs ran tests on them, trying to figure out how their powers worked. The technology for things like the tensors came from those days."

I hadn't heard that, and some things started to click into place for me. We'd made great advances in technology back then, right around the arrival of Calamity. Energy weapons, advanced power sources and batteries, new mobile technology—which was why ours worked underground and at a significant range without using towers.

Of course, we lost much of it when the Epics started to take over. And what we didn't lose, Epics like Steelheart controlled. I tried to imagine those early Epics being tested. Was that why so many were evil? They resented this testing?

"Did any of them go to the testing willingly?" I asked. "How many labs were doing this?"

"I don't know," Cody said. "I reckon it's not very important."

"Why wouldn't it be?"

Cody shrugged, rifle still over his shoulder, the light of his mobile illuminating the tomblike metal corridor. The catacombs smelled of dust and condensation. "Tia is always talking about the scientific foundation of the Epics," he said. "I don't think they can be explained that way. Too much about them breaks what science says should happen. I sometimes wonder if they came along *because* we thought we could explain everything."

It didn't take much longer for us to arrive. I'd noticed that Megan was leading us by way of her mobile, which showed a map on its screen. That was remarkable. A map of the steel catacombs? I didn't think such a thing existed.

"Here," Megan said, waving to a thick patch of wires hanging down like a curtain in front of a wall. Sights like that were common down here, where the Diggers had left things unfinished.

Cody walked up and banged on a plate near the wires. A distant bang came back at him a few moments later.

"In you go, Knees," he said to me, gesturing toward the wires.

I took a breath and stepped forward, pushing them aside with the barrel of my rifle. There was a small tunnel beyond, leading steeply upward. I would have to crawl. I looked back at him.

"It's safe," he promised. I couldn't tell if he was making me go first because of some latent mistrust, or because he liked seeing me squirm. It didn't seem the time to question him or back down. I started crawling.

The tunnel was small enough to make me worry that if I slung my rifle on my back, a good scrape stood a chance of knocking the scope or sights out of alignment. So I kept it in my right hand as I crawled, which made it all the more awkward. The tunnel led toward a distant, soft light, and the crawl took long enough that my knees were aching by the time I reached the light. A strong hand took me by the left arm, helping me out of the tunnel. Abraham. The dark-skinned man had changed into cargo pants and a green tank top, which showed well-muscled arms. I hadn't noticed before, but he was wearing a small silver pendant around his neck, hanging out of his shirt.

The room I stepped into was unexpectedly large. Big enough for the team to have laid out their equipment and several bedrolls without it feeling cramped. There was a large table made of metal that grew right out of the floor, as well as benches at the walls and stools around the table.

They carved it there, I realized, looking at the sculpted walls. *They made this room with the tensors. Carved furniture right into it.*

It was impressive. I gawked as I stepped back and let Abraham help Megan out of the tunnel. The chamber had two doorways into other rooms that looked smaller. It was lit by lanterns, and there were cords on the floor—taped in place and out of the way—leading down another small tunnel.

"You have electricity," I said. "How did you get electricity?"

"Tapped into an old subway line," Cody said, crawling out of the tunnel. "One that was half completed, then forgotten about. The nature of this place is that even Steelheart doesn't know all of its nooks and dead ends."

"Just more proof the Diggers were mad," Abraham said. "They wired things in strange ways. We've found rooms that were sealed completely but had lights left on inside, shining for years by themselves. *Repaire des fantômes.*"

"Megan tells me," Prof said, appearing from one of the other rooms, "that you recovered the information, but that your means were . . . unconventional." The aging but sturdy man still wore his black lab coat.

"Hell yeah!" Cody said, shouldering his rifle.

Prof snorted. "Well, let's see what you recovered before I decide if I should yell at you or not." He reached for the backpack in Megan's hand.

"Actually," I said, stepping toward it, "I can—"

"You'll sit down, son," Prof said, "while I have a look at this. All of it. Then we'll talk."

His voice was calm, but I got the message. I pensively sat down beside the steel table as the others gathered around the pack and began rifling through my life.

12

"WOW," Cody said. "Honestly, lad, I thought you were exaggerating. But y'all really are a full-blown supergeek, aren't you?"

I blushed, still sitting on my stool. They had opened the folders I'd packed and spread out the contents, then moved on to my notebooks, passing them around and studying them. Cody had eventually lost interest and moved over to sit by me, his back to the table and elbows hitched up on it behind him.

"I had a job to do," I said. "I decided to do it well."

"This *is* impressive," Tia said. She sat cross-legged on the floor. She had changed to jeans but was still wearing her blouse and blazer, and her short red hair was still perfectly styled. Tia held up one of my notebooks. "It's rudimentary in organization," she said, "and doesn't use standard classifications. But it is exhaustive."

"There are standard classifications?" I asked.

"Several different systems," she said. "It looks like you've got a few of the terms here that cross between the systems, like High Epic—though I personally prefer the tier system. In other places, what you've come up with is interesting. I do like some of your terminology, like *prime invincibility*."

"Thanks," I said, though I felt a little embarrassed. Of course there were ways of classifying Epics. I hadn't the education—or the resources— to learn such things, so I'd made up my own.

It was surprising how easy it had been. There were outliers, of course— bizarre Epics with powers that didn't fit any of the classifications— but a surprising number of the others showed similarities. There were always individual quirks, like the glimmering of Refractionary's illusions. The core abilities, however, were often very similar.

"Explain this to me," Tia said, holding up a different notebook.

Hesitantly, I slid off my stool and joined her on the floor. She was pointing toward a notation I'd made at the bottom of the entry for a particular Epic named Strongtower.

"It's my Steelheart mark," I said. "Strongtower shows an ability like Steelheart has. I watch Epics like that carefully. If they get killed, or they manifest a limitation to their powers, I want to be aware of them."

Tia nodded. "Why didn't you lump the mental illusionists with the photon-manipulators?"

"I like to make groupings based on limitations," I said, getting out my index and flipping to a specific page for her. Epics with illusion powers fell into two groups. Some created actual changes in the way light behaved, crafting illusions with photons themselves. Others made illusions by affecting the brains of the people around them. They really created hallucinations, not true illusions.

"See," I said, pointing. "The mental illusionists tend to be limited in similar ways to other mentalists—like those with hypnotism powers, or mind-control effects. Illusionists that can alter light work differently. They are far more similar to the electricity-manipulation Epics."

Cody whistled softly. He'd gotten out a canteen and held it in one hand while still leaning back against the table. "Lad, I think we need to have a conversation about how much time you've got on your hands and how we can put it to better use."

"Better use than researching how to kill Epics?" Tia asked with a raised eyebrow.

"Sure," Cody said, taking a swig from his canteen. "Think of what he could do if I got him to organize all of the pubs in town, by brew!"

"Oh please," Tia said drily, turning a page in my notes.

"Abraham," Cody said. "Ask me why it's tragic for the young David to have spent so much time on these notebooks."

"Why is it tragic for the boy to have done such research?" Abraham said, still cleaning his gun.

"That's a very astute question," Cody said. "Thank you very much for asking."

"It is my pleasure."

"Anyway," Cody said, raising his canteen, "why do you want so badly to kill these Epics?"

"Revenge," I said. "Steelheart killed my father. I intend—"

"Yes, yes," Cody said, cutting me off. "Y'all intend to see him bleed again, and all that. Very dedicated and familial of you. But I'm telling you, that ain't enough. You've got passion to kill, but you need to find passion to live. At least that's what I think."

I didn't know how to respond to that. Studying Steelheart, learning about Epics so that I could find a way to kill him, *was* my passion. If there was a place I fit in, wasn't it with the Reckoners? That was their life's work too, wasn't it?

"Cody," Prof said, "why don't you go finish working on the third chamber?"

"Sure thing, Prof," the sniper said, screwing on the lid of his canteen. He sauntered out of the room.

"Don't listen too much to Cody, son," Prof said, setting one of my notebooks on the stack. "He says the same things to the rest of us. He worries we'll focus so hard on killing the Epics that we'll forget to live our lives."

"He might be right," I said. "I . . . I really haven't had much of a life, other than this."

"The work we do," Prof said, "is not about living. Our job is killing. We'll leave the regular people to live their lives, to find joy in them, to enjoy the sunrises and the snowfalls. Our job is to get them there."

I had memories of the world before. It had only been ten years ago, after all. It's just that it was difficult to remember a world of sunshine when darkness was all you saw each day. Remembering that time . . . it was like trying to recall the specifics of my father's face. You forget things like that, gradually.

"Jonathan," Abraham said to Prof, slipping the barrel back onto his gun, "have you considered the things this boy said?"

"I'm not a boy," I said.

They all looked at me. Even Megan, standing beside the doorway.

"I just wanted to note it," I said, suddenly uncomfortable. "I mean, I'm eighteen. I've hit my majority. I'm not a child."

Prof eyed me. Then, surprisingly, he nodded. "Age has nothing to do with it, but you've helped kill two Epics, which is good enough for me. It should be for any of us."

"Very well," Abraham said, voice soft. "But Prof, we have spoken of this before. By killing Epics like Fortuity, are we really achieving anything?"

"We fight back," Megan said. "We're the only ones who do. It's important."

"And yet," Abraham said, snapping another piece onto his gun, "we are afraid to fight the most powerful. And so, the domination of the tyrants continues. So long as they do not fall, the others will not truly fear us. They will fear Steelheart, Obliteration, and Night's

Sorrow. If we will not face creatures such as these, is there any hope that others will someday stand up to them?"

The steel-walled room went quiet, and I held my breath. The words were nearly the same I had used earlier, but coming from Abraham's soft-spoken, lightly accented voice, they seemed to hold more weight.

Prof turned to Tia.

She held up a photograph. "This is really Nightwielder?" she asked me. "You're sure of it?"

The picture was a prize of my possessions, a photograph of Nightwielder beside Steelheart on the Day of Annexation, just before his darkness had come upon the city. As far as I knew, it was one of a kind, sold to me by an urchin whose father had taken it with an old Polaroid camera.

Nightwielder was normally translucent, incorporeal. He could move through solid objects and control darkness itself. He appeared often in the city, but was always in his incorporeal form. In this picture he was solid, wearing a sharp black suit and hat. He had Asian features and black shoulder-length hair. I had other pictures of him in his incorporeal form. The face was the same.

"It's obviously him," I said.

"And the photo wasn't doctored," Tia said.

"I . . ." That I couldn't prove. "I can't promise it wasn't, though its being a Polaroid makes that less likely. Tia, he has to be corporeal *some* of the time. That photo is the best clue, but I have others. People who have smelled phosphorus and spotted someone walking by who matches his description." Phosphorus was one of the signs of him using his powers. "I've found a dozen sources that all match this idea. It's *sunlight* that makes the difference—I suspect it's the ultraviolet part of sunlight that matters. Bathed in it, he turns corporeal."

Tia held the photo before her, contemplating it. Then she began scanning through my other notes on Nightwielder. "I think we need to investigate it, Jon," she said. "If there's a chance we can actually get to Steelheart . . ."

"We can," I said. "I have a plan. It will work."

"This is stupidity," Megan cut in. She stood by the wall with her arms crossed. "Sheer stupidity. We don't even know his weakness."

"We can figure it out," I shot back. "I'm sure of it. We have the clues we need."

"Even if we did figure it out," Megan said, throwing a hand up into the air, "it would be practically useless. The obstacles in even *getting* to Steelheart are insurmountable!"

I locked eyes with her, fighting down my anger. I got the feeling she was arguing with me not because she actually disagreed, but because she found me offensive for some reason.

"I—" I began, but Prof interrupted me.

"Everyone follow me," he said, standing up.

I shared a glare with Megan, and then we all moved, joining him as he walked toward the smaller room to the right of the main chamber. Even Cody made his way in from the third room— unsurprisingly, he'd been listening. He wore a glove on his right hand. It glowed with a soft green light at the palm.

"Is the imager ready?" Prof asked.

"Mostly," Abraham said. "It's one of the first things I set up." He knelt beside a device on the floor connected to the wall by several wires. He turned it on.

Suddenly, all of the metal surfaces in the room turned black. I jumped. It felt like we were floating in darkness.

Prof raised a hand, then tapped on the wall in a pattern. The walls changed to show a view of the city, presenting it as if we were standing atop a six-story building. Lights sparkled in the blackness, shining from the hundreds of steel buildings that made up Newcago. The old buildings were less uniform; the new buildings, spreading out onto what had once been the lake, were more modern. They had been built from other materials, then intentionally transformed to steel. You could do some interesting things with architecture, I'd heard, when you had that option.

"This is one of the most advanced cities in the world," Prof said. "Ruled by arguably the most powerful Epic in North America. If we move against him, we raise the stakes dramatically—and we're already betting up to the limits of what we can pay. Failure could mean the end of the Reckoners completely. It could bring disaster, could end the last bit of resistance against the Epics that mankind has left."

"Just let me tell you the plan," I said. "I think it will persuade you." I had a hunch. Prof *wanted* to go after Steelheart. If I could make my case, he'd side with me.

Prof turned to me, meeting my eyes. "You want us to do this? Fine, I'll give you your shot. But I don't want you to persuade me." He pointed to Megan, who stood beside the doorway, her arms still crossed. "Persuade *her.*"

13

PERSUADE her. *Great,* I thought. Megan's eyes could have drilled holes through . . . well, anything, I guess. I mean, eyes can't normally drill holes through things, so the metaphor works regardless, right?

Megan's eyes could have drilled holes through butter. *Persuade her?* I thought. *Impossible.*

But I wasn't going to give up without trying. I stepped up to the wall of glistening metal overlaid with the outline of Newcago.

"The imager can show us anything?" I asked.

"Anything the basic spynet watches or listens to," Abraham explained, standing up from the imaging device.

"The spynet?" I said, suddenly feeling uncomfortable. I walked forward. This device was remarkable; it made me feel as if we really were standing on top of a building outside in the city, rather than in a box of a room. It wasn't a perfect illusion—if I looked around closely I could still see the corners of the room we were standing in, and the 3-D imaging wasn't great for things nearby.

Still, so long as I didn't look too closely—and didn't pay attention to the lack of wind or scents of the city—I really could imagine I was outside. They were constructing this image using the spynet? That was Steelheart's surveillance system for the city, the means by which Enforcement kept tabs on what the people in Newcago were doing.

"I knew he was watching us," I said, "but I hadn't realized that the cameras were so . . . extensive."

"Fortunately," Tia said, "we've found some ways to influence what the network sees and hears. So don't worry about Steelheart spying on us."

I still felt uncomfortable, but it wasn't worth thinking on at the moment. I stepped up to the edge of the roof, looking down at the street below. A few cars passed, and the imager relayed the sounds of their driving. I reached forward and placed my hand on the wall of the room—seemingly touching something invisible in midair. This was going to be very disorienting.

Unlike the tensors, room imagers I'd heard of—people paid good money to visit imager films. My conversation with Cody left me thinking. Had we learned how to do things like this from Epics with illusion powers?

"I—" I began.

"No," Megan said. "If he has to convince me, then I'm driving this conversation." She stepped up beside me.

"But—"

"Go ahead, Megan," Prof said.

I grumbled to myself and stepped back to where I didn't feel I was on the verge of a multistory plummet.

"It's simple," Megan said. "There's one enormous problem in facing Steelheart."

"One?" Cody asked, leaning back against the wall. It made

him look like he was leaning against open air. "Let's see: incredible strength, can shoot deadly blasts of energy from his hands, can transform anything nonliving around him into steel, can command the winds and fly with perfect control . . . oh, and he's utterly impervious to bullets, edged weapons, fire, radiation, blunt trauma, suffocation, and explosions. That's like . . . *three* things, lass." He held up four fingers.

Megan rolled her eyes. "All true," she said, then turned back to me. "But none of that is even the first problem."

"Finding him is the first problem," Prof said softly. He'd set out a folding chair, Tia as well, and the two were sitting in the center of the imaged rooftop. "Steelheart is paranoid. He makes certain nobody knows where he is."

"Exactly," Megan said, raising her hands and using a thumbs-out gesture to control the imager. We zoomed through the city, the buildings a blur beneath us.

I wobbled, my stomach flip-flopping. I reached for the wall, but I wasn't certain where it was, and stumbled to the side until I found it. Abruptly we halted, hanging in midair, looking at Steelheart's palace.

It was a dark fortress of anodized steel that rose from the edge of the city, built upon the portion of the lake that had been transformed to steel. It spread out in either direction, a long line of dark metal with towers, girders, and walkways. Like some mash-up of an old Victorian manor, a medieval castle, and an oil rig. Violent red lights shone from deep within the various recesses, and smoke billowed from chimneys, black against a black sky.

"They say he intentionally built the place to be confusing," Megan said. "There are hundreds of chambers, and he sleeps in a different one each night, eats in a different one for each meal. Supposedly even the staff doesn't know where he'll be." She turned to me, hostile. "You'll never find him. *That's* the first problem."

I swayed, still feeling as if I were standing in midair, though none of the others seemed to be having trouble. "Could we . . . ," I asked nauseously, looking back at Abraham.

He chuckled, making some gestures and pulling us back to the top of a nearby building. There was a small chimney on it, and as we "landed" the chimney squished flat, becoming two-dimensional on the floor. This wasn't a hologram—so far as I knew, nobody had mimicked that level of illusion power with technology. It was just a very advanced use of six screens and some 3-D imaging.

"Right," I said, feeling steadier. "Anyway, that *would be* a problem."

"Except?" Prof asked.

"Except we don't need to find Steelheart," I said. "He'll come to us."

"He rarely comes out in public anymore," Megan said. "And when he does, it's erratic. How in Calamity's fires are you going to—"

"Faultline," I said. The Epic who had made the earth swallow the bank on that terrible day when my father had been killed, and who had later challenged Steelheart.

"David has a point," Abraham said. "Steelheart *did* come out of hiding to fight her when she tried to take Newcago."

"And when Ides Hatred came here to challenge him," I said. "Steelheart met the challenge personally."

"As I recall," Prof said, "they destroyed an entire city block in that conflict."

"Sounds like quite the party," Cody noted.

"Yes," I said. I had pictures of that fight.

"So you're saying we need to convince a powerful Epic to come to Newcago and challenge him," Megan said, her voice flat. "Then we'll know where he's going to be. Sounds easy."

"No, no," I said, turning to face them, my back to the dark, smoldering expanse of Steelheart's palace. "That's the first part of the plan. We make Steelheart *think* a powerful Epic is coming here to challenge him."

"How would we do that?" Cody asked.

"We've already started," I explained. "Now we spread word that Fortuity was killed by agents of a new Epic. We start hitting more Epics, leaving the impression that it's all the work of the same rival. Then we deliver an ultimatum to Steelheart that if he wants to stop the murder of his followers, he'll need to come out and fight.

"And he *will* come. So long as we're convincing enough. You said he's paranoid, Prof. You're right. He is—and he can't stand a challenge to his authority. He always deals with rival Epics in person, just like he did with Deathpoint all those years ago. If there's one thing that the Reckoners are good at, it's killing Epics. If we hunt down enough of them in the city in a short time, it will be a threat to Steelheart. We can draw him out, choose our own battlefield. We can make him come to us and walk right into our trap."

"Won't happen," Megan said. "He'll just send Firefight or Night-wielder."

Firefight and Nightwielder, two immensely powerful High Epics who acted as Steelheart's bodyguards and right-hand men. They were nearly as dangerous as he was.

"I've shown you Nightwielder's weakness," I said. "It's sunlight— ultraviolet radiation. He doesn't know that anyone is aware of it. We can use that to trap him."

"You haven't proven anything," Megan said. "You've shown us he *has* a weakness. But every Epic does. You don't know it's the sunlight."

"I glanced through his sources," Tia said. "It . . . it really does look like David might have something."

Megan clenched her jaw. If this came down to me convincing her to agree to my plan, I was going to fail. She didn't look like she'd agree no matter how good my arguments.

But I wasn't convinced I needed her support, regardless of what Prof said. I'd seen how the other Reckoners looked to him. If he decided this was a good idea, they'd follow. I just had to hope that my reasoning would be good enough for him, even though he'd said I needed to convince Megan.

"Firefight," Megan said. "What about him?"

"Easy," I said, my mood lifting. "Firefight isn't what he seems."

"What does that mean?"

"I'll need my notes to explain," I said. "But he'll be the easiest of the three to take down—I promise you that."

Megan made a face as if she were offended by this, annoyed that I wasn't willing to engage her without my notes. "Whatever," she said, then made a gesture, spinning the room around in a circle and sending me stumbling again, though there was no momentum. She glanced at me, and I saw a hint of a smile on her lips. Well, at least I knew one thing that broke through her coldness: nearly making me lose my lunch.

When the room stopped rotating, our view pointed upward at an angle. Every part of me said I should be sliding backward into the wall, but I knew it was all just done with perspective.

Directly ahead of us a group of three copters moved through the air low, just above the city. They were sleek and black, with two large rotors each. The sword-and-shield emblem of Enforcement painted in white on their sides.

"It probably won't even come to Firefight and Nightwielder," she said. "I should have brought this up first: Enforcement."

"She's right," Abraham said. "Steelheart is always surrounded by Enforcement soldiers."

"So we take them out first," I said. "It's what a rival Epic would probably do anyway—disable Steelheart's army so they could move in on the city. That will only help convince him that we're a rival Epic. The Reckoners would never do something like take on Enforcement."

"We wouldn't do it," Megan said, "because it would be pure idiocy!"

"It does seem a little outside our capabilities, son," Prof said, though I could tell I had him hooked. He watched with interest. He liked the idea of drawing Steelheart out. It was the sort of thing the Reckoners *did* do, playing on an Epic's arrogance.

I raised my hands, imitating the gestures the others had been making, then thrust them forward to try moving the viewing room toward Enforcement headquarters. The room lurched awkwardly, tipping sideways and streaking through the city to slam into the side of a building. It froze there, unable to continue into the structure because the spynet didn't look there. The entire room quivered, as if desperate to fulfill my demand but uncertain where to go.

I toppled sideways into the wall, then plopped down on the ground, dizzy. "Uh . . ."

"Y'all want me to get that for you?" Cody asked, amused, from the doorway.

"Yeah. Thanks. Enforcement headquarters, please."

Cody made the gestures and raised the room up, leveled it out, then spun it about and moved it over the city until we were hovering near a large black box of a building. It looked vaguely like a prison, though it didn't house criminals. Well, just the state-sanctioned kinds of criminals.

I righted myself, determined not to look like a fool in front of the others. Though I wasn't certain if that was possible at this point. "There's one simple way to neuter Enforcement," I said. "We take out Conflux."

For once an idea of mine didn't prompt an outcry from the others. Even Megan looked thoughtful, standing just a short distance from me, her arms crossed. *I'd love to see her smile again,* I thought, then immediately forced my mind away from that. I had to stay focused. This wasn't a time to let my feet get swept out from underneath me. Well . . . in a figurative sense, at least.

"You've considered this," I guessed, looking around the room. "You hit Fortuity, but you talked about trying for Conflux instead."

"It would be a powerful blow," Abraham said softly, leaning against the wall near Cody.

"Abraham suggested it," Prof said. "He fought for it, actually. Using some of the same arguments that you made—that we weren't doing enough, that we weren't targeting Epics who were important enough."

"Conflux is more than just the head of Enforcement," I said, excited. They finally seemed like they were listening. "He's a gifter."

"A what?" Cody asked.

"It's a slang term," Tia said, "for what we call a transference Epic."

"Yes," I said.

"Great," Cody said. "So what's a transference Epic?"

"Don't you *ever* pay attention?" Tia asked. "We've talked about this."

"He was cleaning his guns," Abraham said.

"I'm an artist," Cody said.

Abraham nodded. "He's an artist."

"And cleanliness is next to deadliness," Cody added.

"Oh please," Tia said, turning back to me.

"A gifter," I said, "is an Epic who has the ability to transfer his powers to other people. Conflux has two powers he can give others, and both are incredibly strong. Maybe even stronger than those of Steelheart."

"So why doesn't *he* rule?" Cody asked.

"Who knows?" I shrugged. "Probably because he's fragile. He isn't said to have any immortality powers. So he stays hidden. Nobody even knows what he looks like. He's been with Steelheart for over half a decade, though, quietly managing Enforcement." I looked back at Enforcement headquarters. "He can create enormous stores of energy from his body. He gives this electricity to team leaders of Enforcement Cores; that's how they run their mechanized suits and their energy rifles. No Conflux means no power armor and no energy weapons."

"It means more than that," Prof said. "Taking out Conflux might knock out power to the city."

"What?" I asked.

"Newcago uses more electricity than it generates," Tia explained. "All of those lights, on all the time . . . it's a huge drain, on a level that would have been hard to sustain even back before Calamity. The new Fractured States don't have the infrastructure to provide Steelheart with enough power to run this city, yet he does."

"He's using Conflux to augment his power stores," Prof said. "Somehow."

"So that makes Conflux an even better target!" I said.

"We talked about this months ago," Prof said, leaning forward, fingers laced before him. "We decided he was too dangerous to hit Even if we succeeded, we'd draw too much attention, be hunted down by Steelheart himself."

"Which is what we want," I said.

The others didn't seem convinced. Take this step, move against Steelheart's empire, and they'd be exposing themselves. No more hiding in the various urban undergrounds, hitting carefully chosen targets. No more quiet rebellion. Kill Conflux, and there would be no backing down until Steelheart was dead or the Reckoners were captured, broken, and executed.

He's going to say no, I thought, looking into Prof's eyes. He looked older than I'd always imagined him being. A man in his middle years, with grey speckling his hair, and with a face that showed he had lived through the death of one era and had worked ten hard years trying to end the next era. Those years had taught him caution.

He opened his mouth to say the words, but was interrupted when Abraham's mobile chirped. Abraham unhooked it from its shoulder mount. "Time for Reinforcement," he said, smiling.

Reinforcement. Steelheart's daily message to his subjects. "Can you show it on the wall here?" I asked.

"Sure," Cody said, turning his mobile toward the projector and tapping a button.

"That won't be ne——" Prof began.

111

The program had already started. It showed Steelheart this time. Sometimes he appeared personally, sometimes not. He stood atop one of the tall radio towers on his palace. A pitch-black cape spread out behind him, rippling in the wind.

The messages were all prerecorded, but there was no way to tell when; as always there was no sun in the sky, and no trees grew in the city any longer to give an indication of the season either. I'd almost forgotten what it was like to be able to tell the time of day just by looking out the window.

Steelheart was illuminated by red lights from below. He placed one foot on a low railing, then leaned forward and scanned his city. His dominion.

I shivered, staring at him, presented in large scale on the wall in front of me. My father's murderer. The tyrant. He looked so calm, so thoughtful, in this picture. Long jet-black hair that curled softly down to his shoulders. Shirt stretched across an inhumanly strong physique. Black slacks, an upgrade from the loose pants he'd worn on that day ten years ago. This shot of him seemed like it wanted to present him as the thoughtful and concerned dictator, like the early communist leaders I'd learned about back in the Factory school.

He raised a hand, staring intently at the city beneath him, and the hand started to glow with a wicked power. Yellow-white, to contrast the violent red below. The power around his hand wasn't electricity but raw *energy*. He built it up for a time, until it was shining so brightly the camera couldn't distinguish anything but the light and the shadow of Steelheart in front of it.

Then he pointed and launched a bolt of blazing yellow force into the city. The power hit a building, blasting a hole through the side, sending flames and debris exploding out the opposite windows. As the building smoldered, people fled from it. The camera zoomed in, making sure to catch sight of them. Steelheart wanted us to know he was firing on an inhabited structure.

Another bolt followed, causing the building to lurch, the steel of one side melting and caving inward. He fired twice more into a building beside it, starting the innards there aflame as well, walls melting from the enormous power of the energy he threw.

The camera pulled back and turned to Steelheart again, still in the same half-crouched stance. He looked down at the city, face impassive, red light from beneath limning a strong jaw and contemplative eyes. There was no explanation of why he'd destroyed those buildings, though perhaps a later message would explain the sins—real or perceived—that the inhabitants were guilty of.

Or perhaps not. Living in Newcago brought risks; one of them was that Steelheart could decide to execute you and your family without explanation. The flip side was that for those risks, you got to live in a place with electricity, running water, jobs, and food. Those were rare commodities in much of the land now.

I took a step forward, walking right up to the wall to study the creature that loomed there. *He wants us to be terrified,* I thought. *It's what this is all about. He wants us to think no one can challenge him.*

Early scholars had wondered if perhaps Epics were some new stage in human development. An evolutionary breakthrough. I didn't accept that. This thing wasn't human. It never had been. Steelheart turned to look toward the camera, and there was a hint of a smile on his lips.

A chair scraped behind me and I turned. Prof had stood up and was staring at Steelheart. Yes, there was hatred there. Deep hatred. Prof looked down and met my eyes. It happened again, that moment of understanding.

Each of us knew where the other stood.

"You haven't said how you'll kill him," Prof said to me. "You haven't convinced Megan. All you've shown is that you have a fragile half of a plan."

"I've seen him bleed," I said. "The secret is in my head somewhere,

Prof. It's the best chance you or anyone will ever have at killing him. Can you pass that up? Can you *really* walk away when you've got a shot?"

Prof met my eyes. He stared into them for a long moment. Behind me Steelheart's transmission ended, and the wall went black.

Prof was right. My plan, clever though it had once seemed to me, depended on a lot of speculation. Draw Steelheart out with a fake Epic. Take down his bodyguards. Upend Enforcement. Kill him using a secret weakness that might be hidden in my memory somewhere.

A fragile half plan indeed. That was why I had needed to come to the Reckoners. They could make it happen. This man, Jonathan Phaedrus, could make it happen.

"Cody," Prof said, turning, "start training the new kid with a tensor. Tia, let's see if we can start tracking Conflux's movements. Abraham, we're going to need some brainstorming on how to imitate a High Epic, if that's even possible."

I felt my heart jump. "We're going to do it?"

"Yes," Prof said. "God help us, we are."

PART TWO

14

"**NOW,** y'all gotta be *gentle* with her," Cody said. "Like caressing a beautiful woman the night before the big caber toss."

"Caber toss?" I said as I raised my hands toward the chunk of steel on the chair in front of me. I sat cross-legged on the floor of the Reckoner hideout, Cody on the ground beside me, his back to the wall and legs stretched out in front of him. It had been a week since the hit on Fortuity.

"Yeah, caber toss," Cody said. Though his accent was purely Southern—and strongly that—he always talked as if he were from Scotland. I guessed his family was from there or something. "It's this sport we had back in the homeland. Involved throwing trees."

"Little saplings? Like javelins?"

"No, no. The cabers had to be so wide that your fingers couldn't

117

touch on the other side when you reached your arms around them. We'd rip 'em out of the ground, then hurl them as far as we could."

I raised a skeptical eyebrow.

"Bonus points if you could hit a bird out of the air," he added.

"Cody," Tia said, walking by with a sheaf of papers, "do you even know what a caber is?"

"A tree," he said. "We used them to build show houses. It's where the word *cabaret* came from, lass." He said it with such a straight face that I had trouble determining if he was sincere or not.

"You're a buffoon," Tia said, sitting down at the table, which was spread with various detailed maps that I hadn't been able to make sense of. They appeared to be city plans and schematics, dating from before the Annexation.

"Thank you," Cody said, tipping his camo baseball cap toward her.

"It wasn't a compliment."

"Oh, you didn't mean it as one, lass," Cody said. "But the word *buffoon,* it comes from the word *buff,* meaning strong and handsome, which in turn—"

"Aren't you supposed to be helping David learn the tensors?" she interrupted. "And *not* bothering me."

"It's all right," Cody said. "I can do both. I'm a man of many talents."

"None of which involve remaining silent, unfortunately," Tia muttered, leaning down and making a few notations on her map.

I smiled, though even after a week with them I wasn't certain what to make of the Reckoners. I'd imagined each pod of them as an elite special forces group, tightly knit and intensely loyal to one another.

There was some of that in this group; even Tia and Cody's banter was generally good-natured. However, there was also a lot of individuality to them. They each kind of . . . did their own thing. Prof didn't seem so much a leader as a middle manager. Abraham worked on the technology, Tia the research, Megan information gathering, and Cody odd jobs—filling in the spaces with mayonnaise, as he liked to call it. Whatever that meant.

It was bizarre to see them as people. A part of me was actually disappointed. My gods were regular humans who squabbled, laughed, got on one another's nerves, and—in Abraham's case—snored when they slept. Loudly.

"Now, *that's* the right look of concentration," Cody said. "Nice work, lad. Y'all've got to keep a keen mind. Focused. Like Sir William himself. Soul of a warrior." He took a bite of his sandwich.

I hadn't been focused on my tensor, but I didn't let on to that fact. Instead I raised my hand, doing as I'd been instructed. The thin glove I wore had lines of metal along the front of each finger. The lines joined in a pattern at the palm and all glowed softly green.

As I concentrated my hand began to vibrate softly, as if someone were playing music with a lot of bass somewhere nearby. It was hard to focus with that strange pulsation running up my arm.

I raised my hand toward the chunk of metal; it was the remnant of a section of pipe. Now, apparently, I needed to *push* the vibrations away from me. Whatever that meant. The technology hooked right into my nerves using sensors inside the glove, interpreting electrical impulses from my brain. So Abraham had explained.

Cody had said it was magic, and had told me not to ask any questions lest I "anger the wee daemons inside who make the gloves work and our coffee taste good."

I still hadn't managed to make the tensors do anything, though I felt I was getting close. I had to remain focused, keep my hands steady, and *push* the vibrations out. Like blowing a ring of smoke, Abraham had said. Or like using your body warmth in a hug—without the arms. That had been Tia's explanation. Everyone thought of it their own way, I guess.

My hand started to shake more vigorously.

"Steady," Cody said. "Don't lose control, lad."

I stiffened my muscles.

"Whoa. Not too stiff," Cody said. "Secure, strong, but calm. Like you're caressing a beautiful woman, remember?"

That made me think of Megan.

I lost control, and a green wave of smoky energy burst from my hand and flew out in front of me. It missed the pipe completely, but vaporized the metal leg of the chair it sat on. Dust showered down and the chair went lopsided, dumping the pipe to the floor with a *clang*.

"Sparks," Cody said. "Remind me to never let you caress me, lad."

"I thought you told him to think of a beautiful woman," Tia said.

"Yeah," Cody replied. "And if that's how he treats one of them, I don't want to *know* what he'd do to an ugly Scotsman."

"I did it!" I exclaimed, pointing at the powdered metal that was the remains of the chair leg.

"Yeah, but you missed."

"Doesn't matter," I said. "I finally made it work!" I hesitated. "It wasn't like blowing smoke. It was like . . . like singing. From my hand."

"That's a new one," Cody said.

"It's different for everyone," Tia said from her table, head still down. She opened a can of cola as she scribbled notes. Tia was useless without her cola. "Using the tensors isn't natural to your mind, David. You've already built neural pathways, and so you have to kind of hotwire your brain to figure out what mental muscles to flex. I've always wondered if we gave a tensor to a child, if they'd be able to incorporate using it better, more naturally, as just another kind of 'limb' to practice with."

Cody looked at me. Then he whispered, "Wee daemons. Don't let her fool you, lad. I think she works for them. I saw her leaving out pie for them the other night."

Trouble was, he was *just* serious enough to make me question whether he really believed that. The twinkle to his eye indicated he was being silly, but he had such a perfectly straight face. . . .

I took off the tensor and handed it over. Cody slipped it on, then absently raised a hand—palm first—to the side and thrust it outward. The tensor began vibrating as his hand moved, and when it stopped a faint, smoky green wave continued on, hitting the fallen chair and the pipe. Both vaporized to dust, falling to the ground in a puff.

Each time I saw the tensors work, I was amazed. The range was very limited, only a few feet at most, and they couldn't affect flesh. They weren't much good in a fight—sure, you could vaporize someone's gun, but only if they were very close to you. In which case taking the time to concentrate and fight with the tensors would probably be less effective than just punching the guy.

Still, the opportunities they afforded were incredible. Moving through the bowels of Newcago's steel catacombs, getting in and out of rooms. If you managed to keep the tensor hidden, you could escape from any bond, any cell.

"You keep training," Cody said. "You show talent, so Prof will want you to get good with these. We need another member of the team who can use them."

"Not all of you can?" I asked, surprised.

Cody shook his head. "Megan can't make them work, and Tia's rarely in a position to use them—we need her back giving support while on missions. So it usually comes down to Abraham and me using them."

"What about Prof?" I asked. "He invented them. He's got to be pretty good with them, right?"

Cody shook his head. "Don't know. He refuses to use them. Something about a bad experience in the past. He won't talk about it. Probably shouldn't. We don't need to know. Either way, you should practice." Cody shook his head and took off the tensor, tucking it into his pocket. "What I'd have given for one of these before. . . ."

The other pieces of Reckoner technology were awesome too. The jackets, which supposedly worked a little like armor, were one.

Cody, Megan, and Abraham each wore a jacket—different on the outside, but with a complicated network of diodes inside that somehow protected them. The dowser, which told if someone was Epic, was another piece of such technology. The only other piece I'd seen was something they called the harmsway, a device that accelerated a body's healing abilities.

It's so sad, I thought, as Cody fetched a broom to clean up the dust. *All of this technology . . . it could have changed the world. If the Epics hadn't done that first.* A ruined world couldn't enjoy the benefits.

"What was your life like back then?" I asked, holding the dustpan for Cody. "Before all of this happened? What did you do?"

"You wouldn't believe me," Cody said, smiling.

"Let me guess," I said, anticipating one of Cody's stories. "Professional footballer? High-paid assassin and spy?"

"A cop," Cody said, subdued, looking down at the pile of dust. "In Nashville."

"What? Really?" I *was* surprised.

Cody nodded, then waved for me to dump the first pile of dust into the trash bin while he swept up the rest of it. "My father was a cop too in his early years, over in the homeland. Small city. You wouldn't know it. He moved here when he married my mother. I grew up over here; ain't never actually been to the homeland. But I wanted to be just like my pa, so when he died, I went to school and joined the force."

"Huh," I said, stooping down again to collect the rest of the dust. "That's a lot less glamorous than I'd been imagining."

"Well, I did take down an entire drug cartel by myself, you understand."

"Of course."

"And there was the time the president's Secret Service were shuttling him through the city, and they all ate a bad mess of scones and got sick, and we in the department had to protect him from an assassination plot." He called over to Abraham, who was tinkering with one of the team's shotguns. "It was them Frenchies who were behind it, you know."

"I'm not French!" Abraham called back. "I'm Canadian, you slontze."

"Same difference!" Cody said, then grinned and looked back at me. "Anyway, maybe it wasn't glamorous. Not all the time. But I enjoyed it. I like doing good for people. Serve and protect. And then . . ."

"Then?" I asked.

"Nashville got annexed when the country collapsed," Cody explained. "A group of five Epics took charge of most of the South."

"The Coven," I said, nodding. "There's actually six of them. One pair are twins."

"Ah, right. Keep forgetting that y'all are freakishly informed about this stuff. Anyway, they took over, and the police department started serving them. If we didn't agree, we were supposed to turn in our badges and retire. The good ones did that. The bad ones stayed on, and they got worse."

"And you?" I asked.

Cody fingered the thing he kept at his waist, tied to his belt on the right side. It looked like a thin wallet. He reached down and undid the snap, showing a scratched—but still polished—police badge.

"I didn't do either one," he said, subdued. "I took an oath. Serve and protect. I ain't going to stop that because some thugs with magic powers start shoving everybody around. That's that."

His words gave me a chill. I stared at that badge, and my mind flipped over and over like a pancake on a griddle, trying to figure out this man. Trying to reconcile the joking, storytelling blowhard with the image of a police officer still on his beat. Still serving after the city government had fallen, after the precinct had been shut down, after everything had been taken from him.

The others probably have similar stories, I thought, glancing at Tia, who was busy working away, sipping her cola. What had drawn her to fighting what most would call a hopeless battle, living a life of constant running, bringing justice to those the law should have condemned—but could not touch? What had drawn Abraham, Megan, the professor himself?

I looked back at Cody, who was moving to close his badge holder. There was something tucked behind the plastic opposite it in the holder—a picture of a woman, but with a section removed, a bar shape that had contained her eyes and much of her nose.

"Who was that?"

"Somebody special," Cody said.

"Who?"

He didn't answer, snapping the badge holder closed.

"It's better if we don't know, or ask, about each other's families," Tia said from the table. "Usually a stint in the Reckoners ends with death, but occasionally one of us gets captured. Better if we can't reveal anything about the others that will put their loved ones in danger."

"Oh," I said. "Yeah, that makes sense." It just wasn't something I'd have considered. I didn't have any loved ones left.

"How is it going there, lass?" Cody asked, sauntering over to the table. I joined him and saw that Tia had spread out lists of reports and ledgers.

"It's not going at all," Tia said with a grimace. She rubbed her eyes beneath her spectacles. "This is like trying to re-create a complex puzzle after being given only one piece."

"What are you doing?" I asked. I couldn't make sense of the ledgers any more than I'd been able to make sense of the maps.

"Steelheart was wounded that day," Tia said. "If your recollection is correct—"

"It is," I promised.

"People's memories fade," Cody said.

"Not mine," I said. "Not about this. Not about that day. I can tell you what color tie the mortgage man was wearing. I can tell you how many tellers there were. I could probably count the ceiling tiles in the bank for you. It's there, in my head. Burned there."

"All right," Tia said. "Well, if you *are* correct, then Steelheart was impervious for most of the fight and only harmed near the end. Something changed. I'm working through all possibilities—something about your father, the location, or the situation. The most likely seems the possibility you mentioned, that the vault was involved. Perhaps something inside it weakened Steelheart, and once the vault was blown open it could affect him."

"So you're looking for a record of the bank vault's contents."

"Yes," Tia said. "But it's an impossible task. Most of the records would have been destroyed with the bank. Off-site records would have been stored on a server somewhere. First Union was hosted by a company known as Dorry Jones LLC. Most of their servers were located in Texas, but the building was burned down eight years back during the Ardra riots.

"That leaves the off chance that they had physical records or a digital backup at another branch, but that building housed the main offices, so the chances of that are slim. Other than that, I've been looking for patron lists—the rich or notable who were known to frequent the bank and have boxes in the vault. Perhaps they stored something in there that will be part of the public record. A strange rock, a specific symbol that Steelheart might have seen, something."

I looked at Cody. Servers? Hosted? What was she talking about? He shrugged.

The problem was, an Epic weakness could be just about anything. Tia mentioned symbols—there were some Epics who, if they saw a specific pattern, lost their powers for a few moments. Others were weakened by thinking certain thoughts, not eating certain foods, or eating the wrong foods. The weaknesses were more varied than the powers themselves.

"If we don't figure out this puzzle," Tia said, "the rest of the plan is useless. We're starting down a dangerous path, but we don't yet know if we'll be capable of doing what we need to at the end. That bothers me greatly, David. If you think of anything—*anything*—that could give me another lead to work on, speak of it."

"I will," I promised.

"Good," she said. "Otherwise, take Cody and *please* let me concentrate."

"You really should learn to do two things at once, lass," Cody said. "Like me."

"It's easy to both be a buffoon and make messes of things, Cody," she replied. "Putting those messes back together while dealing with said buffoon is a much more difficult prospect. Go find something to shoot, or whatever it is you do."

"I thought I *was* doing whatever it is I do," he said absently. He stabbed a finger at a line on one of the pages, which looked like it listed clients of the bank. It read *Johnson Liberty Agency*.

"What are you—" Tia began, then cut herself off as she read the words.

"What?" I asked, reading the document. "Are those people who stored things at the bank?"

"No," Tia said. "This isn't a list of clients. It's a list of people the bank was paying. That's . . ."

"The name of their insurance company," Cody said, smirking.

"Calamity, Cody," Tia swore. "I hate you."

"I know you do, lass."

Oddly, both of them were smiling as they said it. Tia immediately began shuffling through papers, though she noticed—with a dry look—that Cody had left a smudged bit of mayonnaise from his sandwich on the paper where he'd pointed.

He took me by the shoulder and steered me away from the table.

"What just happened?" I asked.

"Insurance company," Cody said. "The people who First Union Bank paid piles of money to cover the stuff they had in their vault."

"So that insurance company . . ."

"Would have kept a detailed, day-by-day record of just what they were insuring," Cody said with a grin. "Insurance people are a wee bit anal about things like that. Like bankers. Like Tia, actually. If we're lucky, the bank filed an insurance claim following the loss of the building. That would leave an additional paper trail."

"Clever," I said, impressed.

"Oh, I'm just good at finding things that are hovering around under my nose. I have keen eyes. I once caught a leprechaun, you know."

I looked at him skeptically. "Aren't those Irish?"

"Sure. He was over in the homeland on an exchange basis. We sent the Irish three turnips and a sheep's bladder in trade."

"Doesn't seem like much of a trade."

"Oh, I think it was a sparking good one, seeing as to how leprechauns are imaginary and all. Hello, Prof. How's your kilt?"

"As imaginary as your leprechaun, Cody," Prof said, walking into the chamber from one of the side rooms, the one he'd appropriated as his "thinking room," whatever that meant. It was the one with the imager in it, and the other Reckoners stayed away from it. "Can I borrow David?"

"Please, Prof," Cody said, "we're friends. You should know by now that you needn't ask something like that . . . you should be *well* aware of my standard charge for renting one of my minions. Three pounds and a bottle of whiskey."

I wasn't sure if I should be more insulted at being called a minion, or at the low price to rent me.

Prof ignored him, taking me by the arm. "I'm sending Abraham and Megan to Diamond's place today."

"The weapons dealer?" I asked, eager. They'd mentioned that he might have some technology for sale that could help the Reckoners pretend to be an Epic. The "powers" manifested would have to be flashy and destructive, to get Steelheart's attention.

"I want you to tag along," Prof said. "It will be good experience for you. But follow orders—Abraham is in charge—and let me know if anyone you meet seems to recognize you."

"I will."

"Go get your gun, then. They're leaving soon."

15

"**WHAT** about the gun?" Abraham said as we walked. "The bank, the vault contents, those could be a false lead, could they not? What if there was something special about the gun that your father fired at him?"

"That gun was dropped by a random security officer," I said. "Smith and Wesson M&P nine-millimeter, semiauto. There was nothing special about it."

"You remember the *exact gun*?"

I kicked a bit of trash as we walked through the steel-walled underground tunnel. "As I said, I remember that day. Besides, I know guns." I hesitated, then admitted more. "When I was young, I assumed the type of gun must have been special. I saved up, planning to buy one, but nobody would sell to a kid my age. I was planning to sneak into the palace and shoot him."

"Sneak into the palace," Abraham said flatly.

"Uh, yes."

"And shoot *Steelheart*."

"I was ten," I said. "Give me a little credit."

"To a boy with aspirations like that, I would extend my respect—but not credit. Or life insurance." Abraham sounded amused. "You are an interesting man, David Charleston, but you sound like you were an even *more* interesting child."

I smiled. There was something invitingly friendly about this soft-spoken, articulate Canadian, with his light French accent. You almost didn't notice the enormous machine gun—with mounted grenade launcher—resting on his shoulder.

We were still in the steel catacombs, where even such a high level of armament didn't draw particular attention. We passed occasional groups of people huddled around burning fires or heaters plugged into pirated electrical jacks. More than a few of the people we passed carried assault rifles.

Over the last few days I'd ventured out of the hideout a couple times, always in the company of one of the other Reckoners. The baby-sitting bothered me, but I got it. I couldn't exactly hope for them to trust me yet. Not completely. Besides—though I would never admit it out loud—I didn't want to walk the steel catacombs alone.

I'd avoided these depths for years. At the Factory they told stories about the depraved people—terrible monsters—who lived down here. Gangs that literally fed on the foolish who wandered into forgotten hallways, killing them and feasting on their flesh. Murderers, criminals, addicts. Not the normal sort of criminals and addicts we had up above, either. Specially depraved ones.

Perhaps those were exaggerations. The people we passed did seem dangerous—but more in a hostile way, not in an insane way. They watched with grim expressions and eyes that tracked your every movement until you passed out of their view.

These people wanted to be alone. They were the outcasts of the outcasts.

"Why does he let them live down here?" I asked as we passed another group.

Megan didn't respond—she was walking ahead of us, keeping to herself—but Abraham glanced over his shoulder, looking toward the firelight and the line of people who had stepped up to make sure we left.

"There will always be people like them," Abraham said. "Steelheart knows it. Tia, she thinks he made this place for them so he would know where they were. It is useful to know where your outcasts are gathering. Better the ones you know about than the ones you cannot anticipate."

That made me uncomfortable. I'd thought we were completely outside Steelheart's view down here. Perhaps this place wasn't as safe as I'd assumed.

"You cannot keep all men confined all the time," Abraham said, "not without creating a strong prison. So instead you allow some measure of freedom for those who really, really want it. That way, they do not become rebels. If you do it right."

"He did it wrong with us," I said softly.

"Yes. Yes, indeed he did."

I kept glancing back as we walked. I couldn't shake the worry that some of those in the catacombs would attack us. They never did, though. They—

I started as I realized that at that moment, some of them *were* following us. "Abraham!" I said softly. "They're following."

"Yes," he said calmly. "There are some waiting for us ahead too."

In front of us the tunnel narrowed. Sure enough, a group of shadowed figures were standing there, waiting. They wore the mismatched cast-off clothing common to many catacombers, and they carried old rifles and pistols wrapped in leather—the type of guns

131

that probably only worked one day out of two and had been carried by a dozen different people over the last ten years.

The three of us stopped walking, and the group behind caught up, boxing us in. I couldn't see their faces. None carried mobiles, and it was dark without their glow.

"That's some nice equipment, friend," said one of the figures in the group in front of us. Nobody made any overtly hostile moves. They held their weapons with barrels pointed to the sides.

I carefully started to unsling my gun, my heart racing. Abraham, however, laid a hand on my shoulder. He carried his massive machine gun in his other hand, barrel pointed upward, and wore one of the Reckoner jackets, like Megan, though his was grey and white, with a high collar and several pockets, while hers was standard brown leather.

They always wore their jackets when they left the hideout. I'd never seen one work, and I didn't know how much protection they could realistically offer.

"Be still," Abraham said to me.

"But—"

"I will deal with this," he said, his voice perfectly calm as he took a step forward.

Megan stepped up beside me, hand on the holster of her pistol. She didn't look any calmer than I was, both of us trying to watch the people ahead and behind us at once.

"You like our equipment?" Abraham asked politely.

"You should leave the guns," the thug said. "Continue on."

"This would not make any sense," Abraham said. "If I have weapons that you want, the implication is that my firepower is greater than yours. If we were to fight, you would lose. You see? Your intimidation, it does not work."

"There are more of us than you, friend," the guy said softly. "And we're ready to die. Are you?"

I felt a chill at the back of my neck. No, these *weren't* the murderers I'd been led to believe lived down here. They were something more dangerous. Like a pack of wolves.

I could see it in them now, in the way they moved, in the way groups of them had watched us pass. These were outcasts, but outcasts who had banded together to become one. They no longer lived as individuals, but as a group.

And for this group, guns like the ones Abraham and Megan carried would increase their chances of survival. They'd take them, even if it meant losing some of their numbers. It looked to be about a dozen men and women against just three, and we were surrounded. They were terrible odds. I itched to lower my rifle and start shooting.

"You didn't ambush us," Abraham pointed out. "You hope to be able to end this without death."

The thieves didn't reply.

"It is very kind of you to offer us this chance," Abraham said, nodding to them. There was a strange sincerity to Abraham; from another person, words like those might have sounded condescending or sarcastic, but from him they sounded genuine. "You have let us pass several times, through territory you consider to be your own. For this also, I give you my thanks."

"The guns," the thug said.

"I cannot give them to you," Abraham said. "We need them. Beyond this, if we were to give them to you, it would go poorly for you and yours. Others would see them, and would desire them. Other gangs would seek to take them from you as you have sought to take them from us."

"That isn't for you to decide."

"Perhaps not. However, in respect of the honor you have shown us, I will offer you a deal. A duel, between you and me. Only one man need be shot. If we win, you will leave us be, and allow us to pass freely through this area in the future. If you win, my friends will deliver up their weapons, and you may take from my body that which you wish."

"These are the steel catacombs," the man said. Some of his companions were whispering now, and he glared at them with shadowed eyes, then continued. "This is not a place of deals."

"And yet, you already offered us one," Abraham said calmly. "You did us honor. I trust that you will show it to us again."

It didn't seem to be about honor to me. They hadn't ambushed us because they were afraid of us; they wanted the weapons, but they didn't want a fight. They aimed to intimidate us instead.

The lead thug, however, finally nodded. "Fine," he said. "A deal." Then he quickly raised his rifle and fired. The bullet hit Abraham right in the chest.

I jumped, cursing as I scrambled for my gun.

But Abraham didn't fall. He didn't even twitch. Two more shots cracked in the narrow tunnel, bullets hitting him, one in the leg, one in the shoulder. Ignoring his powerful machine gun, he calmly reached to his side and took his handgun out of its holster, then shot the thug in the thigh.

The man cried out, dropping his battered rifle and collapsing, holding his wounded leg. Most of the others seemed too shocked to respond, though a few lowered their weapons nervously. Abraham casually reholstered his pistol.

I felt sweat trickle down my brow. The jacket seemed to be doing its job, and doing it better than I'd assumed. But I didn't have one of those yet. If the other thugs opened fire . . .

Abraham handed his machine gun to Megan, then walked forward and knelt beside the fallen thug. "Place pressure here, please," he said in a friendly tone, positioning the man's hand on his thigh. "There, very good. Now if you don't mind, I'll bandage the wound. I shot you where the bullet could pass through the muscle, so it wouldn't get lodged inside."

The thug groaned at the pain as Abraham took out a bandage and wrapped the leg.

"You cannot kill us, friend," Abraham continued, speaking more softly. "We are not what you thought us to be. Do you understand?"

The thug nodded vigorously.

"It would be wise to be our allies, do you not think?"

"Yes," the thug said.

"Wonderful," Abraham replied, tying the bandage tight. "Change that twice a day. Use boiled bandages."

"Yes."

"Good." Abraham stood and took his gun back and turned to the rest of the thug's group. "Thank you for letting us pass," he said to the others.

They looked confused but parted, creating a path for us. Abraham walked forward and we followed in a hurry. I looked over my shoulder as the rest of the gang gathered around their fallen leader.

"That was *amazing*," I said as we got farther away.

"No. It was a group of frightened people, defending what little they can lay claim to—their reputation. I feel bad for them."

"They shot you. Three times."

"I gave them permission."

"Only after they threatened us!"

"And only after we violated their territory," Abraham said. He handed his machine gun to Megan again, then took off his jacket as he walked. I could see that one of the bullets had penetrated it. Blood was seeping out around a hole in his shirt.

"The jacket didn't stop them all?"

"They aren't perfect," Megan said as Abraham took off the shirt. "Mine fails all the time."

We stopped as Abraham cleaned the wound with a handkerchief, then pulled out a little shard of metal. It was all that was left of the bullet, which had apparently disintegrated upon hitting his jacket. Only one little shard had made it through to his skin.

"What if he'd shot you in the face?" I asked.

"The jackets hide an advanced shielding device," Abraham said. "It isn't the jacket itself that protects, really, but the field the jacket extends. It offers some protection for the entire body, an invisible barrier to resist force."

"What? Really? That's amazing."

"Yes." Abraham hesitated, then pulled his shirt back on. "It probably would not have stopped a bullet to the face, however. So I am fortunate they did not choose to shoot me there."

"As I said," Megan interjected, "they are far from perfect." She seemed annoyed with Abraham. "The shield works better with things like falls and crashes—bullets are so small and hit with so much velocity, the shields overload quickly. Any of those shots could have killed you, Abraham."

"But they did not."

"You still could have been hurt." Megan's voice was stern.

"I *was* hurt."

She rolled her eyes. "You could have been hurt worse."

"Or they could have opened fire," he said, "and killed us all. It was a gamble that worked. Besides, I believe they now think we are Epics."

"*I* almost thought you were one," I admitted.

"Normally we keep this technology hidden," Abraham said, putting on his jacket again. "People cannot wonder whether the Reckoners are Epics; it would undermine what we stand for. However, in this case, I believe it will go well for us. Your plan calls for there to be rumors of new Epics in the city, working against Steelheart. These men will hopefully spread that rumor."

"I guess," I said. "It was a good move, Abraham, but *sparks*. For a moment, I thought we were dead."

"People rarely want to kill, David," Abraham said calmly. "It's not basic to the makeup of the healthy human mind. In most situations they will go to great lengths to avoid killing. Remember that, and it will help you."

"I've seen a lot of people kill," I replied.

"Yes, and that will tell you something. Either they felt they had no choice—in which case, if you could give them another choice, they would likely have taken it—or they were not of healthy mind."

"And Epics?"

Abraham reached to his neck and fingered the small silver necklace he wore there. "Epics are not human."

I nodded. With that, I agreed.

"I believe our conversation was interrupted," Abraham said, taking his gun from Megan and casually resting it on his shoulder as we walked onward. "How did Steelheart get wounded? It *could* have been the weapon your father used. You never tried your brave plan of finding an identical gun, then doing . . . what was it you said? Sneaking into Steelheart's palace and shooting him?"

"No, I didn't get to try it," I said, blushing. "I came to my senses. I don't think it was the gun, though. M&P nine-millimeters aren't exactly uncommon. Someone's *got* to have tried shooting him with one. Besides, I've never heard of an Epic whose weakness was being shot by a specific caliber of bullet or make of gun."

"Perhaps," Abraham said, "but many Epic weaknesses do not make sense. It could have something to do with that specific gun manufacturer. Or instead, it could have something to do with the composition of the bullet. Many Epics are weak to specific alloys."

"True," I admitted. "But what would be different about that particular bullet that wasn't the same for all of the others fired at him?"

"I don't know," Abraham said. "But it is worth considering. What do *you* think caused his weakness?"

"Something in the vault, like Tia thinks," I said with only some measure of confidence. "Either that or something about the situation. Maybe my father's specific age let him get through—weird, I know, but there was an Epic in Germany who could only be hurt by someone who was thirty-seven exactly. Or maybe it was the number of people firing on him. Crossmark, an Epic down in Mexico, can only be hurt if five people are trying to kill her at once."

"It doesn't matter," Megan interrupted, turning around in the hallway and stopping in the tunnel to look at us. "You're never going to figure it out. His weakness could be virtually *anything*. Even with David's little story—assuming he didn't just make it up—there's no way of knowing."

Abraham and I stopped in place. Megan's face was red, and she seemed barely in control. After a week of her acting cold and professional, her anger was a big shock.

She spun around and kept walking. I glanced at Abraham, and he shrugged.

We continued on, but our conversation died. Megan quickened her pace when Abraham tried to catch up to her, and so we just left her to it. Both she and Abraham had been given directions to the weapons merchant, so she could guide us just as well as he could. Apparently this "Diamond" fellow was only going to be in town for a short time, and when he came he always set up shop in a different location.

We walked for a good hour through the twisting maze of catacombs before Megan stopped us at an intersection, her mobile illuminating her face as she checked the map Tia had uploaded to it.

Abraham took his mobile off the shoulder of his jacket and did the same. "Almost there," he told me, pointing. "This way. At the end of this tunnel."

"How well do we trust this guy?" I asked.

"Not at all," Megan said. Her face had returned to its normal impassive mask.

Abraham nodded. "Best to never trust a weapons merchant, my friend. They all sell to both sides, and they are the only ones who win if a conflict continues indefinitely."

"Both sides?" I asked. "He sells to Steelheart too?"

"He won't admit it if you ask," Abraham said, "but it is certain that he does. Even Steelheart knows not to harm a good weapons dealer. Kill or torture a man like Diamond, and future merchants won't come here. Steelheart's army will never have good technology compared to the neighbors. That's not saying that Steelheart likes it—Diamond, he could never open his shop up in the overstreets. Down here, however, Steelheart will turn a blind eye, so long as his soldiers continue to get their equipment."

"So . . . whatever we buy from him," I said, "Steelheart will know about it."

"No, no," Abraham said. He seemed amused, as if I were asking questions about something incredibly simple, like the rules to hide-and-seek.

"Weapons merchants don't talk about other clients," Megan said. "As long as those clients live, at least."

"Diamond arrived back in the city just yesterday," Abraham said, leading the way down the tunnel. "He will be open for one week's time. If we are first to get to him, we can see what he has before Steelheart's people do. We can get an advantage this way, eh? Diamond, he often has very . . . interesting wares."

All right, then, I thought. I guess it didn't matter that Diamond was slime. I'd use any tool I could to get to Steelheart. Moral considerations had stopped bothering me years ago. Who had time for morals in a world like this?

We reached the corridor leading to Diamond's shop. I expected guards, perhaps in full powered armor. The only person there, though, was a young girl in a yellow dress. She was lying on a blanket on the floor and drawing pictures on a piece of paper with a silver pen. She looked up at us and began chewing on the end of the pen.

Abraham politely handed the girl a small data chip, which she took and examined for a moment before tapping it on the side of her mobile.

"We are with Phaedrus," Abraham said. "We have an appointment."

"Go on," the girl answered, tossing the chip back to him.

Abraham snatched it from the air, and we continued down the corridor. I glanced over my shoulder at the girl. "That's not very strong security."

"It's always something new with Diamond," Abraham said, smiling. "There is probably something elaborate behind the scenes—some kind of trap the girl can spring. It probably has to do with explosives. Diamond likes explosives."

We turned a corner and stepped into heaven.

"Here we are," Abraham announced.

16

DIAMOND'S shop wasn't set up in a room, but instead in one of the long corridors of the catacombs. I assumed that the other end of the corridor was either a dead end or had guards. The space was lit from above by portable lights that were almost blinding after the general darkness of the catacombs.

Those lights shone on guns—hundreds of them hung on the walls of the hallway. Beautiful polished steel and deep, muted blacks. Assault rifles. Handguns. Massive, electron-compressed beasts like the one Abraham carried, with full gravatonics. Old-style revolvers, grenades in stacks, *rocket launchers*.

I'd only ever owned two guns—my pistol and my rifle. The rifle was a good friend. I'd had her for three years now, and I'd come to rely on her a lot. She worked when I needed her. We had a great relationship—I cared for her, and she cared for me.

At the sight of Diamond's shop, though, I felt like a boy who'd only ever owned a single toy car and had just been offered a showroom full of Ferraris.

Abraham sauntered into the hallway. He didn't give the weapons much of a look. Megan entered and I followed on her heels, staring at the walls and their wares.

"Wow," I said. "It's like . . . a banana farm for guns."

"A banana farm," Megan said flatly.

"Sure. You know, how bananas grow from their trees and hang down and stuff?"

"Knees, you *suck* at metaphors."

I blushed. *An art gallery,* I thought. *I should have said "like an art gallery for guns." No, wait. If I said it that way, it would mean the gallery was intended for guns to come visit. A gallery of guns, then?*

"How do you even know what bananas are?" Megan said quietly as Abraham greeted a portly man standing beside a blank portion of wall. This could only be Diamond. "Steelheart doesn't import from Latin America."

"My encyclopedias," I said, distracted. *A gallery of guns for the criminally destructive. I should have said that. That sounds impressive, doesn't it?* "Read them a few times. Some of it stuck."

"Encyclopedias."

"Yeah."

"Which you read 'a few times.' "

I stopped, realizing what I'd said. "Er. No. I mean, I just browsed them. You know, looking for pictures of guns. I—"

"You are such a nerd," she said, walking ahead to join Abraham. She sounded amused.

I sighed, then joined them and tried to get her attention to show off my new metaphor, but Abraham was introducing us.

". . . new kid," he said, gesturing to me. "David."

Diamond nodded to me. He had on a brightly colored floral-pattern shirt, like people supposedly once wore in the tropics.

Maybe that was where I'd gotten the whole banana metaphor. He had a white beard and long white hair, though he was balding at the front, and wore a huge smile that sparkled in his eyes.

"I assume," he said to Abraham, "you want to see what's new. What's exciting. You know, my—*ahem*—other clients haven't even been through here yet! You're the first. First picks!"

"And highest prices," Abraham said, turning to look at the wall of guns. "Death comes at such a premium these days."

"Says the man carrying an electron-compressed Manchester 451," Diamond said. "With gravatonics and a full grenade dock. Nice explosions on those. Little on the small side, but you can bounce them in really fun ways."

"Show us what you have," Abraham said politely, though his voice seemed strained. I could swear he had sounded more calm talking to the thugs who had shot him. Curious.

"I'm getting some things ready to show you," Diamond said. He had a smile like a parrot fish, which I've always assumed look like parrots, though I've never actually seen either. "Why don't you just have a look around? Browse a bit. Tell me what suits your fancy."

"Very well," Abraham said. "Thank you." He nodded to us—we knew what we were supposed to do. Look for anything out of the ordinary. A weapon that could cause a lot of destruction—destruction that could seem like the work of an Epic. If we were going to imitate one, we'd need something impressive.

Megan stepped up beside me, studying a machine gun that fired incendiary rounds.

"I'm *not* a nerd," I hissed at her softly.

"Why does it matter?" she asked, her tone neutral. "There's nothing wrong with being smart. In fact, if you *are* intelligent, you'll be a stronger asset to the team."

"I just . . . I . . . I just don't like being called that. Besides, who ever heard of a nerd jumping from a moving jet and shooting an Epic in midair while plummeting toward the ground?"

143

"I've never heard of *anyone* doing that."

"Phaedrus did it," I said. "Execution of Redleaf, three years ago up in Canada."

"That story was exaggerated," Abraham said softly, walking by. "It was a helicopter. And it was all part of the plan—we were very careful. Now please, keep focused on our current task."

I shut my mouth and began studying the weapons. Incendiary rounds were impressive, but not particularly original. That wasn't flashy enough for us. In fact, any type of basic gun wouldn't work—whether it shot bullets, rockets, or grenades, it wouldn't be convincing. We needed something more like the energy weapons Enforcement had. A way to mimic an Epic's innate firepower.

I moved down the hallway, and the weapons seemed to grow more unusual the farther I walked. I stopped beside a curious group of objects. They appeared to be innocent enough—a water bottle, a mobile phone, a pen. They were attached to the wall like the weapons.

"Ah . . . you are a discerning man, are you, David?"

I jumped, turning to see Diamond grinning behind me. How could a fat man move so quietly?

"What are they?" I asked.

"Advanced stealth explosives," Diamond answered proudly. He reached up and tapped a section of the wall, and an image appeared on it. He had an imager hooked up here, apparently. It showed a water bottle sitting on a table. A businessman strolled past, looking at some papers in his hand. He set them on the table, then twisted the cap off the water.

And exploded.

I jumped back.

"Ah," Diamond said. "I hope you appreciate the value of this footage—it's rare that I get good shots of a stealth explosive being deployed in the field. This one is quite remarkable. Notice how the explosion flung the body back but didn't damage too much nearby?

That's important in a stealth explosive, particularly if the person to be assassinated might have valuable documents on them."

"That's disgusting," I said, turning away.

"We are in the business of death, young man."

"The video, I mean."

"He wasn't a very nice person, if it helps." I doubted that mattered to Diamond. He seemed affable as he tapped the wall. "Good explosion. I'll be honest—I half keep these to sell just because I like showing off that video. It's one of a kind."

"Do they all explode?" I asked, examining the innocent-looking devices.

"The pen is a detonator," Diamond said. "Click the back and you set off one of those little eraser devices next to it. They're universal blasting caps. Stick them close to something explosive, trigger them, and they can usually set it off. Depends on the substance, but they're programmed with some pretty advanced detection algorithms. They work on most explosive substances. Stick one of those to some guy's grenade, walk away, then click the pen."

"If you could clip one of those to his grenade," Megan said, approaching, "you could have just pulled the pin. Or better yet, shot him."

"It's not for every situation," Diamond said defensively. "But they can be *very* fun. What's better than detonating your enemy's own explosives when he's not expecting it?"

"Diamond," Abraham called from down the corridor. "Come tell me about this."

"Ah! Excellent choice. *Wonderful* explosions from that one . . ." He scuttled off.

I looked at the panel full of innocent yet deadly objects. Something about them felt very wrong to me. I'd killed men before, but I'd done it honestly. With a gun in my hands, and only because I'd been forced to. I didn't have many philosophies about life, but one of them was something my father had taught me: never throw the first punch. If you have to throw the second, try to make sure they don't get up for a third.

"These *could* be useful," Megan said, arms still crossed. "Though I doubt that blowhard really understands what for."

"I know," I said, trying to redeem myself. "I mean, recording some poor guy's death like that? It was totally unprofessional."

"Actually, he sells explosives," she said, "so having a recording like that *is* professional of him. I suspect he has recordings of each of these weapons being fired, as we can't test them hands-on down here."

"Megan, that was a recording of some guy *blowing up*." I shook my head, revolted. "It was awful. You shouldn't show off stuff like that."

She hesitated, looking troubled about something. "Yes. Of course." She looked at me. "You never did explain why you were so bothered by being called a nerd."

"I told you. I don't like it because, you know, I want to do awesome stuff. And nerds don't——"

"That's not it," she said, staring at me coolly. *Sparks,* but her eyes were beautiful. "There's something deeper about it that bothers you, and you need to get over it. It's a weakness." She glanced at the water bottle, then turned and walked over to the thing Abraham was inspecting. It was some kind of bazooka.

I secured my rifle over my shoulder and stuck my hands in my pockets. It seemed that I was spending a lot of time lately getting lectured. I'd thought that leaving the Factory would end all of that, but I guess I should have known better.

I turned from Megan and Abraham and looked across at the wall nearest me. I was having trouble focusing on the guns, which was a first for me. My mind was working over what she'd asked. Why did being called a nerd bother me?

I walked over to her side.

". . . don't know if it's what we want," Abraham was saying.

"But the explosions are *so big*," Diamond replied.

"It's because they took the smart ones away," I said softly to Megan.

I could feel her eyes on me, but I continued staring at the wall.

"A lot of kids at the Factory tried so hard to prove how smart they were," I said quietly. "We had school, you know. You went to school half the day, worked the other half, unless you got expelled. If you did poorly the teacher just expelled you, and after that you worked full days. School was easier than the Factory, so most of the kids tried really hard.

"The smart ones, though . . . the really smart ones . . . the nerds . . . they left. Got taken to the city above. If you showed some skill with computers, or math, or writing, off you went. They got good jobs, I hear. In Steelheart's propaganda corps or his accounting offices or something like that. When I was young I'd have laughed about Steelheart having accountants. He's got a lot of them, you know. You need people like them in an empire."

Megan looked at me, curious. "So you . . ."

"Learned to be dumb," I said. "Rather, to be mediocre. The dumb ones got kicked out of school, and I wanted to learn—knew I *needed* to learn—so I had to stay. I also knew that if I went up above, I'd lose my freedom. He keeps a lot better watch over his accountants than he does his factory workers.

"There were other boys like me. A lot of the girls moved on fast, the smart ones. Some of the boys I knew, though, they started to see it as a mark of pride that they weren't taken above. You didn't want to be one of the smart ones. I had to be extra careful, since I asked so many questions about the Epics. I had to hide my notebooks, find ways to throw off those who thought I was smart."

"But you're not there anymore. You're with the Reckoners. So it doesn't matter."

"It does," I said. "Because it's not who I am. I'm not smart, I'm just persistent. My friends who were smart, they didn't have to study at all. I had to study like a horse for every test I took."

"Like a horse?"

"You know. Because horses work hard? Pulling carts and plows and things?"

"Yeah, I'll just ignore that one."

"I'm *not* smart," I said.

I didn't mention that part of the reason I had to study so hard was because I needed to know the answer to each and every question perfectly. Only then could I ensure that I would get the *exact* number of questions wrong to remain in the middle of the pack. Smart enough to stay in school, but not worthy of notice or attention.

"Besides," I continued. "The people I knew who were really smart, they learned because they loved it. I didn't. I hated studying."

"You read the encyclopedia. *A few times.*"

"Looking for things that could be Epic weaknesses," I said. "I needed to know different types of metal, chemical compounds, elements, and symbols. Practically anything could be a weakness. I hoped something would spark in my head. Something about him."

"So it's all about him."

"Everything in my life is about him, Megan," I said, looking at her. "Everything."

We fell silent, though Diamond continued blabbing on. Abraham had turned to look at me. He seemed thoughtful.

Great, I realized. *He heard. Just great.*

"That will be enough, please, Diamond," Abraham said. "That weapon really won't work."

The weapons merchant sighed. "Very well. But perhaps you can give me a clue as to what *might* work."

"Something distinctive," Abraham said. "Something nobody has seen before, but also something destructive."

"Well, I don't have much that *isn't* destructive," Diamond said. "But distinctive . . . Let me see. . . ."

Abraham waved for us to keep searching. As Megan moved off, however, he took me by the arm. He had quite a strong grip. "Steelheart takes the smart ones," Abraham said softly, "because he fears them. He knows, David. All of these guns, they do not frighten him. They won't be what overthrows him. It will be the person clever enough, *smart* enough, to figure out the chink in his armor. He knows he can't kill them all, so he employs them. When he dies it will be because of someone like you. Remember that."

He released my arm and walked after Diamond.

I watched him go, then walked over to another group of weapons. His words didn't really change anything, but oddly, I did feel myself standing a little taller as I looked at a line of guns and was able to identify each of the manufacturers.

I'm totally not a nerd though. I still know the truth at least.

I looked over the guns for a few minutes, proud of how many I could identify. Unfortunately none of them seemed distinctive enough. Actually, the fact that I could identify them guaranteed that they weren't distinctive enough. We needed something nobody had seen before.

Maybe he won't have anything, I thought. *If he has a rotating stock, then we may have picked the wrong time to visit. Sometimes a grab bag doesn't give anything worthwhile. It—*

I stopped as I noticed something different. Motorcycles.

There were three of them in a row near the far side of the hallway. I hadn't seen them at first, as I'd been focused on the guns. They were sleek, their bodies a deep green with black patterns running up their sides. They made me want to hunch over and crouch down to make myself have less wind resistance. I could imagine shooting through the streets on one of these. They looked so dangerous, like alligators. Really fast alligators wearing black. Ninja alligators.

I decided not to use that one on Megan.

They didn't have any weapons on them that I could see, though there were some odd devices on the sides. Maybe energy weapons? They didn't seem to fit with much of what Diamond had here, but then again, what he had was pretty eclectic.

Megan walked past me and I raised a finger to point at the motorcycles.

"No," she said, not even looking.

"But—"

"No."

"But they're awesome!" I said, holding up my hands, as if that should have been enough of an argument. And, sparks, it should have been. They were *awesome*!

"You could barely drive some lady's sedan, Knees," Megan said. "I don't want to see you on the back of something with gravatonics."

"Gravatonics!" That was even *more* awesome.

"No," Megan said firmly.

I looked toward Abraham, who was inspecting something nearby. He glanced at me, then over at the bikes, and smiled. "No."

I sighed. Wasn't shopping for weapons supposed to be more fun than this?

"Diamond," Abraham called to the dealer. "What is this?"

The weapons merchant began waddling over. "Oh, it's wonderful. Great explosions. It . . ." His face fell as he neared and saw what Abraham was actually looking at. "Oh. That. Um, it is *quite* wonderful, though I don't know if it would suit your needs. . . ."

The item in question was a large rifle with a very long barrel and a scope on top. It looked a little bit like an AWM—one of the sniper rifles the Factory had used as a model in building their products. The barrel was larger, however, and there were some odd coils around the forestock. It was painted a dark black-green and had a big hole where the magazine should have fit.

Diamond sighed. "This weapon is wonderful, but you are a good customer. I should warn you that I don't have the resources to make it work."

"What?" Megan asked. "You're selling a broken gun?"

"It's not that," Diamond said, tapping the section of wall beside the gun. An image displayed of a man set up on the ground, holding the rifle and looking through the scope at some run-down buildings. "This is called a gauss gun, developed using research on some Epic or another who throws bullets at people."

"Rick O'Shea," I said, nodding. "An Irish Epic."

"That's really his name?" Abraham asked softly.

"Yeah."

"That's horrible." He shivered. "Taking a beautiful French word and turning it into . . . into something Cody would say. *Câlice!*"

"Anyway," I said. "He can make objects unstable by touching them; then they explode when subjected to any significant impact. Basically he charges rocks with energy, throws them at people, and they explode. Standard kinetic energy Epic."

I was more interested in the idea that the technology had been developed based on his powers. Ricky was a newer Epic. He wouldn't have been around back in the old days when, as the Reckoners had explained, Epics had been imprisoned and experimented on. Did this mean that kind of research was still going on? There was a place where Epics were being held captive? I'd never heard of such a thing.

"The gun?" Abraham asked Diamond.

"Well, like I said." Diamond tapped the wall and the video started playing. "It's a type of gauss gun, only it uses a projectile that has been charged with energy first. The bullet, once turned explosive, is propelled to extreme speeds using tiny magnets."

The man holding the gun in the video flipped a switch and the coils lit up green. He pulled the trigger and there was a *burst* of energy, though the thing seemed to have almost no recoil. A splash of green light spat from the front of the gun's barrel, leaving a line in the air. One of the distant buildings exploded, giving off a strange shower of green that seemed to warp the air.

"We're . . . not sure why it does that," Diamond admitted. "Or even how. The technology changes the bullet into a charged explosive."

I felt a shiver, thinking about the tensors, the jackets—the technology used by the Reckoners. Actually, a lot of the technology we now used had come with the advent of the Epics. How much of it did we really understand?

We were relying on half-understood technology built from studying mystifying creatures who didn't even know how they did what they did themselves. We were like deaf people trying to dance to a beat we couldn't hear, long after the music actually stopped. Or . . . wait. I don't know what that actually was supposed to mean.

Anyway, the lights given off by that gun's explosion were very distinctive. Beautiful, even. There didn't seem to be much debris, just some green smoke that still floated in the air. Almost as if the building had been transformed directly to energy.

Then it hit me. "Aurora borealis," I said, pointing. "It looks like the pictures I've seen of it."

"Destructive capability looks good," Megan said. "That building was almost completely knocked down by one shot."

Abraham nodded. "It might be what we need. However, Diamond, might I inquire about what you mentioned earlier? You said it didn't work."

"It works just fine," the merchant said quickly. "But it requires an energy pack to fire. A powerful one."

"How powerful?"

"Fifty-six KC," Diamond said, then hesitated. "Per shot."

Abraham whistled.

"Is that a lot?" Megan asked.

"Yeah," I said, in awe. "Like, several thousand standard fuel cells' worth."

"Usually," Diamond said, "you need to hook it up by cord to its own power unit. You can't just plug this bad boy into a wall socket. The shots on this demo were fired using several six-inch cords running back to a dedicated generator." He looked up at the weapon. "I bought it hoping I could trade *a certain client* for some of his high-energy fuel cells, then be able to actually sell the weapon in working condition."

"Who knows about this weapon?" Abraham asked.

"Nobody," Diamond said. "I bought it directly from the lab that created it, and the man who made this video was in my employ. It's never been on the market. In fact, the researchers who developed it died a few months later— blew themselves up, poor fools. I guess that's what you get when you routinely build devices that super-charge matter."

"We'll take it," Abraham said.

"You will?" Diamond looked surprised, and then a smile crossed his face. "Well . . . what an excellent choice! I'm certain you'll be happy. But again, to clarify, this will *not* fire unless you find your own energy source. A very powerful one, likely one you won't be able to transport. Do you understand?"

"We will find one," Abraham said. "How much?"

"Twelve," Diamond said without missing a beat.

"You can't sell it to anyone else," Abraham said, "and you can't make it work. You'll be getting four. Thank you." Abraham got out a small box. He tapped it, and handed it over.

"And we want one of those pen exploder things thrown in," I said on a whim as I held my mobile up to the wall and downloaded the video of the gauss gun in action. I almost asked for one of the motorcycles, but figured that would *really* be pushing things.

"Very well," Diamond said, holding up the box Abraham had given him. What *was* that, anyway? "Is Fortuity in here?" he asked.

"Alas," Abraham said, "our encounter with him did not leave time for proper harvesting. But four others, including Absence."

Harvesting? What did *that* mean? Absence was an Epic the Reckoners had killed last year.

Diamond grunted. I found myself *very* curious as to what was in that box.

"Also, here." Abraham handed over a data chip.

Diamond smiled, taking it. "You know how to sweeten a deal, Abraham. Yes you do."

"Nobody finds out that we have this," Abraham said, nodding toward the gun. "Do not even tell another person that it exists."

"Of course not," Diamond said, sounding offended. He walked over to pull a standard rifle bag out from under his desk, then began to get the gauss gun down.

"What did we pay him with?" I asked Megan, speaking very softly.

"When Epics die, something happens to their bodies," she replied.

"Mitochondrial mutation." I nodded. "Yeah."

"Well, when we kill an Epic, we harvest some of their mitochondria," she said. "It's needed by the scientists who build all this kind of stuff. Diamond can trade it to secret research labs."

I whistled softly. "Wow."

"Yeah," she said, looking troubled. "The cells expire after just a few minutes if you don't freeze them, so that makes it hard to harvest. There are some groups out there who make a living harvesting cells—they don't kill the Epics, they just sneak a blood sample and freeze it. This sort of thing has become a secret, high-level currency."

So *that* was how it was happening. The Epics didn't even need to know about it. It worried me more deeply, however, to learn about this. How much of the process did we understand? What would the Epics think of their genetic material being sold at market?

I'd never heard of any of this, despite my research into Epics. It served as a reminder. I might have figured a few things out, but there was an entire world out there beyond my experience.

"What about the data chip Abraham gave him?" I asked. "The thing Diamond called a deal sweetener?"

"That has explosions on it," she said.

"Ah. Of course."

"Why do you want that detonator?"

"I don't know," I said. "It just sounded fun. And since it looks like a while till I'll get one of those bikes—"

"You'll *never* get one of those bikes."

"—I thought I'd ask for something."

She didn't reply, though it seemed as if I'd unintentionally annoyed her. Again. I was having a tough time deciding what was bothering her—she seemed to have her own special rules for what constituted being "professional" and what didn't.

Diamond packed up the gun and, to my delight, tossed in the pen detonator and a small pack of the "erasers" that worked with it. I was feeling pretty good about getting something extra. Then I smelled garlic.

I frowned. It wasn't *quite* garlic, but it was close. What was . . . Garlic.

Phosphorus smelled like garlic.

"We're in trouble," I said immediately. "Nightwielder is here."

17

"THAT'S impossible!" Diamond said, checking his mobile. "They're not supposed to be here for another hour or two." He paused, then held his ear—he wore a small earpiece—his mobile twinkling in his hand.

He grew pale, likely getting news of an early arrival from the girl outside. "Oh dear."

"Sparks," Megan said, slinging the gauss gun's bag over her shoulder.

"You had an appointment with Steelheart *today*?" Abraham said.

"It won't be him," Diamond said. "Assuming he were a client of mine, he would never come himself."

"He just sends Nightwielder," I said, sniffing the air. "Yeah, he's here. Can you smell that?"

"Why didn't you warn us?" Megan said to Diamond.

"I don't speak of other clients to—"

"Never mind," Abraham said. "We leave." He pointed down the hallway, opposite the way we'd come in. "Where does it lead?"

"Dead end," Diamond said.

"You left yourself without a way out?" I asked, incredulous.

"Nobody would attack me!" Diamond said. "Not with the hardware I've got in here. Calamity! This is *not* supposed to happen. My clients know not to arrive early."

"Stop him outside," Abraham said.

"Stop Nightwielder?" Diamond asked, incredulous. "He's incorporeal. He can walk through walls for Calamity's sake."

"Then keep him from walking all the way down the hallway," Abraham said calmly. "There are some shadows back there. We'll hide."

"I don't—" Diamond started.

"There isn't time to argue, my friend," Abraham said. "Everyone pretends to not care that you sell to all sides, but I doubt Nightwielder will treat you well if he discovers us here. He'll recognize me; he's seen me before. If he finds me here, we all die. Do you understand?"

Diamond, still pale, nodded again.

"Come on," Abraham said, shouldering his gun and jogging down the hallway past the rear of the store. Megan and I joined him. My heart was thumping. Nightwielder would recognize Abraham? What history did they have together?

There were piles of crates and boxes at the other end of the hallway. It was indeed a dead end, but there were no lights. Abraham waved for us to take cover behind the boxes. We could still see the walls full of weapons back where we'd been. Diamond stood there, wringing his hands.

"Here," Abraham said, setting his large gun down on a box and aiming it directly at Diamond. "Man this, David. Don't fire unless you *must*."

"Won't work against Nightwielder anyway," I said. "He has

157

prime invincibility—bullets, energy weapons, explosions all pass through him." Unless we could get him into the sunlight, assuming I was right. I put up a good front for the others, but the truth was, all I had was hearsay.

Abraham dug in the pocket of his cargo pants and pulled something out. One of the tensors.

I immediately felt a surge of relief. He was going to cut us a path to freedom. "So we're not going to wait it out?"

"Of course not," he said calmly. "I feel like a rat in a trap. Megan, contact Tia. We need to know the tunnel nearest to this one. I'll dig us a route to it."

Megan nodded, kneeling down and cupping her mouth as she whispered into her mobile. Abraham warmed up the tensor, and I folded out the scope on his machine gun, flipping the switch to burst mode. He nodded appreciatively at the move.

I sighted through the scope. It was a nice one, far nicer than my own, with distance readouts, wind speed monitors, and optional low-light compensators. I had a pretty good view of Diamond as he welcomed his new customers with hands open and a wide smile on his face.

I grew tense. There were eight of them—two men and a woman in suits alongside four Enforcement soldiers. And Nightwielder. He was a tall Asian man who was only half there. Faint, incorporeal. He wore a fine suit, but the long jacket had an Eastern flair to it. His hair was short, and he walked with hands clasped behind his back.

My finger twitched toward the trigger. This creature was Steelheart's right-hand Epic, the source of the darkness that cut Newcago off from the sun and stars. Similar darkness stirred on the ground around him, sliding toward shadows and pooling there. He could kill with that, could make tendrils of that dark mist turn solid and spear a man.

Those—the incorporeity and the manipulation of that mist— were his only two known powers, but they were doozies. He could move through solid matter, and like all incorporeals, he could fly at a steady speed. He could make a room completely black, then spear you with that darkness. And he could hold an entire city in perpetual night. Many assumed that he dedicated most of his energies to this.

That had always worried me. If he weren't so busy keeping the city in darkness, he might have been as powerful as Steelheart himself. Either way, he'd be more than enough to handle the three of us, unprepared as we were.

He and two of his minions were in conversation with Diamond. I wished I could hear what they were saying. I hesitated, then pulled back from the scope. A lot of advanced guns had . . .

Yes. I flipped the switch on the side, activating the scope's directional sound amplifier. I pulled the earphone out of my mobile and waved it past the chip on the scope to pair it, then stuck it in my ear. I leaned in and aimed the scope right at the group. The receiver picked up what was being said.

". . . is interested in specific kinds of weapons, this time," one of Nightwielder's minions was saying. She wore a pantsuit and had her black hair cut short up over her ears. "Our emperor is worried that our forces rely too much on the armor units for heavy support. What do you have for more mobile troops?"

"Er, plenty," Diamond said.

Sparks, but he looks nervous. He didn't glance at us, but he fidgeted and looked as if he might be sweating. For a man who dealt in the underground weapons trade, he certainly seemed bad at handling stress.

Diamond glanced from the woman toward Nightwielder, whose hands were clasped behind his back. According to my notes, he rarely spoke directly during business interactions. He preferred to use minions. It was some kind of Japanese culture thing.

The conversation continued, and Nightwielder continued to stand straight-backed and silent. They didn't go look at the guns on the walls, even when Diamond hinted that they could. They made him bring the weapons to them, and one of the assistants always handled the inspection and the questions.

That's pretty handy, I thought, a bead of nervous sweat dripping down my temple. *He can focus on Diamond—study and think, without bothering to make conversation.*

"Got it," Megan whispered. I glanced back to see her twisting her mobile around, her hand shading its light, to show Abraham the map Tia had sent. Abraham had to lean in close to make anything out; she had the mobile's screen dimmed almost to black.

He grunted softly. "Seven feet straight back, a few degrees down. That's going to take a few minutes."

"You should get at it, then," Megan said.

"I'll need your help to pile out the dust."

Megan shuffled to the side and Abraham placed his hands against the back wall, near the ground, and engaged the tensor. A large disk of steel began to disintegrate beneath his touch, creating a tunnel we could crawl through. Megan began scooping up and moving the steel dust as Abraham concentrated.

I turned back to watching, trying to breathe as quietly as possible. The tensors didn't make much noise, just a soft buzzing. Hopefully nobody would notice.

". . . master thinks that this weapon is of poor quality," the servant said, handing back a machine gun. "We are growing disappointed in your selection, merchant."

"Well, you want heavy gear, but no launchers. That's a difficult prospect to match. I—"

"What was in this place on the wall?" a soft, eerie voice asked. It sounded something like a loud whisper, faintly accented, yet piercing. It made me shiver.

Diamond stiffened. I shifted the view on the scope slightly. Nightwielder stood beside the wall of weapons. He was pointing toward an open space where hooks jutted from the wall—where the gauss gun had been.

"There was something here, was there not?" Nightwielder asked. He almost never spoke to someone directly like this. It didn't seem to be a good sign. "You only opened today. You have already had business?"

"I . . . don't discuss other clients," Diamond said. "You know this."

Nightwielder looked back at the wall. At that moment, Megan bumped a box as she was moving steel dust. It didn't make a loud noise—in fact, she didn't even seem to notice she'd done it. But Nightwielder swiveled his head in our direction. Diamond followed his gaze; the weapons merchant looked so nervous you could have turned milk into butter by sticking his hand in it.

"He's noticed us," I said softly.

"What?" Abraham said, still concentrating.

"Just . . . keep at it," I said, standing. "And stay quiet."

It was time for a little more improvising.

18

I shouldered Abraham's gun, ignoring Megan's soft curse. I trotted out from behind the boxes before she could restrain me, and at the last moment I remembered to pop the earpiece out of my ear and stow it.

As I left the shadows, Nightwielder's soldiers trained guns on me with quick motions. I felt a spike of anxiety, the prickling sensation of defenselessness. I hate it when people point guns at me . . . though I guess that makes me like pretty much everyone else.

I continued on. "Boss," I called, patting the weapon. "I got it working. Magazine comes out easily now."

Nightwielder's soldiers glanced toward him, as if looking for permission to shoot. The Epic clasped his hands behind his back, studying me with ethereal eyes. He didn't seem to notice, but his elbow brushed the wall and passed right through the solid steel.

He studied me but remained motionless. The goons didn't shoot. Good sign.

Come on, Diamond, I thought, trying to contain my nervousness. *Don't be an idiot. Say someth—*

"Was it the release pin?" Diamond asked.

"No, sir," I said. "The magazine was bent slightly on one side." I gave a respectful nod to Nightwielder and his flunkies, then moved over to set the gun in the spot on the wall. It fit, fortunately. I'd guessed it would, considering it was close to the same size as the gauss gun.

"Well, Diamond," Nightwielder's female attendant said. "Perhaps you can tell us of this new addition. It looks like it—"

"No," Nightwielder said softly. "I will hear it from the boy."

I froze, then turned around, nervous. "Sir?"

"Tell me about this gun," Nightwielder said.

"The boy's a new hire," Diamond said. "He doesn't—"

"It's all right, boss," I said. "That's a Manchester 451. The weapon is a powerhouse—fifty caliber, with electron-compressed magazines. Each holds eight hundred rounds. The select-fire system supports single shot, burst, and full auto capabilities. It has gravatonic recoil reduction for shoulder firing, with optional advanced magnitude scope including audio receiving, range finding, and a remote firing mechanism. It also includes the optional grenade launcher. Equipped rounds are armor-piercing incendiary, sir. You couldn't ask for a better gun."

Nightwielder nodded. "And this?" he said, pointing to the gun next to it.

My palms were sweating. I shoved them in my pockets. That was . . . it was a . . . Yes, I knew. "Browning M3919, sir. An inferior gun, but very good for the price. Also fifty caliber, but without the recoil suppression, the gravatonics, or the electron compression. It is excellent as a mounted weapon—with the advanced heat sinks on the barrel, it can fire around eight hundred rounds a minute. Over a mile effective range with remarkable accuracy."

The corridor fell still. Nightwielder regarded the gun, then turned to his minions and made a curt gesture. That nearly made me jump with alarm, but the others seemed to relax. I'd passed Nightwielder's test, apparently.

"We will want to see the Manchester," the woman said. "This is exactly what we are looking for; you should have mentioned it earlier."

"I . . . was embarrassed about the magazine sticking," Diamond said. "It's a known problem with Manchesters, I'm afraid. Every gun has its quirks. I've heard that if you file down one of the top edges of the magazine, it slides much more easily. Here, let me get that back down for you. . . ."

The conversation continued, but I was forgotten. I was able to step back to where I wouldn't be in the way. *Should I try to slip away?* I wondered. It would seem suspicious if I went to the back of the hallway again, wouldn't it? Sparks. It looked like they were going to buy Abraham's gun. I hoped he'd forgive me for that.

If Abraham and Megan got out through the hole, I could just wait here until Nightwielder left, then meet up with them. Staying put seemed like the best move for the moment.

I found myself staring at Nightwielder's back as his minions continued negotiations. I was . . . what, three steps away from him? One of Steelheart's three most trusted, one of the most powerful living Epics. He was right there. And I couldn't touch him. Well, I couldn't touch him literally, since he was incorporeal—but I meant figuratively too.

That was the way it had always been, ever since Calamity appeared. So few dared resist the Epics. I'd watched children be murdered in front of their parents, with nobody brave enough to lift a hand to try to stop it. Why would they try? They'd just be killed.

He did it to me too, to an extent. I was here with him, but all I wanted to do was escape. *You make us all selfish,* I thought at Nightwielder. *That's why I hate you. All of you.* But Steelheart most of all.

". . . could use some better forensic tools," Nightwielder's female minion said. "I realize it's not your specialty."

"I always bring some along to Newcago," Diamond replied. "Just for you. Here, let me show you what I have."

I blinked. They were done with the conversation about the Manchester, and apparently they'd bought it—and ordered a shipment of three hundred more from Diamond, who'd happily made the sale even though this one wasn't his to sell.

Forensics . . . , I thought. Something about that itched at my memory.

Diamond waddled over to rummage under his desk for a few boxes. He noticed me and waved me away. "You can go back to the stockpile and continue your inventory, kid. I don't need you here any longer."

I should probably have done as he said, but I did something stupid instead. "I'm almost finished with that, boss," I said. "I'd like to stay, if I can. I still don't know a lot about the forensic equipment."

He stopped, studying me, and I tried my best to look innocent, hands stuffed in the pockets of my jacket. A little voice in my head was muttering, *You are so stupid, you are so stupid, you are so stupid.* But when was I going to get a chance like this again?

Forensic equipment would include the kinds of things one used for studying a crime scene. And I knew a little more about that sort of thing than I'd just implied to Diamond. I'd read about it, at least.

And I remembered that you could find DNA and fingerprints by shining UV light on them. UV light . . . the very thing my notes claimed was Nightwielder's weakness.

"Fine." Diamond went back to rummaging. "Just stay out of the Great One's way."

I took a few steps back and kept my eyes down. Nightwielder paid me no heed, and his minions stood with arms crossed as Diamond got out an array of boxes. He began asking what they needed, and I could soon tell from their responses that someone in the

Newcago government—Nightwielder, maybe Steelheart himself—was troubled by Fortuity's assassination.

They wanted equipment to detect Epics. Diamond didn't have such a thing; he said he'd heard of some for sale in Denver, but it had turned out to be only a rumor. It appeared that dowsers like the Reckoners had weren't easy to come by even for someone like Diamond.

They also wanted equipment to better determine the origins of bullet shells and explosives. This request he could accommodate, particularly tracking down explosives. He unpacked several devices from their Styrofoam and cardboard, then showed a scanner that identified the chemicals in an explosive by analyzing the ash produced.

I waited, tense, as one of the minions picked up something that looked like a metal briefcase with locks on the sides. She flipped it open, revealing a bunch of smaller devices situated in foam holes. That looked just like the forensic kits I'd read about.

A small data chip was attached to the top, glowing faintly now that the case was open. That would be the manual. The minion waved her mobile in front of it absently, downloading the instructions. I stepped over and did likewise, and though she glanced at me, she soon dismissed me and turned back to her inspection.

My heart beating more quickly, I scanned through the manual's contents until I found it. UV fingerprint scanner with attached video camera. I skimmed the instructions. Now, if I could just get it out of the case. . . .

The woman took out a device and inspected it. It wasn't the fingerprint scanner, so I didn't pay attention. I snatched that scanner the second she looked away, and then I pretended to just be fiddling with it, trying my best to look idly curious.

In the process I got it turned on. It glowed blue at the front and had a screen on the back—it worked like a digital camcorder, but with a UV light on the front. You shined the light over objects and recorded images of what that revealed. That would be handy if doing a sweep of a room for DNA—it would give you a record of what you'd seen.

I turned on the record function. What I was about to do could easily get me killed. I'd seen men murdered for far less. But I knew Tia wanted stronger proof. It was time to get her some.

I turned the UV light and shined it on Nightwielder.

19

NIGHTWIELDER spun on me immediately.

I turned the UV light to the side, my head down as if I were studying the device and trying to figure out how it worked. I wanted it to seem like I'd shined the light on him by happenstance while fiddling with it.

I didn't look at Nightwielder. I *couldn't* look at Nightwielder. I didn't know if the light had worked on him, but if it had and he so much as suspected that I'd seen, I'd die.

I might die anyway.

It was painful not to know what effect the light had produced, but the device *was* recording. I turned away from Nightwielder, and with one hand I tapped some buttons on the device as if trying to make it work. With the other—fingers trembling nervously—I slid out the data chip and hid it in the palm of my hand.

Nightwielder was still watching me. I could feel his eyes, as if they were drilling holes into my back. The room seemed to grow darker, shadows lengthening. To the side, Diamond continued chatting about the features of the device he was demonstrating. Nobody seemed to have noticed that I'd drawn Nightwielder's attention.

I pretended not to notice either, though my heart was pounding even harder in my chest. I fiddled with the machine some more, then held it up as if I'd finally figured out how it worked. I stepped forward and pressed my thumb on the wall, then stepped back to try to see the thumbprint show up in the UV light.

Nightwielder hadn't moved. He was considering what to do. Killing me would protect him if I'd noticed what the UV light did. He could do it. He could claim that I'd impinged on his personal space, or looked at him wrong. Sparks, he didn't even need to give an excuse. He could do what he wanted.

However, that could be dangerous for him. When an Epic killed erratically or unexpectedly, people always wondered if it was an attempt to hide their weakness. His minions had seen me holding a UV scanner. They might make a connection. And so, to be safe, he'd probably have to kill Diamond and the Enforcement soldiers as well. Probably his own assistants too.

I was sweating now. It felt awful to stand there, to not even be facing him as he considered murdering me. I wanted to spin, look him in the eyes, and spit at him as he killed me.

Steady, I told myself. Keeping the defiance from my face, I looked over and pretended to notice—for the first time—that Nightwielder was staring at me. He stood as he had earlier, hands behind his back, black suit and thin black necktie making him look all lines. Motionless gaze, translucent skin. There was no sign of what had happened, if indeed anything *had* happened.

Upon seeing him I jumped in shock. I didn't have to feign fear; I felt my skin grow pale, the color drain from my face. I dropped the fingerprint scanner and yelped softly. The scanner cracked as it hit the ground. I immediately cursed, crouching down beside the broken device.

"What are you doing, you fool!" Diamond bustled over to me. He didn't seem very worried about the scanner, more about my offending Nightwielder somehow. "I'm so sorry, Great One. He is a bumbling idiot, but he's the best I've been able to find. It—"

Diamond hushed as the shadows nearby lengthened, then swirled upon themselves, becoming thick black cords. He stumbled away and I jumped to my feet. The darkness didn't strike at me, however, but scooped up the fallen fingerprint scanner.

The blackness seemed to pool on the floor, writhing and twisting about itself. Tendrils of it raised the scanner up into the air in front of Nightwielder, and he studied it with an indifferent gaze. He looked to us, and then more of the blackness rose up and surrounded the scanner. There was a sudden *crunch,* like a hundred walnuts being cracked at once.

The intended message was clear. Annoy me, and you will meet the same fate. Nightwielder neatly obscured his fear of the scanner, and his desire to destroy it, behind the guise of a simple threat.

"I . . ." I said softly. "Boss, why don't I just go to the back and keep working on that inventory, like you said?"

"What you should have done from the first," Diamond said. "Off with you."

I turned and scrambled away, hand held to my side, clutching the data chip from the UV scanner. I hurried my pace, not minding how I looked, until I was running. I reached the boxes and the relative safety of their shadows. There, close to the floor, I found a completed tunnel burrowed through the back wall.

I lurched to a stop. I took a breath, got on my hands and knees, and scrambled into the opening. I slid through the seven feet of steel and came out the other side.

Something grabbed my arm and I pulled back by instinct. I looked up, logic fleeing as I thought of how Nightwielder had made the shadows themselves come alive, but was relieved to see a familiar face.

"Hush!" Abraham said, holding my arm. "Are they chasing?"

"I don't think so," I said softly.

"Where's my gun?"

"Um . . . I kind of sold it to Nightwielder."

Abraham raised an eyebrow at me, then towed me to the side, where Megan covered us with my rifle. She was the definition of professional—lips a terse line, eyes searching the tunnels nearby for danger. The only light came from the mobiles she and Abraham wore strapped to their shoulders.

Abraham nodded to her, and there was no further conversation as the three of us made our escape down the corridor. At the next intersection of the catacombs, Megan tossed my rifle to Abraham—ignoring that I'd put my hand out for it—and unholstered one of her handguns. She nodded to him, then took point, hurrying ahead down the steel tunnel.

We continued that way, no talk, for a time. I'd been hopelessly lost before, but now I was turned around so much I barely knew which direction was up.

"Okay," Abraham finally said, holding up a hand to wave Megan back. "Let's take a breather and see if anyone is following." He settled down in a small alcove in the hallway where he could watch the stretch behind us and see if anyone had followed. He seemed to be favoring the arm opposite the shoulder that had been shot.

I crouched beside him and Megan joined us.

"That was an unexpected move you made up there, David," Abraham said softly, calmly.

"I didn't have time to think about it," I said. "They heard us working."

"True, true. And then Diamond suggested you go back, but you said you wanted to stay?"

"So . . . you heard that?"

"I could not have just mentioned it if I hadn't." He continued looking down the hallway.

I glanced at Megan, who gave me a frosty stare. "Unprofessional," she muttered.

I fished in my pocket and brought out the data chip. Abraham glanced at it, then frowned. He obviously hadn't stayed long enough to see what I was doing with Nightwielder. I tapped the chip to my mobile, downloading the information. Three taps later, it started displaying the video from the UV scanner. Abraham glanced over, and even Megan craned her neck to see what it was showing.

I held my breath. I still didn't know for certain if I was right about Nightwielder—and even if I was, there was no telling whether my hasty spin of the scanner had captured any useable images.

The video image showed the ground, with me waving my hand in front of the lens. Then it turned on Nightwielder and my heart leaped. I tapped the screen, freezing the image.

"You clever little slontze," Abraham murmured. There, on the screen, Nightwielder stood with half his body fully corporeal. It was difficult to make out, but it was there. Where the UV light shone, he wasn't translucent, and his body seemed to have *settled* more.

I tapped the screen again and the UV light panned past, letting Nightwielder become incorporeal again. The video was only a second or two, but it was enough. "UV forensics scanner," I explained. "I figured this was the best chance we'd get to know for certain. . . ."

"I can't believe you took that chance," Megan said. "Without asking anyone. You could have gotten *all three* of us killed."

"But he didn't," Abraham said, plucking the data chip from my hand. He studied it, seeming oddly reverent. Then he looked up, as if remembering he'd been planning to watch the hallway for signs of people following. "We need to get this chip to Prof. Now." He hesitated. "Nice work."

He stood up to go, and I found myself beaming. Then I turned to Megan, who gave me an even colder, more hostile look than she had earlier. She rose and followed Abraham.

Sparks, I thought. What would it take to impress that girl? I shook my head and jogged after them.

20

WHEN we returned, Cody was off on a mission to do some scouting for Tia. She waved toward some rations on the back table of the main room, awaiting devourment. Devouration. Whatever that word is.

"Go tell Prof what you found," Abraham said softly, walking toward the storage room. Megan made her way to the rations.

"Where are you going?" I asked Abraham.

"I need a new gun, it seems," he said with a smile, ducking through the doorway. He hadn't chided me for what I'd done with his gun—he saw that I'd saved the team. At least I hoped that was how he viewed it. Still, there was a distinct sense of loss in his voice. He'd liked that gun. And it was easy to see why—I'd *never* owned a weapon as nice as that one.

Prof wasn't in the main room, and Tia glanced at me, raising an eyebrow. "What are you telling Prof?"

"I'll explain," Megan said, sitting down beside her. As usual, Tia had her table covered with papers and cans of cola. It looked like she'd gotten the insurance records Cody mentioned, and she had them up on the screen in front of her.

If Prof wasn't in here, I figured he was probably in his thinking room with the imager. I walked over and knocked softly on the wall; the doorway was only draped with a cloth.

"Come in, David," Prof's voice called from inside.

I hesitated. I hadn't been in the room since I had told the team my plan. The others rarely entered. This was Prof's sanctum, and he usually came out—rather than inviting people in—when they needed to speak to him. I glanced at Tia and Megan, both of whom looked surprised, though neither said anything.

I pushed past the cloth and stepped into the room. I'd imagined what Prof was doing with the wall imagers—maybe exploiting the team's hack of the spy network, moving through the city and studying Steelheart and his minions. It wasn't anything so dramatic.

"Chalkboards?" I asked.

Prof turned from the far wall, where he'd been standing and writing with a piece of chalk. All four walls, along with ceiling and floor, had been turned slate-black, and they were covered in white scribbled writing.

"I know," Prof said, waving me in. "It's not very modern, is it? I have technology capable of representing just about anything I want, in any form I want. And I choose chalkboards." He shook his head, as if in amusement at his own eccentricity. "I think best this way. Old habits, I guess."

I stepped up to him. I could see now that he wasn't actually writing on the walls. The thing in Prof's hand was just a little stylus shaped like a piece of chalk. The machine was interpreting his writings, making the words appear on the wall as he scribbled them.

The drape had fallen back into place, masking the light from the other rooms. I could barely make Prof out; the only light came from the soft glow of the white script on all six walls. I felt as if I were floating in space, the words *stars* and *galaxies* shining at me from distant abodes.

"What *is* this?" I asked, looking upward, reading the script that covered the ceiling. Prof had certain bits of it boxed away from others, and had arrows and lines pointing to different sections. I couldn't make much sense of what it said. It was written in English, kind of. But many of the words were very small and seemed to be in some kind of shorthand.

"The plan," Prof said absently. He didn't wear his goggles or coat—both sat in a pile beside the door—and the sleeves of his black button-up shirt were rolled to the elbows.

"My plan?" I asked.

Prof's smile was lit by the pale glowing chalk lines. "Not any longer. There are some seeds of it here, though."

I felt a sharp sinking feeling. "But, I mean . . ."

Prof glanced at me, then laid a hand on my shoulder. "You did a great job, son. All things considered."

"What was wrong with it?" I asked. I'd spent years . . . really, my *entire life* on that plan, and I was pretty confident in what I'd come up with.

"Nothing, nothing," Prof said. "The ideas are sound. Remarkably so. Convince Steelheart that there's a rival in town, lure him out, hit him. Though there is the glaring fact that you don't know what his weakness is."

"Well, there is that," I admitted.

"Tia is working hard on it. If anyone can tease out the truth, it will be her," Prof said, then paused for a moment before he continued. "Actually, no—I shouldn't have said that this isn't your plan.

176

It is, and there are more than just seeds of it here. I looked through your notebooks. You thought through things very well."

"Thank you."

"But your vision was too narrow, son." Prof removed his hand from my shoulder and walked up to the wall. He tapped it with his imitation chalk stylus, and the room's text rotated. He didn't appear to even notice, but I grew dizzy as the walls seemed to tumble about me, spinning until a new wall of text popped up in front of Prof.

"Let me start with this," he said. "Other than not specifically knowing Steelheart's weakness, what's the biggest flaw in your plan?"

"I . . ." I frowned. "Taking out Nightwielder, maybe? But Prof, we just—"

"Actually," Prof said, "that's not it."

My frown deepened. I hadn't thought there *was* a flaw in my plan. I'd worked all those out, smoothing them away like cleanser removing the pimples from a teenager's chin.

"Let's break it down," Prof said, raising his arm and sweeping an opening on the wall, like he was wiping mud from a window. The words scrunched to the side, not vanishing but bunching up like he'd pulled a new section of paper from a spool. He raised his chalk to the open space and started to write. "Step one, imitate a powerful Epic. Step two, start killing Steelheart's important Epics to make him worried. Step three, draw him out. Step four, kill him. By doing this you restore hope to the world and encourage people to fight back."

I nodded.

"Except there's a problem," Prof said, still scribbling on the wall. "If we *actually* manage to kill Steelheart, we'll have done it by imitating a powerful Epic. Everyone's going to assume, then, that an *Epic* was behind the defeat. And so, what do we gain?"

"We could announce it was the Reckoners after the fact."

Prof shook his head. "Wouldn't work. Nobody would believe us, not after all the trouble we'll need to go through to make Steelheart believe."

"Well, does it matter?" I asked. "He'll be dead." Then, more softly, I added, "And I get revenge."

Prof hesitated, chalk pausing on the wall. "Yes," he said. "I guess you'd still have that."

"You want him dead too," I said, stepping up beside him. "I know it. I can see it."

"I want all Epics dead."

"It's more than that," I said. "I've seen it in you."

He glanced at me, and his gaze grew stern. "That doesn't matter. It is *vital* that people know we were behind this. You've said it yourself—we can't kill every Epic out there. The Reckoners are spinning in circles. The only hope we have, the only hope that humankind has, is to convince people that we *can* fight back. For that to happen, Steelheart has to fall by human hands."

"But for him to come out, he has to believe an Epic is threatening him," I said.

"You see the problem?"

"I . . ." I was starting to. "So we're not going to imitate an Epic?"

"We are," Prof said. "I like the idea, the spark of that. I'm just pointing out problems we have to work through. If this . . . Limelight is going to kill Steelheart, we need a way to make certain that after the fact, we can convince people it was really us. Not impossible, but it is why I had to work more on the plan, expand it."

"Okay," I said, relaxing. So we were still on track. A false Epic . . . the soul of my plan was there.

"There's a bigger problem, unfortunately," Prof said, tapping his chalk against the wall. "Your plan calls for us to kill Epics in Steelheart's administration to threaten him and draw him out. You indicate that we should do this to prove that a new Epic has come to town. Only, that's not going to work."

"What? Why?"

"Because it's what the Reckoners would do," Prof said. "Killing Epics quietly, never coming out into the open? It'll make him suspicious. We need to think like a *real* rival would. Anyone who wants Newcago would think bigger than that. Any Epic out there can have a city of his own; it's not that hard. To want Newcago, you'd have to be ambitious. You'd have to want to be a *king*. You'd have to want Epics at your beck and call. And so, killing them off one by one wouldn't make sense. You see?"

"You'd want them alive so they'd follow you," I said, slowly understanding. "Every Epic you kill would lessen your power once you actually took Newcago."

"Exactly," Prof said. "Nightwielder, Firefight, maybe Conflux . . . they'll have to go. But you'd be very careful who to kill and who to try to bribe away."

"Only we *can't* bribe them away," I said. "We wouldn't be able to convince them that we're an Epic, not long term."

"So you see another problem," Prof said.

He was right. I wilted, like soda going flat in a cup left out overnight. How had I not seen this hole in my plan?

"I've been working on these two problems," Prof said. "If we're going to imitate an Epic—and I think we still should—we need to be able to prove that we were behind it all along. That way the truth can flood Newcago and spread across the Fractured States from there. We can't just kill him; we have to film ourselves doing so. And we need to, at the last minute, send information about our plan to the right people around the city—so that they know and can vouch for us. People like Diamond, non-Epic crime magnates, people with influence but no direct connection to his government."

"Okay. But what about the second problem?"

"We need to hit Steelheart where it hurts," Prof said, "but we can't spread it out over too much time, and we can't focus on Epics. We need one or two massive hits that make him bleed, make him see us as a threat, and we need to do it as a rival seeking to take his place."

"So . . ."

Prof tapped the wall, rotating the text from the floor up in front of him. He tapped a section and some of the text started glowing green.

"Green?" I said, amused. "What was that about liking things old-fashioned?"

"You can use colored chalk on a chalkboard," he said gruffly as he circled a pair of words: *sewage system*.

"Sewage system?" I said. I'd been expecting something a little more grand, and a little less . . . crappy.

Prof nodded. "The Reckoners never attack facilities; we focus only on Epics. If we hit one of the city's main points of infrastructure, it will make Steelheart believe it's not the Reckoners working against him, but some other force. Someone specifically trying to take down Steelheart's rule—either rebels in the city, or another Epic moving on his territory.

"Newcago works on two principles: fear and stability. The city has the basic infrastructure that many others don't, and that draws people here. The fear of Steelheart keeps them in line." He rolled the words on the walls again, bringing over a network of drawings he'd done in "chalk" on the far wall. It looked like a crude blueprint. "If we start attacking his infrastructure he'll move on us faster than if we'd attacked his Epics. Steelheart is smart. He knows why people come to Newcago. If he loses the basic things—sewage, power, communications—he'll lose the city."

I nodded slowly. "I wonder why."

"Why? I just explained. . . ." Prof trailed off, looking at me. He frowned. "That's not what you mean."

"I wonder why he cares. Why does he go to so much trouble to create a city where people want to live? Why does he care if they have food, or water, or electricity? He kills them so callously, yet he also sees that they're provided for."

Prof fell silent. Eventually he shook his head. "What is it to be a king if you have nobody to follow you?"

I thought back to that day, the day when my father died. *These people are mine. . . .* As I considered it I realized something about the Epics. Something that, despite all my years of study, I'd never quite understood before.

"It isn't enough," Prof whispered. "It isn't *enough* to have godly powers, to be functionally immortal, to be able to bend the elements to your will and soar through the skies. It isn't enough unless you can use it to make others follow you. In a way, the Epics would be nothing without the regular people. They need someone to dominate; they need some way to show off their powers."

"I hate him," I hissed, though I hadn't meant to say it out loud. I hadn't even realized I'd been thinking it.

Prof looked at me.

"What?" I asked. "Are you going to tell me that my anger doesn't do any good?" People had tried to tell me that in the past, Martha foremost among them. She claimed the thirst for vengeance would eat me alive.

"Your emotions are your own business, son," Prof said, turning away. "I don't care *why* you fight, so long as you do fight. Maybe your anger will burn you away, but better to burn yourself away than to shrivel up beneath Steelheart's thumb." He paused. "Besides, telling you to stop would be a little like a hearth telling the oven to cool down."

I nodded. He understood. He felt it too.

"Regardless, the plan is now realigned," Prof said. "We'll strike at the wastewater treatment plant, as it's the least well guarded. The trick will be making sure Steelheart connects the attack to a rival Epic, rather than just rebels."

"Would it be so bad if people thought there was a rebellion?"

"It wouldn't draw Steelheart out, for one," Prof said. "And if he thought the people were rebelling, he'd make them pay. I won't have innocents dying in retaliation for things we've done."

"But, I mean, isn't that the point? To show the others that we can fight back? Actually, as I think about it, maybe we could set up here in Newcago for good. If we win, maybe we could lead the place once—"

"Stop."

I frowned.

"We kill Epics, son," Prof said, his voice suddenly quiet, intense. "And we're good at it. But don't get it into your mind that we're revolutionaries, that we're going to tear down what's out there and put ourselves in its place. The *moment* we start to think like that, we derail.

"We want to make others fight back. We want to inspire them. But we dare not take that power for ourselves. That's the end of it. We're killers. We'll rip Steelheart from his place and find a way to pull his heart from his chest. After that, let someone else decide what to do with the city. I want no part of it."

The ferocity of those words, soft though they were, quieted me. I didn't know how to respond. Maybe Prof did have a point, though. This was about killing Steelheart. We had to stay focused.

It still felt odd that he hadn't challenged me on my passion for vengeance. He was pretty much the first person who hadn't served me some platitude on revenge.

"Fine," I said. "But I think the sewage station is the wrong place to hit."

"Where would you go?"

"The power station."

"Too well guarded." Prof examined his notes, and I could see that he had a schematic of the power station as well, with notations around the perimeter. He'd considered it.

I got a thrill from the idea that the two of us thought along the same lines.

"If it's well guarded," I said, "then blowing it up will look that much more impressive. And we could steal one of Steelheart's power cells while we're there. We brought back a gun from Diamond, but it's dry. It needs a powerful energy source to run." I raised my mobile to the wall and uploaded the video of the gauss gun firing. The video appeared on the wall, shoving aside some of Prof's chalk writings, and played.

He watched in silence, and when it was done he nodded. "So our fake Epic will have energy powers."

"And that's why he'd destroy the power station," I said. "It's in theme." Epics liked themes and motifs.

"It's too bad that removing the power station wouldn't stop Enforcement," Prof said. "Conflux powers them directly. He powers some of the city directly too, but our intel says he does it by charging power cells that are stored here." He pulled up his schematics of the power station. "One of those cells could power this gun—they're extremely compact, and they each have more juice packed into them than should be physically possible. If we blow the station, and the rest of those cells, it will cause serious damage to the city." He nodded. "I like it. Dangerous, but I like it."

"We'll still have to hit Conflux," I said. "It would make sense, even for a rival Epic. First remove the power station, then take out the police force. Chaos. It will work particularly well if we can kill Conflux using that gun, giving off a big light show."

Prof nodded. "I'll need to do more planning," he said, raising a hand and wiping away the video. It came off like it had been drawn in chalk. He pushed aside another pile of writing and raised his stylus to start working. He stopped, however, then looked at me.

"What?" I asked.

He walked over to his Reckoner jacket, which sat on a table, and took something out from under it. He walked back and handed it to me. A glove. One of the tensors. "You've been practicing?" he asked me.

"I'm not very good yet."

"Get better. Fast. I won't have the team underpowered, and Megan can't seem to make the tensors work."

I took the glove, saying nothing, though I wanted to ask the question. *Why not you, Prof? Why do you refuse to use your own invention?* Tia's warning not to pry too much made me hold my tongue.

"I confronted Nightwielder," I blurted out, only now remembering the reason I'd come to talk with Prof.

"What?"

"He was there, at Diamond's place. I went out and pretended to be one of Diamond's helpers. I . . . used a UV fingerprint scanner he had to confirm Nightwielder's weakness."

Prof studied me, his face betraying no emotions. "You've had a busy afternoon. I assume you did this at great risk to the entire team?"

"I . . . Yes." Better he heard it from me, rather than Megan, who would undoubtedly report—in great detail—of how I'd deviated from the plan.

"You show promise," Prof said. "You take risks; you get results. You have proof of what you said about Nightwielder?"

"I got a recording."

"Impressive."

"Megan wasn't very happy with it."

"Megan liked the way things were before," Prof said. "Adding a new team member always upends the dynamic. Besides, I think she's worried you're showing her up. She's still smarting from being unable to make the tensors work."

Megan? Worried that *I* was showing *her* up? Prof must not know her very well.

"Out with you, then," Prof said. "I want you up to speed with the tensor by the time we hit the power plant. And don't worry too much about Megan . . ."

"I won't. Thank you."

". . . worry about me."

I froze.

Prof started writing on the board and didn't turn back when he spoke, but his words were sharp. "You got results by risking the lives of my people. I assume nobody was hurt, otherwise you'd have mentioned it by now. You show promise, as I said. But if you brashly get one of my people killed, David Charleston, Megan will not be your problem. I won't leave enough of you for her to bother with."

I swallowed. My mouth had suddenly gone dry.

"I trust you with their lives," Prof said, still writing, "and them with yours. Don't betray that trust, son. Keep your impulses in check. Don't just act because you can; act because it's the right thing to do. If you keep that in mind, you'll be all right."

"Yes sir," I said, leaving with a quick step out the cloth-covered doorway.

21

"HOW'S the signal?" Prof asked through the earpiece.

I raised my hand to my ear. "Good," I said. I wore my mobile—newly tuned to the Reckoner mobiles and made completely secure from Steelheart's prying—on my wrist mount. I'd also been given one of the jackets. It looked like a thin black and red sports-style jacket—though it had wiring all around the inside lining and a little power pack sewn into the back. That was the part that would extend a concussion field around me if I was hit hard.

Prof had built it for me himself. He said it would protect me from a short fall or a small explosion, but I shouldn't try jumping off any cliffs or getting shot in the face. Not like I was intending to do either.

I wore it proudly. I'd never been officially told I was a member of the team, but these two changes seemed essentially the same thing. Of course, going on this mission was probably a good indication too.

I glanced at my mobile; it showed that I was only on the line with Prof. Tapping the screen could move me to a line to everyone in the team, cycle me to a single member, or let me pick a few of them to talk to.

"You in position?" Prof asked.

"We are." I stood in a dark tunnel of pure steel, the only light that of my mobile and Megan's up ahead. She wore a pair of dark jeans and her brown leather jacket, open at the front, over a tight T-shirt. She was inspecting the ceiling.

"Prof," I said softly, turning away, "you sure I can't pair up with Cody for this mission?"

"Cody and Tia are interference," Prof said. "We've been over this, son."

"Maybe I could go with Abraham, then. Or you." I glanced over my shoulder, then spoke even more softly. "She doesn't really like me much."

"I won't have two members of my crew not getting along," Prof said sternly. "You will learn to work together. Megan is a professional. It'll be fine."

Yes, she's professional, I thought. *Too professional.* But Prof wasn't hearing any of it.

I took a deep breath. Part of my nervousness, I knew, was because of the job. One week had passed since my conversation with Prof, and the rest of the Reckoners had agreed that hitting the power station—and imitating a rival Epic while doing so—was the best plan.

Today was the day. We'd sneak in and destroy Newcago's power plant. This would be my first real Reckoner operation. I was finally a member of the team. I didn't want to be the weak one.

"You good, son?" Prof asked.

"Yeah."

"We're moving. Set your timer."

I set my mobile for a ten-minute countdown. Prof and Abraham were going to break in first on the other side of the station, where all the huge equipment was. They'd work their way upward, setting charges. At the ten-minute mark, Megan and I would go in and steal a power cell to use with the gauss gun. Tia and Cody would come in last, entering through the hole Prof and Abraham had made. They were a support team; ready to move and help us extract if we needed to, but otherwise hanging back and giving us information and guidance.

I took another deep breath. On the hand opposite my mobile, I wore the black leather tensor, with glowing green strips from the fingertips to the palm. Megan eyed me as I strode up to the end of the tunnel that Abraham had dug the day before during a scouting mission.

I showed her the countdown.

"You're sure you can do this?" she asked me. There was a hint of skepticism in her voice, though her face was impassive.

"I've gotten a lot better with the tensors," I said.

"You forget that I've watched most of your practice sessions."

"Cody didn't need those shoes," I said.

She raised an eyebrow at me.

"I can do it," I said, stepping up to the end of the tunnel, where Abraham had left a pillar of steel jutting from the ground. It was short enough that I could step up on it to reach the low ceiling. The clock ticked down. We didn't speak. I mentally sounded out a few ways to start conversation, but each one died on my lips as I opened my mouth. Each time I was confronted by Megan's glassy stare. She didn't want to chat. She wanted to do the job.

Why do I even care? I thought, looking up at the ceiling. *Other than that first day, she's never shown me anything other than coldness and the occasional bit of disdain.*

Yet . . . there was something about her. More than the fact that she was beautiful, more than the fact that she carried tiny grenades in her top—which I still thought was awesome, by the way.

There had been girls at the Factory. But, like everyone else, they were complacent. They'd just call it living their lives, but they were afraid. Afraid of Enforcement, afraid that an Epic would kill them.

Megan didn't seem afraid of anything, ever. She didn't play games with men, fluttering her eyes, saying things she didn't mean. She did what needed to be done, and she was very good at it. I found that *incredibly* attractive. I wished I could explain that to her. But getting the words out of my mouth felt like trying to push marbles through a keyhole.

"I—" I began.

My mobile beeped.

"Go," she said, looking upward.

Trying to tell myself I wasn't relieved by the interruption, I raised my hands up to the ceiling and closed my eyes. I *was* getting better with the tensor. I still wasn't as good as Abraham, but I wasn't an embarrassment any longer. At least not most of the time. I pressed my hand flat against the metal ceiling of the tunnel and pushed, holding my hand in place as the vibrations began.

The buzzing was like the eager purr of a muscle car that had just been started, but left in neutral. That was another of Cody's metaphors for it; I'd said the sensation felt like an unbalanced washing machine filled with a hundred epileptic chimpanzees. Pretty proud of that one.

I pushed and kept my hand steady, humming softly to myself in the same tone as the tensor. That helped me focus. The others didn't do it, and they didn't always have to keep their hand pressed against a wall either. I eventually wanted to learn to do it like they did, but this would work for now.

The vibrations built, but I contained them, held them in my hand. Kept hold of them until it felt like my fingernails were going to rattle free. Then I pulled my hand back and *pushed* somehow.

Imagine holding a swarm of bees in your mouth, then spitting them out and trying to keep them pointed in a single direction by the sheer force of your breath and will. It's kind of like that. My hand flew back and I launched the half-musical vibrations away, into the ceiling, which rattled and shook with a quiet hum. Steel dust fell down around my arm, showering to the ground below like someone had taken a cheese grater to a refrigerator.

Megan crossed her arms and watched, a single eyebrow raised. I prepared myself for some cold, indifferent comment. She nodded and said, "Nice work."

"Yeah, well, you know, I've been practicing a lot. Hitting the old wall-vaporizing gym."

"The what?" She frowned as she pulled over the ladder we'd brought with us.

"Never mind," I said, climbing up the ladder and peeking my head into the basement of Station Seven, the power station. I'd never been inside any of the city stations, of course. They were like bunkers, with high steel walls and fences surrounding them. Steelheart liked to keep things under a watchful eye; a place like this wouldn't just be a power station but would have government offices on the upper floors as well. All carefully fenced, guarded, and observed.

The basement, fortunately, had no cameras watching it. Most of those were in the hallways.

Megan handed me my rifle, and I climbed out into the room above. We were in a storage chamber, dark save for a few of those glowing "always on" lights that places tend to . . . well, always leave on. I moved to the wall and tapped my mobile. "We're in," I said softly.

"Good," Cody's voice came back.

I blushed. "Sorry. I meant to send that to Prof."

"You did. He told me to watch over y'all. Turn on the video feed from your earpiece."

The earpiece was one of those wraparound kinds and had a little camera sticking out over my ear. I tapped a few times on my mobile screen, activating it.

"Nice," Cody said. "Tia and I have set up here at Prof's entrance point." Prof liked contingencies, and that usually meant leaving a person or two back to create diversions or enact plans if the main teams got pinned down.

"I don't have much to do here," Cody continued, his Southern drawl as thick as ever, "so I'm going to bother you."

"Thanks," I said, glancing back at Megan as she climbed up out of the hole.

"Don't mention it, lad. And stop looking down Megan's shirt."

"I'm not—"

"Just teasing. I hope you keep doing it. It'll be fun to watch her shoot you in the foot when she catches you."

I looked away pointedly. Fortunately it didn't appear that Cody had included Megan in that particular conversation. I actually found myself breathing a little easier, knowing that Cody was watching over us. Megan and I were the two newest members of the team; if anyone could use coaching it would be us.

Megan carried our pack on her back, filled with the things we'd need for the infiltration. She had out a handgun, which honestly would be more useful in close quarters than my rifle. "Ready?" she asked.

I nodded.

"How much 'improvising' do I have to be ready for from you today?" she asked.

"Only as much as needed," I grumbled, raising my hand to the wall. "If I knew when it would be needed, it wouldn't be improvising, would it? It would be planning."

She chuckled. "A foreign concept to you."

"Foreign? Did you not see all the notebooks of plans I brought to the team? You know, the ones we all almost died retrieving?"

She turned away, not looking at me, and her posture grew stiff.

Sparking woman, I thought. *Try making some sense for once.* I shook my head, placing my hand against the wall.

One of the reasons that the city stations were considered

impregnable was because of the security. Cameras in all of the hallways and stairwells; I had thought we'd hack into security and change the camera feeds. Prof said we'd certainly hack the feeds to watch them, but changing those feeds to cover sneaking rarely worked as well as it did in the old movies. Steelheart didn't hire stupid security officers, and they'd notice if their video looped. Besides, soldiers patrolled the hallways.

However, there was a much simpler way to make sure we weren't seen. We just had to stay out of the hallways. There weren't cameras in most of the rooms, as the research and experiments done there were kept secret, even from the security watching the building. Besides, logically, if you kept really close watch on all the hallways, you could catch intruders. How else would people move from room to room?

I raised my hand and, with some concentration, vaporized a four-foot-wide hole in the wall. I glanced through it, shining my mobile. I'd ruined some computer equipment on the wall, and I had to shove a desk out of the way to get in, but there was nobody inside. At this hour of the night much of the station was unoccupied, and Tia had drawn up our path very carefully, with the goal of minimizing the chances that we'd run into anyone.

After we crawled through, Megan took something from the pack and placed it on the wall beside the hole I'd made. It had a small red light that blinked ominously. We were to place explosive charges beside each hole we created so that when we detonated the building, it would be impossible to find out about the tensors from the wreckage.

"Keep moving," Cody said. "Every minute y'all are in there is a minute longer that someone might wander into a room and wonder where all those bloody holes came from."

"I'm on it," I said, sliding my finger across my mobile's screen and bringing up Tia's map. If we continued straight ahead through three rooms, we'd reach an emergency stairwell with fewer security cameras. We could avoid those, hopefully, by looping through some walls and moving up two floors. Then we needed to make our way into the main storage chamber for energy cells. We'd set the rest of our charges, steal a power cell or two, and bolt.

"Are you talking to yourself?" Megan asked, watching the door, her gun at chest level and arm straight and ready.

"Tell her you're listening to ear demons," Cody suggested. "Always works for me."

"Cody is on the line," I said, working on the next wall. "Giving me a delightful running commentary. And telling me about ear demons."

That almost provoked a smile from her. I swore I saw one, for a moment at least.

"Ear demons are totally real," Cody said. "They're what make microphones like these ones work. They're also what tell you to eat the last slice of pie when you know Tia wanted it. Hold for a second. I'm patched into the security system, and there's someone coming down the hall. Hold."

I froze, then hastily quieted the tensor.

"Yeah, they're entering that room next to you," Cody said. "Lights were already on. Might be someone else in it too—can't tell from the security feed. Y'all might have just dodged a bullet. Or rather, dodged having to dodge quite a few of them."

"What do we do?" I asked tensely.

"About Cody?" Megan asked, frowning.

"Cody, could you just patch her in too?" I asked, exasperated.

"You really want to talk about her cleavage when she's on the line?" Cody asked innocently.

"No! I mean. Don't talk about that at all."

"Fine. Megan, there's someone in the next room."

"Options?" she asked, calm.

"We can wait, but the lights were already on. My guess is some late-night scientists still working."

Megan raised her gun.

"Uh . . . ," I said.

"No, lass," Cody said. "You know how Prof feels about that. Shoot guards if you have to. Nobody else." The plan included pulling an alarm and evacuating the building before we detonated our charges.

"I wouldn't have to shoot the people next door," Megan said calmly.

"And what else would you do, lass?" Cody asked. "Knock them out, then leave them for when we blow up the building?"

Megan hesitated.

"Okay," Cody said. "Tia says there's another way. You're going to have to go up an elevator shaft, though."

"Lovely," Megan said.

We hurried back to the first room we'd come through. Tia uploaded a new map for me, with tensor points, and I got to work. I was a little more nervous this time. Were we going to find random scientists and workers just hanging around all over? What *would* we do if someone surprised us? What if it was some innocent custodian?

For the first time in my life, I found myself nearly as worried about what I might end up doing as I was about what someone might do to me. It was an uncomfortable situation. What we were doing was, basically, terrorism.

But we're the good guys, I told myself, breaking open the wall and letting Megan slide through first. Of course, what terrorist *didn't* think he or she was the good guy? We were doing something important, but what would that matter to the family of the cleaning woman we accidentally killed? As I hastened through the next darkened room—this one was a lab chamber, with some beakers and other glasswork set up—I had trouble shaking off these questions.

And so, I focused on Steelheart. That awful, hateful sneer. Standing there with the gun he'd taken from my father, barrel pointed down at the inferior human.

That image worked. I could forget everything else when I thought of it. I didn't have all the answers, but at least I had a goal. Revenge. Who cared if it would eat me up inside and leave me hollow? So long as it drove me to make life better for everyone else. Prof understood that. I understood it too.

We reached the elevator shaft without incident, entering it through a storage room that bordered it. I vaporized a large hole in the wall, and then Megan poked her head in and looked up the tall, dark shaft. "So, Cody, there's supposed to be a way up?"

"Sure. Handholds on the sides. They put them in all elevator shafts."

"Looks like someone forgot to inform Steelheart of that," I said, looking in beside Megan. "These walls are completely slick. No ladder or anything like that. No ropes or cords either."

Cody cursed.

"So we're back to going the other way?" Megan asked.

I scanned the walls again. The blackness seemed to extend forever above and below us. "We could wait for the elevator to come."

"The elevators have cameras," Cody said.

"So we ride on top of it," I said.

"And alert the people inside when we drop onto it?" Megan asked.

"We just wait for one that doesn't have anyone in it," I said. "Elevators are empty about half the time, right? They're responding to calls people make."

"All right," Cody said. "Prof and Abraham have hit a small snag—waiting for a room to clear out so they can move through. Prof says you have five minutes to wait. If nothing happens by then, we're scrapping the job."

"Okay," I said, feeling a stab of disappointment.

"I'm going to run some visuals for them," Cody said. "I'll be offline from you for a bit; call me if you need me. I'll watch the elevator. If it moves, I'll let you know." The line clicked as Cody switched frequencies, and we started waiting.

We both sat quietly, straining to hear any sounds of the elevator moving, though we'd never spot it before Cody did with his video feeds.

"So . . . how often is it like this?" I asked after a few minutes of kneeling beside Megan, stuck in the room beside the hole I'd burrowed into the side of the elevator shaft.

"Like what?" she asked.

"The waiting."

"More than you'd think," she said. "The jobs we do, they're often all about timing. Good timing requires a lot of waiting around." She glanced at my hand, and I found that I'd been nervously tapping the side of the wall.

I forced myself to stop.

"You sit," she said, voice growing softer, "and you wait. You go over and over the plan, picture it in your mind. Then it usually goes wrong anyway."

I eyed her suspiciously.

"What?" she asked.

"The thing you just said. It's exactly what I think too."

"So?"

"So if something usually goes wrong, why are you always on my back about improvising?"

She grew thin-lipped.

"No," I said. "It's time you leveled with me, Megan. Not just about this mission, but about everything. What is with you? Why do you treat me like you hate me? *You* were the one who originally spoke up for me when I wanted to join! You sounded impressed with me at first—Prof might never have listened to my plan at all if you hadn't said what you did. But since then you've acted like I was a gorilla at your buffet."

"A . . . *what?*"

"Gorilla at your buffet. You know . . . eating all your food? Making you annoyed? That kind of thing?"

"You're a very special person, David."

"Yeah, I take a specialness pill each morning. Look, Megan, I'm *not* letting go of this. The whole time I've been with the Reckoners, it seems like I've been doing something that bothers you. Well, what is it? What made you turn on me like that?"

She looked away.

"Is it my face?" I asked. "Because that's the only thing I can think of. I mean, you were all for me after the Fortuity hit. Maybe it's my face. I don't think it's too bad a face, as far as faces go, but it does look kind of stupid sometimes when I—"

"It's not your face," she interrupted.

"I didn't think it was, but I need you to talk to me. Say something." *Because I think you're hotter than hell and I can't understand what went wrong.* Fortunately I stopped myself from saying that part out loud. I also kept my eyes straight at her head, just in case Cody was watching in.

She said nothing.

"Well?" I prompted.

"Five minutes is up," she said, checking her mobile.

"I'm not going to let this go so easily, this—"

"Five minutes is up," Cody suddenly said, cutting in. "Sorry, kids. This mission is a bust. Nobody is moving the elevators."

"Can't you send one for us?" I asked.

Cody chuckled. "We're tapped into the security feed, lad, but that's a far cry from being able to control things in the building. If Tia could hack us in that far, we could blow the building from the inside by overpowering the plants or something."

"Oh." I looked up the cavernous shaft. It resembled an enormous throat, stretching upward . . . one we needed to get up . . . which made us . . .

Bad analogy. Very bad. Regardless, there was a twisting feeling in my gut. I hated the idea of backing down. Above lay the path to destroying Steelheart. Behind lay more waiting, more planning. I'd been planning for years.

"Oh no," Megan said.

"What?" I asked absently.

"You're going to improvise, aren't you?"

I reached out into the shaft with the hand that wore the tensor, pressed it flat against the wall, and began a small vibrative burst. Abraham had taught me to make bursts of different sizes; he said that a master with the tensors could control the vibrations, leaving patterns or even shapes in your target.

I pushed my hand hard, flat, feeling the glove shake. It wasn't just the glove, though. It was my whole hand. That had confused me at first. It seemed like *I* was creating the power, not the glove—the glove just helped shape the blast somehow.

I couldn't fail at this. If I did the operation was over. I should have felt stress at that, but I didn't. For some reason, I was realizing, when things got really, really tense I found it easier to relax.

Steelheart looming above my father. A gunshot. I *would not back down*.

The glove vibrated; dust fell away from the wall in a little patch around my hand. I slipped my fingers forward and felt what I'd done.

"A handhold," Megan said softly, shining the light of her mobile.

"What, really?" Cody asked. "Turn on your camera, lass." A moment later he whistled. "You've been holding back on me, David. I didn't think you were nearly practiced enough to do something like that. I might have suggested it myself if I'd thought you could."

I moved my hand to the side and made another handhold, placing it beside the other in the shaft just next to the hole in the wall. I made two more for my feet, then swung out of the hole in the wall and into the elevator shaft, placing my hands and feet in the handholds.

I stretched up and made another set of holds above. I climbed up, rifle slung over my shoulder. I did *not* look down but made another set of holds and continued. Climbing and carving with the tensor wasn't by any means easy, but I was able to shape the tensor blasts to leave a ridge at the front of each handhold, making them easy to grip.

"Can Prof and Abraham stall for a little longer?" Megan asked from below. "David seems to be working at a good clip, but it might take us about fifteen minutes to get up."

"Tia's calculating," Cody said.

"Well, I'm going after David," Megan said. She sounded muffled. I glanced over my shoulder; she'd wrapped a scarf around her face.

The dust from the handholds; she doesn't want to breathe it in. Smart. I was having trouble avoiding it, and steel dust did *not* seem like a smart thing to inhale. Abraham said tensor dust wasn't as dangerous as it seemed, but I still didn't think it would be a good idea, so I ducked my head and held my breath each time I made a new hole.

"I'm impressed," a voice said in my ear. Prof's voice. It nearly made me leap in shock, which would have been a very bad thing. He must have patched into my visual feed with his mobile, and could see the images made by the camera on my earpiece.

"Those holes are crisp and well formed," Prof continued. "Keep at it and you'll soon be as good as Abraham. You might already have passed up Cody."

"You sound worried about something," I said between making handholds.

"Not troubled. Just surprised."

"It needed to be done," I said, grunting as I pulled myself up past another floor.

Prof was silent for a few moments. "That it did. Look, we can't have you extract down this same route. It will take too long, so you'll have to go out another way. Tia will let you know where. Wait for the first explosion."

"Affirmative," I said.

"And, David," Prof added.

"Yeah?"

"Good work."

I smiled, pulling myself up again.

We continued at it, climbing up the elevator shaft. I worried that the elevator would come down at some point, though if it did it should miss us by a few inches. We were on the side of the shaft where there *should* have been a ladder. They just hadn't installed one.

Perhaps Steelheart has watched the same movies that we have, I thought with a grimace as we finally passed the second floor. One more to go.

My mobile clicked in my ear. I glanced at it on my wrist—someone had muted our channel.

"I don't like what you've done to the team," Megan called up, her voice muffled.

I glanced over my shoulder at her. She wore the backpack with our equipment in it, and her nose and mouth were covered with the scarf. Those eyes of hers glared at me, softly lit by the glow of the mobile strapped to her forearm. Beautiful eyes, peeking out above the shroud of a scarf.

With a huge, black pit stretching behind her. Whoa. I lurched woozily.

"Slontze," she called. "Stay focused."

"You're the one who said something!" I whispered, turning back around. "What do you mean you don't like what I did to the team?"

"Before you showed up we were going to move out of Newcago," Megan said from below. "Hit Fortuity, then leave. You made us stay."

I continued climbing. "But—"

"Oh, just shut up and let me talk for once."

I shut up.

"I joined the Reckoners to kill Epics who deserved it," Megan continued. "Newcago is one of the safest, most stable places in the entire Fractured States. I don't think we should be killing Steelheart, and I don't like how you've hijacked the team to fight your own personal war against him. He's brutal, yes, but he's doing a better job than most Epics. He doesn't deserve to die."

The words stunned me. She didn't think we should kill Steelheart? He didn't *deserve* to die? It was insanity. I resisted the urge to look down again. "Can I talk now?" I asked, making another pair of handholds.

"Okay, fine."

"Are you *crazy*? Steelheart is a monster."

"Yes. I'll admit that. But he's an *effective* monster. Look, what are we doing today?"

"Destroying a power plant."

"And how many cities out there still have power plants?" she asked. "Do you even know?"

I kept climbing.

"I grew up in Portland," she said. "Do you know what happened there?"

I did, though I didn't say. It hadn't been good.

"The turf wars between Epics left the city in ruins," Megan continued, her voice softer now. "There is nothing left, David. *Nothing.* All of Oregon is a wasteland; even the trees are gone. There aren't any power plants, sewage treatment plants, or grocery stores. That was what Newcago would have become, if Steelheart hadn't stepped in."

I continued climbing, sweat tickling the back of my neck. I thought about the change in Megan—she'd grown cold toward me right after I'd first talked about taking down Steelheart. The times when she'd treated me the worst had been when we'd been making breakthroughs. When we'd gone to fetch my plans and when I'd found out how to kill Nightwielder.

It hadn't been my "improvising" that had set her against me. It had been my intentions. My successes in getting the team to target Steelheart.

"I don't want to be the cause of something like Portland

happening again," Megan continued. "Yes, Steelheart is terrible. But he's a kind of terrible that people can live with."

"So why haven't you quit?" I asked. "Why are you here?"

"Because I'm a Reckoner," she said. "And it's not my job to contradict Prof. I'll do my job, Knees. I'll do it well. But this time, I think we're making a mistake."

She was using that nickname of hers for me again. It actually seemed like a good sign, as she only seemed to use it when she was less annoyed at me. It was kind of affectionate, wasn't it? I just wished the nickname hadn't been a reference to something so embarrassing. Why not . . . Super-Great-Shot? That kind of rolled off the tongue, didn't it?

We climbed the rest of the way in silence. Megan turned our audio feed to the rest of the team back on, which seemed an indication that she thought the conversation was over. Maybe it was—I certainly didn't know what else to say. How could she possibly think that living under Steelheart was a *good* thing?

I thought of the other kids at the Factory, of the people in the understreets. I guessed that many of them thought the same way—they'd come here knowing that Steelheart was a monster, but they still thought life was better in Newcago than in other places.

Only they were complacent—Megan was anything but that. She was active, incredible, capable. How could *she* think like they did? It shook what I knew of the world—at least, what I thought I knew. The Reckoners were supposed to be different.

What if she was right?

"Oh *sparks*!" Cody suddenly said in my ear.

"What?"

"Y'all've got trouble, lad. It's—"

At that moment the doors to the elevator shaft just above—the ones on the third floor—slid open. Two uniformed guards stepped up to the ledge and peered down into the darkness.

22

"**I'M** telling you, I heard something," one of the guards said, squinting downward. He seemed to be looking right at me. But it was dark in the elevator shaft—darker than I'd thought it would be, with the doors open.

"I don't see anything," the other said. His voice echoed softly.

The first pulled his flashlight off his belt.

My heart lurched. *Uh-oh*.

I pressed my hand against the wall; it was the only thing I could think to do. The tensor started vibrating, and I tried to concentrate, but it was *hard* with them up there. The flashlight clicked.

"See? Hear that?"

"Sounds like the furnace," the second guard said drily.

My hand rattling against the side of the wall did have a kind of mechanical sound to it. I grimaced but kept on. The light of the flashlight shone in the shaft. I nearly lost control of the vibration.

There was no way they could have missed seeing me with that light. They were too close.

"Nothing there," the guard said with a grunt.

What? I looked up. Somehow, despite being only a short distance away, it seemed they hadn't seen me. I frowned, confused.

"Huh," the other guard said. "I do hear a sound, though."

"It's coming from . . . you know," the first guard said.

"Oh," the other said. "Right."

The first guard stuffed the flashlight back into place on his belt. How could he have missed seeing me? He'd shined it right in my direction.

The two backed away from the opening and let the doors slide shut.

What in Calamity's fires? I thought. Could they have actually missed us in the darkness?

My tensor went off.

I'd been preparing to vaporize a pocket into the wall to hide in—get us out of their line of fire if it came to that. But because I wasn't focusing the blast, I took a large chunk out of the wall in front of me, and in an instant my handhold disappeared. I grabbed at the side of the hole I'd made, barely finding a grip.

A burst of dust fell back over me and cascaded over Megan in an enormous shower. Holding tight to the side of the hole, I glanced down to find her glaring up at me, blinking dust from her eyes. Her hand actually seemed to be inching toward her gun.

Calamity! I thought with a start. Her scarf and skin were dusted silver, and her eyes were *angry*. I don't think I'd ever seen an expression like that in a person's eyes before—not directed at me at least. It was like I could feel the hate coming off her.

Her hand kept inching toward the handgun at her side.

"M-Megan?" I asked.

204

Her hand stopped. I didn't know what I'd seen, but it was gone in a moment. She blinked, and her expression softened. "You need to watch what you're destroying, Knees," she snapped, reaching up to wipe some of the dust off her face.

"Yeah," I said, then looked back up into the hole I was hanging onto. "Hey, there's a room here." I raised my mobile, shining light into it to get a better look.

It was a small room—a few orderly desks outfitted with computer terminals lined one wall and filing cabinets ran along the other. There were two doors, one a reinforced metal security door with a keypad.

"Megan, there's definitely a room here. And it doesn't look like there's anyone in it. Come on." I pulled myself up and crawled through.

As soon as I was in I helped Megan up and out of the shaft. She hesitated before taking my hand, then once she was out she walked past me without a word. She seemed to have gone back to being cold toward me, maybe even a little mean.

I knelt beside the hole back into the elevator shaft. I couldn't shake the feeling that something very strange had just happened. First the guard hadn't seen us, then Megan went from opening up to me to totally closing off in seconds flat. Was she having second thoughts about what she'd shared with me? Was she worried I'd tell Prof that she didn't support killing Steelheart?

"What *is* this place?" Megan said from the center of the small room. The ceiling was low enough that she almost had to stoop—I would definitely have to. She unwrapped her scarf, releasing a puff of metal dust, grimaced, and then began shaking out her clothing.

"No idea," I said, checking my mobile and the map Tia had uploaded. "The room's not on the map."

"Low ceilings," Megan said. "Security door with a code. Interesting." She tossed her pack to me. "Put an explosive on the hole you made. I'll check things out here."

I fished in the pack for an explosive as she cracked open the door that didn't have the security pad and then stepped through.

I attached the small device to the hole I'd made, then noticed some exposed wires in the lower part of the wall.

I followed them down and was prying up a section of the floor when Megan came back.

"There are two other rooms like this," she said. "No people in them, small and built up against the elevator shaft. Best I can figure, this is where furnace equipment and elevator maintenance is supposed to be, but they hid some rooms here instead and took them off the building schematics. I wonder if there's space between other floors—if there are rooms hidden there too."

"Look at this," I said, pointing at what I'd discovered.

She knelt beside me and eyed the wall and the wiring.

"Explosives," she said.

"The room's *already* set to blow," I said. "Creepy, eh?"

"Whatever is in here," Megan said, "it must be important. Important enough that it's worth destroying the entire power plant to keep it from being discovered."

We both looked up at the computers.

"What are you two doing?" Cody's voice came back onto our feed.

"We found this room," I said, "and—"

"Keep moving," Cody said, cutting me off. "Prof and Abraham just ran into some guards and were forced to shoot them. The guards are down, bodies hidden, but they'll be missed soon. If we're lucky we'll have a few minutes before someone realizes they're not on their patrol anymore."

I cursed, fishing in my pocket.

"What's that?" Megan asked.

"One of the universal blasting caps I got from Diamond," I said. "I want to see if they work." I nervously used my electrical tape to stick the little round nub on the explosives we'd found under the floor. In my pocket I carried its detonator—the one that looked like a pen.

"By the map Tia gave us," Megan said, "we're only two rooms

over from the storage area with the energy cells, but we're a little below it."

We shared a glance, then split up to scour the hidden room. We might not have much time, but we needed to at least *try* to find out what information this place contained. She pulled open a filing cabinet and grabbed a handful of folders. In an instant I was up and opening desk drawers. One had a couple of data chips. I grabbed them, waved them at Megan, then tossed them in her bag. She threw the folders in, then searched another desk while I raised a hand to the right wall and made us a hole.

Since the hidden room was halfway between two floors, I wasn't certain how that related to the rest of the building. I made a hole in the wall in the direction we wanted to go, but I made it near the ceiling.

That opened up into a room on the third floor, but near the floor. So there was some overlap between our hidden room and the third floor. With a glance at the map, I could see how they'd hidden the room. On the schematics the elevator shaft was shown as slightly bigger than it actually was. It also included a maintenance shaft that wasn't actually there—and that explained the lack of handholds in the elevator. The builders assumed the maintenance shaft would provide a way to service the elevator, not knowing that the hidden room would actually go in that space.

Megan and I climbed through the hole and onto the third floor. We crossed that room—a conference room of some sort—and passed through another, which was a monitoring station. I vaporized the wall and opened a hole into a long, low-ceilinged storage area. This was our target: the room where the power cells were kept.

"We're in," Megan said to Cody as we slipped inside. The room was filled with shelves, and on them were various pieces of electrical equipment, none of which we wanted.

We went in different directions, searching hastily.

"Awesome," Cody said. "The power cells should be in there

somewhere. Look for cylinders about a handspan wide and about as tall as a boot."

I spied some large storage lockers on the far wall, with locks on the doors. "Might be in here," I said to Megan, moving toward them. I made quick work of the locks with the tensor and pulled the doors open as she joined me. Inside one was a tall column of green cylinders stacked on top of one another on their sides. Each cylinder looked vaguely like a cross between a very small beer keg and a car battery.

"Those are the power cells," Cody said, sounding relieved. "I was half worried there wouldn't be any. Good thing I brought my four-leaf clover on this operation."

"Four-leaf clover?" Megan said with a snort as she fished something out of her pack.

"Sure. From the homeland."

"That's the Irish, Cody, not the Scottish."

"I know," Cody said without missing a beat. "I had to kill an Irish dude to get mine."

I pulled out one of the power cells. "They aren't as heavy as I thought they'd be," I said. "Are we sure these will have enough juice to power the gauss gun? That thing needs a *lot* of energy."

"Those cells were charged by Conflux," Cody said in my ear. "They're more powerful by magnitudes than anything we could make or buy. If they won't work, nothing will. Grab as many as you can carry."

They might not have been as heavy as I'd thought, but they were still kind of bulky. We took the rest of the equipment out of Megan's pack, then retrieved the smaller sack we had stuffed in the bottom. I managed to stuff four of the cells in the pack while Megan transferred the rest of our equipment—a few explosive charges, some rope, and some ammunition—to her smaller sack. There were also some lab coats for disguises. I left these out—I suspected we'd need them to escape.

"How are Prof and Abraham?" I asked.

"On their way out," Cody said.

"And our extraction?" I asked. "Prof said we shouldn't go back down the elevator shaft."

"You have your lab coats?" Cody asked.

"Sure," Megan said. "But if we go in the hallways, they might record our faces."

"That's a risk we'll have to take," Cody said. "First explosion is a go in two minutes."

We threw on the lab coats, and I squatted down and let Megan help me put on the backpack with the power cells. It was heavy, but I could still move reasonably well. Megan threw on her lab coat. It looked good on her, but pretty much anything would. She swung her own lighter pack over her shoulder, then eyed my rifle.

"It can be disassembled," I explained as I pulled the stock from the rifle, then popped out the magazine and removed the cartridge from the chamber. I slid on the safety just in case, then stuffed the pieces in her sack.

The coats were embroidered with Station Seven's logo, and we both had fake security badges to go with them. The disguises would never have worked getting us in—security was far too tight—but in a moment of chaos, they should get us out.

The building shook with an ominous rumble—explosion number one. That was mostly to prompt an evacuation rather than to inflict any real damage.

"Go!" Cody yelled in our ears.

I vaporized the lock on the door to the room and the two of us burst out into the hallway. People were peeking out of doors—it seemed to be a busy floor, even at night. Some of the people were cleaning staff in blue overalls, but others were technicians in lab coats.

"Explosion!" I did my best to seem panicked. "Someone's attacking the building!"

The chaos started immediately, and we were soon swept up into the crowd fleeing from the building. About thirty seconds later, Cody triggered the second explosion, on an upper floor. The ground trembled and people in the hallway around us screamed, glancing at the ceiling. Some of the dozen or so people clutched small computers or briefcases.

There wasn't actually anything to be frightened of. These initial explosions had been set in unpopulated locations that wouldn't bring down the building. There would be four of those early blasts, and they'd been placed to shepherd all the civilians out of the structure. Then the real explosions could begin.

We made a hasty flight through hallways and down stairwells, being careful to keep our heads down. Something felt odd about the place, and as we ran I realized what it was. The building was clean. The floors, the walls, the rooms . . . too clean. It had been too dark for me to notice it when we were making our way in, but in the light, it seemed stark to me. The understreets weren't ever this clean. It didn't feel right for everything to be so scrubbed, so neat.

As we ran it became clear that the place was big enough that any one employee wouldn't know everyone else who worked there, and though our intelligence said that the security officers had the faces of all employees in portfolios that they checked against security feeds, no one challenged us.

Most of the security officers were running with the growing crowd, just as worried about the explosions as everyone else, and that dampened my fears even more.

As a group we flooded down the last flight of stairs and burst out into the lobby. "What's going on?" a security officer yelled. He was standing by the exit with his gun out and aimed. "Did anyone see anything?"

"An Epic!" Megan said breathlessly. "Wearing green. I saw him walking through the building throwing out blasts of energy!"

The third explosion went off, shaking the building. It was followed by a series of smaller explosions. Other groups of people flooded out of adjacent stairwells and from the ground-floor hallways.

The guard cursed, then did the smart thing. He ran too. He wouldn't be expected to face an Epic—indeed, he could get in trouble for doing it, even if that Epic was working against Steelheart. Ordinary men left Epics alone, end of story. In the Fractured States that was a law greater than any other.

We burst out of the building and onto the grounds. I glanced back to see trails of smoke rising from the enormous structure. Even as I watched, another series of small explosions went off in an upper row of windows, each one flashing green. Prof and Abraham hadn't just planted bombs, they'd planted a light show.

"It *is* an Epic," a woman near me breathed. "Who would be so foolish . . ."

I flashed a smile at Megan, and we joined the flood of people running to the gates in the wall surrounding the grounds. The guards there tried to hold people in, but when the next explosion went off they gave up and opened the gates. Megan and I followed the others out into the dark streets of the city, leaving the smoldering building behind.

"Security cameras are still up," Cody reported on the open channel to everyone. "Building is still evacuating."

"Hold the last explosions," Prof said calmly. "But blow the leaflets."

There was a soft pop from behind, and I knew that the leaflets proclaiming that a new Epic had come to town had been blasted from the upper floors and were floating down to the city. Limelight, we were calling him—the name I'd chosen. The flyer was filled with propaganda calling Steelheart out, claiming that Limelight was the new master of Newcago.

Megan and I were to our car before Cody gave the all clear. I climbed in the driver's side, and Megan followed through the same door, shoving me over into the passenger seat.

"I can drive," I said.

"You destroyed the last car going around one block, Knees," she said, starting the vehicle. "Knocked down two signs, I believe. And I think I saw the remains of some trash cans as we fled." There was a faint smile on her lips.

"Wasn't my fault," I said, thrilled by our success as I looked back at Station Seven rising into the dark sky. "Those trash cans were totally asking for it. Cheeky slontzes."

"I'm triggering the big one," Cody said in my ear.

A line of blasts sounded in the building, including the explosives Megan and I had placed, I guessed. The building shook, fires burning out the windows.

"Huh," Cody said, confused. "Didn't bring it down."

"Good enough," Prof answered. "Evidence of our incursion is gone, and the station won't be operating anytime soon."

"Yeah," Cody said. I could hear the disappointment in his voice. "I just wish it had been a little more dramatic."

I pulled the pen detonator from my pocket. It probably wouldn't do anything—the explosives we'd placed on the walls had probably already set off the ones in the floor. I clicked the top of the pen anyway.

The following explosion was about ten times as strong as the previous one. Our car shook and debris sprayed out over the city, dust and bits of rock raining down. Megan and I both spun around in our seats in time to catch the building collapse in an awful-sounding crunch.

"Wow," Cody said. "Look at that. I guess some of the power cells went up."

Megan glanced at me, then at the pen, then rolled her eyes. In seconds we were racing down the street in the opposite direction of fire trucks and emergency responders, heading for the rendezvous point with the other Reckoners.

PART THREE

23

I grunted, hauling the rope hand over hand. A plaintive squeak came from the pulley system with each draw, as if I had strapped some unfortunate mouse to a torture device and was twisting with glee.

The construction had been set up around the tunnel into the Reckoner burrow, which was the only way in or out. It had been five days since our attack on the power station, and we'd been lying low during most of that, planning our next move—the hit on Conflux to undermine Enforcement.

Abraham had just gotten back from a supply run. Which meant that I'd stopped being one of the team's tensor specialists and started being their source of free teenage labor.

I continued pulling, sweat dripping from my brow and beginning to soak through my T-shirt. Eventually the crate appeared from the depths of the hole, and Megan pulled it off its rollers and heaved it into the room. I let go of the rope, sending the roller board and rope back down the tunnel so Abraham could tie on another crate of supplies.

"You want to do the next one?" I asked Megan, wiping my brow with a towel.

"No," she said lightly. She heaved the crate onto a dolly and wheeled it over to stack it with the others.

"You sure?" I asked, arms aching.

"You're doing such a fine job," she said. "And it's good exercise." She settled the crate, then sat down on a chair, putting her feet up on the desk and sipping a lemonade while reading a book on her mobile.

I shook my head. She was unbelievable.

"Think of it as being chivalrous," Megan said absently, tapping the screen to scroll down more text. "Protecting a defenseless girl from pain and all that."

"Defenseless?" I asked as Abraham called up. I sighed, then started pulling the rope again.

She nodded. "In an abstract way."

"How can someone be *abstractly* defenseless?"

"Takes a lot of work," she said, then sipped her drink. "It only *looks* easy. Just like abstract art."

I grunted. "Abstract art?" I asked, heaving on the rope.

"Sure. You know, guy paints a black line on a canvas, calls it a metaphor, sells it for millions."

"That never happened."

She looked up at me, amused. "Sure it did. You never learned about abstract art in school?"

"I was schooled at the Factory," I said. "Basic math, reading, geography, history. Wasn't time for anything else."

"But before that. Before Calamity."

"I was eight," I said. "And I lived in inner-city Chicago, Megan.

My education mostly involved learning to avoid gangs and how to keep my head down at school."

"That's what you learned when you were *eight*? In grade school?"

I shrugged and kept pulling. She seemed troubled by what I'd said, though I'll admit, I was troubled by what she'd said. People hadn't really paid that much money for such simple things, had they? It baffled me. Pre-Calamity people had been a strange lot.

I hauled the next crate up, and Megan hopped down from her chair again to move it. I couldn't imagine that she was getting much reading done, but she didn't seem bothered by the interruptions. I watched her, taking a long gulp from my cup of water.

Things had been . . . different between us since her confession in the elevator shaft. In a lot of ways she was more relaxed around me, which didn't make that much sense. Shouldn't things have been more awkward? I knew she didn't support our mission. That felt like a pretty big deal to me.

She really *was* a professional, though. She didn't agree that Steelheart should be killed, but she didn't abandon the Reckoners, or even ask for a transfer to another Reckoner cell. I didn't know how many of those there were—apparently only Tia and Prof knew—but there was at least one other.

Either way, Megan stayed on board and didn't let her feelings distract her from her job. She might not agree that Steelheart needed to die, but from what I'd pried from her, she believed in fighting the Epics. She was like a soldier who believed a certain battle wasn't tactically sound, yet supported the generals enough to fight it anyway.

I respected her for that. Sparks, I was liking her more and more. And though she hadn't been particularly affectionate toward me lately, she wasn't openly hostile and cold any longer. That left me room to work some seductive magic. I wished I knew some.

She got the crate in place, and I waited for Abraham to call up that I should start pulling again. Instead he appeared at the mouth of the tunnel and started to unhook the pulley system. His shoulder had been healed from the gunshot using the harmsway, the Reckoner device that helped flesh heal extraordinarily fast.

I didn't know much about it, though I'd spoken to Cody—he'd called it the "last of the three." Three bits of incredible technology brought to the Reckoners from Prof's days as a scientist. The tensors, the jackets, the harmsway. From what Abraham told me, Prof had developed each technology and then stolen them from the lab he'd worked in, intent on starting his own war against the Epics.

Abraham got the last parts of the pulley down.

"Are we done?" I asked.

"Indeed."

"I counted more crates than that."

"The others are too big to fit through the tunnel," Abraham said. "Cody's going to drive them over to the hangar."

That was what they called the place where they kept their vehicles. I'd been there; it was a large chamber with a few cars and a van inside. It wasn't nearly as secure as this hideout was—the hangar had to have access to the upper city and couldn't be part of the understreets.

Abraham walked over to the stack of a dozen crates we'd heaved into the hideout. He rubbed his chin, inspecting them. "We might as well unload these," he said. "I've got another hour to spare."

"Before what?" I asked, joining him at the crates.

He didn't reply.

"You've been gone a lot these last few days," I noted.

Again, he didn't reply.

"He's not going to tell you where he's been, Knees," Megan said from her lounging position at the desk. "And get used to it. Prof sends him out on secret errands a lot."

"But . . . ," I said, feeling hurt. I'd thought I'd earned my place on the team.

"Do not be saddened, David," Abraham said, grabbing a crowbar to crack open one of the crates. "It is not a matter of trust. We must keep some things secret, even within the team, should one of us be taken captive. Steelheart has his way of getting to what one hides—nobody except Prof should know everything we are doing."

It was a good rationale, and it was probably why I couldn't know about other Reckoner cells either, but it was still annoying. As Abraham cracked open another crate, I reached to the pouch at my side and slipped out my tensor. With that, I vaporized the wooden lids off a few crates.

Abraham raised an eyebrow at me.

"What?" I said. "Cody told me to keep practicing."

"You are growing quite good," Abraham said. Then he reached into one of the crates I'd opened and fished out an apple, which was now covered in sawdust. It made something of a mess getting it out. "Quite good," he continued. "But sometimes, the crowbar is more effective, eh? Besides, we may wish to reuse these crates."

I sighed, but nodded. It was just . . . well, hard. The sense of strength I'd felt during the power station infiltration was difficult to forget. Opening the holes in the walls and creating those handholds, I'd been able to bend matter to my will. The more I used the tensor, the more excited I grew about the possibilities it offered.

"It is also important," Abraham said, "to avoid leaving traces of what we can do. Imagine if everyone knew about these things, eh? It would be a different world, more difficult for us."

I nodded, reluctantly putting the tensor away. "Too bad we had to leave that hole for Diamond to see."

Abraham hesitated, just briefly. "Yes," he said. "Too bad."

I helped him unload the supplies, and Megan joined us, working with characteristic efficiency. She ended up doing a lot of supervising, telling us where to stow the various foodstuffs. Abraham accepted her direction without complaint, even though she was the junior member of the team.

About halfway through the unloading, Prof came out of his planning room. He walked over to us while scanning through some papers in a folder.

"Did you learn anything, Prof?" Abraham asked.

"Rumors are going our way, for once," Prof said, tossing the folder onto Tia's desk. "The city's buzzing with the news of a new Epic come to challenge Steelheart. Half the city is talking about it, while the other half is bunkering down in their basements, waiting for the fighting to blow over."

"That's great!" I said.

"Yes." Prof seemed troubled.

"What's wrong, then?" I asked.

He tapped the folder. "Did Tia tell you what was on those data chips you brought back from the power plant?"

I shook my head, trying to hide my curiosity. Was he going to tell me? Perhaps it would give me a clue to what Abraham had been up to the last few days.

"It's propaganda," Prof said. "We think you found a hidden public manipulation wing of Steelheart's government. The files you brought back included press releases, outlines of rumors planned to be started, and stories of things Steelheart has done. Most of those stories and rumors are false, so far as Tia can determine."

"He wouldn't be the first ruler to fabricate a grand history for himself," Abraham noted, stowing some canned chicken on one of the shelves that had been carved to fill the entire wall of the back room.

"But why would Steelheart need to do that?" I asked, wiping my brow. "I mean . . . he's practically immortal. It's not like he needs to look more powerful than he is."

"He's arrogant," Abraham said. "Everybody knows this. You can see it in his eyes, in how he speaks, in what he does."

"Yes," Prof said. "Which is why these rumors are so confusing. The stories aren't meant to bolster him—or if they are, he has an odd way of going about it. Most of the stories are about atrocities he's committed. People he's murdered, buildings—even small towns—he has supposedly wiped out. But none of it has actually happened."

"He's spreading rumors about having slaughtered towns full of people?" Megan asked, sounding troubled.

"So far as we can tell," Prof said. He joined in, helping unload the crates. Megan had stopped giving orders, I noticed, now that he was around. "Someone, at least, wants Steelheart to sound more terrible than he really is."

"Maybe we found some kind of revolutionary group," I said, eager.

"Doubtful," Prof said. "Inside one of the major government buildings? With that kind of security? Besides, what you told me seems to imply the guards knew of the place. Anyway, many of these stories are accompanied by documentation claiming they were devised by Steelheart himself. It even notes their falsehood, and the need to substantiate them with made-up facts."

"He's been bragging," Abraham said, "and making things up—only now, his ministry has to make all of his claims sound true. Otherwise he'll look foolish."

Prof nodded, and my heart sank. I'd assumed that we'd found something important. Instead all I'd discovered was a department dedicated to making Steelheart look good. And more evil. Or something.

"So Steelheart is not as terrible as he would like us to think," Abraham said.

"Oh, he's pretty terrible," Prof said. "Wouldn't you say, David?"

"Over seventeen thousand confirmed deaths to his name," I said absently. "It's in my notes. Many were innocents. They can't all be fabrications."

"And they're not," Prof said. "He's a terrible, awful individual. He just wants to make sure that we all know it."

"How strange," Abraham said.

221

I dug into a crate of cheeses, getting out the paper-wrapped blocks and loading them in the cold-storage pit on the far side of the room. So many of the foods the Reckoners ate were things I'd never been able to afford. Cheese, fresh fruit. Most food in Newcago had to be shipped in because of the darkness. It was impossible to grow fruit and vegetables outside, and Steelheart was careful to keep a firm hold on the farmlands surrounding the city.

Expensive foods. I was already getting used to eating them. Odd, how quickly that could happen.

"Prof," I said, placing a cheese wheel in the pit, "do you ever wonder if maybe Newcago will be worse without Steelheart than it is with him?"

At the other side of the room, Megan turned sharply to look at me, but I didn't look at her. *I won't tell him what you said, so stop glaring at me. I just want to know.*

"It probably will be," Prof said. "For a while at least. The infrastructure of the city will probably collapse. Food will get scarce. Unless someone powerful takes Steelheart's place and secures Enforcement, there will be looting."

"But—"

"You want your revenge, son? Well, that's the cost. I won't sugarcoat it. We try to keep from hurting innocents, but when we kill Steelheart, we'll cause suffering."

I sat down beside the cold-storage hole.

"Did you never think of this?" Abraham asked. He'd gotten that necklace out from underneath his shirt and was rubbing his finger on it. "In all those years of planning, preparing to kill the one you hated, did you never consider what would happen to Newcago?"

I blushed, but then I shook my head. I hadn't. "So . . . what do we do?"

"Continue as we have," Prof said. "Our job is to cut out the infected flesh. Only then can the body start to heal—but it's going to hurt a lot first."

"But . . ."

Prof turned to me, and I saw something in his expression. A deep exhaustion, the tiredness of one who had been fighting a war for a long, long time. "It's good for you to think of this, son. Ponder. Worry. Stay up nights, frightened for the casualties of your ideology. It will do you good to realize the price of fighting.

"I need to warn you of something, however. There aren't any answers to be found. There are no good choices. Submissiveness to a tyrant or chaos and suffering. In the end I chose the second, though it flays my soul to do so. If we don't fight, humankind is finished. We slowly become sheep to the Epics, slaves and servants—stagnant.

"This isn't just about revenge or payback. It's about the survival of our race. It's about men being the masters of their own destiny. I choose suffering and uncertainty over becoming a lapdog."

"That's all well and good," Megan said, "to choose for yourself. But Prof, you're *not* just choosing for yourself. You're choosing for everyone in the city."

"So I am." He slid some cans onto the shelf.

"In the end," Megan said, "they *don't* get to be masters of their own destinies. They get to be dominated by Steelheart or left to fend for themselves—at least until another Epic comes along to dominate them again."

"Then we'll kill him too," Prof said softly.

"How many can you kill?" Megan said. "You can't stop all of the Epics, Prof. Eventually another one will set up here. You think he'll be *better* than Steelheart?"

"Enough, Megan," Prof said. "We've spoken of this already, and I made my decision."

"Newcago is one of the best places in the Fractured States to live," Megan continued, ignoring Prof's comment. "We should be focusing on Epics who *aren't* good administrators, places where life is worse."

"No," Prof said, his voice sounding gruffer.

"Why not?"

"Because that's the problem!" he snapped. "Everyone talks about how great Newcago is. But it's *not* great, Megan. It's good by comparison only! Yes, there are worse places, but so long as this hellhole is considered the ideal, we'll never get anywhere. *We cannot let them convince us this is normal!*"

The room fell still, Megan looking taken aback by Prof's outburst. I sat down, my shoulders slumping.

This wasn't anything like I'd imagined. The glorious Reckoners, bringing justice to the Epics. I hadn't once thought of the guilt they'd bear, the arguments, the uncertainty. I could see it in them, the same fear I'd had in the power plant. The worry that we might be making things worse, that we might end up as bad as the Epics.

Prof stalked away, waving a hand in frustration. I heard the curtain rustle as he retreated back to his thinking room. Megan watched him go, red-faced with anger.

"It is not so bad, Megan," Abraham said quietly. He still seemed calm. "It will be all right."

"How can you say that?" she asked.

"We don't need to defeat all of the Epics, you see," Abraham said. He was holding a chain in his dark-skinned hand, with a small pendant dangling from it. "We just need to hold out long enough."

"I'm not going to listen to your foolishness, Abraham," she said. "Not right now." With that she turned and left the storage room. She crawled into the tunnel that led down to the steel catacombs and vanished.

Abraham sighed, then turned to me. "You look unwell, David."

"I feel sick," I said honestly. "I thought . . . well, if anyone had the answers, I thought it would be the Reckoners."

"You mistake us," Abraham said, walking over to me. "You mistake Prof. Do not look to the executioner for the reason his blade falls. And Prof *is* society's executioner, the warrior for mankind. Others will come to rebuild."

224

"But doesn't it bother you?" I asked.

"Not unduly," Abraham answered simply, putting his necklace back on. "But then, I have a hope the others do not."

I could now see the pendant he wore. It was small and silver, with a stylized *S* symbol on it. I thought I recognized that symbol from somewhere. It reminded me of my father.

"You're one of the Faithful," I guessed. I'd heard of them, though I'd never met one. The Factory raised realists, not dreamers, and to be one of the Faithful you had to be a dreamer.

Abraham nodded.

"How can you still believe that good Epics will come?" I asked. "I mean, it's been over ten years."

"Ten years is not so long," Abraham said. "Not in the big picture of things. Why, humankind is not so old a species, compared to the big picture! The heroes *will* come. Someday we will have Epics that do not kill, do not hate, do not dominate. We will be protected."

Idiot, I thought. It was a gut reaction, though I immediately felt bad about it. Abraham wasn't an idiot. He was a wise man, or had seemed so until this moment. But . . . how could he really still think there would be *good* Epics? It was the same reasoning that had gotten my father killed.

Though at least he has something to look forward to, I thought. Would it be so bad, to wish for some mythical group of heroic Epics—to wait for them to come and provide salvation?

Abraham squeezed my shoulder and gave me a smile, then walked away. I stood and caught sight of him following Prof into the thinking room, something I'd never seen any of the others do. I soon heard soft conversation.

I shook my head. I considered continuing with the unloading, but found I didn't have a heart for it. I glanced at the tunnel down to the catacombs. On a whim I climbed in and went to see if I could find Megan.

24

MEGAN hadn't gone far. I found her at the bottom of the tunnel, sitting on a pile of old crates just outside the hideout. I walked up, hesitantly, and she shot me a suspicious glance. Her expression softened after a moment, and she turned back to studying the darkness in front of her. She had her mobile turned all the way up to give light.

I climbed up on the crates beside her and sat, but didn't speak. I wanted to have the perfect thing to say, and—as usual—I couldn't figure out what that would be. Trouble was, I basically agreed with Prof, even though it made me feel guilty that I did. I didn't have the schooling to predict what would happen to Newcago if its leader were killed. But I *did* know Steelheart was evil. No court would convict him, but I had a right to seek justice for the things he had done to me and mine.

So I just sat there, trying to formulate something to say that wouldn't offend her but that also wouldn't sound lame. It's harder than it seems—which is probably why I just say what comes to me most of the time. When I stop to think, I can never come up with anything.

"He really is a monster," Megan eventually said. "I know that he is. I hate sounding like I'm defending him. I just don't know if killing him is going to be good for the very people we're trying to protect."

I nodded. I got it, I really did. We fell silent again. As we sat I could hear distant sounds in the corridors, distorted by the bizarre composition and acoustics of the steel catacombs. Sometimes you could hear water rushing, as the city sewage pipes ran nearby. Other times I swore I could hear rats, though it baffled me what they could be living on down here. Other times the land seemed to be groaning softly.

"What *are* they, Megan?" I asked. "Have you ever wondered that?"

"You mean the Epics?" she asked. "Lots of people have theories."

"I know. But what do you think?"

She didn't reply immediately. Lots of people did have theories, and most would be happy to tell you about them. The Epics were the next stage in human evolution, or they were a punishment sent by this god or that, or they were really aliens. Or they were the result of a secret government project. Or it was all fake and they were using technology to pretend they had powers.

Most of the theories fell apart when confronted by facts. Normal people had gained powers and become Epics; they weren't aliens or anything like that. There were enough direct stories of a family member manifesting abilities. Scientists claimed to be baffled by the genetics of Epics, but I didn't know much about that kind of thing. Besides, most of the scientists were either gone now or worked for one of the more powerful Epics.

Anyway, a lot of the rumors were silly, but that had never stopped them from spreading, and probably never would.

"I think they're a test of some kind," Megan said.

I frowned. "You mean, like religiously?"

"No, not a test of faith or anything like that," Megan said. "I mean a test of what we'll do, if we have power. Enormous power. What would it do to us? How would we deal with it?"

I sniffed. "If the Epics are an example of what we'd do with power, then it's better if we never get any."

She fell silent. A few moments later I heard another odd sound. Whistling.

I turned and was surprised to see Cody walking down the corridor. He was alone, and on foot, which meant he'd left the industrial scooter—which had pulled the crates of supplies—in the hangar. He had his gun over his shoulder and wore his baseball cap embroidered with the supposed coat of arms of his Scottish clan. He tipped the cap to us.

"So . . . we having a party?" he asked. He checked his mobile. "Is it time for tea?"

"Tea?" I asked. "I've never seen you drink tea."

"I usually have some fish sticks and a bag of potato chips," Cody said. "It's a British thing. Y'all are Yanks and wouldn't understand."

Something seemed off about that statement, but I didn't know enough to call him on it.

"So why the dour expressions?" Cody asked, hopping up beside us on the crates. "You two look like a pair of coon hunters on a rainy day."

Wow, I thought. *Why can't I come up with metaphors like that?*

"Prof and I got into an argument," Megan said with a sigh.

"Again? I thought you two were past that. What was it about this time?"

"Nothing I want to talk about."

"Fair enough, fair enough." Cody got out his long hunter's knife and began trimming his fingernails. "Nightwielder's been out in the city. People are reporting him all over, passing through walls, looking in on dens of miscreants and lesser Epics. It has everyone on edge."

"That's good," I said. "It means Steelheart is taking the threat seriously."

"Maybe," Cody said. "Maybe. He ain't said anything about the challenge we left him yet, and Nightwielder is checking in on a lot of regular folks. Steelheart might suspect that someone's trying to blow smoke up his kilt."

"Maybe we should hit Nightwielder," I said. "We know his weakness now."

"Might be a good idea," Cody said, fishing a long, slender device out of his hip pack. He tossed it to me.

"What's this?"

"UV flashlight," he said. "I managed to find a place that sold them— or, well, bulbs anyway, which I put in the flashlights and fixed us up a few. Best to be ready in case Nightwielder surprises us."

"Do you think he'll come here?" I asked.

"He'll start in on the steel catacombs eventually," Cody said. "Maybe he's started already. Having a defensible base means nothing if Nightwielder just decides to phase through the walls and strangle us in our sleep."

Cheery thoughts. I shivered.

"At least we can fight him now," Cody said, fishing out another flashlight for Megan. "But I think we're poorly prepared. We still don't know what Steelheart's weakness is. What if he *does* challenge Limelight?"

"Tia will find the answer," I said. "She has a lot of leads in discovering what was in that bank vault."

"And Firefight?" Cody said. "We haven't even *started* planning how to deal with him."

Firefight, the other of Steelheart's High Epic bodyguards. Megan looked at me, obviously curious as to what I'd say next.

"Firefight won't be a problem," I said.

"So you said before, when you pitched this whole thing to us. But you ain't said why yet."

"I've talked it over with Tia," I said. "Firefight's not what you think he is." I was reasonably confident about that. "Come on, I'll show you."

Cody raised an eyebrow but followed as I crawled back up the tunnel. Prof already knew what my notes said, though I wasn't certain he believed. I knew he was planning a meeting to talk about Firefight and Nightwielder, but I *also* knew that he was waiting on Tia before moving too far ahead in the plan. If she didn't come up with the answer to how to kill Steelheart, nothing else would matter.

I didn't want to think about that. Giving up now because we didn't know his weakness . . . it would be like finding out that you'd drawn lots for dessert at the Factory and been only one number off. Only it didn't matter, because Pete already snuck in to steal the dessert, so nobody was going to get any anyway—not even Pete, because it turns out that there had never been any dessert in the first place. Well, something like that. That metaphor's a work in progress.

At the top of the tunnel I led Cody to the box where we kept my notes. I flipped through them for a few minutes, noting that Megan had followed us up. She had an unreadable expression on her face.

I grabbed the folder on Firefight and brought it over to the desk, spreading out some pictures. "What do you know about Firefight?"

"Fire Epic," Cody said, pointing at a photo. It showed a person made of flames, the heat so intense the air around him warped. No photo could capture the details of Firefight's features, as they were composed of solid flames. In fact, each photo I pulled out showed him glowing so brightly that it distorted the picture.

"He's got standard fire Epic powers," Megan said. "He can turn to flame—in fact, he pretty much always remains in fire form. He can fly, throw fire from his hands, and manipulate existing flames. He creates an intense heat field around him, capable of melting bullets—though they likely couldn't hurt him even if they didn't melt. It's a basic fire Epic portfolio."

"Too basic," I said. "Every Epic has quirks. Nobody has *exactly* the same portfolio of powers. That was what first tipped me off. Here's the other clue." I tapped the series of photographs—each was a shot of Firefight taken on a different day, usually with Steelheart and his retinue. Though Nightwielder often went out on missions, Firefight usually remained near Steelheart to act as first-line body-guard.

"Do you see it?" I asked.

"See what?" Cody asked.

"Here," I said, pointing to a man standing with Steelheart's guards in one of the pictures. He was slender and clean-shaven and wore a stiff suit, a pair of dark shades, and a wide-brimmed hat that obscured his face.

I pointed to the next photo. The same person was there. And the next photo. And the next. His face was hard to make out in the other pictures too—none of them were focused on him specifically, and the hat and shades always masked his features.

"This person is always there when Firefight appears," I said. "It's suspicious. Who is it, and what is he doing there?"

Megan frowned. "What are you implying?"

"Here," I said, "take a look at these." I got out a sequence of five photos, a rapid-fire series of shots capturing a few moments. The scene was Steelheart flying through the city with a procession of his minions. He did that sometimes. Though he always looked like he was going somewhere important, I suspected these were really just his version of a parade.

Nightwielder and Firefight were with him, flying about ten feet above the ground. A cavalcade of cars drove beneath, like a military convoy. I couldn't make out any faces, though I suspected the suspicious person was among them.

Five pictures. Four of them showed the trio of Epics flying side by side. And in one of them—right in the middle of the sequence—Firefight's shape had fuzzed and gone translucent.

"Firefight can go incorporeal, like Nightwielder?" Cody guessed.

"No," I said. "Firefight's not real."

Cody blinked. "What?"

"He's not real. At least, not in the way we think. Firefight is an incredibly intricate—and incredibly clever—illusion. I suspect that the person we're seeing in those photos, the one wearing the suit and hat, is the true Epic. He's an illusionist, capable of manipulating light to create images, a lot like Refractionary—only on a much more powerful level. Together the real Firefight and Steelheart concocted the idea of a fake Epic much the same way we're concocting Limelight. In these photos we're catching a moment of distraction, when the real Epic wasn't concentrating on his illusion and it wobbled and nearly vanished."

"A fake Epic?" Megan said, dismissive. "What would be the point? Steelheart wouldn't need to do that."

"Steelheart has a strange psychology," I said. "Trust me. I'll bet I know him better than anyone other than his closest allies. He's arrogant, like Abraham said, but he's *also* paranoid. Much of what he does is about holding on to power, about forcing people into line. He moves the location of his sleeping quarters. Why would he need to do that? He's immune to harm, right? He's paranoid, scared that someone will discover his weakness. He destroyed the entire bank because we might have had a *hint* at how he was hurt."

"Lots of Epics would do that," Cody noted.

"That's because most Epics are equally paranoid. Look, what better way to surprise would-be assassins than to make them prepare for an Epic that isn't there? If they spend all their time planning how to kill Firefight, then go up against an illusionist instead, they'll be caught totally off guard."

"So will we, if you're right," Cody said. "Fighting illusionists is tough. I hate not being able to trust my eyes."

"Look, an illusionist Epic can't explain everything," Megan said. "There are recorded events of Firefight melting bullets."

"Firefight made the bullets vanish when they reached the illusion, then made illusory melted bullets drop to the ground. Later some of Steelheart's minions went and spread some actual melted bullets down as proof." I took out another pair of pictures. "I've got evidence of them doing just that. I have mountains of documentation on this, Megan. You're welcome to read through it. Tia agrees with me."

I picked up a few more pictures from the stack. "Take this. Here, we've got photos of a time that Firefight 'burned' down a building. I took these pictures myself; see how he's throwing fire? If you look at the scorch marks on the walls the following day in this next set, they're different from the blasts Firefight created. The real scorch marks were added by a team of workers in the night. They cleared everyone from the scene, so I couldn't get pictures of them, but the next day's evidence is clear."

Megan looked deeply troubled.

"What?" Cody said.

"It's what you said," she replied. "Illusionists. They're annoying. I'm just hoping we don't have to face one."

"I don't think we'll have to," I said. "I've thought it through and, despite Firefight's reputation, he doesn't seem terribly dangerous. I can't squarely attribute any deaths to him, and he rarely fights. It has to be because he wants to be careful not to reveal what he really is. I've got the facts in these folders. As soon as Firefight appears, all we have to do is shoot the one creating the illusion—this man in the photos—and all of his illusions will go down. It shouldn't be too hard."

"Y'all might be right about the illusions," Cody said, looking through another group of photos. "But I'm not sure about this person you think is making them. If Firefight were smart, he'd create the illusion, then turn himself invisible."

"It's possible he can't," I said. "Not all illusionists are capable of that, even powerful ones." I hesitated. "But you're right. We can't know for certain who's making the fake Firefight, but I still think Firefight won't be a problem. All we need to do is spook him—set up a trap that will expose his illusion as fake. When he's threatened with being revealed, I'll bet he bolts. From what I've been able to determine about him, he seems like something of a coward."

Cody nodded thoughtfully.

Megan shook her head. "I think you're taking this too lightly." She sounded angry. "If Steelheart really has been fooling everyone all this time, then it's likely that Firefight is even more dangerous than we thought. Something about this bothers me; I don't think we're prepared for it."

"You're looking for a reason to call off this mission anyway," I said, annoyed at her.

"I never said that."

"You didn't need to. It—"

I was interrupted by motion at the tunnel into the hideout and I turned in time to see Tia climbing through, wearing old jeans and her Reckoner jacket. Her knees were dusty. She stood up, smiling. "We've found it."

My heart leaped in my chest and sent what felt like electricity jolting through my body. "Steelheart's weakness? You found out what it is?"

"No," she said, her eyes seeming to glow with excitement. "But this should lead to the answers. I found *it*."

"What, Tia?" Cody asked.

"The bank vault."

25

"I first started considering this possibility when you told your story, David," Tia explained. The entire team of Reckoners was following her down a tunnel in the steel catacombs. "And the more I investigated the bank, the more curious I became. There are oddities."

"Oddities?" I asked. The group moved in a tense huddle, Cody taking point, Abraham watching our tail. He had replaced his very nice machine gun with a similar one, only without quite as many bells and whistles.

I felt pretty comfortable with him at our back. These narrow confines would make a heavy machine gun especially deadly to anyone trying to approach us; the walls would work like bumpers on the sides of a bowling lane, and Abraham wouldn't have any trouble at all getting strikes.

"The Diggers," Prof said. He was at my side. "They weren't allowed to excavate the area beneath where the bank had stood."

"Yes," Tia said, speaking eagerly. "It was very irregular. Steelheart barely gave them any direction. The chaos of these lower catacombs proves that; their madness made them hard to control. But one order he was firm on: the area beneath the bank was to be left alone. I wouldn't have thought twice about that if it hadn't been for what you described, that Steelheart had most of the main room of the bank turned to steel by the time Faultline came that afternoon. Her powers had two parts, it—"

"Yes," I said, too excited not to interrupt. Faultline—the woman Steelheart had brought to bury the bank after I'd escaped. "I know. Power duality—melding two second-tier abilities creates a first-tier one."

Tia smiled. "You've been reading my classification system notes."

"I figure we might as well use the same terminology." I shrugged. "I have no trouble switching over."

Megan glanced at me, the hint of a smile on the corners of her lips.

"What?" I asked.

"Nerd."

"I am not—"

"Stay focused, son," Prof said, shooting a hard look at Megan, whose eyes shone with amusement. "I happen to have a fondness for nerds."

"I never said that I didn't," Megan replied lightly. "I'm just interested whenever someone pretends to be something they're not."

Whatever, I thought. Faultline was a tier-one Epic, by Tia's classification, without an immortality benefit. That made her powerful, but fragile. She should have realized that; when she'd tried to seize Newcago a few years back, she'd never had a chance.

Anyway, she was an Epic who had several smaller powers that worked together to create what seemed to be a single, more impressive power. In her case, she could move earth—but only if it wasn't too rigid. However, she *also* had the ability to turn ordinary stone and earth into a kind of sandy dust.

What had looked like her creating an earthquake had actually been her softening the ground, then pulling back the earth. There were true earthquake-creating Epics, but they were ironically less powerful—or at least less useful. The stronger ones could destroy a city with their powers but couldn't bury a single building or group of people at will. Plate tectonics just worked on too massive a scale to allow for precision.

"Don't you see?" Tia asked. "Steelheart turned the bank's main room—walls, much of the ceiling, floor—to steel. Then Faultline softened the ground beneath it and let it sink. I began thinking, there might be a chance that—"

"—that it would still be there," I said softly. We turned a corner in the catacombs, and then Tia stepped forward, moving some pieces of junk to reveal a tunnel. I had enough practice by now to tell it was probably tensor-made. The tensors, unless controlled precisely, always created circular tunnels, while the Diggers had created square or rectangular corridors.

This tunnel burrowed through the steel at a slight decline. Cody walked up, shining his light in. "Well, I guess now we know what you and Abraham have been working on for the last few weeks, Tia."

"We had to try several different avenues of approach," Tia explained. "I wasn't certain how deep the bank room ended up sinking, or even if it retained structural integrity."

"But it did?" I asked, suddenly feeling a strange numbness.

"It did!" Tia said. "It's amazing. Come see." She led the way down the tunnel, which was tall enough to walk through, though Abraham would have to stoop.

I hesitated. The others waited for me to follow, so I forced myself forward, joining Tia. The rest of them came along behind, our mobiles providing the only light.

No, wait. There was light up ahead; I could barely make it out, around the shadows of Tia's slender figure. We eventually reached the end of the tunnel, and I stepped into a memory.

Tia had set up a few lights in corners and on tables, but they did little more than give a ghostly cast to the large, dark chamber. The room had settled at an angle, with the floor sloping downward. The skewed perspective only enhanced the surreal sensation of this place.

I froze in the mouth of the tunnel. The room was as I remembered it, shockingly well preserved. Towering pillars—now made of steel—and scattered desks, counters, rubble. I could still make out the tile mosaic on the floor, though only its shape. Instead of marble and stone it was now all a uniform shade of silver broken by ridges and bumps.

There was almost no dust, though some motes dodged lazily in the air, creating little halos around the white lanterns Tia had set up.

Realizing that I was still standing in the mouth of the tunnel, I stepped down into the room. *Oh sparks . . . ,* I thought, my chest constricting. I found my hands gripping my rifle, though I knew I was in no danger. The memories were coming back in a flood.

"In retrospect," Tia was explaining—I listened with only half an ear—"I shouldn't have been surprised to find it so well preserved. Faultline's powers created a kind of cushion of earth as the room sank, and Steelheart turned almost all of that earth to metal. The other rooms in the building were destroyed in his assault on the bank, and they broke off as the structure sank. But this one, and the attached vault, were ironically preserved by Steelheart's own powers."

By coincidence we'd entered through the front of the bank. There had been wide, beautiful glass doors here; those had been destroyed in the gunfire and energy blasts. Steel rubble and some steel bones from Deathpoint's victims littered the ground to both sides. As I stepped forward I followed the path Steelheart had taken into the building.

Those are the counters, I thought, looking directly ahead. *The ones where the tellers worked.* One section had been destroyed; as a child I'd crawled through that gap before making my way to the vault. The ceiling nearby was broken and misshapen, but the vault itself had been steel before Steelheart's intervention. Now that I thought about it, that might have helped preserve its contents, because of how his transfersion abilities worked.

"Most of the rubble is from where the ceiling fell in," Tia said from behind, her voice echoing in the vast chamber. "Abraham and I cleaned as much out as we could. A large amount of dirt had tumbled through the broken wall and ceiling, filling one part of the chamber over by the vault. We used the tensors on that pile, then made a hole in the corner of the floor—it opens into a pocket of space under-neath the building—and shoved the dust in there."

I moved down three steps to the lower section of the floor. Here, in the center of the room, was where Steelheart had faced Death-point. *These people are mine. . . .* By instinct, I turned to the left. Huddling beside the pillar I found the body of the woman whose child had been killed in her arms. I shivered. She was now a statue made of steel. When had she died? How? I didn't remember. A stray bullet, maybe? She wouldn't have been turned to steel unless she'd already been dead.

"What *really* saved this place," Tia continued, "was the Great Transfersion, when Steelheart turned everything in the city to steel. If he hadn't done that, dirt would have filled this room completely. Beyond that, the settling of the ground probably would have caved in the ceiling. However, the transfersion turned the remaining things in the room to steel, as well as the earth around it. In effect he locked the room into place, preserving it, like a bubble in the middle of a frozen pond."

I continued forward until I could see the sterile little mortgage cubicle I'd hidden in. Its windows were now opaque, but I could see in through the open front. I walked in and ran my fingers along the desk. The cubicle felt smaller than I remembered.

"The insurance records were inconclusive," Tia continued. "But there *was* a claim submitted on the building itself, an earthquake claim. I wonder if the bank owners really thought the insurance company would pay out on that. Seems ridiculous—but of course, there was still a lot of uncertainty surrounding Epics in those days. Anyway, that made me investigate records surrounding the bank's destruction."

"And that led you here?" Cody asked, his voice coming from the darkness as he poked around the perimeter of the room.

"No, actually. It led me to find something curious. A cover-up. The reason I couldn't find anything in the insurance reports, and why I couldn't find any lists of what was in the vault, was because some of Steelheart's people had already gathered and hidden the information. I realized that since he had made a dedicated attempt to cover this up, I would never discover anything of use in the records. Our only chance would be to come to the bank, which Steelheart had assumed was buried beyond reach."

"It's a good assumption," Cody said, sounding thoughtful. "Without the tensors—or some kind of Epic power like the Diggers had—getting here would have been near impossible. Burrowing through fifty feet of solid steel?" The Diggers had started out as normal humans and had been granted their strange powers by an Epic known as Digzone, who was a gifter like Conflux. It . . . hadn't gone well for them. Not all Epic powers were meant to be used by mortal hands, it appeared.

I was still standing in the cubicle. The mortgage man's bones were there, scattered on the floor around the desk, peeking out from some rubble. All of it was metal now.

I didn't want to look, but I had to. I *had to.*

I turned around. For a moment I couldn't tell the past from the present. My father stood there, determined, gun raised to defend a monster. Explosions, shouts, dust, screams, fire.

Fear.

I blinked, trembling, hand to the cold steel of the cubicle wall. The room smelled of dust and age, but I thought I could smell blood. I thought I could smell terror.

I stepped out of the cubicle and walked to where Steelheart had stood, holding a simple pistol, arm extended toward my father. Bang. One shot. I could remember hearing it, though I didn't know if my mind had constructed that. I'd been deafened by the explosions by then.

I knelt beside the pillar. A mound of silvery rubble covered everything in front of me, but I had my tensor. The others continued talking, but I stopped paying attention, and their words became nothing more than a low hum in the background. I put on my tensor, then reached forward and—very carefully—began vaporizing bits of rubble.

It didn't take long; the bulk of it was made of one large piece of ceiling panel. I destroyed it, then froze.

There he was.

My father lay slumped against the pillar, head to the side. The bullet wound was frozen in the steel folds of his shirt. His eyes were still open. He looked like a statue, cast with incredible detail—even the pores of the skin were clear.

I stared, unable to move, unable to even lower my arm. After ten years, the familiar face was almost crushing to me. I didn't have any pictures of him or my mother; I hadn't dared go home after surviving, though Steelheart couldn't have known who I was. I'd been paranoid and traumatized.

Seeing his face brought that all back to me. He looked so . . . normal. Normal in a way that hadn't existed for years; normal in a way that the world didn't deserve any longer.

I wrapped my arms around myself, but I kept looking at my father's face. I couldn't turn away.

"David?" Prof's voice. He knelt down beside me.

"My father . . . ," I whispered. "He died fighting back, but he also died protecting Steelheart. And now here I am, trying to kill the thing he rescued. It's funny, eh?"

Prof didn't respond.

"In a way," I said, "this is all his fault. Deathpoint was going to kill Steelheart from behind."

"It wouldn't have worked," Prof said. "Deathpoint didn't know how powerful Steelheart was. Nobody knew back then."

"I guess that's true. But my father was a fool. He couldn't believe that Steelheart was evil."

"Your father believed the best about people," Prof said. "You could call that foolish, but I'd never call it a fault. He was a hero, son. He stood up to, and killed, Deathpoint—an Epic who had been slaughtering wantonly. If, in doing so, he let Steelheart live . . . well, Steelheart hadn't done terrible things at that point. Your father couldn't know the future. You can't be so frightened of what *might* happen that you are unwilling to act."

I stared into my father's dead eyes, and I found myself nodding. "That's the answer," I whispered. "It's the answer to what you and Megan were arguing about."

"It isn't her answer," Prof said. "But it's mine. And maybe yours too." He gave my shoulder a squeeze, then went to join the rest of the Reckoners, who were standing near the vault.

I'd never expected to see my father's face again; I'd left that day feeling like a coward, seeing him mouth the plea for me to run and escape. I'd lived ten years with a single dominating emotion: the need for vengeance. The need to prove I was not a coward.

Now, here he was. Looking into those steel eyes, I knew my father wouldn't care about vengeance. But he'd kill Steelheart all the same if he had the chance, to stop the murders. Because sometimes, you need to help the heroes along.

I stood up. Somehow I knew, in that moment, that the bank vault and its contents were a false lead. That hadn't been the source of Steelheart's weakness. It had been my father, or something about him.

I left the corpse for the moment, joining the others. ". . . very careful as we open the vault boxes," Tia was saying. "We don't want to destroy what might be inside."

"I don't think it will work," I said, drawing all of their eyes. "I don't think the vault contents are to blame."

"You said Steelheart looked at the vault after the rocket blew it open," Tia said. "And his agents worked very hard to obtain and hide any lists of what was in here."

"I don't think he knew how he got hurt," I said. "A lot of Epics don't know their weaknesses at first. He quietly had his people gather those records and analyze them so he could try to figure it out."

"So maybe he found the answer there," Cody said with a shrug.

I raised an eyebrow. "If he'd found out this vault contained something that made him vulnerable, do you think this place would still be here?"

The others grew silent. No, it wouldn't still be there. If that had been the case, Steelheart would have burrowed down and destroyed the place, no matter the difficulty in doing so. I was increasingly certain that it wasn't an object that had made him weak; it was something about the situation.

Tia's face looked dark; she probably wished I'd mentioned this before she spent days excavating. I couldn't help it, though, since nobody had told me what she was doing.

"Well," Prof said. "We're going to search this vault. David's theory has merit, but so does the theory that something in here weakened him."

"Will we even be able to find anything?" Cody asked. "Everything's been turned to steel. I don't know that I'll be able to recognize much if it's all fused together."

"Some things might have survived in their original form," Megan said. "In fact, it's likely that they did. Steelheart's transfersion powers are insulated by metal."

"They're what?" Cody asked.

"Insulated by metal," I repeated. "He exerts a kind of . . . ripple of transfersion that travels through and changes nonmetal substances like sound travels through air or waves move through a pool of water. If the wave hits metal—particularly iron or steel—it stops. He can affect other kinds of metal, but the wave moves more slowly. Steel stops it entirely."

"So these safe-deposit boxes . . . ," Cody said, stepping into the vault.

"Might have insulated their contents," Megan finished, following him in. "Some of it will have been transformed—the wave that created the transfersion was enormously powerful. I think we might find something, though, particularly since the vault itself was metal and would work as a primary insulator." She glanced over her shoulder and caught me looking at her. "What?" she demanded.

"Nerd," I said.

Uncharacteristically, she blushed furiously. "I pay attention to Steelheart. I wanted to be familiar with his powers, since we were coming into the city."

"I didn't say it was a bad thing," I said lightly, stepping into the vault and raising my tensor. "I just pointed it out."

Never has getting glared at felt so good.

Prof chuckled. "All right," he said. "Cody, Abraham, David, vaporize the fronts of the safe-deposit boxes but *don't* destroy the contents. Tia, Megan, and I will start pulling them out and going through them for anything that looks interesting. Let's get to work; this is going to take a while. . . ."

26

"**WELL,**" Cody said, looking over the heap of gemstones and jewelry, "if this achieved nothing else, it at least made me rich. That's a failure I can live with."

Tia snorted, picking through the jewelry. We four, including Prof, sat around a large desk in one of the cubicles. Megan and Abraham were on guard duty, watching the tunnel into the bank chamber.

There was a hallowed feeling to the room—like I somehow had to show respect—and I think the others must have sensed it too. They spoke in low, muted voices. All except Cody. He tried to lean back on his chair as he held up a large ruby, but—of course—the steel chair legs were fused to the steel floor.

"That once might have made you rich, Cody," Tia said, "but you'd have some trouble selling it now."

That was true. Jewelry was practically worthless these days. There were a couple Epics who could create gemstones.

"Maybe," Cody said, "but gold remains a standard." He scratched his head. "Not sure why, though. You can't eat it, which is all most people are interested in."

"It's familiar," Prof said. "It doesn't rust, it's easy to shape, and it's hard to fake. There aren't any Epics who can make it. Yet. People need to have a way to trade, particularly across kingdom or city boundaries." He fingered a gold chain. "Cody's actually right."

"I am?" Cody looked surprised.

Prof nodded. "Whether or not we take on Steelheart, the gold we've recovered here can fund the Reckoners for a few years on its own."

Tia set her notebook on the desk, tapping it absently with her pen. On the other mortgage cubicle desks we'd arranged what we'd found in the vault. About three-quarters of the boxes' contents had been recoverable.

"Mostly we have a lot of wills," Tia said, opening a can of cola, "stock certificates, passports, copies of driver's licenses . . ."

"We could fill a whole city with fake people if we wanted," Cody said. "Imagine the fun."

"The second-largest grouping," Tia continued, "is the aforementioned pile of jewelry, both valuable and worthless. If something in there affected Steelheart, then by pure volume this is the most likely group."

"But it's not," I said.

Prof sighed. "David, I know what you—"

"What I mean," I interrupted, "is that jewelry doesn't make sense. Steelheart didn't attack other banks, and he hasn't done anything— either directly or indirectly—to forbid people from wearing jewelry in his presence. Jewelry is common enough among Epics that he'd have to take measures."

"I agree," Tia said, "though only in part. It's possible we've missed something. Steelheart has proven subtle in the past; perhaps he has a secret embargo on a certain type of gemstone. I'll look into it, but I think David's right. If something *did* affect Steelheart, then it's likely one of the oddities."

"How many of those are there?" Prof asked.

"Over three hundred," Tia said with a grimace. "Mostly mementos or keepsakes of no intrinsic value. Anything among them could be our culprit, theoretically. But then there's a chance it was something one of the people in the room was carrying on them. Or it could be, as David seems to think, something about the situation."

"It's very rare for an Epic's weakness to be influenced just by proximity to something mundane," I said, shrugging. "Unless an object in the vault emitted a kind of radiation or a light or a sound—something that actually reached Steelheart—the chances are slim it was the culprit."

"Look through the items anyway, Tia," Prof said. "Maybe we can find a correlation to something Steelheart has done in the city."

"What about the darkness?" Cody asked.

"Nightwielder's darkness?"

"Sure," Cody said. "I've always thought it was strange that he kept it so dark here."

"That's probably because of Nightwielder himself," I said. "He doesn't want sunlight shining on him and making him corporeal. I wouldn't be surprised if that was part of the deal between them, one of the reasons Nightwielder serves beneath Steelheart. Steelheart's government provides infrastructure—food, electricity, crime prevention—to compensate for it always being dark."

"I suppose that makes sense," Cody said. "Nightwielder needs darkness, but can't have it unless he's got a good city to work from. Kind of like a piper needs a good city to support him, so he can stand on the cliff tops and play."

"A . . . piper?" I asked.

"Oh please, don't get him started," Tia said, raising a hand to her head.

"Bagpiper," Cody said.

I looked at him blankly.

"You've never heard of *bagpipes*?" Cody asked, sounding aghast. "They're as Scottish as kilts and red armpit hair!"

"Um . . . yuck?" I said.

"That's it," Cody said. "Steelheart has to fall so we can get back to educating children properly. This is an offense against the dignity of my motherland."

"Great," Prof said, "I'm glad we now have proper motivation." He tapped the desk idly.

"You're worried," Tia said. She seemed to be able to read Prof pretty well.

"We're getting closer and closer to a confrontation. If we continue on this course we'll draw Steelheart out but will be unable to fight him."

The people at the desk grew still. I looked up, gazing at the high ceiling; the sterile white lights around the room provided insufficient glow to reach the room's farthest corners. It was cold in this room, and quiet. "When's the last moment we could pull out?"

"Well," Prof said, "we could draw him to a confrontation with Limelight, then not show."

"That might be kind of fun on its own merits," Cody noted. "I doubt Steelheart gets stood up very often."

"He'd react poorly to the embarrassment," Prof said. "Right now the Reckoners are a thorn—an annoyance. We've only done three hits in his city and have never killed anyone vital to his organization. If we run, what we've been doing will get out. Abraham and I set in place evidence that will prove we're behind this—that is the only way to make sure our victory, if we obtain one, isn't attributed to an Epic instead of ordinary men."

"So if we run . . . ," Cody said.

"Steelheart will know that Limelight was a fake and that the Reckoners were working on a way to assassinate him," Tia said.

"Well," Cody said, "most Epics already want to kill the lot of us. So maybe nothing will change."

"This will be worse," I said, still looking up at the ceiling. "He killed the *rescue workers,* Cody. He's paranoid. He'll hunt us actively if he finds out what we've been up to. The thought that we tried to get to him . . . that we were researching his weakness . . . he won't take that sitting down."

The shadows flickered, and I looked down to see Abraham walking up to our cubicle. "Prof, you asked me to warn you when we reached the hour."

Prof checked his mobile, then nodded. "We should be getting back to the hideout. Everyone grab a sack and fill it with the things we found. We'll sort through them further in a more controlled environment."

We got up from our seats, Cody patting the head of the dead— and steel-frozen—bank patron who slumped beside the wall of this particular cubicle. As they left, Abraham set something down on the desk. "For you."

It was a handgun. "I'm no good with . . ." I trailed off. It looked familiar. *The gun . . . the one my father picked up.*

"I found it in the rubble beside your father," Abraham said. "The transfersion turned the grip and frame to metal, but most of the parts were already good steel. I removed the magazine and cleared the chamber, and the slide and trigger still function as expected. I wouldn't completely trust it until I give it a thorough once-over back at base, but there's a good chance it will fire reliably."

I picked up the gun. This was the weapon that had killed my father. Holding it felt wrong.

But it was also, so far as I knew, the only weapon ever to have wounded Steelheart.

"We can't know if it was something about the gun that allowed Steelheart to be hurt," Abraham said. "I felt it would be worth digging out. I'll take it apart and clean it for you, check over the cartridges. They should still be good, though I might need to change the powder, if the casings didn't insulate against the transfersion. If it all checks out, you can carry it. If the opportunity presents itself, you can try shooting him with it."

I nodded in thanks, then ran to get a sack and haul out my part of what we'd found.

"Piping is the most sublime sound y'all have ever heard," Cody explained, gesturing widely as we walked down the corridor toward the hideout. "A sonorous mix of power, frailty, and wonder."

"It sounds like dying cats being stuffed into a blender," Tia said to me.

Cody looked wistful. "Aye, and a beauteous melody that is, lass."

"So, wait," I said, holding up a finger. "These bagpipes. To make them, you . . . what was it you said? 'Y'all need to kill yourself a wee dragon, which are totally real and not at all mythological—they live in the Scottish Highlands to this day.' "

"Aye," Cody said. "It's important y'all pick a *wee* one. The big ones are too dangerous, you see, and their bladders don't make good pipes. But you have to kill it yourself, you see. A piper needs to have slain his own dragon. It's part of the code."

"After that," I said, "you need to cut out the bladder, and attach . . . what was it?"

"Carved unicorn horns to make the pipes," Cody said. "I mean, you *could* use something less rare, like ivory. But if you're going to be a purist, it has to be unicorn horns."

"Delightful," Tia said.

"A grand word to choose," Cody said. "It, of course, is originally a Scottish term. *Del* coming from Dál Riata, the ancient and

great Scottish kingdom of myth. Why, I think one of the great piping songs is from that era. *'Abharsair e d' a chois e na Dùn Èideann.'*"

"Ab . . . ha . . . what?" I asked.

"Abharsair e d' a chois c na Dùn Èideann," Cody said. "It is a
sweetly poetic name that doesn't really translate to English—"

"It means 'The Devil Went Down to Edinburgh' in Scottish
Gaelic," Tia said, leaning in toward me but speaking loudly enough
that Cody could hear.

Cody, for once, missed a step. "You speak Scottish Gaelic, lass?"

"No," Tia said. "But I looked that up *last* time you told this story."

"Er . . . you did, eh?"

"Yes. Though your translation is questionable."

"Well, now. I always did say you were a smart one, lass. Yes indeed." He coughed into his hand. "Ah, look. We're at the base. I'll
continue the story later." The others had arrived at the hideout just
ahead and Cody scurried up to meet them, then followed Megan up
the tunnel.

Tia shook her head, then walked with me to the tunnel. I went
last, making sure the cords and cables that hid the entrance were in
place. I turned on the hidden motion sensors that would alert us if
someone came in, then crawled up myself.

". . . just don't know, Prof," Abraham was saying in his soft
voice. "I just don't know." The two of them had spent the trip back
walking ahead, speaking softly. I'd tried to edge up to hear them,
but Tia had pointedly placed a hand on my shoulder and drawn me
back.

"So?" Megan asked, crossing her arms as we all gathered around
the main table. "What's going on?"

"Abraham doesn't like the way the rumors are going," Prof said.

"The general public does seem to accept our tale of Limelight,"
Abraham said. "They are scared, and our hit on the power station
has had an effect—there are rolling blackouts all over the city. However, I see no proof that Steelheart believes. Enforcement is sweeping

the understreets. Nightwielder is scouring the city. Everything I hear from informants is that Steelheart is searching for a group of rebels, not a rival Epic."

"So we hit back with a fury," Cody said, crossing his arms and leaning back against the wall beside the tunnel. "Kill a few more Epics."

"No," I said, remembering my conversation with Prof. "We need to be more focused. We can't just take out random Epics; we have to think like someone trying to capture the city."

Prof nodded. "Each and every hit we make without having Limelight appear in the open will make Steelheart more suspicious."

"We're giving up?" Megan said, a hint of eagerness in her voice, though she obviously tried to cover it.

"Not by a mile," Prof said. "Perhaps I will still decide we need to pull out—if we aren't confident enough about Steelheart's weakness, I might do just that. We aren't there yet. We're going to keep on with this plan, but we need to do something big, preferably with an appearance by Limelight. We need to squeeze Steelheart as hard as we can and drive that temper of his. *Force* him out."

"And we do that how?" Tia asked.

"It's time to kill Conflux," Prof said. "And bring down Enforcement."

27

CONFLUX.

In many ways he was the backbone of Steelheart's rule. A mysterious figure, even when compared to the likes of Firefight and Nightwielder.

I had no good photos of Conflux. The few I'd paid dearly to get were blurry and unspecific. I couldn't even know if he was real.

The van thumped as it moved through the dark streets of Newcago; it was stuffy inside. I sat in the passenger seat, with Megan driving. Cody and Abraham were in the back. Prof was running point in a different vehicle, and Tia was running support back at our base, watching the spy videos of the city streets. It was a frigid day and the heater in our van didn't work—Abraham hadn't gotten around to fixing it.

Prof's words ran through my mind. *We've considered hitting*

Conflux before, but discarded the idea because we thought it would be too dangerous. We still have the plans we made. It's no less dangerous now, but we're in deep. No reason not to move forward.

Was Conflux real? My gut said he was. Much as the clues pointed to Firefight being a fabrication, the clues surrounding Conflux added up to *something* being there. A powerful but fragile Epic.

Steelheart moves Conflux around, Prof had said, *never letting him stay long in the same place. But there's a pattern to how he's moved. He often uses an armored limo with six guards and a two-motorcycle escort. If we watch for that, wait until he uses that convoy to move, we can hit him on the streets in transit.*

The clues. Even with power plants Steelheart didn't have enough electricity to run the city, and yet he somehow produced those fuel cells. The mechanized armor units didn't pack power sources, and neither did many of the copters. The fact that they were powered directly by high-ranking members of Enforcement wasn't much of a secret. Everyone knew it.

He was out there. A gifter who could make energy in a form that could power vehicles, fill fuel cells, even light a large chunk of the city. That level of power was awesome, but no more so than what Nightwielder or Steelheart held. The most powerful Epics set their own scale of strength.

The van bumped, and I gripped my rifle—held low, safety on, barrel pointed down and toward the door. Out of sight, but handy. Just in case.

Tia had spotted the right kind of limo convoy today, and we'd scrambled. Megan drove us toward a point where our road would intersect with Conflux's limo. Her eyes were characteristically intense, though there was a particular edge to her today. Not fear. Just . . . worry, maybe?

"You don't think we should be doing this, do you?" I asked.

"I think I made that clear," Megan said, her voice even, eyes ahead. "Steelheart doesn't need to fall."

"I'm talking about Conflux specifically," I said. "You're nervous. You're normally not nervous."

"I just don't think we know enough about him," she said. "We shouldn't be hitting an Epic we don't even have photographs of."

"But you *are* nervous."

She drove, eyes forward and hands tight on the wheel.

"It's okay," I said. "I feel like a brick made of porridge."

She looked at me, brow scrunching up. The van's cab fell silent. Then Megan started to laugh.

"No, no," I said. "It makes sense! Listen. A brick is supposed to be strong, right? But if one were secretly made of porridge, and all of the other bricks didn't know, he'd sit around worrying that he'd be weak when the rest of them were strong. He'd get smooshed when he was placed in the wall, you see, maybe get some of his porridge mixed with that stuff they stick between bricks."

Megan was laughing even harder now, so hard she was actually gasping for breath. I tried to keep explaining but found myself smiling. I don't think I'd ever heard her laugh, *really* laugh. Not chuckle, not part her lips in wry mockery, but truly laugh. She was almost in tears by the time she got control of herself. I think we were fortunate she didn't crash into a post or something.

"David," she said between gasps, "I think that is the most ridiculous thing I've ever heard anyone say. The most outlandishly, audaciously ridiculous."

"Um . . ."

"Sparks," she said, exhaling. "I needed that."

"You did?"

She nodded.

"Can we . . . pretend that's why I said it, then?"

She looked at me, smiling, eyes sparkling. The tension was still there, but it had retreated somewhat. "Sure," she said. "I mean, bad puns are something of an art, right? So why not bad metaphors?"

"Exactly."

"And if they're an art, you are a master painter."

"Well, actually," I said, "that won't work, you see, because the metaphor makes too much sense. I'd have to be, like, the ace pilot or something." I cocked my head. "Actually, that makes a little bit of sense too." Sparks, doing it badly intentionally was hard too. I found that decidedly unfair.

"Y'all okay up there?" Cody said in our ears. The back of the van was separated from the cab by a metal partition, like a service van. There was a little window in it, but Cody preferred to use the mobiles to communicate.

"We're fine," Megan said. "Just having an abstract conversation about linguistic parallelism."

"You wouldn't be interested," I said. "It doesn't involve Scotsmen."

"Well, actually," Cody said, "the original tongue of my motherland . . ."

Megan and I looked at each other, then both pointedly reached to our mobiles and muted him.

"Let me know when he's done, Abraham," I said into mine.

Abraham sighed on the other end of the line. "Want to trade places? I'd sure like to be able to mute Cody myself right about now. It is regrettably difficult when he's sitting beside you."

I chuckled, then glanced at Megan. She was still grinning. Seeing her smile made me feel like I'd done something grand.

"Megan," Tia said in our ears, "keep on straight as you are. The convoy is progressing along the road, without deviations. You should meet up in another fifteen minutes or so."

"Affirmative."

Outside the streetlights flickered, as did the lights inside an apartment complex we were passing. Another brownout.

So far there hadn't been any looting. Enforcement walked the streets, and people were too frightened. Even as we drove past an intersection, I saw a large, mechanized armor unit lumbering down a side street. Twelve feet tall with arms that were little more than machine-gun barrels, the mechanized armor was accompanied by a five-man Enforcement Core. One soldier bore a distinctive energy weapon, painted bright red in warning. A few blasts from that could level a building.

"I've always wanted to pilot one of those armor units," I noted as we drove on.

"It's not much fun," Megan said.

"You've done it?" I asked, shocked.

"Yeah. They're stuffy inside, and they respond very sluggishly." She hesitated. "I'll admit that firing both rotary guns with wild abandon can be rather fulfilling, in a primal sort of way."

"We'll convert you away from those handguns yet."

"Not a chance," she said, reaching over and patting her under-arm holster. "What if I got stuck in close confines?"

"Then you hit 'em with the stock of the gun," I said. "If they're too far away for that, it's always better to have a gun you can actually *hit* with."

She gave me a flat stare as she drove. "Rifles take too much time. They're not . . . spontaneous enough."

"This from the woman who complains when people improvise."

"I complain when *you* improvise," she said. "That's different from improvising myself. Besides, not all handguns are inaccurate. Have you ever fired an MT 318?"

"Nice gun, that," I admitted. "If I *had* to carry a handgun, I'd consider an MT. Problem is, the thing is so weak, you might as well just be throwing the bullets at someone. Likely to hurt them about as much."

"If you're a good shot, it doesn't matter how much stopping power a gun has."

"If you're a good shot," I said solemnly, raising a hand to my breast, "you're probably already using a rifle."

She snorted. "And what handgun *would* you pick, given the choice?"

"Jennings .44."

"A Spitfire?" she asked, incredulous. "Those things shoot about as accurately as tossing a handful of bullets into a fire."

"Sure. But if I'm using a handgun, that means someone is in my face. I might not have a chance for a second shot, so I want to down them fast. At that point accuracy doesn't matter, since they're so close anyway."

Megan just rolled her eyes and shook her head. "You're hopeless. You're buying into assumptions. You can be just as accurate with a handgun as you can with a rifle, and you can use it at more immediate ranges. In a way, because it's harder, *truly* skilled people use the handgun. Any slontze can hit with a rifle."

"You did *not* just say that."

"I did, and I'm driving, so I get to decide when the argument is over."

"But . . . but that makes no sense!"

"It doesn't need to," she said. "It's a brick made out of porridge."

"You know," Tia said in our ears, "you two *could* just each carry both a rifle *and* a handgun."

"That's not the point," I said at exactly the same time that Megan said, "You don't understand."

"Whatever," Tia answered. I could hear her sipping cola. "Ten minutes." Her tone said she was bored with our arguing. She, however, couldn't see that both of us were grinning.

Sparks, I like this girl, I thought, eyeing Megan. Who seemed to think she'd won the argument.

I tapped the mute-all button on my mobile. "I'm sorry," I found myself saying.

Megan raised an eyebrow at me.

"For doing what I did to the Reckoners," I said. "For making everything go a different way than you wanted it to. For dragging you into this."

She shrugged, then tapped her own mute button. "I'm past it."

"What changed?"

"Turns out I like you too much to hate you, Knees." She eyed me. "Don't let it go to your head."

I wasn't worried about my head. My heart, on the other hand, was another matter. A wave of shock ran through me. Had she really just said that?

Before I could melt too far, however, my mobile flashed. Prof was trying to contact us. I tapped it with a quick snap.

"Stay sharp, you two," he told us. He sounded a little suspicious. "Keep the lines up."

"Yes sir," I said immediately.

"Eight minutes," Tia said. "The convoy has taken a left on Frewanton. Turn right at the next intersection to continue on an intercept course."

Megan focused on her driving, and so—to keep *me* from focusing too much on *her*—I went over the plan a few times in my head.

We're going to do this one simply, Prof had said. *Nothing fancy at all. Conflux is fragile. He's a schemer, an organizer, a string puller, but he has no powers that will protect him.*

We pull up close to the motorcade, and Abraham uses the dowser to determine if a powerful Epic is really in the car. The van pulls forward in front of the convoy; we throw open the back doors, where Cody stands in costume.

Cody raises his hands; Abraham fires the gauss gun from behind. In the confusion, we'll hope it looks like he launched the bolt from his hand. We hit the entire limo, leave nothing but slag, and then flee. The surviving motorcycle guards can spread the story.

It *would* work. Hopefully. And without Conflux gifting his abilities to high-level Enforcement soldiers, the mechanized armor, the energy weapons, and the copters would all stop working. Fuel cells would run dry, and the city would run out of power.

"We're getting close," Tia said softly in our ears. "The limo is turning right on Beagle. Prof, use the beta formation; I'm pretty sure they're heading uptown, and that means they'll turn onto Finger Street. Megan, you're still on target."

"Got it," Prof said. "I was heading that way."

We passed an abandoned park from the old days. You could tell because of the frozen weeds and fallen branches transformed to steel. Only the dead ones had been changed—Steelheart couldn't affect living matter. In fact, his pulses had trouble with anything too close to a living body. A person's clothing often wouldn't be transformed, but the ground around them would change.

That kind of oddity was common in Epic powers; it was one of the things that didn't make scientific sense. A dead body and a living one could be very similar, scientifically. But one could be affected by many of the odder Epic powers while the other could not.

My breath fogged the window as we passed the playground, which was no longer safe for play. The weeds were now jagged bits of metal. Steelheart's steel didn't rust, but it could break, leaving sharp edges.

"Okay," Prof said a few minutes later. "I'm here. Climbing up the outside of the building. Megan, I want you to repeat back to me our contingencies."

"Nothing is going to go wrong," Megan said, her voice sounding both beside me and in my ear comm.

"Something always goes wrong," Prof said. I could hear him puffing as he climbed, though he had a gravatonic belt to help him. "Contingencies."

"If you or Tia give the word," Megan said, "we'll pull out and split up. You'll create a distraction. The four of us in the van will break into two squads and go opposite directions, heading for rally point gamma."

"That's what I don't get," I said. "How exactly are we going to go separate directions? We've only got one van."

"Oh, we've got a little surprise back here, lad," Cody said; I'd unmuted him when I'd unmuted Prof and the rest. "I'm actually hoping something goes wrong. I kinda want to use it."

"Never hope for something to go wrong," Tia said.

"But always expect it to," Prof added.

"You're paranoid, old man," Tia said.

"Damn right," Prof said, voice muffled, probably because he was hunkering down with his rocket launcher. I had assumed they'd put Cody in that position with a sniper rifle, but Prof said that he'd rather have something heavier when Enforcement might be involved. Diamond would have been proud.

"You're getting close, Megan," Tia said. "You should be on them in another few minutes. Maintain your speed; the limo is driving faster than it usually does."

"Do they suspect something?" Cody asked.

"They'd be fools not to," Abraham said softly. "Conflux will take extra care these days, I should think."

"It's worth the risk," Prof said. "Just be careful."

I nodded. With widespread power outages in the city, disabling Enforcement would leave the city in disorder. It would force Steelheart to step forward and take a firm hand to prevent looting or riots. That would mean revealing himself one way or another.

"He's never afraid to fight other Epics," I said.

"What are you talking about?" Prof asked.

"Steelheart. He'll face other Epics, no problem. But he doesn't like putting down riots by himself. He always uses Enforcement. We assumed it's because he doesn't want to bother, but what if it's something more? What if he's afraid of crossfire?"

"Who's that?" Abraham asked.

"No, not an Epic. It just occurred to me—what if Steelheart is afraid of getting hit accidentally? What if that's his weakness? He got hurt by my father, but my father wasn't aiming for him. What if he can only be hurt if the bullet was meant for someone else?"

"Possible," Tia said.

"We need to stay focused," Prof answered. "David, shelve that idea for the moment. We'll come back to it."

He was right. I was letting myself get distracted, like a rabbit doing math problems instead of looking for foxes.

Still . . . *If I'm right, he wouldn't ever be in danger in a one-on-one fight. He's faced other Epics with impunity. What he seems to be afraid of is a big battle, where bullets are flying around.* There was a sense to it. It was a simple thing, but most Epic weaknesses *were* simple.

"Slow down just a tad," Tia said softly.

Megan complied.

"Here it comes. . . ."

A sleek black car pulled out onto the dark street in front of us, going the same direction we were. It was flanked by a couple of motorcycles—good security, but not great. We knew from the Reckoners' original plan to hit Conflux that this convoy was probably his. We'd use the dowser to make sure, though.

We continued along behind the limo. I was impressed; even though they didn't know where the limo was going, Tia and Megan had timed it so that the limo came onto *our* street, not the other way around. We'd look far less suspicious this way.

My job was to keep my eyes open and, if things went wrong, to return fire so Megan could drive. I slipped a small pair of binoculars out of my pocket and hunkered down, sighting through them and inspecting the limo ahead.

"Well?" Prof asked in my ear.

"Looks good," I said.

"I'm going to pull up beside them at the next light," Megan said. "It will feel natural. Be ready, Abraham."

I slipped the binoculars into my pocket and tried to look nonchalant. The next light was green when we hit it, so Megan kept trailing the limo at a safe distance. The light after that, however, turned red before the limo reached it.

We pulled up slowly beside the limo, on the left side.

"There's an Epic near us for sure," Abraham said from the back of our van. He whistled softly. "A powerful one. *Very* powerful. The dowser is focusing in. I'll have more in a second."

One of the motorcycle drivers looked us over. He wore an Enforcement helmet and had an SMG strapped to his back. I tried to peer through the windows of the limo and catch a glimpse of Conflux. I'd always wondered what he looked like.

I couldn't see through the tinted rear glass. But as we pulled forward, I caught sight of someone sitting in the passenger seat. A woman who was vaguely familiar. She met my eyes but then looked away.

Business suit, black hair cut short over her ears. She was Nightwielder's assistant, the one who had been with him at Diamond's. She was probably a liaison to Enforcement; it made sense for her to be in the limo.

Something still made me suspicious. She'd met my eyes; she should have recognized me. Maybe . . . she *had* recognized me, but hadn't been surprised to see me.

We pulled forward, the light green, and I felt a spike of alarm. "Prof, I think it's a trap."

At that moment Nightwielder himself flew through the top of the limo, his arms spread wide, lines of darkness stretching from his fingers out into the night.

28

MOST people have never seen a High Epic in their glory. That's what we call it when they summon their powers in earnest—when they rise up in their might, their emotions kindled to wrath and fury.

There is a *glow* about them. The air grows sharp, like it's become full of electricity. Heartbeats still. The wind holds its breath. Nightwielder's rising made this the third time I'd seen something like it.

He was clothed in night, and blackness writhed and twisted about him. His face was pale, translucent, but his eyes were alight, his lips drawn in a sneer of hatred. It was the sneer of a god, barely tolerant of even his allies. He had come to destroy.

Looking upon him, I found myself terrified.

"Calamity!" Megan cursed, slamming her foot down on the gas and swerving the van to the side as shadows leaped from around Nightwielder toward us. They moved like ghostly fingers.

"Abort!" Tia called. "Get out of there!"

There was no time. Nightwielder moved in the air, ignoring things like wind and gravity. He flew like a specter out in front of his car and toward us. He wasn't the true danger, though—the true danger was those tendrils of blackness. The van could not avoid them; there were dozens.

Shoving aside my fear, I raised my rifle. The van rattled and jolted around me. Wisps of darkness moved up, wrapping around the vehicle.

Idiot, I thought. I dropped my rifle and shoved my hand into my coat pocket. The flashlight! Panicked, I flipped it on and shined it right in Nightwielder's face as he floated up beside my window. He was flying face-first, like he was swimming in the air.

The reaction was immediate. Though the flashlight gave off little light that I could see, Nightwielder's face immediately lost its incorporeity. His eyes stopped glowing, and the shadows vanished from around his head. The beam of invisible light pierced the dark tendrils like a laser through a pile of sheep.

In that UV light, Nightwielder's face didn't look divine. It looked frail, human, and very, very surprised. I struggled to get my gun up to fire at him, but the rifle was too unwieldy and my father's handgun was strapped under my arm where I couldn't get at it while holding the flashlight.

Nightwielder looked at me for the space of a single heartbeat, his eyes wide with terror. Then he fled in a blink, streaking sideways away from the van. I wasn't sure, but it seemed like he'd been losing altitude as I shined the light on him, as if all his powers were weakening.

He vanished down a side street, and the shadows that had been moving around the van retreated with him. I had a feeling he wasn't going to be back anytime soon, not after the scare I'd just given him.

Submachine-gun fire erupted around us, bullets pelting the side of the van with metallic *ping*s. I cursed, ducking down as my window shattered. The motorcyclists had opened fire. Though I was crouched low, I could still see a terrible sight: a sleek black Enforcement copter was rising from behind the commercial buildings in front of us.

"Calamity, Tia!" Megan screamed, twisting the wheel. "How did you miss *that*?"

"I don't know," Tia said. "I—"

A ball of light propelled by a long smoke trail snaked through the sky, exploding into the side of the copter. It tipped in the air, flames chewing its side, bits of debris fluttering through the sky.

Rotors slowing, it began to fall.

Rocket launcher, I realized. *Prof.*

"Don't panic." Prof's voice was steady. "We can survive this. Cody, Abraham, prep for the split."

"Prof!" Abraham said. "I think you—"

"Four more copters coming!" Tia cut in. "It looks like they had them hidden in warehouses all along the limo's route. They didn't know where we'd hit them; that one was just the closest. I . . . Megan, what are you *doing*?"

The copter was out of control. Smoke billowing from one side, it was spinning in a crooked circle and coming down toward the roadway right in front of us. Megan wasn't turning; she'd punched up the speed, leaning over the wheel and driving the van forward in a frenzied, insane rush right toward where the copter would hit.

I tensed, pushing myself back in my seat and grabbing the side of my door in a panic. She'd lost her mind!

There was no time to object. Bullets pelting us, streets outside a blur, Megan drove the van right under the copter as it crashed to the street with force enough to make the earth beneath us tremble.

Something clipped the top of the van with a ghastly screech of metal on metal, and we spun out to the side, hitting the wall of a brick building and grinding my side of the van along it. Noise, chaos, sparks. My door ripped free. Bricks ground against steel mere inches from me. It seemed to last forever.

Then, a second later, the van lurched to a halt. Trembling, I took a deep breath. I was covered in pebbles of safety glass; the windshield had shattered.

Megan sat breathing hard in the driver's seat—a mad grin on her face, eyes wide. She looked at me.

"Calamity!" I said, looking in Megan's side mirror back at the burning copter. It had hit the roadway right after we passed under it, blocking off the bikers and the pursuit. "Calamity, Megan! *That was awesome!*"

Megan's grin broadened. "You two okay back there?" she called, looking through the little window into the back of the van.

"I feel like I've been in a centrifuge," Cody complained, groaning. "I think the Scotsman drained to my feet and the American floated up to my ears."

"Prof," Abraham said. "I still had the dowser on as Nightwielder fled, and it was focusing on Epic locations. I got confusing readings, but there is *another Epic* in that limo. Maybe a third. That doesn't make sense. . . ."

"No, it does," Megan said, hurriedly pushing open her door and hopping out onto the street. "They really *were* transporting Conflux; they didn't know if we'd strike. They just wanted to be ready if we did. He was in that car. That's what you're sensing, Abraham. Probably a third, lesser Epic as another safety measure."

I hastily reached to undo my seat belt, then realized the right half had been ripped free as we skidded against the wall. I shivered, then scrambled out of the van through Megan's side.

"Hurry up, you four," Prof said. I heard an engine revving on his side of the link. "Those other copters are almost upon you, and those cycles will circle around."

"I'm watching them," Tia said. "You've got maybe a minute."

"Where's Nightwielder?" Prof asked.

"David scared him off with a flashlight," Megan said, reaching the back of the van and pulling the doors open.

"Nice work," Prof said.

I grinned in satisfaction as I reached the back of the van. I was just in time to see Cody and Abraham push the back off a huge crate inside. I hadn't seen them load up the van—that had happened in the hangar.

Cody was wearing a dark green jacket and glasses, the uniform we'd devised for Limelight. My eyes were drawn to the items in the crate: three shiny green motorcycles.

"The cycles from Diamond's shop!" I exclaimed, pointing. "You *did* buy them!"

"Sure did," Abraham said, running his hand along the sleek, dark green finish on one of the cycles. "Wasn't about to let machines like *this* pass us by."

"But . . . you told me no!"

Abraham laughed. "I've heard how you drive, David." He pushed a ramp out from the back of the van and rolled one of the bikes down to Megan. She climbed on, starting it up. Small ovals mounted to the sides of the cycles glowed a bright green. I'd noticed those at Diamond's.

Gravatonics, I thought. *To make the cycles lighter, maybe?* Gravatonics couldn't make things fly; they were just used to reduce recoil or to make heavy items easier to move.

Abraham rolled the next vehicle down.

"You *were* going to get to drive one, David," Cody said, quickly gathering things out of the back of the van, including the dowser. "But somebody wrecked the van."

"It would never stay ahead of the copters anyway," Megan said. "Two of us will have to ride tandem."

"I'll take David on mine," Cody said. "Grab that pack, lad. Where are the helmets?"

"Hurry!" Tia exclaimed, her voice urgent.

I jumped to grab the pack Cody pointed out. It was heavy. "I can drive!" I said.

Megan glanced at me as she pulled on her helmet. "You took out two signs trying to drive around *one* corner."

"Small ones!" I said, slinging on the pack and dashing toward Cody's cycle. "And I was under a lot of pressure!"

"Really?" Megan said. "Kind of like we are now?"

I hesitated. *Wow. I walked into that one, didn't I?*

Cody and Abraham started up their cycles. There were only three helmets. I didn't ask for one—hopefully my Reckoner jacket would be enough.

Before I could reach Cody, I heard the thumping sounds of a copter overhead. An Enforcement armored van appeared out of a side street, a man in the machine-gun turret on the top. He opened fire.

"Calamity!" Cody said, kicking his cycle forward with a burst of speed as the bullets hit the ground near him. I fell back beside the wreckage of our van.

"Get on," Megan yelled to me; she was closest. "Now!"

I ducked down and ran to her cycle, throwing myself up behind her and grabbing her waist as she revved the engine. We lurched away, zipping down an alleyway as Enforcement cycles came roaring out of another side street.

We lost Cody and Abraham in a flash. I held tight to Megan—something I'll admit I wished I could have done under less insane circumstances. Cody's bag thumped against my back.

I left my rifle in the van, I realized with a sinking feeling. I hadn't noticed in the panic to grab Cody's bag and get to a cycle.

I felt terrible, like I'd abandoned a friend.

We burst out of the alleyway and Megan turned onto a dark city street, increasing our speed to what I felt was a pretty ridiculous level. The wind blew against my face so powerfully, I had to squeeze in close and low against her back.

"Where are we going?" I yelled.

Fortunately we still had our mobiles and our earpieces. Though I couldn't hear her naturally, her voice spoke in my ear. "There's a plan! We all go different ways and meet up!"

"Except you're going the wrong way," Tia said, sounding exasperated. "And so is Abraham!"

"Where is the limo?" Abraham asked; even with his voice in my ear, it was hard to hear him over the wind.

"Forget the limo," Prof ordered.

"I can still get to Conflux," Abraham said.

"It doesn't matter," Prof said.

"But—"

"It's over," Prof said, voice harsh. "We ran."

We ran.

Megan hit a bump and I jolted, but hung on tight. My mind reeled as I realized what Prof meant. An Epic who truly sought to defeat Steelheart wouldn't have run from Enforcement; he'd have been able to handle a few squads of them on his own.

By fleeing, we proved what we really were. Steelheart would never face us in person now.

"Then I want to do something," Abraham said, "make him hurt before we abandon the city. Half of Enforcement is going to be out chasing us. That limo is unguarded, and I've got some grenades."

"Jon, let him try," Tia said. "This is already a disaster. At least we can make it cost Steelheart."

Streetlights were a blur. I could hear cycles behind us, and I risked glancing over my shoulder. *Calamity!* I thought. They were close, their headlights illuminating the street.

"You'll never make it," Prof said to Abraham. "Enforcement is on you."

"We'll draw them off him," I said.

"Wait," Megan said. "We'll *what?*"

"Thanks," Abraham said. "Meet up with me at Fourth and Nodell; see if you can take the pressure away from me."

Megan tried to twist around and glare at me through her helmet's visor.

"Keep driving!" I said urgently.

"Slontze," she said, then took the next turn. *Without slowing down.*

I screamed, certain we were dead. The bike went almost parallel to the ground, skidding against the street, but the gravatonics on the side glowed brightly, keeping us from toppling. We half skidded, half drove around the corner, almost like we were tethered to it.

We came upright, my scream dying off.

There was an explosion from behind us and the steel street trembled. I looked over my shoulder, hair whipping in the wind. One of the black Enforcement cycles had just failed to take the corner at speed, and was now a smoking wreck pasted to the side of a steel building. Their gravatonics didn't seem as good as ours, if they even had any.

"How many are there?" Megan asked.

"Three now. No, wait, there are two more. *Five.* Sparks!"

"Great," Megan muttered. "How exactly do you expect us to take heat off Abraham?"

"I don't know. Improvise!"

"They're setting up roadblocks on nearby streets," Tia warned in our ears. "Jon, copter on Seventeenth."

"On my way."

"What are you doing?" I asked.

"Trying to keep you kids alive," Prof said.

"Sparks," Cody cursed. "Roadblock on Eighth. Taking an alleyway over to Marston."

"No," Tia said. "They're trying to get you to go that way. Circle back around. You can escape into the understreets on Moulton."

"Right," Cody said.

Megan and I burst out onto a large roadway, and a second later Abraham's cycle came skidding out of a side street in front of us, almost level to the ground, the gravatonics keeping it from tipping over completely. It was impressive; the bike turned almost on its side, wheels spinning, sparks spraying out from underneath it. The gravatonic mechanisms cushioned the momentum so the wheels could grip the road and the cycle could turn, but only after an extended skid.

I'll bet I could drive one of these things, I told myself. *It doesn't look too hard.* Like slipping on a banana peel around a corner at eighty miles an hour. Piece of cake.

I glanced over my shoulder. There were at least a dozen black cycles behind us now, though we were going too fast for them to dare shooting at us. Everyone needed to concentrate on their driving. That was probably the idea behind going so fast in the first place.

"Armored unit!" Tia exclaimed. "Just ahead!"

We barely had time to react as a juggernaut of an armor unit, on two legs and standing fifteen feet high, lumbered out onto the street and opened fire with both rotary guns. Bullets hit the steel building wall beside us, creating a spray of sparks. I kept my head down and my jaw clenched as Megan kicked a lever on the cycle and sent us down in a long gravatonic skid, almost parallel to the ground, to pass under the bullets.

Wind ripped at my jacket, sparks blinded my vision. I could barely make out two enormous feet of steel on either side as we slid between the armor's legs. Megan brought the cycle up in a wide spin as we turned a corner. Abraham got around the armor to one side, but his cycle was trailing smoke.

"I'm hit," Abraham said.

"Are you all right?" Tia asked, alarmed.

"Jacket kept me in one piece," Abraham said with a grunt.

"Megan," I said softly. "He doesn't look good." Abraham was slowing, one hand holding his side.

She glanced at him, then turned quickly back to the road. "Abraham, as we take the next curve, I want you to break right into the first alleyway. They're far enough behind that they might not see. I'll keep straight and draw them after."

"They'll wonder where I went," Abraham said. "It—"

"Do it!" Megan said sharply.

He didn't object further. We took the next corner but had to slow down to keep from outpacing Abraham. I could see he was trailing blood, his cycle riddled with bullet holes. It was a wonder it was still moving.

As we came around, Abraham turned and darted right. Megan punched her cycle and the wind rose to a howl as we raced down a dark street. I risked a glance behind me and almost lost Cody's pack as it slipped down my shoulder. I had to release Megan for a moment with one hand and hold it, which threw me off balance and nearly sent me tumbling to the ground.

"Be careful," Megan said with a curse.

"Right," I said, confused. In that jumbled moment, I *thought* I'd seen another green cycle like our own, following us close behind.

I looked again. The Enforcement cycles seemed to have taken the bait and were following us and not Abraham. Their headlights were a wave of light on the street, helmets reflecting streetlights. Of the phantom cycle I'd thought I'd seen, there was no sign.

"Sparks," Tia said. "Megan, they've got blockades going up all around you, particularly in places that lead to the understreets. They seem to have guessed that's where we're trying to run."

In the distance I saw the flash of an explosion in the sky, and another copter began trailing smoke. There was yet another heading our way, however—a black form with blinking lights against the dark sky.

Megan sped up.

"Megan?" Tia said, her voice laced with urgency. *"You're heading straight for a blockade."*

Megan gave no response. I could feel her body growing more

and more rigid in my grip. She leaned forward, and intensity seemed to *stream* off her.

"Megan!" I said, noticing the lights flashing ahead as Enforcement set up their blockade. Cars, vans, trucks. A dozen or more soldiers, a mechanized unit.

"MEGAN!" I screamed.

She seemed to shake for a moment, then cursed and punched us to the side as gunfire pelted the street around us. We tore down an alleyway, the wall an inch from my elbow, then hit the next street and went down in a long turn, throwing sparks as we took the corner.

"I'm out," Abraham said softly, grunting. "Abandoning the cycle. I can make it to one of the bolt-holes. They didn't spot me, but some soldiers came down and started setting up in the stairway after I passed."

"Sparks," Cody murmured. "Are you monitoring the Enforcement audio lines, Tia?"

"Yeah," Tia said. "They're confused. They think this is a full-out assault on the city. Prof keeps blasting copters out of the air, and we all went different directions. Enforcement seems to think they're fighting dozens, maybe hundreds of insurgents."

"Good," Prof said. "Cody, are you clear?"

"I'm still dodging a few cycles," he said. "I've ended up looping around." He hesitated. "Tia, where's the limo? Is it still out?"

"It's breaking for Steelheart's palace," she said.

"I'm heading along that way too," Cody said. "What street?"

"Cody . . . ," Prof said.

Gunfire from behind distracted me from the rest of the conversation. I caught a glimpse of cycles, their drivers holding out SMGs and firing. We were going more slowly now; Megan had driven us into a slum neighborhood where the streets were smaller, and she was weaving us through lots of twists and turns.

"Megan, that's dangerous," Tia said. "There are a lot of dead ends in there."

"The other way is all dead ends," Megan answered. She seemed to have recovered from whatever lapse had almost led her to drive us right into a blockade.

"I'm going to have trouble leading you," Tia said. "Try to take the next right."

Megan started to break that direction, but an approaching cycle moved to cut us off, the soldier firing an SMG one-handed toward us in a spray. Megan cursed and slowed, sending the soldier on ahead, then she broke left down an alleyway. We nearly slammed into a large garbage bin, but she managed to weave around it. I guessed that we were barely going twenty.

Barely going twenty, I thought. Twenty mph down narrow alleys while being shot at. It was still insane, just a different kind of insane.

I could hold on pretty well with one arm at these speeds, Cody's pack thumping against my back. I probably should have dropped that by now. I didn't even know what was . . .

I felt at the pack, realizing something. I carefully slung it down in front of me, between Megan and myself. I gripped the cycle between my knees, let go of Megan, and unzipped the pack.

The gauss gun lay inside. Shaped like a regular assault rifle, perhaps a little longer, it had one of the power cells we'd recovered hooked up at the side. I pulled it out. With the power cell it was heavy, but I could still maneuver it.

"Megan!" Tia said. "Blockade ahead."

We turned into another alley, and I nearly lost the gun as I grabbed onto Megan with one arm.

"No!" Tia said. "Not right. That's— "

A motorcycle followed us into the alleyway. Bullets hit the wall just above my head. And right in front of us the alley ended in a wall. Megan tried to brake.

I didn't think. I grabbed the gun with both hands, leaned back, and raised the barrel right over Megan's shoulder.

Then I fired at the wall.

29

THE wall before us went up in a flash of green energy. Megan tried to turn the cycle and stop. We skidded through the churning green smoke, pebbles scattering under our tires, and slid out onto the street on the other side, where we came to a halt. Megan's body was braced for impact. She seemed stunned.

The Enforcement cyclist burst from the smoke. I swung the gauss gun and blasted his cycle out from underneath him. The shot turned the whole motorcycle into a flash of green energy, vaporizing it and part of the officer on it. His body went rolling.

The gun was amazing—there was no recoil, and the shots *vaporized* instead of really *exploding*. That left little debris, but gave a great light show and a lot of smoke.

Megan turned toward me, a grin splitting her lips. "About time you started doing something useful back there."

"Go," I said. The sound of more cycles was coming from the alleyway.

Megan revved our motorcycle, then led us in a darting, stomach-churning pattern through the narrow streets of the slum. I couldn't turn to fire the gun behind us as we drove, so instead I clung to her waist with one hand and settled the gun on her shoulder to steady it, using the iron sights, scope folded down to the side.

We roared out of an alleyway and skidded toward a blockade. I blasted a hole through a truck for us, then for good measure hit the armored unit with a shot to the leg. Soldiers scattered, yelling, some trying to fire as we sped through the opening I'd made. The armor unit collapsed and Megan dodged to the side, down a dark alley. Shouts and curses sounded behind as some of the cycles chasing us got caught up in the confusion.

"Nice work," Tia said in our ears, her voice calm again. "I think I can get you to the understreets. There's an old tunnel up ahead at the bottom of a flood gulley. You might have to blast your way through some walls, though."

"I think I can hit a wall or two," I said. "So long as they aren't good at dodging."

"Be careful," Prof said. "That gun drinks energy like Tia with a six-pack of cola. That power cell could run a small city, but it will give you only a dozen shots at best. Abraham, you still with us?"

"I'm here."

"You in the bolt-hole?"

"Yes. Bandaging my wound. It's not too bad."

"I'll be the judge of that. I'm almost to you. Cody, status?"

"I can see the limo," Cody said in my ear as Megan took another corner. "I've mostly shaken pursuit. I've got a tensor; I'll hit the limo with a grenade, then use the tensor to drill myself down to the understreets."

"Not an option," Prof said. "It'll take you too long to drill down that far."

"Wall!" Tia said.

"Got it," I said, blasting a hole through a wall at the end of an alleyway. We roared out into a backyard, and I blasted a hole in another wall, letting us cut into the next yard. Megan turned us to the right, then drove us through a very narrow slot between two houses.

"Go left," Tia said as we reached the street.

"Prof," Cody said. "I can *see* the limo. I can hit it."

"Cody, I don't—"

"I'm taking the shot, Prof," Cody said. "Abraham's right. Steelheart's going to come for us after this. We need to hurt him as much as we can, while we can."

"All right."

"Turn right," Tia said.

We turned.

"I'm sending you through a large building," Tia said. "Can you handle that?"

Gunfire sprayed against the wall beside us, and Megan cursed, hunkering down farther. I held the gauss gun in a sweaty grip, feeling terribly exposed with my back to the enemy. I could hear the cycles back there.

"They *really* seem to want you two," Tia said softly. "They're pulling a lot of resources toward you, and . . . Calamity!"

"What?" I said.

"My video feed just went out," Tia said. "Something's wrong. Cody?"

"Little busy," he grunted.

More gunfire sounded from behind. Something hit the cycle, jarring us, and Megan cursed.

"The building, Tia!" I said. "How do we find that building? We'll lose them inside."

"Second right," Tia told us. "Then straight to the end of the road. It's an old mall, and the gulley is just behind it. I was looking for other routes, but—"

"This will work," Megan said curtly. "David, be ready to open the place up for us."

"Got it," I said, steadying the gun, though it was harder now that she'd picked up speed. We took a corner, then turned toward a large, flat structure at the end of the road. I vaguely remembered malls from the days before Calamity. They'd been marketplaces, all enclosed.

Megan was driving fast and heading right at it. I took aim carefully and blasted through a set of steel doors in the front. We shot through the smoke, entering the heavy blackness of an abandoned building. The headlight of the cycle showed shops on either side of us.

The place had been looted long ago, though a lot of wares remained in the shops. Clothing that had been turned to steel wasn't particularly useful.

Megan wove easily through the mall's open corridors, taking us up a frozen escalator onto the second floor. Engines echoed throughout the building as Enforcement cycles followed us in.

Tia couldn't guide us any longer, it appeared, but Megan seemed to have an idea of what she was doing. From the balcony above, I got a shot at the cycles following us. I hit the ground in front of them, taking a chunk out of the floor and causing several to skid out, the others scattering for cover. None seemed to have drivers as skilled as Megan.

"Wall up ahead," Megan said.

I blasted it, then glanced at the energy meter on the side of the gauss gun. Prof was right; I'd drained it pretty quickly. We had maybe a couple of shots left.

We roared out into open air and the gravatonics on the cycle engaged, softening our landing as we fell one story to the street below. We still hit hard; the cycle wasn't intended to take jumps that high. I grunted, my backside and legs hammered from the impact. Megan immediately punched the vehicle forward down a narrow alleyway behind the mall.

I could see the ground fall away up ahead. The gulley. We only had to—

A sleek black copter rose out of the gulley in front of us, and the rotary guns on its sides began to spin up.

Not a chance, I thought, raising the gauss gun with both hands, sighting. Megan ducked lower and the cycle hit the edge of the gulley. The copter started firing. I could see the pilot's helmet through the glass of the cockpit.

I took the shot.

I'd often dreamed of doing incredible things. I'd imagined what it would be like to work with the Reckoners, to fight the Epics, to actually *do* things instead of sitting around thinking about them. With that shot, I finally got my chance.

I hung in the air, staring down a hundred-ton death machine, and squeezed the trigger. I popped the copter's canopy dead on, vaporizing it and the pilot inside. For a moment I felt like the Epics must. Like a god.

And then I fell out of the seat.

I should have expected it—going into free fall in a twenty-foot ravine with two hands on my gun and none on my ride made it kind of inevitable. I won't say I was happy to find myself plummeting toward broken legs and probably worse.

But that shot . . . That shot had been worth it.

I didn't feel much of the fall. It happened so fast. I hit mere moments after realizing I'd lost my seat, and I heard a crunch. That was followed by a *boom* that deafened me, and that was followed by a wave of heat.

I lay there, stunned, as my vision swam. I found myself facing the wreckage of the copter, which burned nearby. I felt numb.

Suddenly Megan was shaking me. I coughed, rolling over, and looked up at her. She'd pulled off her helmet, so I could see her face. Her beautiful face. She actually seemed concerned about me. That made me smile.

She was saying something. My ears rang, and I squinted, trying to read her lips. I could barely hear the words. ". . . up, you slontze! Get up!"

"You aren't supposed to shake someone who's suffered a fall," I mumbled. "Might have a broken back."

"You'll have a broken head if you don't *start moving*."

"But—"

"Idiot. Your jacket absorbed the blow. Remember? The one you wear to keep you from getting killed? They're supposed to make up for you doing stupid things like letting go of me in midair."

"It's not my intention to let go of you," I mumbled. "Not ever."

She froze.

Wait. Had I just said that out loud?

Jacket, I thought, wiggling my toes, then raising both arms. *The jacket's shielding device protected me. And . . . and we're still being chased.*

Calamity! I *was* a slontze. I rolled onto my knees and let Megan help me to my feet. I coughed a few times but felt more stable by the moment. I let go of her and was pretty steady by the time we reached the cycle, which she'd landed without crashing.

"Wait," I said, looking around. "Where is . . ."

The gauss gun lay in several pieces where it had fallen and hit a steel rock. I felt a sinking feeling, though I knew the gun wasn't nearly as useful to us now. We couldn't use it to pretend to be an Epic any longer, not now that Enforcement had seen me shooting it.

Still, it was a pity to lose such a nice weapon. Particularly after leaving my own rifle in the van. I was making a real habit of that sort of thing.

I climbed onto the cycle behind Megan, who pulled on her helmet again. The poor machine was looking pretty ragged, scratched and dented, the windshield cracked. One of the gravatonics—a palm-size oval on the right side—didn't light up like the others anymore. But the cycle still started, and the engine roared as Megan drove us down the ravine toward a large tunnel up ahead. It looked like it led into the sewage system, but a lot of things like that were misleading in Newcago, what with the Great Transfersion and the creation of the understreets.

"Hey, all y'all?" Cody said softly in our ears. By some miracle I'd kept my mobile and earpiece through the fall. "Something strange is going on. Something very, very strange is going on."

"Cody," Tia said. "Where are you?"

"Limo's down," he said. "I shot out one of the tires and it drove itself into a wall. I had to eliminate six soldiers before I could approach."

Megan and I passed into the tunnel, the darkness deepening. The ground sloped downward. I was vaguely familiar with the area, and I figured this would lead us into the understreets near Gibbons Street, a relatively unpopulated area.

"What about Conflux?" Prof asked Cody.

"He wasn't inside the limo."

"Maybe one of the Enforcement officers you shot was actually Conflux," Tia said.

"Nah," Cody said. "I found him. In the trunk."

The line was quiet for a moment.

"You're sure it's him?" Prof asked.

"Well, no," Cody said. "Maybe they had some *other* Epic tied up in their trunk. Either way, the dowser says this lad's *very* powerful. But he's unconscious."

"Shoot him," Prof said.

"No," Megan said. "Bring him."

"I think she's right, Prof," Cody said. "If he's tied up, he can't be that strong. Either that, or they've used his weakness to make him impotent."

"We don't know his weakness, though," Prof said. "Put him out of his misery."

"I'm not shooting an unconscious fellow, Prof," Cody said. "Not even an Epic."

"Then leave him."

I was torn. Epics deserved to die. All of them. But why was he unconscious—what were they doing with him? Was it even Conflux?

"Jon," Tia said. "We might need this. If it *is* Conflux, he could tell us things. We might even be able to use him against Steelheart, or bargain for our escape."

"He's not supposed to be very dangerous," I admitted, speaking into the line. My lip was bleeding. I'd bit it when I'd fallen, and now that I was a little more aware of things I realized my leg was aching and my side was *throbbing*. The jackets helped, but they were far from perfect.

"Fine," Prof said. "Bolt-hole seven, Cody. Don't take him to the base. Leave him tied up, blindfolded, and gagged. Do *not* talk to him. We need to deal with him together."

"Right," Cody said. "I'm on it."

"Megan and David," Prof said, "I want you to—"

I lost the rest as gunfire erupted around us. The cycle—battered as it was—spun out and went down.

Right onto the side where the gravatonics were broken.

30

WITHOUT the gravatonics, the cycle reacted like any normal motor-cycle would when falling onto its side at very high speed.

Which isn't a good thing.

I was immediately ripped free, the cycle skidding out from underneath me as my leg hit the ground and the friction pulled me backward. Megan wasn't so lucky. She got pinned under the cycle, its weight grinding her against the ground. It collided with the wall of the tubular steel corridor.

The tunnel wavered, and my leg burned with pain. As I rolled to a halt and things stopped shaking, I realized that I was still alive. I actually found that surprising.

Behind us, from an alcove we had driven past, two men in full Enforcement armor stepped out of the shadows. There were some small, faint lights ringing the edge of the alcove. By that light I could see that the soldiers looked relaxed. I swore I could hear one chuckling inside his helmet as he said something over the comm unit to his companion. They assumed Megan and I would both be dead—or at least knocked out of fighting shape—by such a crash.

To Calamity with that, I thought, cheeks hot with anger. Before I'd had time to think, I'd unholstered the pistol under my arm—the pistol that had killed my father—and unloaded four shots at nearly point-blank range into the men. I didn't aim for their chests, not with their armor. The sweet spot was the neck.

Both men fell. I breathed in a deep, ragged breath, my hand and gun shaking in front of me. I blinked a few times, shocked that I'd managed to hit them. Maybe Megan was right about handguns.

I groaned, then managed to sit up. My Reckoner jacket was in tatters; many of the diodes along its inside—the ones that generated the protective field—were smoking or entirely ripped free. My leg was scraped badly along one side. Though it hurt fiercely, the lacerations weren't too deep. I was able to stumble to my feet and walk. Kind of.

The pain was . . . rather unpleasant.

Megan! The thought came through the daze, and—stupid though it was—I didn't check to see if the two soldiers were actually dead. I limped over to where the fallen cycle had skidded up against the wall. The only light here was from my mobile. I pushed aside the wreckage and found Megan sprawled beneath, her jacket in even worse shape than mine.

She didn't look good. She wasn't moving, her eyes were closed, and her helmet was cracked, only halfway on. Blood trailed down her cheek. It was the color of her lips. Her arm was twisted at an awkward angle, and her entire side—leg up to torso—was bloodied. I knelt, aghast, the cool, calm light of my mobile revealing horrible wounds everywhere I turned it.

"David?" Tia's voice came softly from my mobile, which hung in its place from my jacket. It was a miracle it still functioned, though I'd lost my earpiece. "David? I can't reach Megan. What's going on?"

"Megan's down," I said numbly. "Her mobile is gone. Shattered, probably." It had been attached to her jacket, which was mostly gone also.

Breathing. I have to see if she's breathing. I leaned down, trying to use my mobile screen to catch her breath. Then I thought to check for a pulse. *I'm in shock. I'm not thinking right.* Could you think that, when you weren't thinking right?

I pressed my fingers against Megan's neck. The skin felt clammy.

"David!" Tia said urgently. "David, there's chatter on the Enforcement channels. They know where you are. There are multiple units converging on you. Infantry and armor. Go!"

I felt a pulse. Shallow, light, but there.

"She's alive," I said. "Tia, she's alive!"

"You *have* to get out of there, David!"

Moving Megan could make things worse for her, but leaving her would definitely make things worse. If they took her she'd be tortured and executed. I pulled off my tattered jacket and used it to wrap my leg. As I worked I felt something in the pocket. I pulled it out. The pen detonator and blasting caps.

In a moment of lucidity I stuck one of the blasting caps on the cycle's fuel cell. I'd heard you could destabilize and blow those, if you knew what you were doing—which I didn't. It seemed like a good idea, though. My *only* idea. I took my mobile and attached it to my wrist mount. Then, sucking in a deep breath, I shoved aside the broken motorcycle—the front wheel had been ripped clean off—and lifted Megan.

Her broken helmet slipped free, falling off and cracking against the ground. That made her hair cascade down over my shoulder. She was heavier than she looked. People always are. Though she was small, she was compact, *dense*. I decided she'd probably not like hearing me describe her that way.

I got her up over my shoulders, then began an unsteady hike down the tunnel. Tiny yellow lights hung from the ceiling periodically, giving barely enough light to see by, even for an understreeter like me.

Soon my shoulders and back were complaining. I kept on going, one foot after another. I wasn't moving very quickly. I wasn't thinking very well either.

"David." Prof's voice. Quiet, intense.

"I'm *not* leaving her," I said through clenched teeth.

"I wouldn't have you do something like that," Prof said. "I'd much sooner have you stand your ground and make Enforcement gun you both down."

Not very comforting.

"It's not going to come to that, son," Prof said. "Help is on its way."

"I think I can hear them," I said. I'd finally reached the end of the tunnel; it opened onto a narrow crossroads in the understreets. There were no buildings here, just steel corridors. I didn't know this part of town well.

The ceiling was solid, with no gaps up to the air above like there were in the area where I'd grown up. Those were definitely shouts I heard echoing from the right. I heard *clank*s from behind, steel feet pounding against the steel ground. More shouts. They'd found the cycle.

I leaned up against the wall, shifting Megan's weight, then pressed the button on my pen detonator. I was relieved to hear a *pop* from behind as the cycle's fuel cell blew. The shouts rose. Maybe I'd caught a few of them in the blast; if I was really lucky they'd assume I was hiding somewhere near the wreckage and had tossed a grenade or something.

I hefted Megan, then took the left turn at the crossroads. Her blood had soaked my clothing. She was probably dead by—

No. I wouldn't think about that. One foot in front of the other. Help was coming. Prof *promised* help was coming. It would come. Prof didn't lie. Jonathan Phaedrus, founder of the Reckoners, a man I somehow understood. If there was anything in this world I felt I could trust, it was him.

I walked a good five minutes before I was forced to pull up short. The tunnel in front of me ended in a flat wall of steel. Dead end. I glanced over my shoulder to see flashlights and shadows moving. No escape that way.

The corridor around me was wide, maybe twenty paces across, and tall. There was some old construction equipment on the ground, though most of it looked to have been picked over by opportunists. There were a few heaps of broken bricks and cinder blocks. Someone had been building more rooms down here recently. Well, those might provide some cover.

I stumbled over and laid Megan down behind the largest of the piles, then I flipped my mobile to manual response. Prof and the others wouldn't be able to hear me unless I touched the screen to broadcast, but it also meant they wouldn't give away my position by trying to contact me.

I crouched down behind the bricks. The pile didn't give me complete cover, but it was better than nothing. Cornered, outgunned, with no way to . . .

Suddenly I felt like an idiot. I dug in the zip pocket on my trouser leg, fishing for my tensor. I pulled it out triumphantly. Maybe I could dig down to the steel catacombs, or even just dig out to the side and find a safer path.

I pulled on the glove, and only then did I realize that the tensor had been shredded. I stared at it with a sinking despair. It had been in the pocket on the leg I'd landed on when falling, and the pouch had been ripped at the bottom. The tensor was missing two fingers, and the electronics had been shattered, pieces hanging off like eyes drooping out of a zombie's sockets in an old horror movie.

I almost laughed as I settled back down. The Enforcement soldiers were searching the corridors. Shouts. Footsteps. Flashlights. Getting closer.

My mobile blinked softly. I turned the volume way down, then pressed the screen and leaned in. "David?" Tia asked in a very quiet voice. "David, where are you?"

"I reached the bottom of the tunnel," I whispered back, holding the mobile up to my mouth. "I turned left."

"Left? That's a dead end. You need to—"

"I know," I said. "There were soldiers the other directions." I glanced at Megan, lying slumped on the floor. I tested her neck again.

Still a pulse. I closed my eyes in relief. *Not that it matters now.*

"Calamity," Tia swore. I heard gunfire and jumped, thinking it was from my position. But it wasn't. It was from the line.

"Tia?" I hissed.

"They're here," she said. "Don't worry about me. I can hold this place. David, you have to—"

"Hey, you!" a voice called from the intersection.

I ducked down, but the mound of bricks wasn't large enough to hide me completely unless I was practically lying flat.

"There's someone over there!" the voice shouted. Powerful, Enforcement-issue flashlights pointed my direction. Most of those would be on the ends of assault rifles.

My mobile flashed. I tapped it. "David." Prof's voice. He sounded winded. "Use the tensor."

"Broken," I whispered. "I ruined it in the crash."

Silence.

"Try it anyway," Prof urged.

"Prof, it's dead." I peeked over the bricks. A large crowd of soldiers was gathering at the other end of the hall. Several were kneeling with guns pointed in my direction, eyes to scopes. I kept low.

"Just do it," Prof ordered.

I sighed, then pressed my hand against the ground. I closed my eyes, but it wasn't easy to concentrate.

"Hold up your arms and walk forward slowly!" a voice shouted down the hall toward me. "If you do not show yourself, we will be forced to open fire."

I tried as best I could to ignore them. I focused on the tensor, on the vibrations. For a moment I thought I felt something, a low hum—deep, powerful.

It was gone. This was stupid. Like trying to saw a hole in a wall using only a bottle of soda.

"Sorry, Prof," I said. "It's busted up good." I checked the magazine on my father's gun. Five rounds left. Five precious rounds that might be able to hurt Steelheart. I'd never have the chance to find out.

"You are running out of time, friend!" the soldier called toward me.

"You have to hold out," Prof said urgently. His voice sounded frail with the volume down so low.

"You should go to Tia," I said, preparing myself.

"She'll be fine," Prof said. "Abraham is on his way to help her, and the hideout was designed with an attack in mind. She can seal the entrance and wait them out. David, you *must* hang on long enough for me to arrive."

"I'll see that they don't take us alive, Prof," I promised. "The safety of the Reckoners is more important than I am." I fished at Megan's side, getting out her handgun and then flipping off its safety. SIG Sauer P226, .40 caliber. A nice gun.

"I'm coming, son," Prof said softly. *"Hold out."*

I peeked up. The officers were advancing, guns raised. They probably wanted to take me alive. Well, maybe that would let me take a few of them out before I fell.

I lifted Megan's gun and let loose a burst of rapid-fire shots. They had the intended effect; the officers scattered, seeking cover.

Some fired back, and chips sprayed across me as bricks exploded to automatic-weapon fire.

Well, so much for hoping they wanted me alive.

I was sweating. "Hell of a way to go, eh?" I found myself saying to Megan as I ducked around and fired on an officer who'd gotten too close. I think one of the bullets actually got through his armor—he was limping as he jumped behind a few rusty barrels.

I hunkered down again, assault-rifle fire sounding like fire-crackers in a tin can. Which was, as I thought about it, kind of what this was. *I'm getting better.* I smiled wryly as I dumped the magazine from Megan's gun and locked a new one in.

"I'm sorry to let you down," I said to her immobile form. Her breathing had grown more shallow. "You deserved to live through this, even if I didn't."

I tried to fire off more rounds, but gunfire drove me back to cover before I could get off a single shot. I breathed hard, wiping some blood from my cheek. Some of the exploding rubble had hit hard enough to cut me.

"You know," I said, "I think I fell for you that first day. Stupid, huh? Love at first sight. What a cliché." I got off three shots, but the soldiers were acting less scared now. They had figured out there was only one of me, and that my gun was only a handgun. I was prob-ably only alive because I'd blown the cycle, which made them worry about explosives.

"I don't even know if I can call it love," I whispered, reloading. "Am I in love? Is it just infatuation? We've known each other for less than a month, and you've treated me like dirt about half that time. But that day fighting Fortuity and that day in the power plant, it seems like we had something. A . . . I don't know. Something to-gether. Something I wanted."

I glanced at her pale, motionless figure.

"I think," I said, "that a month ago, I would have left you by the cycle. Because I wanted so badly to get my vengeance on *him.*"

Bam, bam, bam!

The pile of bricks shook, as if the officers were trying to cut through them to get to me.

"That scares me about myself," I said softly, not looking at Megan. "For what it's worth, thank you for making me care about something other than Steelheart. I don't know if I love you. But whatever the emotion is, it's the strongest one I've felt in years. Thank you." I fired widely but fell back as a bullet grazed my arm.

The magazine was empty. I sighed, dropping Megan's gun and raising my father's. Then I pointed it at her.

My finger hesitated on the trigger. It would be a mercy. Better a quick death than to suffer torture and execution. I tried to force myself to pull the trigger.

Sparks, she looks beautiful, I thought. Her unbloodied side was toward me, her golden hair fanning out, her skin pale and eyes closed as if asleep.

Could I really do this?

The gunshots had paused. I risked glancing over my crumbling pile of bricks. Two enormous forms were mechanically clomping down the hallway. So they *had* brought in armor units. A piece of me felt proud that I was such a problem for them. The chaos the Reckoners had caused this day, the destruction we'd brought to Steelheart's minions, had driven them to overkill. A squad of twenty men and two mechanized armors had been sent to take down one guy with a pistol.

"Time to die," I whispered. "I think I'll do it while firing a handgun at a fifteen-foot-tall suit of powered armor. At least it will be dramatic."

I took a deep breath, nearly surrounded by Enforcement forms creeping forward in the dark corridor. I began to stand, my gun leveled at Megan more firmly this time. I'd shoot her, then force the soldiers to gun me down.

I noticed that my mobile was blinking.

"Fire!" a soldier yelled.

The ceiling melted.

I saw it distinctly. I was looking down the tunnel, not wanting to watch Megan as I shot her. I had a clear view of a circle in the ceiling becoming a column of black dust, cascading in a shower of disintegrated steel. Like sand from an enormous spigot, the particles hit the floor and billowed outward in a cloud.

The haze cleared. My finger twitched, but I had not pulled the trigger. A figure stood from a crouch amid the dust; he had fallen from above. He wore a black coat—thin, like a lab coat—dark trousers, black boots, and a small pair of goggles over his eyes.

Prof had come, and he wore a tensor on each hand, the green light glowing with a phantom cast.

The officers opened fire, releasing a storm of bullets down the hallway. Prof raised his hand and thrust forward the glowing tensor. I could almost *feel* the device hum.

Bullets burst in midair, crumbling. They hit Prof as little shavings of fluttering steel, no more dangerous than pinches of dirt. Hundreds of them pelted him and the ground around him; the ones that missed flew apart in the air, catching the light. Suddenly I understood why he wore the goggles.

I stood up, slack jawed, gun forgotten in my fingers. I'd assumed *I* was getting good with my tensor, but destroying those bullets . . . that was beyond anything I'd been able to comprehend.

Prof didn't give the baffled soldiers time to recover. He carried no weapon that I could see, but he leaped free of the dust and dashed right toward them. The mechanized units started firing, but they used their rotary guns—as if they couldn't believe what they'd seen and figured a higher caliber was the answer.

More bullets popped in the air, shattered by Prof's tensors. His feet skidded across the ground on the dust, and then he reached the Enforcement troops.

He attacked fully armored men with his fists.

293

My eyes widened as I saw him drop a soldier with a fist to the face, the man's helmet melting to powder before his attack. *He's vaporizing the armor as he attacks.* Prof spun between two soldiers, moving gracefully, slamming a fist into the gut of one, then spinning and slamming an arm into the leg of the other. Dust sprayed out as their armor failed them, disintegrating just before Prof hit.

As he came up from the spin he pounded a hand against the side of the steel chamber. The pulverized metal poured away, and something long and thin fell from the wall into his hand. A sword, carved from the steel by an incredibly precise tensor blast.

Steel flashed as Prof struck at the disordered officers. Some tried to keep firing, and others were going in with batons—which Prof destroyed just as easily as he had the bullets. He wielded the sword in one hand, and his other hand sent out near-invisible blasts that reduced metal and kevlar to nothing. Dust streamed off soldiers who got too close to him, making them slip and stumble, suddenly unbalanced as helmets melted around their heads and body armor fell away.

Blood flew in front of high-powered flashlights, and men collapsed. It had been mere heartbeats since Prof had dropped into the room, but a good dozen of the soldiers were down.

The armored units had drawn their shoulder-mounted energy cannons, but Prof had gotten too close. He hit a patch of steel dust at a sprint, then slid in a crouch forward, moving on the dust with obvious familiarity. He twisted to the side and swung his forearm, *smashing* through the armored unit's leg. Powder sprayed out the back as Prof's arm passed completely through it.

He slid to a stop, still on one knee. The armor collapsed with a resounding *thud* as Prof leaped forward and drilled his fist through the second armor's leg. He pulled his hand out and the leg bent, then snapped, the unit collapsing sideways. It fired a yellow-blue blast into the ground as it fell, melting a portion of the floor.

One foolhardy member of Enforcement tried to charge Prof, who stood over the fallen armors. Prof didn't bother with the sword. He dodged to the side, then slammed his fist forward. I could see the fist approach the soldier's face, could see the helmet's visor vaporizing just in front of Prof's punch.

The soldier dropped. The hallway grew silent. Sparkling steel flakes floated in beams of light like snow at midnight.

"I," Prof said in a powerful, self-assured voice, "am known as Limelight. Let your master know that I am *more* than aggravated by being forced to bother myself with you worms. Unfortunately, my minions are fools, and are incapable of following the simplest of orders.

"Tell your master that the time for dancing and playing is through. If he does not come to face me himself, I will dismantle this city piece by piece until I find him." Prof strode past the remaining soldiers without sparing them a glance.

He walked toward me, his back to the soldiers. I grew tense, waiting for them to try something. But they didn't. They cowered. Men did not fight Epics. They had been taught this, had it drilled into them.

Prof reached me, face shrouded in shadows, light shining from behind.

"That was *genius*," I said softly.

"Get the girl."

"I can't believe that you—"

Prof looked at me, and I finally caught sight of his features. Jaw clenched, eyes seeming to blaze with intensity. There was *contempt* in those eyes, and the sight of it caused me to stumble back in shock.

Prof seemed to be shaking, his hands forming fists, as if he were holding back something terrible. "Get. The. Girl."

I nodded dumbly, stuffing my gun back in my pocket and picking up Megan.

"Jon?" Tia's voice came from his mobile; mine was still on silent. "Jon, the soldiers have pulled out from my position. What's going on?"

Prof didn't reply. He waved a tensored hand and the ground before us melted away. The dust drained, like sand in an hourglass, revealing an improvised tunnel to the lower levels below.

I followed him through the tunnel, and we made our escape.

PART FOUR

31

"**ABRAHAM,** more blood," Tia said, working with a frantic urgency. Abraham—his arm in a sling, which was stained red with his own blood—hastened to the cooler.

Megan lay on the steel conference table in the main room of our hideout. Stacks of paper and some of Abraham's tools lay on the floor where I'd swept them. Now I sat to the side, feeling helpless, exhausted, and terrified. Prof had burrowed us a path into the hideout from the back; the front entrance had been sealed by Tia using some metal plugs and a special type of incendiary grenade.

I didn't understand much of what Tia was doing as she worked on Megan. It involved bandages and attempts to stitch wounds. Apparently Megan had internal injuries. Tia found those even more distressing than the huge amounts of blood Megan had lost.

I could see Megan's face. It was turned toward me, angel's eyes closed softly. Tia had cut free most of Megan's clothing, revealing the extent of her wounds. Horrible wounds.

It seemed strange that her face was so serene. But I felt like I understood. I felt numb myself.

One step after another . . . I'd carried her back to the hideout. That time was a blur, a blur of pain and fright, of aching and dizziness.

Prof hadn't offered to help a single time. He'd almost left me behind at several points.

"Here," Abraham said to Tia, arriving with another pouch of blood.

"Hook it up," Tia said distractedly, working on Megan's side opposite me. I could see her bloodied surgical gloves reflecting the light. She hadn't had time to change, and her regular clothing—a cardigan over a blouse and jeans—was now stained with streaks of red. She worked with intense concentration, but her voice betrayed panic.

Tia's mobile beeped a soft rhythm; it had a medical package, and she had set it on Megan's chest to detect her heartbeat. Tia occasionally picked it up to take quick ultrasounds of Megan's abdomen. With the part of my brain that could still think, I was impressed by the Reckoners' preparations. I hadn't even known that Tia had medical training, let alone that we had blood and surgical equipment in storage.

She shouldn't look that way, I thought, blinking out tears I hadn't realized were forming. *So vulnerable. Naked on the table. Megan is stronger than that. Shouldn't they cover her a little with a sheet or something as they work?*

I caught myself rising to fetch something to cover her, something to give a semblance of modesty, but then realized how stupid I was being. Each moment was crucial here, and I couldn't go blundering in and distract Tia.

I sat down. I was covered in Megan's blood. I couldn't smell it anymore; I guess my nose had gotten used to it.

She has to be okay, I thought, dazed. *I saved her. I brought her back. She has to be all right, now. That's the way it works.*

"This shouldn't be happening," Abraham said softly. "The harmsway . . ."

"It doesn't work on everyone," Tia said. "I don't know why. I *wish* I knew why, dammit. But it has never worked well on Megan, just like she always had trouble working the tensors."

Stop talking about her weaknesses! I screamed at them in my head.

Megan's heartbeat was getting even weaker. I could hear it, amplified by Tia's phone—*beep, beep, beep.* Before I knew it, I was standing up. I turned toward Prof's thinking room. Cody hadn't returned to the hideout; he was still watching the captured Epic in a separate location, as he'd been ordered. But Prof was here, in the other room. He'd walked straight there after arriving, not once looking at Megan or me.

"David!" Tia said sharply. "What are you doing?"

"I . . . I . . . ," I stammered, trying to get out the words. "I'm going to get Prof. He'll do something. He'll save her. He knows what to do."

"Jon can't do anything here," Tia said. "Sit back down."

The sharp order cut through my dazed confusion. I sat and watched Megan's closed eyes as Tia worked, swearing softly to herself. The curses almost matched the beat of Megan's heart. Abraham stood to the side, looking helpless.

I watched her eyes. Watched her serene, calm face as the beeps slowed. Then stopped. There was no flatline sound from the mobile. Just silence that carried a weight of meaning. Nothingness laden with data.

"This . . . ," I said, blinking tears. "I mean, I carried her all the way here, Tia. . . ."

"I'm sorry," Tia said. She raised a hand to her face, leaving a bloody mark on her forehead. Then she sighed and leaned back against the wall, looking exhausted.

"Do something," I said. Not an order. A plea.

"I've done what I can," Tia said. "She's gone, David."

Silence.

"Those wounds were bad," Tia continued. "You did everything you could. It's not your fault. To be honest, even if you'd been able to get her here immediately, I don't know if she'd have made it."

"I . . ." I couldn't think.

Cloth rustled. I glanced to the side. Prof stood in the doorway to his room. He'd dusted off his clothing, and he looked clean and dignified, a sharp contrast to the rest of us. His eyes flickered to Megan. "She's gone?" he asked. His voice had softened a little from before, though he still didn't sound like I felt he should.

Tia nodded.

"Gather what you can," Prof said, slinging a pack over his shoulder. "We're abandoning this position. It's been compromised."

Tia and Abraham nodded, as if they'd been expecting this order. Abraham did pause to lay a hand on Megan's shoulder and bow his head, and then he moved his hand to the pendant at his neck. He hurried off to gather his tools.

I took a blanket from Megan's bedroll—it didn't have sheets—and brought it back to lay over her. Prof looked at me, and he seemed about to object to the frivolous action, but he held his tongue. I tucked the blanket around Megan's shoulders but left her head exposed. I don't know why people cover the face after someone dies. The face is the only thing left that is still right. I brushed it with my fingers. The skin was still warm.

This isn't happening, I thought numbly. *The Reckoners don't fail like this.*

Unfortunately, facts—my own facts—flooded my mind. The

Reckoners *did* fail; members of the Reckoners *did* die. I'd researched this. I'd studied this. It happened.

It just shouldn't have happened to Megan.

I need to see her body cared for, I thought, bending down to pick her up.

"Leave the corpse," Prof said.

I ignored him, then felt him gripping my shoulder. I looked up through bleary eyes and found his expression harsh, eyes wide and angry. They softened as I looked at him.

"What's done is done," Prof said. "We'll burn out this hole, and that will be a fitting burial for her. Regardless, trying to bring the body would just slow us down, maybe get us killed. The soldiers are probably still watching the front position. We can't know how long it will take them to find the new hole I cut in here." He hesitated. "She's gone, son."

"I should have run faster," I whispered, in direct contrast to what Tia had said. "I should have been able to save her."

"Are you angry?" Prof asked.

"I . . ."

"Abandon the guilt," Prof said. "Abandon the denial. Steelheart did this to her. He's our goal. That has to be your focus. We don't have time for grief; we only have time for vengeance."

I found myself nodding. Many would have called those the wrong words, but they worked for me. Prof was right. If I moped and grieved, I'd die. I needed something to replace those emotions, something strong.

Anger at Steelheart. That would do it. He'd taken my father from me, and now he'd taken Megan too. I had a lurking understanding that so long as he lived, he'd take everything I loved from me.

Hate Steelheart. Use that to keep me going. Yes . . . I could do that. I nodded.

"Gather your notes," Prof said, "and then pack up the imager.

We're leaving in ten minutes, and we'll destroy anything we leave behind."

I looked back down the new tunnel Prof had cut into the hideout. Harsh red light glowed at its end, a funeral pyre for Megan. The blast Abraham had rigged was hot enough to melt steel; I could feel the heat from here, far away.

If Enforcement managed to cut into the hideout, all they'd find would be slag and dust. We had carried out what we could, and Tia had stashed a little more in a hidden pocket she'd had Abraham cut into a nearby corridor. For the second time in a month, I watched a home I'd known burn.

This one took something very dear with it. I wanted to say good-bye, to whisper it or at least think it. I couldn't get the word to form. I just . . . I guess I just wasn't ready.

I turned and followed the others, hiking away into the darkness.

An hour later I was still walking through the dark corridor, head down, pack slung on my back. I was so tired I could barely think.

It was odd, though—as strong as my hatred had been for a short time, now it was just lukewarm. Replacing Megan with hatred seemed a poor trade.

There was motion ahead and Tia fell back. She'd changed quickly from her bloodstained clothing. She'd also forced me to do so before abandoning the hideout. I'd washed my hands too, but there was still blood crusted under my fingernails.

"Hey," Tia said. "You're looking pretty tired."

I shrugged.

"Do you want to talk?"

"Not about her. Just . . . not right now."

"Okay. Then something else, maybe?" Something to distract you, her tone implied.

Well, maybe that would be nice. Except the only other thing I wanted to talk about was nearly as distressing. "Why is Prof so mad at me?" I asked softly. "He looked . . . He looked *indignant* that he had to come rescue me."

That made me sick. When he'd spoken to me via mobile, he'd seemed encouraging, determined to help. And then after . . . he felt like another person. It lingered with him still, as he walked alone at the front of the group.

Tia followed my gaze. "Prof has some . . . bad memories attached to the tensors, David. He hates using them."

"But—"

"He's not mad at you," Tia said, "and he's *not* bothered by having to rescue you, regardless of how it might have seemed. He's mad at himself. He just needs some time alone."

"But he was so *good* with them, Tia."

"I know," she said softly. "I've seen it. There are troubles there you can't understand, David. Sometimes doing things we used to do reminds us of who we used to be, and not always in good ways."

That didn't make much sense to me. But then, my mind wasn't exactly the most crisp it had ever been.

We eventually reached the new bolt-hole, which was much smaller than the hideout—only two small rooms. Cody met us but spoke with a subdued tone. He'd been briefed, obviously, about what had happened. He helped us carry our equipment up into the main chamber of the new hideout.

Conflux, the head of Enforcement, was captive in there somewhere. Were we foolhardy to think we could hold him? Was this all part of another trap? I had to assume that Prof and Tia knew what they were doing.

As he worked, Abraham flexed his arm—the one that had taken a bullet. The little diodes of the harmsway flashed on his biceps, and the bullet holes had scabbed over already. A night sleeping with those diodes on and he'd be able to use the arm without trouble in the morning. A few days and the wound would only be a scar.

And yet, I thought, handing my pack to Cody and crawling through the tunnel to the upper chamber, *it didn't help Megan. Nothing we did helped Megan.*

I had lost a lot of people in the last ten years. Life in Newcago wasn't easy, particularly for orphans. But none of those losses had affected me this profoundly since my father's death. I guess it was a good thing—it meant I was learning to care again. Still, it felt pretty crappy at the moment.

When I came out of the entry tunnel and into the new hideout, Prof was telling everyone to bed down for the night. He wanted us to have some sleep in us before we dealt with the captive Epic. As I arranged my bedroll, I heard him speaking with Cody and Tia. Something about injecting the captive Epic with a sedative so that he remained unconscious.

"David?" Tia asked. "You're wounded. I should hook up the harmsway to you and . . ."

"I'll live," I said. They could heal me tomorrow. I didn't care at the moment. Instead I lay down on my bedroll and turned over to face the wall. Then I finally let the tears come in force.

32

ABOUT sixteen hours later I sat on the floor of the new hideout, eating a bowl of oatmeal sprinkled with raisins, harmsway diodes flashing on my leg and side. We'd had to leave most of our good food behind and were relying on storage that had been packed in the bolt-hole.

The other Reckoners gave me space. I found that odd, since they'd all known Megan longer than I had. It wasn't like she and I had actually shared anything special, even if she *had* begun warming up to me.

In fact, as I looked back on it, my reaction to her death seemed silly. I was just a boy with a crush. It still hurt, though. Badly.

"Hey, Prof," Cody said, sitting in front of a laptop. "You should see this, mate."

"Mate?" Prof asked.

"I've got a little bit of Australian in me," Cody said. "My father's grandfather was one-quarter Aussie. Been meaning to try it out for a spin."

"You're a bizarre little man, Cody," Prof said. He was back to his normal self, for the most part—maybe a little more solemn today. So were the rest of them, even Cody. Losing a teammate wasn't a pleasant experience, though I got the sense that they'd been through all of this before.

Prof studied the screen for a moment, then raised an eyebrow. Cody tapped, then tapped again.

"What is it?" Tia asked.

Cody turned the laptop around. None of us had chairs; we were all just sitting on our bedrolls. Even though this hideout was smaller than the other, it felt empty to me. There weren't enough of us.

The screen was blue, with simple block letters in black. PICK A TIME AND LOCATION. I WILL COME.

"This," Cody said, "is all people can see on any of the one hundred entertainment channels in Steelheart's network. It's displayed on every mobile that logs on, and on every information screen in the city. Something makes me think we got through to him."

Prof smiled. "This is good. He's letting us pick the place for the fight."

"He usually does that," I said, staring into my oatmeal. "He let Faultline choose. He thinks it sends a message—this city is his, and he doesn't care if you try to find a place that gives you the better ground. He'll kill you anyway."

"I just wish I didn't feel blind," Tia said. She was sitting in the far corner with her datapad. It had her mobile stuck to the back so its display expanded what was on the mobile's screen. "It's baffling. How did they find out that I'd hacked their camera system? I'm locked out on all sides, every hole plugged. I can't see a thing of what's going on in the city."

"We'll pick a place where we can set up our own cameras," Prof said. "You won't be blind when we face him, Tia. It—"

Abraham's mobile beeped. He raised it up. "Proximity alarms say that our prisoner is stirring, Prof."

"Good," Prof said, standing up and looking toward the entrance to the smaller room that held our captive. "That mystery has been itching at me all day." As he turned, his eyes fell on me, and I caught a flash of guilt from him.

He moved past me quickly and began giving orders. We'd interrogate the prisoner with a light shining directly on him, Cody standing behind him with a gun to the Epic's head. Everyone was to wear their jackets. They'd replaced mine with a spare. It was black leather, too large for me by a size or two.

The Reckoners began moving to set things up. Cody and Tia entered the prisoner's room, eventually followed by Prof. I shoved a spoonful of oatmeal in my mouth, then noticed Abraham, who was lingering in the main room.

He walked over to me and knelt on one knee. "Live, David," he said softly. "Live your life."

"I'm doing that," I grumbled.

"No. You are letting Steelheart live your life for you. He controls it, each step of the way. Live your own life." He patted my shoulder, as if that made everything all right, then waved for me to come with him into the next room.

I sighed, climbed to my feet, and followed.

The captive was a spindly older man—perhaps in his sixties— balding and dark skinned. He was turning his head about, trying to figure out where he was, though he was still blindfolded and gagged. He certainly didn't look threatening, strapped into his chair as he was. Of course many an "unthreatening" Epic could kill with little more than a thought.

Conflux wasn't supposed to have powers like that. But then,

Fortuity wasn't supposed to have had heightened dexterity. Besides, we didn't even know if this *was* Conflux. I found myself pondering the situation, which was good. At least it kept me from thinking about her.

Abraham aimed a large floodlight right at the captive's face. Many Epics needed line of sight to use their powers on someone, so keeping the man disoriented had a very real and useful purpose. Prof nodded to Cody, who cut off the prisoner's blindfold and gag, then stepped back and leveled a wicked .357 at the man's head.

The prisoner blinked against the light, then looked about. He cringed in his chair.

"Who are you?" Prof asked, standing by the light where the prisoner wouldn't be able to make out his features.

"Edmund Sense," the prisoner said. He paused. "And you?"

"That is not important to you."

"Well, seeing as to how you have me captive, I suspect it's of *utmost* importance to me." Edmund had a pleasant voice, with a faint Indian accent. He seemed nervous—his eyes kept darting from side to side.

"You're an Epic," Prof said.

"Yes," Edmund answered. "They call me Conflux."

"Head of Steelheart's Enforcement troops," Prof said. The rest of us remained quiet, as instructed, to not give the man an indication of how many were in the room.

Edmund chuckled. "Head? Yes, I suppose you could call me that." He leaned back, closing his eyes. "Though, more appropriately, I might be the heart. Or maybe just the battery."

"Why were you in the trunk of that car?" Prof asked.

"Because I was being transported."

"And you suspected your limo might be attacked, so you hid yourself in the trunk?"

"Young man," Edmund said pleasantly, "if I had wanted to hide, would I have had myself tied up, gagged, and blindfolded?"

Prof was silent.

"You wish for proof that I am who I say," Edmund said with a sigh. "Well, I'd rather not force you to beat it out of me. Do you have a mechanical device that has been drained of energy? No battery power at all?"

Prof looked to the side. Tia fished in her pocket and handed over a penlight. Prof tried it and no light came out. Then he hesitated. Finally he waved us out of the room. Cody remained, gun on Edmund, but the rest of us—Prof included—gathered in the main chamber.

"He might be able to overload it and make it explode," Prof said softly.

"We *will* need proof of who he is, though," Tia said. "If he can power that by touching it, then he's either Conflux or a different Epic with a *very* similar power."

"Or someone who Conflux gifted his abilities to," I said.

"He registers as a powerful Epic on the dowser," Abraham said. "We've tried it on Enforcement officers before who had powers given to them by Conflux, and it didn't register them."

"What if he's a different Epic?" Tia asked. "With some powers gifted by Conflux to show he can give energy to things and make us think he's Conflux? He could act harmless, then when we aren't expecting, turn his full powers on us."

Prof slowly shook his head. "I don't think so. That's just too convoluted, and too dangerous. Why would they think we would decide to kidnap Conflux? We could just as easily have killed him right there when we found him. I think this man is who he says he is."

"Why was he in the trunk, though?" Abraham asked.

"He'll probably answer if we ask him," I said. "I mean, he hasn't exactly been difficult so far."

"That's what worries me," Tia said. "It's too easy."

"Easy?" I asked. "Megan died so we could capture that guy. I want to hear what he has to say."

Prof glanced at me, tapping the penlight against his palm. He nodded, and Abraham fetched a long wooden rod, which we tied the light to. We returned to the room, and Prof used the rod to touch the light to Edmund's cheek.

Immediately the flashlight's bulb started glowing. Edmund yawned, then tried to settle himself in his bonds.

Prof pulled the flashlight back; it continued to shine.

"I recharged the battery for you," Edmund said. "Might that be enough to persuade you to get me a drink . . . ?"

"Two years ago," I said, stepping forward despite Prof's orders, "in July, you were involved in a large-scale project on Steelheart's behalf. What was it?"

"I don't really have a good sense of time . . . ," the man said.

"It shouldn't be hard to remember," I said. "The people of the city don't know about it, but something odd happened to Conflux."

"Summer? Hmm . . . was that when I was taken out of the city?" Edmund smiled. "Yes, I remember the sunlight. He needed me to power some of his war tanks for some reason."

It had been an offensive against Dialas, an Epic in Detroit who had angered Steelheart by cutting off some of his food supplies. Conflux's part had been handled very covertly. Few knew of it.

Prof was looking at me, lips drawn to a tight line. I ignored him. "Edmund," I said, "you came to the city on what date?"

"Spring of 04 AC," he said.

Four years after Calamity. That clinched it for me—most people assumed that Conflux had joined Steelheart in 05 AC, when Enforcement had first gained mechanized units and the power outages of 04 AC had finally begun to stabilize. But inside sources that I'd carefully gathered claimed Steelheart hadn't trusted Conflux at first, and hadn't used him for important projects for nearly a year.

As I looked at this man, a lot of things from my notes about Conflux were starting to make sense. Why was Conflux never seen? Why was he transported as he was? Why the shroud, the mystery? It wasn't just because of Conflux's frailty.

"You're a prisoner," I said.

"Of course he is," Prof said, but Conflux nodded.

"No," I said to Prof. "He's always been a prisoner. Steelheart isn't using him as a lieutenant, but as a power source. Conflux isn't in charge of Enforcement, he's just . . ."

"A battery," Edmund said. "A slave. It's all right, you can say it. I'm quite accustomed to it. I'm a valuable slave, which is actually an enviable position. I suspect it won't be too long before he finds us and kills you all for taking me." He grimaced. "I *am* sorry about that. I hate it terribly when people fight over me."

"All this time . . . ," I said. "Sparks!"

Steelheart *couldn't* let it be known what he was doing to Conflux. In Newcago Epics were all but sacred. The more powerful they were, the more rights they had. It was the foundation of the government. The Epics lived by the pecking order because they knew, even if they were at the bottom, they were still far more important than the ordinary people.

But here was an Epic who was a slave . . . nothing more than a power plant. This had huge ramifications for everyone in Newcago. Steelheart was a liar.

I guess I shouldn't be too surprised, I thought. *I mean, after everything else he's done, this is a minor issue.* Still, it seemed important. Or maybe I was just latching on to the first thing that drew my attention away from Megan.

"Shut it down," Prof said.

"Excuse me?" Edmund said. "Shut down what?"

"You're a gifter," Prof said. "A transference Epic. Draw your power back from the people you've given it to. Remove it from the mechanized armors, the copters, the power stations. I want you to cut off every person you've granted your power."

"If I do that," Edmund said hesitantly, "Steelheart will *not* be pleased with me when he recovers me."

"You can tell him the truth," Prof said, raising a handgun in one hand so that it pointed out in front of the spotlight. "If I kill you, the power will go away. I'm not afraid to take that step. Recover your power, Edmund. Then we'll talk further."

"Very well," Edmund said.

And just like that, he all but shut down Newcago.

33

"I don't really think of myself as an Epic," Edmund said, leaning forward across the makeshift table. We'd made it out of a box and a plank, and we sat on the floor to eat at it. "I was captured and used for power only a month after my transformation. Bastion was my first owner's name. I'll tell you, was *he* unpleasant after we discovered I couldn't transfer my power to him."

"Why do you suppose that is?" I asked, chewing on some jerky.

"I don't know," Edmund said, raising his hands in front of himself. He liked to gesture a lot when he talked; you had to watch yourself, lest you get an accidental ninja punch to the shoulder during a particularly emphatic exclamation about the taste of a good curry.

That was about as dangerous as he got. Though Cody stayed near, his rifle never too far from him, Edmund hadn't been the least bit provocative. He actually seemed pleasant, at least when he wasn't mentioning our inevitable gruesome deaths at Steelheart's hands.

"That's the way it has always worked for me," Edmund continued, pointing at me with his spoon. "I can only gift them to ordinary humans, and I have to touch them to do it. I've never been able to give my powers to an Epic. I've tried."

Nearby, Prof—who had been carrying some supplies past—stopped in place. He turned to Edmund. "What was that you said?"

"I can't gift to other Epics," Edmund said, shrugging. "It's just the way the powers work."

"Is it that way for other gifters?" Prof asked.

"I've never met any," Edmund said. "Gifters are rare. If there are others in the city, Steelheart never let me meet them. He wasn't bothered by not being able to get my powers for himself; he was plenty happy using me as a battery."

Prof looked troubled. He continued on his way, and Edmund looked to me, his eyebrows raised. "What was that about?"

"I don't know," I said, equally confused.

"Well, anyway, continuing my story. Bastion didn't like that I couldn't gift him, so he sold me to a fellow named Insulation. I always thought that was a stupid Epic name."

"Not as bad as the El Brass Bullish Dude," I said.

"You're kidding. There's really an Epic named that?"

I nodded. "From inner LA. He's dead now, but you'd be surprised at the stupid names a lot of them come up with. Incredible cosmic powers do not equate with high IQ . . . or even a sense of what is dramatically appropriate. Remind me to tell you about the Pink Pinkness sometime."

"That name doesn't sound so bad," Edmund said, grinning. "It's actually a little self-aware. Has a smile to it. I'd like to meet an Epic who likes to smile."

I'm talking to one, I thought. I still hadn't quite accepted that.

"Well," I said, "she didn't smile for long. She thought the name was clever, and then . . ."

"What?"

"Try saying it a few times really quickly," I suggested.

He moved his mouth, then a huge grin split his mouth. "Well, well, well . . ."

I shook my head in wonder as I continued eating my jerky. What to make of Edmund? He wasn't the hero people like Abraham and my father were looking for, not by a long shot. Edmund paled when we talked of fighting Steelheart; he was so timid, he often asked for permission to speak before voicing an opinion.

No, he wasn't some heroic Epic born to fight for the rights of men, but he was nearly as important. I'd *never* met, read of, or even caught a story of an Epic who so blatantly broke the stereotype. Edmund had no arrogance, no hatred, no dismissiveness.

It was baffling. Part of me kept thinking, *This is what we get? I finally find an Epic who doesn't want to kill or enslave me, and it's an old, soft-spoken Indian man who likes to put sugar in his milk?*

"You lost someone, didn't you?" Edmund asked.

I looked up sharply. "What makes you ask?"

"Reactions like that one, actually. And the fact that everyone in your team seems to be walking on crumpled tinfoil and trying not to make any sound."

Sparks. Good metaphor. Walking on crumpled tinfoil. I'd have to remember that one.

"Who was she?" Edmund asked.

"Who said it was a she?"

"The look on your face, son," Edmund said, then smiled.

I didn't respond, though that was in part because I was trying to banish the flood of memories washing through my mind. Megan, glaring at me. Megan, smiling. Megan, laughing just a few hours before she died. *Idiot. You only knew her for a couple of weeks.*

"I killed my wife," Edmund said absently, leaning back, staring at the ceiling. "It was an accident. Electrified the counter while trying to power the microwave. Stupid thing, eh? I wanted a frozen burrito. Sara died for that." He tapped the table. "I hope yours died for something greater."

That will depend, I thought, *on what we do next.*

I left Edmund at the table and nodded to Cody, who was standing by the wall and doing a very good job of pretending he wasn't playing guard. I wandered into the other room, where Prof, Tia, and Abraham were sitting around Tia's datapad.

I almost went looking for Megan, my instincts saying she'd be standing guard outside the hideout, since all of the others were in here. Idiot. I joined the team, looking over Tia's shoulder at the screen of the enlarged mobile datapad. She was running it from one of the fuel cells we'd stolen from the power station. Once Edmund had withdrawn his abilities, the city power had gone out, including those wires that sometimes ran through the steel catacombs.

Her pad showed an old steel apartment complex. "No good," Prof said, pointing to some numbers at the side of the screen. "The building next to it is still populated. I'm not going to have a showdown with a High Epic when there are bystanders so close."

"What about in front of his palace?" Abraham asked. "He won't expect that."

"I doubt he's expecting anything in particular," Tia said. "Besides, Cody's done some scouting. The looting has started, so Steelheart has pulled Enforcement in close to his palace. He's really only got infantry left, but that's enough. We'll never get in to make any preparations. And we're going to *need* to prepare the area if we're going to face him."

"Soldier Field," I said softly.

They turned to me.

"Look," I said, reaching over and scrolling along Tia's map of the city. It felt downright primitive compared to the real-time camera views we'd been using.

I got the screen to an old portion of the city that was mostly abandoned. "The old football stadium," I said. "Nobody lives nearby, and there's nothing in the area to loot, so nobody will be around. We can use the tensors to tunnel in from a nearby point in the understreets. That will let us make preparations quietly, without worry that we're being spied on."

"It's so open," Prof said, rubbing his chin. "I'd rather face him in an old building, where we can confuse him and hit him from a lot of sides."

"That will still work here," I said. "He'll almost certainly fly down into the middle of the field. We could put a sniper in the upper seats, and could carve ourselves a few unexpected tunnels—with rope lines—down through the seats into the stadium's innards. We could baffle Steelheart and his minions by putting tunnels where they aren't expected, and the terrain will be unfamiliar to his people—far more so than a simple apartment complex."

Prof nodded slowly.

"We still haven't addressed the real question," Tia said. "We're all thinking it. We might as well talk about it."

"Steelheart's weakness," Abraham said softly.

"We're too effective for our own good," Tia said. "We've got him positioned, and we can bring him out to fight us. We can ambush him perfectly. But will that even matter?"

"So it comes to this," Prof said. "Listen well, people. These are the stakes. We *could* pull out now. It would be a disaster—everyone would find out we'd tried to kill him and failed. That could do as much harm as killing him would do good. People would think that the Epics really are invincible, that even we can't face someone like Steelheart.

"Beyond that, Steelheart would take it upon himself to personally hunt us down. He is not the type to give up easily. Wherever we go, we'd always have to watch and worry about him. But we could go. We don't know his weakness, not for certain. It might be best to pull out while we can."

"And if we don't?" Cody asked.

"We continue with the plan," Prof said. "We do everything we can to kill him, try out every possible clue from David's memory. We set up a trap in this stadium that combines all of those possibilities, and we take a chance. It will be the most uncertain hit I've ever been part of. One of those things could work, but more likely none of them will, and we will have entered into a fight with one of the most powerful Epics in the world. He'll probably kill us."

Everyone sat in silence. No. It couldn't end here, could it?

"I want to try," Cody said. "David's right. He's been right all along. Sneaking about, killing little Epics . . . that's not changing the world. We've got a chance at Steelheart. We have to at least *try*."

I felt a flood of relief.

Abraham nodded. "Better to die here, with a chance at defeating this creature, than to run."

Tia and Prof shared a look.

"You want to do it too, don't you, Jon?" Tia asked.

"Either we fight him here, or the Reckoners are finished," Prof said. "We'd spend the rest of our lives running. Besides, I doubt I could live with myself if I ran, after all we've been through."

I nodded. "We do have to at least try. For Megan's sake."

"I'll bet she would find that ironic," Abraham noted. We looked at him, and he shrugged. "She was the one who didn't want to do this job. I don't know what she'd think of us dedicating the end of it to her memory."

"You can be a downer, Abe," Prof said.

"The truth is not a downer," Abraham said in his lightly accented voice. "The lies that you pretend to accept are the true downer."

"Says the man who still believes the Epics will save us," Prof said.

"Gentlemen," Tia cut in. "Enough. I think we're all in agreement. We're going to try this, ridiculous though it is. We'll try to kill Steelheart without any real idea what his weakness is."

One by one, we all nodded. We had to try.

"I'm not doing this for Megan," I finally said. "But I'm doing it, in part, *because* of her. If we have to stand up and die so that people will know that someone still fights, so be it. Prof, you said that you worry our failure will depress people. I don't see that. They'll hear our story and realize that there's an option other than doing what the Epics command. We may not be the ones to kill Steelheart. But even if we fail, we might be the cause of his death. Someday."

"Don't be so sure we'll fail," Prof said. "If I thought this was suicide for certain, I wouldn't let us continue. As I said, I don't intend to pin our hopes of killing him on a single guess. We'll try everything. Tia, what do your instincts say will work?"

"Something from the bank vault," she said. "One of those items is special. I just wish I knew which one."

"Did you bring them with you when we abandoned the old hideout?"

"I brought the most unusual ones," she said. "I stowed the rest in the pocket we made outside. We can fetch them. So far as I know, Enforcement hasn't found them."

"We take everything and spread it all out here," Prof said, pointing at the steel floor of the stadium, which had once been soil. "David's right; that's where Steelheart will probably land. We don't have to know specifically what weakened him—we can just haul it all over and use it."

Abraham nodded. "A good plan."

"What do you think it is?" Prof asked him.

"If I had to guess? I would say it was David's father's gun or the bullets it shot. Every gun is slightly distinctive in its own way. Perhaps it was the precise composition of the metal."

"That's easy enough to test," I said. "I'll bring the gun, and when I get a chance I'll shoot him. I don't think it will work, but I'm willing to try."

"Good," Prof said.

"And you, Prof?" Tia asked.

"I think it was because David's father was one of the Faithful," Prof said softly. He didn't look at Abraham. "Fools though they are, they're earnest fools. People like Abraham see the world differently than the rest of us do. So maybe it was the way David's father viewed the Epics that let him hurt Steelheart."

I sat back, thinking it over.

"Well, it shouldn't be too hard for me to shoot him too," Abraham said. "In fact, we should probably all try it. And anything else we can think of."

They looked at me.

"I still think it's crossfire," I said. "I think Steelheart can only be harmed by someone who isn't intending to hurt him."

"That's tougher to arrange," Tia said. "If you're right, it probably won't activate if any of us hit him, since we actually want him dead."

"Agreed," Prof said. "But it's a good theory. We'd need to find a way to get his own soldiers to hit him by accident."

"He'd have to *bring* the soldiers first," Tia said. "Now that he's convinced there's a rival Epic in town, he might just bring Nightwielder and Firefight."

"No," I said. "He'll come with soldiers. Limelight has been using minions, and Steelheart will want to be ready—he'll want to have his own soldiers to deal with distractions like that. Besides, while he'll want to face Limelight himself, he'll also want witnesses."

"I agree," Prof said. "His soldiers will probably have orders not to engage unless fired upon. We can make certain they feel they need to start fighting back."

"Then we'll need to be able to stall Steelheart long enough to set up a good crossfire," Abraham said. He paused. "Actually, we'll need to stall him *during* the crossfire. If he assumes this is just an ambush of soldiers, he'll fly off and let Enforcement deal with it." Abraham looked at Prof. "Limelight will have to make an appearance."

Prof nodded. "I know."

"Jon . . . ," Tia said, touching his arm.

"It's what must be done," he said. "We'll need a way to deal with Nightwielder and Firefight too."

"I'm telling you," I said, "Firefight won't be an issue. He's—"

"I know he's not what he seems, son," Prof said. "I accept that. But have you ever fought an illusionist?"

"Sure," I said. "With Cody and Megan."

"That was a weak one," Prof said. "But I suppose it gives you an idea what to expect. Firefight will be stronger. *Much* stronger. I almost wish he was just another fire Epic."

Tia nodded. "He should be a priority. We'll need code phrases, in case he sends in illusory versions of the other members of the team to confuse us. And we'll have to watch for false walls, fake members of Enforcement intended to confuse, things like that."

"Do you think Nightwielder will even show?" Abraham asked. "From what I heard, David's little flashlight show sent him running like a rabbit before the hawk."

Prof looked to me and Tia.

I shrugged. "He might not," I said.

Tia nodded. "Nightwielder's a hard one to read."

"We should be ready for him anyway," I said. "But I'll be perfectly fine if he stays away."

"Abraham," Prof said, "you think you can rig up a UV floodlight or two using the extra power cells? We should arm everyone with some of those flashlights as well."

We fell silent, and I had a feeling we were all thinking the same thing. The Reckoners liked extremely well-planned operations, executed only after weeks or months of preparation. Yet here we were going to try to take down one of the strongest Epics in the world with little more than some trinkets and flashlights.

It was what we had to do.

"I think," Tia said, "we should come up with a good plan for extraction in case none of these things work."

Prof didn't look like he agreed. His expression had grown grim; he knew that if none of these ideas let us kill Steelheart, our chances of survival were slim.

"A copter will work best," Abraham said. "Without Conflux, Enforcement is grounded. If we can use a power cell, or even make him power a copter for us . . ."

"That will be good," Tia said. "But we'll still have to disengage."

"Well, we've still got Diamond in custody," Abraham said. "We could grab some of his explosives—"

"Wait," I said, confused. "In *custody*?"

"I had Abraham and Cody grab him the evening of your little encounter," Prof said absently. "Couldn't risk letting him say what he knew."

"But . . . you said he'd never . . ."

"He saw a hole made by the tensors," Prof said, "and you were linked to him in Nightwielder's mind. The moment they saw you at one of our operations, they'd grab Diamond. It was for his safety as much as our own."

"So . . . what are you doing with him?"

"Feeding him a lot," Prof said, "and bribing him to lie low. He was pretty unsettled by that run-in, and I think he was happy we took him." Prof hesitated. "I promised him a look at how the tensors work in exchange for him remaining in one of our bolt-holes until this all blows over."

I sat back against the wall of the room, disturbed. Prof hadn't said it, but I could read the truth from his tone. The emergence of knowledge of the tensors would change the way the Reckoners worked.

Even if we beat Steelheart, they had lost something great—no longer would they be able to sneak into places unexpectedly. Their enemies would be able to plan, watch, prepare.

I'd brought about the end of an era. They didn't seem to blame me, but I couldn't help feeling some guilt. I was like the guy who had brought the spoiled shrimp cocktail to the party, causing everyone to throw up for a week straight.

"Anyway," Abraham said, tapping the screen of Tia's datapad, "we could dig out a section under the field here with the tensors, leave an inch or so of steel, then pack the hole with explosives. If we have to punch out, we blow the thing, maybe take out some soldiers and use the confusion and smoke to cover our escape."

"Assuming Steelheart doesn't just chase us down and shoot the copter out of the sky," Prof said.

We fell silent.

"I believe you said *I* was a downer?" Abraham asked.

"Sorry," Prof replied. "Just pretend I said something self-righteous about truth instead."

Abraham smiled.

"It's a workable plan," Prof said. "Though we might want to try to set up some kind of decoy explosion, maybe back at his palace, to draw him off. Abraham, I'll let you handle that. Tia, can you send a message to Steelheart through these networks without being traced?"

"I should be able to," she replied.

"Well, give him a response from Limelight. Tell him: 'Be ready on the night of the third day. You'll know the place when the time comes.'"

She nodded.

"Three days?" Abraham said. "Not much time."

"We really don't have much we need to prepare," Prof said. "Besides, anything longer would be too suspicious; he probably expects us to face him tonight. This will have to do, though."

The Reckoners nodded, and the preparations for our last fight began. I sat back, my anxiety rising. I was *finally* going to have my chance to face him. Killing him with this plan seemed almost as much a longshot as ever.

But I would finally get my chance.

34

THE vibrations shook me to the soul. It seemed that my soul vibrated back. I breathed in, shaping the sound with a thought, then thrust my hand forward and sent the music outward. Music only I could hear, music only I could control.

I opened my eyes. A portion of the tunnel in front of me collapsed into fine, powdery dust. I wore a mask, though Prof continued to assure me the stuff wasn't as bad to breathe as I thought.

I wore my mobile strapped to my forehead, shining brightly. The small tunnel through the steel was cramped, but I was alone, so I was able to move as much as I needed to.

As always, using the tensor reminded me of Megan and that day when we'd infiltrated the power station. It reminded me of the elevator shaft, where she'd shared with me things it seemed she hadn't shared with many. I'd asked Abraham if he'd known she was from

Portland, and he'd seemed surprised. He said she never spoke about her past.

I scooped the steel dust into a bucket, then hauled it down the tunnel and dumped it. I did that a few more times, then got back to digging with the tensor. The others were hauling the dust the rest of the way out.

I added a few feet to the tunnel, then checked my mobile to see how I was doing. Abraham had set up three others above to create a kind of triangulation system that let me cut this tunnel with precision. I needed to go a bit more to the right, then I needed to angle upward.

Next time I pick a location to ambush a High Epic, I thought, *I'm going to choose one that's closer to established understreet tunnels.*

The rest of the team agreed with Abraham that they should wire the field with explosives from below, and they also wanted a few hidden tunnels leading up to the perimeter. I was pretty sure we'd be happy to have those when we faced Steelheart, but building all of it was getting *very* tiring.

I almost regretted that I'd shown so much talent with the tensor. Almost. It was still pretty awesome to be able to dig through solid steel with just my hands. I couldn't hack like Tia, scout as well as Cody, or fix machinery like Abraham. This way, at least, I had a place in the team.

Of course, I thought as I vaporized another section of the wall, *Prof's ability makes mine look like a piece of rice. And not even a cooked one.* I was basically only useful in this role because he refused to take it. That dampened my satisfaction.

A thought occurred to me. I raised my hand, summoning the tensor's vibrations. How had Prof done it to make that sword? He'd pounded the wall, hadn't he? I tried to mimic the motion, pounding my fist against the side of the tunnel and directing the burst of energy in my mind from the tensor.

I didn't get a sword. I caused several handfuls of dust to stream out of a pocket in the wall, followed by a long lump of steel that looked vaguely like a bulbous carrot.

Well, it's a start. I guess.

I reached down to pick up the carrot, but caught sight of a light moving up the small tunnel. I quickly kicked the carrot into the pile of dust, then got back to work.

Prof soon moved up behind me. "How's it going?"

"Another couple of feet," I said. "Then I can carve out the pocket for the explosives."

"Good," Prof said. "Try to make it long and thin. We want to channel the explosion upward, not back down the tunnel here."

I nodded. The plan was to weaken the "roof" of the pocket, which would lie just below the center of Soldier Field. Then we'd seal the explosives in with some careful welding by Cody, directing the blast the direction we wanted it to go.

"You keep at it," Prof said. "For now I'll take care of carting off the dust for you."

I nodded, grateful for the chance to just spend more time with the tensor. It was Cody's. He'd given it up for me, as mine was still a ripped, zombie-droopy-eyed mess. I hadn't asked Prof about the two he carried. It didn't seem prudent.

We worked in silence for a time, me carving out chunks of steel, Prof carting off the dust. He found my carrot sword and gave me an odd look. I hoped he didn't see me blush in the faint light.

Eventually my mobile beeped, telling me I was nearing the right depth. I carefully crafted a long hole at shoulder level. Then I reached in and began creating a small "room" to stuff the explosives into.

Prof walked back, carrying his bucket, and saw what I'd done. He checked his mobile, looking up at the ceiling, then rapped softly at the metal with a small hammer. He nodded to himself, though I couldn't tell any difference in the way it sounded.

"You know," I said, "I'm pretty sure these tensors defy the laws of physics."

"What? You mean destroying solid metal with your fingers isn't normal?"

"More than that," I said. "I think we get less dust than we should. It always seems to settle down and take up less space than the steel did—but it couldn't do that unless it was denser than the steel, which it can't possibly be."

Prof grunted, filling another bucket.

"Nothing about the Epics makes sense," I said, pulling a few armfuls of dust out of the hole I was making. "Not even their powers." I hesitated. "Particularly not their powers."

"True enough," Prof said. He continued filling his buckets. "I owe you an apology, son. For how I acted."

"Tia explained it," I said quickly. "She said you've got some things in your past. Some history with the tensors. It makes sense. It's okay."

"No, it's not. But it *is* what happens when I use the tensors. I . . . well, it's like Tia said. Things in my past. I'm sorry for how I acted. There was no justification for it, especially considering what you'd just been through."

"It wasn't so bad," I said. "What you did, I mean." *The rest was horrible.* I tried not to think about that long march with a dying girl in my arms. A dying girl I didn't save. I pushed forward. "You were amazing, Prof. You shouldn't just use the tensors when we face Steelheart. You should use them all the time. Think of what—"

"STOP."

I froze. The tone of his voice sent a spike of shock down my spine.

Prof breathed in and out deeply, his hands buried in steel dust. He closed his eyes. "Don't speak like that, son. It doesn't do me any good. Please."

"All right," I said carefully.

"Just . . . accept my apology, if you are willing."

"Of course."

Prof nodded, turning back to his work.

"Can I ask you something?" I said. "I won't mention . . . you know. Not directly, at least."

"Go ahead, then."

"Well, you invented these things. Amazing things. The harmsway, the jackets. From what Abraham tells me, you had these devices when you founded the Reckoners."

"I did."

"So . . . why not make us something else? Another kind of weapon, based off the Epics? I mean, you sell knowledge to people like Diamond, and he sells it to scientists who are working to create technology like this. I figure you've got to be as good at it as any of them are. Why sell the knowledge and not use it yourself?"

Prof worked in silence for a few minutes, then walked over to help me pull dust out of the hole I was making. "That's a good question. Have you asked Abraham or Cody?"

I grimaced. "Cody talks about daemons or fairies—which he claims the Irish totally stole from his ancestors. I can't tell if he's serious."

"He's not," Prof said. "He just likes to see how people react when he says things like that."

"Abraham thinks it's because you don't have a lab now, like you used to. Without the right equipment, you can't design new technology."

"Abraham is a very thoughtful man. What do *you* think?"

"I think that if you can find the resources to buy or steal explosives, cycles, and even copters when you need them, you could get yourself a lab. There's got to be another reason."

Prof dusted off his hands and turned to look at me. "All right. I can see where this is going. You may ask one question about my past." He said it as if it were a gift, a kind of . . . penance. He had treated me poorly, in part because of something in his past. The recompense he gave was a piece of that past.

I found myself completely unprepared. What did I want to know? Did I ask how he'd come up with the tensors? Did I ask what it was that made him not want to use them? He seemed to be bracing himself.

I don't want to drag him through that, I thought. *Not if it affects him so profoundly.* I wouldn't want to do that any more than I would have wanted someone to drag me through memories of what had happened to Megan.

I decided to pick something more benign. "What *were* you?" I asked. "Before Calamity. What was your job?"

Prof seemed taken aback. "That's your question?"

"Yes."

"You're sure you want to know?"

I nodded.

"I was a fifth-grade science teacher," Prof said.

I opened my mouth to laugh at the joke, but the tone of his voice made me hesitate.

"Really?" I finally asked.

"Really. An Epic destroyed the school. It . . . it was still in session." He stared at the wall, emotion bleeding from his face. He was putting a mask up.

And here I thought it had been an innocent question. "But the tensors," I said. "The harmsway. You worked at a lab at some point, right?"

"No," he said. "The tensors and the harmsway don't belong to me. The others just assume I invented them. I didn't."

That revelation stunned me.

Prof turned away to gather up his buckets. "The kids at the school called me Prof too. It always sticks, though I'm not a professor—I didn't even go to graduate school. I only ended up teaching science by accident. It was the teaching itself that I loved. At least, I loved it back when I thought it would be enough to change things."

He walked off down the tunnel, leaving me to wonder.

• • •

"That's it. Y'all can turn around now."

I turned, adjusting the pack I was toting on my back. Cody, balanced on a ladder above me, lifted the welding mask from his face and wiped his brow with the hand not holding the torch. It was a few hours after I had carved out the pocket under the field. Cody and I had spent those hours carving smaller tunnels and holes throughout the stadium, with Cody spot welding where support was needed.

Our most recent project was making the sniper's nest that would be my post at the beginning of the battle. It was at the front of the third level of seats on the west side of the stadium, at about the fifty-yard line, overhanging the top of the first deck. We didn't want it to be visible from above, so I'd used the tensor to carve away a space under the floor, leaving only an inch of metal on top, except for two feet right near the front for my head and shoulders to poke out so I could aim a rifle through a hole in the low wall at the front of the deck.

Cody reached up from his perch on the ladder and jiggled the metal framework he had just welded to the bottom of the area I had hollowed out. He nodded, apparently satisfied it would support me when I lay in wait there in the sniper's nest. The floor of that section of seating was too thin to hollow out a hole deep enough to hide in; the framework was our solution to that problem.

"Where to next?" I asked as Cody climbed down the ladder. "How about we do that escape hole farther up in the third deck?"

Cody slung his welding gear over his shoulder and cracked some kinks out of his back. "Abraham called to say he's going to take care of the UV floodlights now," he said. "He finished packing the explosives under the field a while ago, so it's time for me to go weld down there. Y'all can handle the next hole on your own—but I'll help you carry the ladder there. Good job on these holes so far, lad."

"So you're back to *lad*?" I asked. "What happened to *mate*?"

"I realized something," Cody said, collapsing the ladder and tilting the top to one side. "My Australian ancestors?"

"Yeah?" I lifted the lower end of the ladder and followed him as he walked from the first deck of seats into the stadium innards.

"They came from Scotland originally. So if I want to be *really* authentic, I need to be able to speak Australian with a Scottish accent."

We kept walking through the pitch-black space beneath the stands that was kind of like a large, curved hallway—I think it was called a concourse. The planned lower end for the next escape hole was in one of the restrooms down the hall. "An Australian-Scottish-Tennessean accent, eh?" I said. "You practicing it?"

"Hell no," Cody said. "I'm not crazy, lad. Just a little eccentric."

I smiled, then turned my head to look in the direction of the field. "We're really going to try this, aren't we?"

"We'd better. I bet Abraham twenty bucks that we'd win."

"I just . . . It's hard to believe. I've spent ten years planning for this day, Cody. Over half my life. Now it's here. It's nothing like what I'd pictured, but it's here."

"You should feel proud," Cody said. "The Reckoners have been doing what they've been doing for over half a decade. No changes, no real surprises, no big risks." He reached up to scratch his left ear. "I often wondered if we were getting stagnant. Never could gather the arguments to suggest a change. It took someone coming in from the outside to shake us up a wee bit."

"Attacking Steelheart is just a 'wee bit' of a shakeup?"

"Well, it's not like you've gotten us to do something *really* crazy, like trying to steal Tia's cola."

Outside the restroom, we set the ladder down and Cody wandered over to check on some explosives on the opposite wall. We intended to use them as distractions; Abraham was going to blow them when needed. I paused, then pulled out one of my eraser-like blasting caps. "Maybe I should put one of these on them," I said. "In case we need a secondary person to blow the explosives."

Cody eyed it, rubbing his chin. He knew what I meant. We'd only need a secondary person to blow the explosives if Abraham fell. I didn't like thinking about it, but after Megan . . . Well, we all seemed a whole lot more frail to me now than we once had.

"You know," Cody said, taking the blasting cap from me, "where I'd *really* like to have a backup is on the explosives under the field there. Those are the most important ones to detonate; they're going to cover our escape."

"I suppose," I said.

"Do you mind if I take this and stick it down there before I weld it closed?" Cody asked.

"No, assuming Prof agrees."

"He likes redundancy," Cody said, slipping the blasting cap into his pocket. "Just keep that pen-dealy of yours handy. And *don't* push it by accident."

He sauntered back toward the tunnel under the field, and I took the ladder into the restroom to get to work.

I punched my fist out into open air, then ducked as the steel dust fell around me. *So that's how he did it,* I thought, flexing my fingers. I hadn't figured out the sword trick, but I was getting good at punching and vaporizing things in front of my fist. It had to do with crafting the tensor's sound waves so that they followed my hand in motion, creating kind of an . . . envelope around it.

Done right, the wave would course along with my fist. Kind of like smoke might follow your hand if you punch through it. I smiled, shaking my hand. I'd finally figured it out. Good thing too. My knuckles were feeling pretty sore.

I finished off the hole with a more mundane tensor blast, reaching up from the top of my ladder to sculpt the hole. Through it I could see a pure black sky. *Someday I'd like to see the sun again,* I thought. The only thing up there was blackness. Blackness and Calamity, burning in the distance directly above, like a terrible red eye.

I climbed up off the ladder and out into the upper third deck. I had a sudden, surreal flash of memory. This was near where I'd sat the one time I'd come to this stadium. My father had scrimped and saved to buy us the tickets. I couldn't remember which team we'd played, but I could remember the taste of the hot dog my father bought. And his cheering, his excitement.

I crouched down among the seats, keeping low just in case. Steelheart's spy drones were probably out of commission now that the city was without power, but he might have people scouting the city and looking for Limelight. It would be wise to remain out of sight as much as possible.

Fishing a rope out of my pack, I tied it around the leg of one of the steel seats, then sneaked back to the hole and down the ladder, returning to the bathroom below the second deck. Leaving the rope hanging for a quicker escape than the ladder would allow, I stowed the ladder and my empty pack in one of the stalls and walked out toward the seats.

Abraham was waiting there for me, leaning against the entryway to the lower seating with his muscled arms crossed, his expression thoughtful.

"So, I take it the UV lights are hooked up?" I asked.

Abraham nodded. "It would have been beautiful to use the stadium's own floodlights."

I laughed. "I'd have liked to see that, making a bunch of lights work that had their bulbs turned to steel and fused to their sockets."

The two of us stood there for a time, looking out at our battlefield. I checked my mobile. It was early morning; we planned to summon Steelheart at 5:00 a.m. Hopefully his soldiers would be exhausted from preventing lootings all night without any vehicles or power armor. The Reckoners usually worked on a night schedule anyway.

"Fifteen minutes until projected go time," I noted. "Did Cody finish the welding? Prof and Tia back yet?"

"Cody completed the weld and is moving to his position," Abraham said. "Prof will arrive momentarily. They were able to procure a copter, and Edmund has gifted Tia the ability to power it. She flew it outside of town to park it, so as to not give away our location."

If things went sour, she'd time her flight back in so that she could sweep down and pick us up as the explosives went off. We'd also blast a smokescreen from the stands to cover our escape.

I agreed with Prof, though. You couldn't outfly or outgun Steelheart in a copter. This was the showdown. We defeated him here or we died.

My mobile flashed, and a voice spoke into my ear. "I'm back," Prof said. "Tia's set too." He hesitated a moment. "Let's do this."

35

SINCE my post was right up against the front of the third deck, if I'd been standing I could have looked down over the edge toward the lowest level of seats. Huddled in my improvised hole, however, I couldn't see those—though I had a good view of the field.

This put me high enough to watch what was going on around the stadium, but I also had a route to ground if I needed to try firing my father's gun at Steelheart. The tunnel and rope farther up the deck would get me there quickly.

I'd drop down, then try to sneak up on him, if it came to that. It would be like trying to sneak up on a lion while armed only with a squirt gun.

I huddled in my spot, waiting. I wore my tensor on my left hand, my right hand holding the grip of the pistol. Cody had given me a replacement rifle, but for now it lay beside me.

Overhead, fireworks flared in the air. Four posts around the top of the stadium released enormous jets of sparks. I don't know where Abraham had found fireworks that were pure green, but the signal would undoubtedly be seen and recognized.

This was the moment. Would he really come?

The fireworks began to die down. "I've got something," Abraham said in our ears, his light French accent subtly emphasizing the wrong syllables. He had the high-point sniping position and Cody had the low-point sniping position. Cody was the better shot, but Abraham needed to be farther away, where he could be outside the fight. His job was to remotely turn on the floodlights or blow strategic explosives. "Yes, they're coming indeed. A convoy of Enforcement trucks. No sign of Steelheart yet."

I holstered my father's gun, then reached to the side to pick up the rifle. It felt too new to me. A rifle should be a well-used, well-loved thing. Familiar. Only then can you know that it's trustworthy. You know how it shoots, when it might jam, how accurate the sights are. Guns, like shoes, are worst when they're brand-new.

Still, I couldn't rely on the pistol. I had trouble hitting anything smaller than a freight train with one of those. I'd need to get close to Steelheart if I wanted to try it. It had been decided that we'd let Abraham and Cody test out the other theories first before risking sending me in close.

"They're pulling up to the stadium," Abraham said in my ear. "I've lost them."

"I can see them, Abraham," Tia said. "Camera six." Though she was outside of the city in the copter, with Edmund's gifted abilities to power it, she was monitoring a rig of cameras we'd set up for spying and for recording the battle.

"Got it," Abraham said. "Yes, they're fanning out. I thought they'd come straight in, but they're not."

"Good," Cody said. "That'll make it easier to get a crossfire going."

If Steelheart even comes, I thought. That was both my fear and my hope. If he didn't come, it would mean he didn't believe that Limelight was a threat—which would make it far easier for the Reckoners to escape the city. The operation would be a bust, but not for any lack of trying. I almost wanted that to be the case.

If Steelheart came and killed us all, the Reckoners' blood would be on my hands for leading them on this path. Once that wouldn't have bothered me, but now it itched at my insides. I peered toward the football field but couldn't see anything. I glanced back behind me, toward the upper stands.

I caught a hint of motion in the darkness—what looked like a flash of gold.

"Guys," I whispered. "I think I just saw someone up here."

"Impossible," Tia said. "I've been watching all the entrances."

"I'm telling you, I *saw* something."

"Camera fourteen . . . fifteen . . . David, there's nobody up there."

"Stay calm, son," Prof said. He was hiding in the tunnel we'd made beneath the field, and would come out only when Steelheart appeared. It had been decided that we wouldn't try blowing the explosives down there until after we'd tried all the other ways to kill Steelheart.

Prof wore the tensors. I could tell he hoped he wouldn't have to use them.

We waited. Tia and Abraham gave a quiet running explanation of Enforcement's movements. The ground troops surrounded the stadium, secured all the exits they knew about, then slowly started to infiltrate. They set up gunnery positions at several points in the stands, but they didn't find any of us. The stadium was too large, and we were hidden too well. You could build a lot of interesting hiding places when you could tunnel through what everyone else assumed was un-tunnel-through-able.

"Tap me into the speakers," Prof said softly.

"Done," Abraham replied.

"I am not here to fight worms!" Prof bellowed, his voice echoing through the stadium, blasted from speakers we'd set up. "This is the bravery of the mighty Steelheart? To send little men with popguns to annoy me? Where are you, Emperor of Newcago? Do you fear me so?"

The stadium fell silent.

"You see that pattern the soldiers set up in the stands?" Abraham asked over our line. "They're being very deliberate. It's intended to ensure they don't hit one another with friendly fire. We're going to have trouble catching Steelheart in a crossfire."

I kept glancing over my shoulder. I saw no other movement in the seats behind me.

"Ah," Abraham said softly. "It worked. He's coming. I can see him in the sky."

Tia whistled softly. "This is it, kids. Time for the real party."

I waited, raising my rifle and using the scope to scan the sky. I eventually spotted a point of light in the darkness, getting closer. Gradually it resolved into three figures flying down toward the center of the stadium. Nightwielder floated amorphously. Firefight landed beside him, a burning humanoid form that was so bright he left afterimages in my eyes.

Steelheart landed between them. My breath caught in my throat, and I fell utterly still.

He'd changed little in the decade since he destroyed the bank. He had that same arrogant expression, that same perfectly styled hair. That inhumanly toned and muscled body, shrouded in a black and silver cape. His fists glowed a soft yellow, wisps of smoke rising from them, and there was a hint of silver in his hair. Epics aged far more slowly than regular people, but they did age.

Wind swirled about Steelheart, blowing up dust that had collected on the silvery ground. I found I couldn't look away. My father's murderer. He was here, *finally*. He didn't seem to notice the junk from the bank vault. We'd strewn it around the center of the field and mixed it with garbage we'd brought in to mask what we'd done.

The items were easily as close to him now as they had been when he'd been in the bank. My finger twitched on the trigger of my rifle—I hadn't even realized it had moved to the trigger. I carefully removed it. I would see Steelheart dead, but it didn't *have* to be by my hand. I needed to remain hidden; my duty was to hit him with the pistol, and he was too far away for that at the moment. If I shot now, and the shot failed, I'd be revealing myself.

"Guess I get to start this party," Cody said softly. He was going to fire first to test the theory about the vault contents, as his position was the easiest to retreat from.

"Affirmative," Prof said. "Take the shot, Cody."

"All right, you slontze," Cody said softly to Steelheart. "Let's see if that junk was worth the trouble of hauling up here. . . ."

A shot rang in the air.

36

I was zoomed in on Steelheart's face in the rifle scope. I could swear that I saw, quite distinctly, the bullet hit the side of his head, disturbing his hair. Cody was right on target, but the bullet didn't even break the skin.

Steelheart didn't flinch.

Enforcement reacted immediately, men shouting, trying to determine the source of the shot. I ignored them, staying focused on Steelheart. He was all that mattered.

More shots fired; Cody was making certain he had hit his mark. "Sparks!" Cody said. "I didn't catch sight of any of the shots. One of those has to have landed, though."

"Can anyone confirm?" Prof asked urgently.

"Hit confirmed," I said, eye still to my scope. "It didn't work."

I heard muttered cursing from Tia.

"Cody, move," Abraham said. "They've caught your location."

"Phase two," Prof said, voice firm—anxious, but in control.

Steelheart turned about with a leisurely air—hands glowing—and regarded the stadium. He was a king inspecting his domain. Phase two was for Abraham to blow some distractions and try to get a crossfire going. My role was to sneak forward with the pistol and get in position. We wanted to keep Abraham's position secret as long as possible, so he could use explosions to try to move the Enforcement officers around.

"Abraham," Prof said. "Get those—"

"Nightwielder's moving!" Tia interrupted. "Firefight too!"

I forced myself to pull back from my scope. Firefight had become a streak of burning light heading toward one of the entrances to the concourse beneath the stands. Nightwielder was moving up into the air.

He was flying right toward where I was hiding.

Impossible, I thought. *He can't—*

Enforcement started firing from the positions they had set up, but they weren't shooting toward Cody. They were shooting toward other areas in the stands. I was confused for a moment until the first hidden UV floodlight exploded.

"They're on to us," I cried, pulling back. "They're shooting out the floodlights!"

"Sparks!" Tia said as each of the other floodlights exploded in a row, shot out by various members of Enforcement. "There's no way they spotted all of those!"

"Something's wrong here," Abraham said. "I'm blowing the first distraction." The stadium shook as I slung my rifle over my shoulder and climbed out of my hole. I raced up a flight of steps in the stands.

The gunfire below sounded soft compared to what I'd experienced a few days ago in the corridors.

"Nightwielder is on to you, David!" Tia said. "He *knew* where you were hiding. They must have been watching this place."

"That doesn't make sense," Prof said. "They'd have stopped us earlier, wouldn't they?"

"What's Steelheart doing?" Cody asked, breathing hard as he ran.

I was barely listening. I dashed for the escape hole in the ground up ahead, not looking over my shoulder. The shadows from the seats around me began to lengthen. Tendrils grew like elongating fingers. In the middle of that, something splashed sparks along the steps in front of me.

"Enforcement sharpshooter!" Tia said. "Targeting you, David."

"Got him," Abraham said. I couldn't pick Abraham's sniper shot out of the gunfire, but no further shots came after me. Abraham might have just revealed himself, though.

Sparks! I thought. This was all going to Calamity really quickly. I hit the rope and fumbled with my flashlight. Those shadows were alive, and they were getting close. I got the flashlight on, shining it to destroy the shadows around the hole, then grabbed the rope with one hand and slid down. Fortunately the UV light affected Nightwielder's shadows as well as it did him personally.

"He's still after you," Tia said. "He . . ."

"What?" I asked urgently, holding the rope with the tensor glove, feet wrapped around it to slow my fall. I passed through open air beneath the third deck of seats, above the second deck. My hand grew hot with the friction, but Prof claimed the tensor could handle that without ripping.

I dropped through the hole in the second deck and through the ceiling of the restroom, emerging into the complete darkness of the concourse. This was where things like the concession stands were. At one time the outside of the place had all been glass—but that was now steel, of course, and so the stadium felt enclosed. Like a warehouse.

I could still hear gunshots, faint, echoing slightly in the hollow confines of the stadium. My flashlight shone mostly UV light through its filter, but it did glow a faint, quiet blue.

"Nightwielder sank into the stands," Tia whispered to me. "I lost track of him. I think he did it to hide from cameras."

So we're not the only ones with that trick, I thought, heart thumping in my chest. He'd come for me. He had a vendetta—he knew I'd been the one to figure out his weakness.

I shined the flashlight about anxiously. Nightwielder would be on me in a second, but he would know that I was armed with UV light. Hopefully that would keep him wary. I unholstered my father's pistol, wielding the flashlight in one hand and the gun in the other, my new rifle slung over my shoulder.

I have to keep moving, I thought. *If I can stay ahead of him, I can lose him.* We had tunnels in and out of places like the restrooms, the offices, the locker rooms, and the concession stands.

The UV flashlight gave off very little visible illumination, but I was an understreeter. It was enough. It did have the odd effect of making things that were white glow with a phantom light, and I worried that would give me away. Should I turn off the flashlight and go by touch?

No. It was also my only weapon against Nightwielder. I wasn't about to go around blind when facing an Epic who could strangle me with shadows. I crept down the tomblike hallway. I needed to—

I froze. What had that been in the shadows ahead? I turned my flashlight back toward it. The light shone across discarded bits of trash that had fused to the ground in the Great Transfersion, some formerly retractable stanchions for line control, a few posters frozen on the wall. Some more recent trash, glowing white and ghostly. What had I . . .

My light fell on a woman standing quietly in front of me. Beautiful hair I knew would be golden if I were seeing it under normal light. A face that seemed too perfect, tinged blue in the UV beam, as if sculpted from ice by a master artist. Curves and full lips, large eyes. Eyes I knew.

Megan.

37

BEFORE I had a chance to do more than gape, the shadows around me started to writhe. I dodged to the side as several of them speared through the air where I'd been standing. Though it seemed as if Nightwielder could animate shadows, really he exuded a black mist that pooled in darkness. That was what he could manipulate.

He could have very fine control over a few tendrils of it, but usually he opted for large numbers of them, probably because it was more intimidating. Controlling so many was more difficult, and he could basically just grab, constrict, or stab. Every patch of darkness around me started forming spears that sought my blood.

I dodged between them, eventually having to roll to the ground to get under a group of attacks. Doing a dodging roll on a steel floor is *not* a comfortable experience. When I came up, my hip was smarting.

I leaped over several of the steel crowd control stanchions, sweating and shining my flashlight at any suspicious shadows. I couldn't turn it all directions at once, though, and I had to keep spinning to avoid the ones at my back. I paid vague attention to the chatter from the other Reckoners in my ear, though I was too busy trying to not be killed to digest much of it. It seemed that things were in chaos. Prof had revealed himself to hold Steelheart's attention; Abraham had been located because of his shot to save me. Both he and Cody were on the run, fighting Enforcement soldiers.

A blast rocked the stadium, the sound traveling down the hallway and washing over me like stale cola through a straw. I threw myself over the last of the steel stanchions and found myself shining the light frantically about me to stop spear after spear of blackness.

Megan was no longer where she'd been standing. I could almost believe she'd been a trick of my mind. Almost.

I can't keep this up, I thought as a black spear struck my jacket and was rebuffed by the shielding. I could feel the hit through my sleeve, and the diodes on the jacket were beginning to flash. This jacket seemed a *lot* weaker than the one I'd worn before. Maybe it was a prototype.

Sure enough, the next spear that caught me ripped through the jacket and sliced my skin. I cursed, shining the light on another patch of inky, oily blackness. Nightwielder was going to have me soon if I didn't change tactics.

I had to fight smarter. *Nightwielder has to be able to see me to use his spears on me,* I thought. So he was nearby—yet the hallway seemed empty.

I stumbled, which saved me from a spear that nearly took off my head. *Idiot,* I thought. He could move through walls. He wouldn't just stand in the open; he'd barely be peeking out. All I needed to do was . . .

There! I thought, catching a glimpse of a forehead and eyes peering out from the far wall. He looked pretty stupid, actually, like a kid in the deep end of a pool thinking he was invisible because he was mostly submerged.

I shined the light on him and tried to get a shot off at the same time. Unfortunately I'd switched hands so I could have the flashlight in my right hand—which meant I was firing with my left. Have I mentioned my thoughts on pistols and their accuracy?

The shot went wild. Like, *way* wild. Like I came closer to hitting a bird flying above the stadium outside than I did Nightwielder. But the flashlight worked. I wasn't sure what would happen if his powers vanished while he was phasing through an object. Unfortunately it looked like it didn't kill him—his face was jerked back through the wall as he became corporeal again.

I didn't know what was on the other side of that wall. It was opposite the field. Was he outside, then? I couldn't stop to look up the map on my phone. Instead I ran for a nearby concession stand. We'd dug a tunnel through there, wrapping down through the floor. Hopefully, if I could keep moving while Nightwielder was outside, he'd have trouble tracking me down once he peeked in again.

I got into the concession stand and crawled inside the tunnel. "Guys," I whispered into my mobile as I moved, "I saw Megan."

"You *what*?" Tia asked.

"I saw *Megan*. She's alive."

"David," Abraham said. "She's dead. We all know this."

"I'm telling you I saw her."

"Firefight," Tia said. "He's trying to get to you."

As I crawled I felt a sharp sinking feeling. Of course—an illusion. But . . . something felt wrong about that.

"I don't know," I said. "The eyes were *right*. I don't think an illusion could be that detailed—that lifelike."

"Illusionists wouldn't be worth much if they weren't able to create realistic puppets," Tia said. "They need to— Abraham, not left! The other way. In fact, throw a grenade down there if you can."

349

"Thanks," he said, puffing slightly. I could hear an explosion twice—once through his microphone. A distant portion of the stadium shook. "Phase three is a failure, by the way. I got a shot off on Steelheart right after I revealed myself. It didn't do anything."

Phase three was Prof's theory—that one of the Faithful could hurt Steelheart. If Abraham's bullets had bounced off, then it wasn't viable. We only had two other ideas. The first was my theory of crossfire; the other was the theory that my father's gun or bullets were in some way special.

"How's Prof holding up?" Abraham asked.

"He's holding up," Tia said.

"He's *fighting* Steelheart," Cody said. "I've only been able to see a little, but— Sparks! I'm going offline for a moment. They're almost on me."

I crouched in the narrow tunnel, trying to sort through what was happening. I could still hear a lot of gunfire and the occasional blast.

"Prof's keeping Steelheart distracted," Tia said. "We still don't have any confirmed crossfire hits, though."

"We're trying," Abraham said. "I'll get this next group of soldiers to follow me around the corridor, and then let Cody goad them into firing across the field at him. That might work. David, where are you? I might need to set off a distraction blast or two to flush out the soldiers behind cover on your side."

"I'm taking the second concessions tunnel," I said. "I'll be coming out on the ground floor, near the bear. I'll head westward after that." *The bear* meant a giant stuffed bear that had been part of some promotion during the football season, but which was now frozen in place like everything else.

"Got it," Abraham said.

"David," Tia said. "If you saw an illusion, it means you've got both Firefight and Nightwielder on you. On one hand that's good—we were wondering where Firefight ran off to. It's bad for you, though—you've got two powerful Epics to deal with."

"I'm telling you, that wasn't an illusion," I said, cursing as I tried to juggle the gun and the flashlight. I searched in my cargo pocket, fishing out my industrial tape. My father had told me to always keep that industrial tape handy; I'd been surprised, as I grew older, how good that advice had been. "She was real, Tia."

"David, think about that for a moment. How would Megan have gotten here?"

"I don't know," I said. "Maybe they . . . did something to revive her. . . ."

"We flash-burned everything in the hideout. She'd have been cremated."

"There would have been DNA, maybe," I said. "Maybe they have an Epic who can bring someone back or something like that."

"Durkon's Paradox, David. You're searching too hard."

I finished taping the flashlight to the side of the barrel of my rifle—not on the top, as I wanted to be able to use the sights. That left the weapon off balance and clunky, but I felt I'd still be better with it than the handgun. I stuffed that into its holster under my arm.

Durkon's Paradox referred to a scientist who had studied and pondered the Epics during the early days. He'd pointed out that, with Epics breaking known laws of physics, literally anything was possible—but he warned against the practice of theorizing that every little irregularity was caused by an Epic's powers. Often that kind of thinking led to no actual answers.

"Have you *ever* heard of an Epic who could restore another person to life?" Tia said.

"No," I admitted. Some could heal, but none could reanimate someone else.

"And weren't you the one who said we were probably facing an illusionist?"

"Yes. But how would they know what Megan looked like? Why wouldn't they use Cody or Abraham to distract me, someone they know is here?"

"They would have her on video from the Conflux hit," Tia said. "They're using her to confuse you, unhinge you."

Nightwielder *had* nearly killed me while I was staring at the phantom Megan.

"You were right about Firefight," Tia continued. "As soon as that fire Epic was out of sight of the Enforcement officers, it vanished from my video feeds. That was just an illusion, meant to distract. The real Firefight is someone else. David, they're trying to play you so that Nightwielder can kill you. You *have* to accept this. You're letting your hopes cloud your judgment."

She was right. Sparks, but she was right. I halted in the tunnel, breathing in and out deliberately, forcing myself to confront it. Megan was dead. Now Steelheart's minions were playing with me. It made me angry. No, it made me *furious*.

It also brought up another problem. Why would they risk revealing Firefight like that? Letting him vanish after getting out of sight when it was likely we had the place under surveillance? Using an illusion of Megan? These things exposed Firefight for what he was.

That gave me a chill. They knew. They *knew* we were on to them, so they didn't need to pretend. *They also knew where we'd placed the UV floodlights,* I thought, *and where some of us were hiding.*

Something strange was going on. "Tia, I think—"

"Will you fools stop blathering," Prof said, his voice rough, harsh. "I need to concentrate."

"It's all right, Jon," Tia said comfortingly. "You're doing all right."

"Bah! Idiots. All of you."

He's using the tensors, I thought. *It's almost like they turn him into another person.*

There wasn't time to think about that. I simply hoped we all lived long enough for Prof to apologize. I climbed out of the tunnel behind some tall steel equipment cases and panned my rifle with mounted flashlight around the corridor.

I was saved from the strike by a fluke. I thought I saw something in the distance, and I lunged toward it, trying to get more light on it. As I did, three spears of darkness struck at me. One sliced clean through the back of my jacket and cut a line through my flesh. Just another fraction of an inch and it would have severed my spine.

I gasped, spinning around. Nightwielder stood nearby in the cavernous room. I fired a shot at him, but nothing happened. I cursed, getting closer, rifle to my shoulder and the UV light streaming before me.

Nightwielder smiled a devilish grin as I put a bullet through his face. Nothing. The UV wasn't working. I froze in place, panicked. Was I wrong about his weakness? But it had worked before. Why—

I spun about, barely stopping a group of spears. The light dispersed them as soon as it touched them, so it was still working. So what was happening?

Illusion, I thought, feeling stupid. *Slontze. How many times am I going to fall for that?* I scanned the walls. Sure enough, I caught a glimpse of Nightwielder staring out from one of them toward me. He pulled back before I could fire, and the darkness fell motionless again.

I waited, sweating, focused on that point. Maybe he'd peer out again. The fake Nightwielder was just to my right, looking impassive. Firefight was in the room somewhere. Invisible. He could gun me down. Why didn't he?

Nightwielder peeked out again, and I fired, but he was gone in an eyeblink and the shot ricocheted off the wall. He'd probably come at me from another direction, I decided, so I took off running. As I ran I swiped the butt of my gun through the fake Nightwielder. As I expected, it passed right through, the apparition wavering faintly like a projected image.

Explosions sounded. Abraham cursed in my ear.

"What?" Tia asked.

"Crossfire doesn't work," Cody said. "We got a big group of soldiers to fire on each other through the smoke, without their realizing that Steelheart was in the middle."

"At *least* a dozen shots hit him," Abraham said. "That theory is dead. I repeat, accidental fire does *not* hurt him."

Calamity! I thought. And I'd been so sure about that theory. I ground my teeth, still running. *We're not going to be able to kill him,* I thought. *This is all going to be meaningless.*

"I'm afraid that I can confirm," Cody said. "I saw the bullets hit too, and he didn't even notice." He paused. "Prof, you're a machine. Just thought I'd say that."

Prof's only response was a grunt.

"David, how are you handling Nightwielder?" Tia asked. "We need you to activate phase four. Shoot Steelheart with your father's gun. It's all we have left."

"How am I handling Nightwielder?" I asked. "*Poorly.* I'll get out there when I can." I continued jogging down the large, open concourse beneath the seating. Maybe if I could get outside I'd have a better time of it. There were too many hiding places in here.

He was waiting *for me when I came out of that tunnel,* I thought. *They've got to be listening in on our conversations. That's how they knew so much about our initial setup.*

That, of course, was impossible. Mobile signals were unhackable. The Knighthawk Foundry made sure of that. And beyond that, the Reckoners were on their own network.

Except . . .

Megan's mobile. It was still connected to our network. Had I ever mentioned to Prof and the others that she'd lost it in the fall? I'd assumed it was broken, but if it hadn't been . . .

They listened in on our preparations, I thought. *Did we mention over the lines that Limelight wasn't real?* I thought hard, trying to remember our conversations over the last three days. I came up blank.

Maybe we'd talked about it, but maybe not. The Reckoners tended to be circumspect about their conversations over the network, just to be extra careful.

Further speculation was cut off as I spotted a figure in the hall way in front of me. I slowed, rifle to shoulder, drawing a bead on it. What would Firefight try this time?

Another image of Megan, just standing there. She wore jeans and a tight red button-up shirt—but no Reckoner jacket—her golden hair pulled back in a shoulder-length ponytail. Wary, in case Nightwielder attacked me from behind, I moved past the illusion. It watched me with a blank expression but didn't move otherwise.

How could I find Firefight? He'd be invisible, probably. I wasn't certain he had that power, but it made sense.

Ways of revealing an invisible Epic ran through my mind. Either I had to listen for him or I had to fog the air with something. Flour, dirt, dust . . . maybe I could use the tensor somehow? Sweat trickled down my brow. I *hated* knowing that someone was watching me, someone I couldn't see.

What to do? My initial plan to deal with Firefight had been to reveal I knew his secret, to scare him off as I had Nightwielder during the Conflux hit. That wouldn't work now. He knew we were on to him. He needed to see the Reckoners dead to hide his secret. *Calamity, Calamity, Calamity!*

The illusion of Megan turned its head, following me as I tried to watch all corners of the room and listen for movement.

The illusion frowned. "I know you," she said.

It was her voice. I shivered. *A powerful Epic illusionist would be able to create sounds with their images,* I told myself. *I know that's true. No need to be surprised.*

But it was her voice. How did Firefight know her voice?

"Yes . . . ," she said, walking toward me. "I do know you. Something about . . . about knees." Her eyes narrowed at me. "I should kill you now."

Knees. Firefight couldn't know about that, could he? Had Megan called me that name over the mobile? They couldn't have been listening back then, could they?

I wavered, my gun's sights on her. The illusion. Or was it Megan? Nightwielder would be coming. I couldn't just stand there, but I couldn't run either.

She was walking toward me. Her arrogant expression made her look like she owned the world. Megan had acted like that before, but there was something more here. Her bearing was more confident, even though she had pursed her lips, perplexed.

I had to know. I *had* to.

I lowered the gun and leaped forward. She reacted, but too slowly, and I grabbed her arm.

It was real.

A second later, the hallway exploded.

38

I coughed, rolling over. I was on the ground, my ears ringing. Bits of trash burned nearby. I blinked away the afterimages in my eyes, shaking my head.

"What was that?" I croaked.

"David?" Abraham said in my ear.

"An explosion," I said, groaning and pulling myself up to my feet. I looked around the hallway. Megan. Where was she? I couldn't see her anywhere.

She'd been real. I had felt her. That meant it wasn't an illusion, right? Was I losing my mind?

"Calamity!" Abraham said. "I thought you were down the other end of the concourse. You said you'd go westward!"

"I ran to get away from Nightwielder," I said. "I ran the wrong way. I'm a slontze, Abraham. Sorry."

My rifle. I saw the stock sticking out of a nearby pile of trash. I pulled it out. The rest of the gun wasn't attached. *Sparks!* I thought. *I'm having a devil of a time holding on to these lately.*

I found the rest of the gun nearby. It *might* still work, but without a stock I'd be firing from the hip. The flashlight was still strapped to it, however, and still shining, so I snatched the whole thing up.

"What's your condition?" Tia asked, voice tense.

"A little stunned," I said, "but all right. It wasn't close enough to hit me with anything more than the concussion."

"Those will be amplified in these hallways," Abraham said. "Calamity, Tia. We're losing control of this situation."

"Damn you all," Prof's voice said, sounding feral. "I want David *out here now*. Bring me that gun!"

"I'm coming to help you, lad," Cody said. "Stay put."

A sudden thought struck me. If Steelheart and his people really were listening in on our private line, I could use that.

The idea warred with my desire to hunt for Megan. What if she was hurt? She had to be around here somewhere, and there seemed to be a lot more rubble in the hallway now. I needed to see if . . .

No. I *couldn't* afford to be tricked. Maybe that had been Firefight, wearing Megan's face to distract me.

"Okay," I said to Cody. "You know the restrooms near the fourth bomb position? I'm going to hide in there until you arrive."

"Got it," Cody said.

I dashed away, hoping that Nightwielder, wherever he was, had been disoriented by the blast. I neared the restrooms I'd mentioned to Cody, but I didn't go into them as I'd said. Instead I found a spot nearby and used my tensor to blast a hole into the ground. This was a place where I'd be relatively well hidden but would also have a good view of the rest of the corridor—restrooms included.

I dug the hole deep, then burrowed down in it as Prof had taught me, using the dust to cover up. Soon I was like a soldier in a foxhole, carefully hidden. I turned my mobile to silent and buried my half rifle just under the surface of the dust, so the light from the flashlight was concealed.

Then I watched the door to that restroom. The corridor fell silent. Lit only by burning scraps.

"Is anyone there?" a voice called into the hallway. "I . . . I'm hurt."

I tensed. That was Megan.

It's a trick. It has to be.

I scanned the dim room. There, on the other side of the hallway, I saw an arm wedged in a mountain of rubble from the blast. Chunks of steel, some fallen girders from above. The arm twitched, and blood ran down the wrist. As I looked closer, I could see her face and torso in the shadows. She looked like she was only now beginning to stir, as if she'd been briefly knocked unconscious by the blast.

She was pinned. She was hurt. I had to move, to go help her! I stirred but then forced myself down.

"Please," she said. "Please, someone. Help me."

I didn't move.

"Oh Calamity. Is that my blood?" She struggled. "I can't move my legs."

I squeezed my eyes shut. How were they doing this? I didn't know what to trust.

Firefight is doing it somehow, I told myself. *She's not real.*

I opened my eyes. Nightwielder was emerging from the floor in front of the bathroom. He looked confused, as if he'd been inside looking for me. He shook his head and walked through the corridor, searching about him.

Was that really him, or was it an illusion? Was any of this real? The stadium shook with another blast, but the gunfire outside was dying down. I needed to do something, quickly, or Cody would stumble into Nightwielder.

Nightwielder stopped in the center of the hallway and crossed his arms. His normal calm had been shattered and he looked annoyed. Finally he spoke. "You're in here somewhere, aren't you?"

Dared I take the shot? What if he was the illusion? I could get myself killed by the real Nightwielder if I exposed myself. I turned carefully, examining the walls and floor. I saw nothing other than some darkness creeping from the shadows nearby, tendrils moving like hesitant animals seeking food. Testing the air.

If Firefight was really pretending to be Megan, then shooting her would stop the illusions. I'd be left only with the real Nightwielder, wherever he was. But there was a good chance that the fallen Megan was a full illusion. Sparks, the *girders* could be an illusion. Would a distant blast have really knocked those down?

What if that was Firefight, though, wearing Megan's face so that if I touched her I'd feel something real? I raised my father's gun and sighted on her bloodied face. I hesitated, heart pounding in my ears. Surely Nightwielder could hear that pounding. It was all that I could hear. What would I do to get to Steelheart? Shoot Megan?

She's not real. She can't be real.

But what if she is?

Heartbeats, like thunder.

My breath, held.

Sweat on my brow.

I made my decision and leaped from the foxhole, bringing up the rifle in my left hand—light shining forward—and the handgun in my right. I let loose with both.

On Nightwielder, not Megan.

He spun toward me as the light hit him, eyes wide, and the bullets ripped through him. He opened his mouth in horror and blood sprayed out his back. His *solid* back. He dropped, turning translucent again the moment he got out of the direct line of my flashlight. He hit the ground and began to sink into it.

He only sank halfway. He froze there, mouth open, chest bleeding. He solidified slowly—it was almost like the view from a camera coming into focus—half sunken in the steel floor.

I heard a click and turned. Megan stood there, a gun in her hand. A handgun, a P226 just like she preferred to carry. The other version of her, the one trapped by rubble, vanished in a heartbeat. So did the girders.

"I never did like him," Megan said indifferently, glancing toward Nightwielder's corpse. "You just did me a favor. Plausible deniability and all of that."

I looked into her eyes. I knew those eyes. I *did*. I didn't understand how it was happening, but it was her.

Never did like him . . .

"Calamity," I whispered. "*You're* Firefight, aren't you? You always were."

She said nothing, though her eyes flickered down toward my weapons—the rifle still held at my hip, the handgun in my other hand. Her eye twitched.

"Firefight wasn't male," I said. "He . . . she was a woman." I felt my eyes go wide. "That day in the elevator shaft, when the guards almost caught us . . . they didn't see anything in the shaft. You made an illusion."

She was still staring at my guns.

"And then, when we were on the cycles," I said. "You created an illusion of Abraham riding with us to distract the people following, to keep them from seeing the real him flee to safety. That's what I saw behind us after he split off."

Why was she looking at my guns?

"But the dowser," I said. "It tested you, and it said you weren't an Epic. No . . . wait. Illusions. You could just make it display anything you wanted. Steelheart must have known the Reckoners were coming to town. He sent you to infiltrate. You were the newest of the Reckoners, before me. You never wanted to attack Steelheart. You said you believed in his rule."

She licked her lips, then whispered something. She didn't seem to have been listening to anything I said. "Sparks," she murmured. "I can't believe that actually worked. . . ."

What?

"You checkmated him . . . ," she whispered. "That was amazing. . . ."

Checkmated him? Nightwielder? Was that what she talking about? She looked up at me, and I remembered. She was repeating one of our first conversations, following her shooting Fortuity. She'd held a rifle at her hip and a handgun out forward. Just like I had done to gun down Nightwielder. The sight seemed to have triggered something in her.

"*David,*" she said. "*That's* your name. And I think you're very aggravating." She seemed to only just be recalling who I was. What had happened to her memory?

"Thank you?" I said.

A blast rocked the stadium and she looked over her shoulder. She still had the gun pointed at me.

"Whose side are you on, Megan?" I asked.

"My own," she said immediately, but then she held her other hand to her head, seeming uncertain.

"Someone betrayed us to Steelheart," I said. "Someone warned him we were going to hit Conflux, and someone told him we were hacking the city cameras. Today someone's been listening in on us, reporting to him what we've been doing. It was you."

She looked back at me, and didn't deny it.

"But you also used your illusions to save Abraham," I said. "And you killed Fortuity. I can buy that Steelheart wanted us to trust you, so he let you kill off one of his lesser Epics. Fortuity was out of favor anyway. But why would you betray us, *then* help Abraham escape?"

"I don't know," she whispered. "I . . ."

"Are you going to shoot me?" I asked, looking down the barrel of her gun.

She hesitated. "Idiot. You really don't know how to talk to women, do you, Knees?" She cocked her head as if surprised the words had come out.

She lowered the gun, then turned and ran off.

I've got to follow her, I thought, taking a step forward. Another explosion sounded outside.

No. I ripped my eyes away from her fleeing form. *I've got to get outside and help.*

I dashed past Nightwielder's corpse—still half submerged in steel, frozen, blood seeping down his chest—and headed for the nearest exit out onto the playing field.

Or in this case, the battlefield.

39

"... find that idiot boy and shoot him for me, Cody!" Prof screamed into my ear as I unmuted my mobile.

"We're pulling out, Jon," Tia said, talking over him. "I'm on my way in the copter. Three minutes until I arrive. Abraham will blow the cover explosion."

"Abraham can go to hell," Prof spat. "I'm seeing this to the end."

"You *can't* fight a High Epic, Jon," Tia said.

"I'll do whatever I want! I'm—" His voice cut out.

"I've removed him from the feed," Tia said to the rest of us. "This is bad. I've never heard him go this far. We need to pull him out somehow or we'll lose him."

"Lose him?" Cody asked, sounding confused. I could hear gunfire through the line near him, and could hear the same gunfire up ahead echoing in the wide corridor. I kept running.

"I'll explain later," Tia said in the type of voice that really meant "I'll find a better way to dodge that question later."

There, I thought, catching a bit of light up ahead. It was dark outside, but not as pitch-black as it was in the tunnellike confines of the stadium's innards. The gunfire was louder.

"I'm pulling us out," Tia continued. "Abraham, I need you to blow that explosion in the ground when I say. Cody . . . have you found David yet? Be warned, Nightwielder might be on your back."

She thinks I'm dead, I thought, *because I haven't been answering.* "I'm here," I said.

"David," Tia said, sounding relieved. "What is your status?"

"Nightwielder is down," I said, reaching the tunnel out onto the field, one of the ones that the teams had used when running out to play. "The UV worked. I think Firefight is gone too. I . . . drove him off."

"What? How?"

"Um . . . I'll explain later."

"Fair enough," Tia said. "We have about two minutes until I extract. Get to Cody."

I didn't reply—I was taking in the field. *Battlefield is right,* I thought, stunned. The bodies of Enforcement soldiers lay scattered like discarded trash. Fires burned in several locations, sending smoke twisting up into the dark sky. Red flares blazed across the field, thrown by soldiers to get better light. Chunks had been blown out of the seating and the ground, and blackened scars marred the once-silver steel.

"You guys have been fighting a war," I whispered. Then I caught sight of Steelheart.

He strode across the field, lips parted and teeth clenched in a sneer. His glowing hand was forward, and he blasted shot after shot toward something in front of him. Prof, running behind one of the team benches. Blast after blast nearly hit him, but he ducked and dodged between them, incredibly nimble. He pushed through a wall in the side of the stadium, his tensors vaporizing an opening for him.

Steelheart bellowed in aggravation, firing blasts into the hole. Prof appeared a moment later, breaking out of another wall, steel dust pouring down around him. He whipped his hand forward, throwing a series of crude daggers toward Steelheart; they had likely been cut from the steel itself. They just bounced off the High Epic.

Prof looked frustrated, as if he were annoyed he couldn't hurt Steelheart. For my part, I was amazed. "Has he been doing this the whole time?" I asked.

"Yeah," Cody said. "Likc I said, man's a machine."

I scanned the field to my right and picked out Cody behind some rubble. He was leaning forward on his rifle and tracking a group of Enforcement soldiers in the first-level seats. They had set up a large machine gun behind some blast shields, and Cody looked pinned down, which explained why he hadn't been able to come find me. I stuffed my handgun into its holster and unwrapped the flashlight from the stock of my rifle.

"I'm almost there, gentlemen," Tia said. "No more attempts to kill Steelheart. All phases aborted. We need to take this chance and leave while we can."

"I don't think Prof is going to go," Abraham said.

"I'll deal with Prof," Tia said.

"Fine," Abraham answered. "Where are you going to—"

"Guys," I cut in. "Be careful what you say in the general link. I think our lines may be hacked."

"Impossible," Tia said. "Mobile networks are secure."

"Not if you have access to an authorized mobile," I answered. "And Steelheart might have recovered Megan's."

There was silence on the line. "Sparks," Tia said. "I'm an idiot."

"Ah, finally something makes sense," Cody said, firing a shot at the soldiers. "That mobile—"

Something moved in the opening to the building behind Cody. I cursed, raising my rifle—but without the stock it was *very* hard to aim properly. I pulled the trigger as an armed Enforcement soldier leaped out. I missed. He fired a staccato burst.

There was no sound from Cody, but I could see the blood spray. *No, no, NO!* I thought, taking off at a run. I fired again, this time clipping the soldier on the shoulder. It didn't get past his armor, but he turned from Cody, sighting on me.

He fired. I raised my left hand, the one with the tensor. I did it almost by instinct. It was tougher to make the song this time, and I didn't know why.

But I made it work. I let the song out.

I felt something thump against my palm, and a puff of steel dust sprayed off my hand. It smarted something incredible, and the tensor started sparking. A moment later a series of gunshots sounded, and the soldier dropped. Abraham came around the corner behind the man.

Gunfire from above. I dashed and skidded against the ground, sliding behind Cody's cover. He was there, gasping, eyes wide. He'd been hit several times, three in the leg, one in the gut.

"Cover us," Abraham said in his calm voice, whipping out a bandage. He tied it around Cody's leg. "Tia, Cody is hit badly."

"I'm here," Tia said. In the chaos I hadn't noticed the sounds of the copter. "I've created new mobile channels using a direct feed to each of you; that's what we should have done the moment Megan lost her mobile. Abraham, we *need* to extract. Now."

I peeked up over the rubble. Soldiers were climbing down from the stands to move on us. Abraham casually pulled a grenade off his belt and tossed it into the hallway behind us in case someone was trying to sneak up again. It exploded, and I heard shouts.

I swapped my rifle for Cody's, then opened fire on those advancing soldiers. Some went for cover, but others continued moving, bold. They knew we were at the end of our resources. I kept firing but was rewarded with a series of clicks. Cody had been almost out of ammo.

"Here," Abraham said, dropping his large assault rifle beside me. "Tia, where are you?"

"Near your position," she said. "Just outside the stadium. Head straight back and out."

"I'm bringing Cody," Abraham said.

Cody was still conscious, though he was mostly just cursing at the moment, with his eyes squeezed shut. I nodded to Abraham. I'd cover their retreat. I took up Abraham's assault rifle. To be honest, I'd always wanted to fire the thing.

It was a very satisfying weapon to use. The recoil was soft, and the weapon felt lighter than it should have. I set it on the small front tripod and let loose on fully automatic, dozens of rounds ripping through the soldiers trying to get to us. Abraham carried Cody out the back way.

Prof and Steelheart were still fighting. I downed another soldier, Abraham's high-caliber rounds ignoring most of the soldier's armor. As I fired I could feel the handgun under my arm pressing against my side.

We'd never tried firing that, the last of our guesses at how to beat Steelheart. There was no way I could hit Steelheart at this range, though. And Tia had decided to pull us out before we tried it, calling the operation.

I gunned down another soldier. The stadium trembled as Steelheart fired a series of blasts at Prof. *I can't extract now,* I thought, *despite what Tia said—I've got to try the gun.*

"We're in the copter," Abraham said in my ear. "David, time to move."

"I still haven't tried phase four," I said, climbing up to a kneeling position and firing on the soldiers again. One tossed a grenade my direction, but I was already pulling back into the corridor. "And Prof is still out there."

"We're aborting," Tia said. "Retreat. Prof will escape using the tensors."

"He'll never stay ahead of Steelheart," I said. "Besides, do you really want to run without trying this?" I ran my finger along the gun in its holster.

Tia was silent.

"I'm going for it," I said. "If you take heat, pull out." I ran off the field and back into the hallways beneath the stands, holding Abraham's assault rifle and listening to soldiers shout behind me. *Steelheart and Prof were moving this direction,* I thought. *I just need to wrap around and get close enough to fire on him. I can do it from behind.*

It would work. It *had* to work.

Those soldiers were following me. Abraham's gun had a grenade launcher underneath. Any ammunition? Those were meant to be fired before exploding, but I could use my remote detonator pen and an eraser tab to make one go off.

No luck. The gun was out of grenades. I cursed, but then saw the remote fire switch on the gun. I grinned, then stopped, spun, and put the gun on the ground, wedged back against a chunk of steel. I flipped the switch and ran.

It started firing like crazy, spraying the corridor behind me with bullets. It probably wouldn't do much damage, but all I needed was a short breather. I heard soldiers yelling at one another to take cover.

That would do. I reached another opening and left the hallway, dashing out onto the playing field.

Smoke curled in patches from the ground. Steelheart's blasts seemed to smolder after they hit, starting fires on things that shouldn't burn. I raised the pistol, and in a fleeting moment I wondered what Abraham would say when he learned that I'd lost his gun. Again.

I spotted Steelheart, who was turned away from me, distracted by Prof. I ran for all I was worth, passing through clouds of smoke, leaping over rubble.

Steelheart started to turn as I approached. I could see his eyes, imperious and arrogant. His hands seemed to burn with energy. I pulled to a halt in the whipping smoke, arms shaking as I raised the gun. The gun that had killed my father. The only weapon that had ever wounded this monster in front of me.

I fired three shots.

40

EACH one hit . . . and each one bounced free of Steelheart, like pebbles thrown at a tank.

I lowered the gun. Steelheart raised a hand toward me, energy glowing around his palm, but I didn't care.

That's it, I thought. *We've tried everything.* I didn't know his secret. I never had.

I had failed.

He released a blast of energy, and some primal part of me wouldn't just stand there. I threw myself to the side, and the blast hit the ground beside me, spraying up a shower of molten metal. The ground shook and the blast threw my roll out of control. I tumbled hard on the unyielding ground.

I came to a stop and lay there, dazed. Steelheart stepped forward. His cape had been torn in places from Prof's attacks, but he didn't seem to be anything more than inconvenienced. He loomed above me, hand forward.

He was majestic. I could recognize that, even as I readied myself for death at his hands. Silver and black cape flapping, the rips making it look more *real* somehow. Classically square face, a jaw that any linebacker would have envied, a body that was toned and muscled—but not in the way of a bodybuilder. This wasn't exaggeration; it was perfection.

He studied me, his hand glowing. "Ah yes," he said. "The child in the bank."

I blinked, shocked.

"I remember everyone and everything," he said to me. "You needn't be surprised. I am divine, child. I do not forget. I thought you well and dead. A loose end. I *hate* loose ends."

"You killed my father," I whispered. A stupid thing to say, but it was what came out.

"I've killed a lot of fathers," Steelheart said. "And mothers, sons, daughters. It is my right."

The glow of his hand grew brighter. I braced myself for what was coming.

Prof tackled Steelheart from behind.

I rolled to the side by reflex as the two hit the ground nearby. Prof came up on top. His clothing was burned, ripped, and bloodied. He had his sword, and began slamming it down in Steelheart's face.

Steelheart laughed as the weapon hit; his face actually *dented* the sword.

He was talking to me to draw Prof out, I realized in a daze. *He . . .*

Steelheart reached up and shoved Prof, throwing him backward. What seemed like a tiny bit of effort from Steelheart tossed Prof a good ten feet. He hit and grunted.

The winds picked up, and Steelheart floated up to a standing position. Then he leaped, soaring into the air. He came down on one knee, slamming a fist into Prof's face.

Red blood splashed out around him.

I screamed, scrambling to my feet and running for Prof. My ankle wasn't working properly though, and I fell hard, hitting the ground. Through tears of pain, I saw Steelheart punch down again.

Red. So much red.

The High Epic stood up, shaking his bloodied hand. "You have a distinction, little Epic," he said to the fallen Prof. "I believe you agitated me more than any before you."

I crawled forward, reaching Prof's side. His skull was crushed in on the left, his eyes bulging out the front, staring sightlessly. Dead.

"David!" Tia said in my ear. There was gunfire on her side of the line. Enforcement had found the copter.

"Go," I whispered.

"But—"

"Prof is dead," I said. "I am too. Go."

Silence.

From my pocket, I took the detonator pen. We were in the middle of the field. Cody had placed my blasting cap on the dump of explosives, and it was just beneath us. Well, I'd blow Steelheart into the sky, for what good it would do.

Several Enforcement soldiers rushed up to Steelheart, reporting on the perimeter. I heard the copter thumping as it ascended to leave. I also heard Tia weeping on the line.

I pulled myself up to a kneeling position beside Prof's corpse.

My father dying before me. Kneeling at his side. Go . . . run . . .

At least this time I hadn't been a coward. I raised the pen, fingering the button on the top. The blast would kill me, but it wouldn't harm Steelheart. He'd survived explosions before. I might take a few soldiers with me, though. That was worth it.

"No," Steelheart said to his troops. "I'll deal with him. This one is . . . special."

I looked over at him, blinking dazed eyes. He'd raised his arm to ward away the Enforcement officers.

There was something strange in the distance behind him, over the stadium rim, above the luxury suites. I frowned. Light? But . . . that wasn't the right direction. I wasn't facing the city. Besides, the city had never produced a light that grand. Reds, oranges, yellows. The very sky seemed on fire.

I blinked through the haze of smoke. Sunlight. Nightwielder was dead. The *sun* was rising.

Steelheart spun about. Then he stumbled back, raising an arm against the light. His mouth opened in awe; then he shut it, grinding his teeth.

He turned back on me, eyes wide with anger. "Nightwielder will be difficult to replace," he growled.

Kneeling in the middle of the field, I stared at the light. That beautiful glow, that powerful *something* beyond.

There are *things greater than the Epics,* I thought. *There is life, and love, and nature herself.*

Steelheart strode toward me.

Where there are villains, there will be heroes. My father's voice. *Just wait. They* will *come.*

Steelheart raised a glowing hand.

Sometimes, son, you have to help the heroes along. . . .

And suddenly, I knew.

An awareness opened my mind, like the burning radiance of the sun itself. I knew. I understood.

Not looking down, I gathered up my father's gun. I fiddled with it a moment, then raised it directly at Steelheart.

Steelheart sniffed and stared it down. "Well?"

My hand quivered, wavering, my arm trembling. The sun back-lit Steelheart.

"Idiot," Steelheart said, and reached forward, grabbing my hand and crushing the bones. I barely felt the pain. The gun dropped to the ground with a clank. Steelheart held out a hand and the air spun around on the ground, forming a little whirlwind underneath the gun that raised it into his fingers. He turned it on me.

I looked up at him. A murderer outlined in brilliant light. Seen like that, he was just a shadow. Darkness. A nothingness before *real* power.

The men in this world, Epics included, would pass from time. I might be a worm to him, but he was a worm himself in the grand scheme of the universe.

His cheek bore a tiny sliver of a scar. The only imperfection on his body. A gift from a man who had believed in him. A gift from a better man than Steelheart would ever be, or ever understand.

"I should have been more careful that day," Steelheart said.

"My father didn't fear you," I whispered.

Steelheart stiffened, gun pointed to my head as I knelt, bloodied, before him. He always liked to use his enemy's own weapon against him. That was part of the pattern. The wind stirred the smoke rising around us.

"That's the secret," I said. "You keep us in darkness. You show off your terrible powers. You kill, you allow the Epics to kill, you turn men's own weapons against them. You even spread false rumors about how horrible you are, as if you can't be bothered to be as evil as you want to be. You want us to be afraid . . ."

Steelheart's eyes widened.

". . . because you can only be hurt by someone who doesn't fear you," I said. "But such a person doesn't really exist, do they? You make sure of it. Even the Reckoners, even Prof himself. Even me. We are all afraid of you. Fortunately I know someone who isn't afraid of you, and never has been."

"You know nothing," he growled.

"I know everything," I whispered. Then I smiled.

Steelheart pulled the trigger.

Inside the gun, the hammer struck the back of the bullet's

casing. Gunpowder exploded, and the bullet sprang forward, summoned to kill.

In the barrel, it struck the thing I had lodged there. A slender pen, with a button you can click on the top. It was just small enough to fit into the gun. A detonator. Connected to explosives beneath our feet.

The bullet hit the trigger and pushed it in.

I swore I could watch the explosion unfold. Each beat of my heart seemed to take an eternity. Fire channeled upward, steel ground ripping apart like paper. Terrible redness to match the peaceful beauty of the sunrise.

The fire consumed Steelheart and all around him; it ripped his body apart as he opened his mouth to scream. Skin flayed, muscles burned, organs shredded. He turned eyes toward the heavens, consumed by a volcano of fire and fury that opened at his feet. In that fraction of a sliver of a moment, Steelheart—greatest of all Epics—died.

He could only be killed by someone who didn't fear him.

He had pulled the trigger himself.

He had caused the detonation himself.

And as that arrogant, self-confident sneer implied, Steelheart did *not* fear himself. He was, perhaps, the only person alive who did not.

I didn't really have time to smile in that frozen moment, but I was feeling it nonetheless as the fire came for me.

41

I watched the shifting pattern of red, orange, and black. A wall of fire and destruction. I watched it until it vanished. It left a black scar on the ground in front of me, surrounding a hole five paces wide— the blast crater of the explosion.

I watched it all, and found myself still alive. I'll admit, it was the most baffling moment in my life.

Someone groaned behind me. I spun to see Prof sitting up. His clothing was covered in blood and he had a few scratches on his skin, but his skull was whole. Had I mistaken the extent of his injuries?

Prof had his hand forward, palm out. The tensor he'd been wearing was in tatters. "Sparks," he said. "Another inch or so and I wouldn't have been able to stop it." He coughed into his fist. "You're a lucky little slontze."

Even as he spoke, the scratches on his skin pulled together, healing. *Prof's an Epic,* I thought. *Prof's an* Epic. *That was an energy shield he created to block the explosion!*

He stumbled to his feet, looking around the stadium. A few Enforcement soldiers were running away, fleeing as they saw him rise. They seemed to want no part of whatever was happening in the center of the field.

"How . . . ," I said. "How long?"

"Since Calamity," Prof said, cracking his neck. "You think an ordinary person could have stood against Steelheart as long as I did tonight?"

Of course not. "The inventions are all fakes, aren't they?" I said, realization dawning. "You're a gifter! You *gave* us your abilities. Shielding abilities in the form of jackets, healing ability in the form of the harmsway, and destructive powers in the form of the tensors."

"Don't know why I did it," Prof said. "You pathetic little . . ." He groaned, raising his hand to his head, then gritted his teeth and roared.

I scrambled back, startled.

"It's so hard to fight," he said through clenched teeth. "The more you use it, the . . . Arrrrr!" He knelt down, holding his head. He was quiet for a few minutes, and I let him be, not knowing what to say. When he raised his head, he seemed more in control. "I give it away," he said, "because if I use it . . . it does this to me."

"You can fight it, Prof," I said. It felt right. "I've seen you do it. You're a good man. Don't let it consume you."

He nodded, breathing in and out deeply. "Take it." He reached out his hand.

I hesitantly took his hand with my good one—the other was crushed. I should have felt pain from that. I was too much in shock.

I didn't feel any different, but Prof seemed to grow more in control. My wounded hand re-formed, bones pulling together. In seconds I could flex it again, and it worked perfectly.

"I have to split it up among you," he said. "It doesn't seem to . . .

seep into you as quickly as it does me. But if I give it all to one person, they'll change."

"That's why Megan couldn't use the tensors," I said. "Or the harmsway."

"What?"

"Oh, sorry. You don't know. Megan's an Epic too."

"What?"

"She's Firefight," I said, cringing back a bit. "She used her illusion powers to fool the dowser. Wait, the dowser—"

"Tia and I programmed it to exclude me," Prof said. "It gives a false negative on me."

"Oh. Well, I think Steelheart must have sent Megan to infiltrate the Reckoners. But Edmund said that he couldn't gift his powers to other Epics, so . . . yeah. That's why she couldn't ever use the tensors."

Prof shook his head. "When he said that, in the hideout, it made me wonder. I'd never tried to give mine to another Epic. I should have seen . . . Megan . . ."

"You couldn't have known," I said.

Prof breathed in and out, then nodded. He looked at me. "It's okay, son. You don't need to be afraid. It's passing quickly this time." He hesitated. "I think."

"Good enough for me," I said, climbing to my feet.

The air smelled of explosives—of gunpowder, smoke, and burned flesh. The growing sunlight was reflecting off the steel surfaces around us. I found it almost blinding, and the sun wasn't even fully up yet.

Prof looked at the sunlight as if he hadn't noticed it before. He actually smiled, and seemed more and more like his old self. He strode out across the field, walking toward something in the rubble.

Megan's personality changed when she used her powers too, I thought. *In the elevator shaft, on the cycle . . . she changed. Became brasher, more arrogant, even more hateful.* It had passed quickly each time, but she'd barely used her powers, so maybe the effects on her had been weaker.

If that was true, then spending time with the Reckoners—when she needed to be careful not to use her abilities lest she give herself away—had served to keep her from being affected. The people she was meant to have infiltrated had instead turned her more human.

Prof came walking back with something in his hand. A skull, blackened and charred. Metal glinted through the soot. A steel skull. He turned it toward me. There was a groove in the right cheekbone, like the trail left by a bullet.

"Huh," I said, taking the skull. "If the bullet could hurt his bones, why couldn't the blast?"

"I wouldn't be surprised if his death triggered his tranfersion abilities," Prof said. "Turning what was left of him as he died—his bones, or some of them—into steel."

Seemed like a stretch to me. But then, strange things happened around Epics. There were oddities, especially when they died.

As I regarded the skull, Prof called Tia. I distractedly caught the sounds of weeping, exclamations of joy, and an exchange that ended with her turning the copter back for us. I looked up, then found myself walking toward the tunnel entrance into the stadium innards.

"David?" Prof called.

"I'll be right back," I said. "I want to get something."

"The copter will be here in a few minutes. I suggest we *not* be here when Enforcement comes in earnest to see what happened."

I started running, but he didn't object further. As I entered the darkness, I turned my mobile's light up to full, illuminating the tall, cavernous corridors. I ran past Nightwielder's body suspended in steel. Past the place where Abraham had detonated the explosion.

I slowed, peeking into concession stands and restrooms. I didn't have long to look, and I soon felt like a fool. What did I expect to find? She'd left. She was . . .

Voices.

I froze, then turned about in the dim corridor. There. I walked forward, eventually finding a steel door frozen open and leading into what appeared to be a janitorial chamber. I could almost make out the voice. It was familiar. Not Megan's voice, but . . .

". . . deserved to live through this, even if I didn't," the voice said. Gunfire followed, sounding distant. "You know, I think I fell for you that first day. Stupid, huh? Love at first sight. What a cliché."

Yes, I knew that voice. It was mine. I stopped at the doorway, feeling like I was in a dream as I listened to my own words. Words spoken as I defended Megan's dying body. I continued listening as the entire scene played out. Right up until the end. "I don't know if I love you," my voice said. "But whatever the emotion is, it's the strongest one I've felt in years. Thank you."

The recording stopped. Then it started playing again from the beginning.

I stepped into the small room. Megan sat on the floor in the corner, staring at the mobile in her hands. She turned down the volume when I entered, but she didn't stop looking at the screen.

"I keep a secret video and audio feed," she whispered. "The camera's embedded in my skin, above my eye. It starts up if I close my eyes for too long, or if my heart rate goes too high or too low. It sends the data to one of my caches in the city. I started doing that after I died the first few times. It's always disorienting to reincarnate. It helps if I can watch what happened leading up to my death."

"Megan, I . . ." What could I say?

"Megan is my real name," she said. "Isn't that funny? I felt I could give it to the Reckoners because that person, the person I was, is dead. Megan Tarash. She's never had any connection to Firefight. She was just another ordinary human."

She looked up at me, and in the light of her mobile screen I could see tears in her eyes. "You carried me all that way," she whispered. "I watched it, when I was first reborn this time. Your actions didn't make sense to me. I thought you must have needed something from me. Now I see something different in what you did."

"We've got to go, Megan," I said, stepping forward. "Prof can explain better than I can. But right now, just come with me."

"My mind *changes,*" she whispered. "When I die, I am reborn out of light a day later. Somewhere random, not where my body was, not where I died, but nearby. Different each time. I . . . I don't feel like myself, now that that's happened. Not the self I want to be. It doesn't make sense. What do you trust, David? What do you trust when your own thoughts and emotions seem to hate you?"

"Prof can—"

"Stop," she said, raising a hand. "Don't . . . don't come closer. Just leave me. I need to think."

I stepped forward.

"Stop!" The walls faded, and fires seemed to flame up around us. The floor warped beneath me, making me nauseous. I stumbled.

"You've *got* to come with me, Megan."

"Take another step and I'll shoot myself," she said, reaching for a gun on the floor beside her. "I'll do it, David. Death is nothing to me. Not anymore."

I backed away, hands up.

"I need to think about this," she mumbled again, looking back at her mobile.

"David." A voice in my ear. Prof's voice. "David, we're leaving *now.*"

"Don't use your powers, Megan," I said to her. "Please. You *have* to understand. They're what change you. Don't use them for a few days. Hide, and your mind will get clearer."

She kept staring at the screen. The recording started over.

"Megan . . ."

She raised the gun toward me without shifting her gaze. The tears dripped down her cheeks.

"David!" Prof yelled.

I turned and ran for the copter. I didn't know what else to do.

382

Epilogue

I'VE seen Steelheart bleed.

I've seen him scream. I've seen him burn. I've seen him die in an inferno, and I was the one who killed him. Yes, the hand that pushed the detonator was his own, but I don't care—and have never cared—which hand actually took his life. I made it happen. I've got his skull to prove it.

I sat strapped in the copter's chair, looking out the open door to the side, my hair blowing as we lifted off. Cody was stabilizing quickly in the back seat, much to Abraham's amazement. I knew Prof had given the man a large portion of his healing power. From what I knew of Epic regeneration abilities, that would be able to heal Cody from practically anything, so long as he was still breathing when the power was transferred.

We soared up into the air before a blazing yellow sun, leaving the stadium scorched, burned, blasted, but with the scent of triumph. My father told me that Soldier Field had been named in honor of the military men and women who had fallen in battle. Now it had hosted the most important battle since Calamity. The field's name had never seemed more appropriate to me.

We rose above a city that was seeing real light for the first time in a decade. People were in the streets, looking upward.

Tia piloted the copter, one hand reaching over to hold Prof's arm, as if she were unable to believe he was really there with us. He looked out his window, and I wondered if he saw what I did. We hadn't rescued this city. Not yet. We'd killed Steelheart, but other Epics would come.

I didn't accept that we just had to abandon the people now. We'd removed Newcago's source of authority; we'd have to take responsibility for that. I wouldn't abandon my home to chaos, not now, not even for the Reckoners.

Fighting back had to be about more than just killing Epics. It had to be about something greater. Something, perhaps, that had to do with Prof and Megan.

The Epics *can* be beaten. Some, maybe, can even be rescued. I don't know how to manage it exactly. But I intend to keep trying until either we find an answer or I'm dead.

I smiled as we turned out of the city. *The heroes will come . . . we might just have to help them along.*

I always assumed that my father's death would be the most transformative event of my life. Only now, with Steelheart's skull in my hand, did I realize that I hadn't been fighting for vengeance, and hadn't been fighting for redemption. I hadn't been fighting because of my father's death.

I fought because of his dreams.

ACKNOWLEDGMENTS

THIS one has been a long time brewing. I had the first idea for it while on book tour in . . . oh, 2007? With a long ride like that involved in getting the book finished, a *lot* of people have given me feedback over the years. I hope I don't miss any of you!

Notably, thanks go out to my delightful editor, Krista Marino, for her extremely capable direction of this project. She's been a wonderful resource, and her editing was top-notch, taking this book from plucky upstart to polished product. Also, we should make note of that rascal James Dashner, who was kind enough to call her up and get me an introduction.

Others who deserve a cheer are: Michael Trudeau (who did a superb copyedit); and at Random House, Paul Samuelson, Rachel Weinick, Beverly Horowitz, Judith Haut, Dominique Cimina, and Barbara Marcus. Also, Christopher Paolini, for his feedback and help on the book.

As always, I wish to give big thanks to my agents, Joshua Bilmes, who didn't laugh too hard when I told him I had this book I wanted to write instead of working on the twenty other projects I needed to do at the time, and Eddie Schneider, whose jobs include dressing better than the rest of us and having a name I have to look up every time I want to put it in acknowledgments. On the *Steelheart* film front (we're trying hard), thanks go to Joel Gotler, Brian Lipson, Navid McIlhargey, and the superhuman Donald Mustard.

A big thumbs-up goes to the incandescent Peter Ahlstrom, my editorial assistant, who was part of this book's cheering section from the get-go. He was, editorially, the first one who got his hands on this project—and much of its success is due to him.

I also don't want to forget my UK/Ireland/Australia publishing team, including John Berlyne and John Parker of the Zeno Agency, and Simon Spanton and my publicist/mother-in-the-UK, Jonathan Weir of Gollancz.

Others with Epic-level powers in reading and giving feedback (or just great support) include: Dominique Nolan (Dragonsteel's official Gun-Nut super-reference man), Brian McGinley, David West, Peter (again) and Karen Ahlstrom, Benjamin Rodriguez and Danielle Olsen, Alan Layton, Kaylynn ZoBell, Dan "I Wrote Postapocalyptic Before You" Wells, Kathleen Sanderson Dorsey, Brian Hill, Brian "By Now You Owe Me Royalties, Brandon" Delambre, Jason Denzel, Kalyani Poluri, Kyle Mills, Adam Hussey, Austin Hussey, Paul Christopher, Mi'chelle Walker, and Josh Walker. You're all awesome.

Finally, as always, I wish to thank my lovely wife, Emily, and my three destructive little boys, who are constant inspiration for how an Epic might go about blowing up a city. (Or the living room.)

Brandon Sanderson

The battle for mankind continues in

FIREFIGHT